A Line Too Far

A LINE TOO FAR

B. C. Colman

The Liberty Publishing Company

This edition first published in 2016

Copyright © The Liberty Publishing Company
www.alinetoofar.com

B. C. Colman asserts his moral right to be identified as the author of this work.

ISBN 978-0-473-35956-0 (Paperback)
ISBN 978-0-473-35957-7 (EPUB)

Cover design by Craig Violich, CVD Graphics.

Digital and print preparation by Martin Taylor, Digital Strategies

For Kati Clara, Geoff and Libby

Either we must accomplish the peopling
of the Northern Territory or submit to its
transfer to some other nation.
— *Australian Prime Minister Alfred*
Deakin, 1910

It's not a question of people being goodies
or baddies … countries will do things to
try to give themselves security.
— *former Bank of England Governor,*
Lord Mervyn King, Diggers and Dealers
Conference, Kalgoorlie, Western
Australia, 2014

CONTENTS

PROLOGUE

It was almost two in the morning when he spotted the lights bumping toward the guardhouse.

Sergeant Keith Patterson felt a flash of annoyance. The Sunday graveyard shift was supposed to be the most peaceful.

The vehicle laboured closer, its engine protesting, as though locked accidentally in a low gear. Patterson shook his head: it was no Australian Army-trained driver behind the wheel.

It finally burst from the night into the base's floodlit entrance. Patterson narrowed his eyes against the glare of its headlights.

He could make out the shape of a bus. A brightly coloured bus. A garish logo ran down its side: "Happy Tours Queensland".

It shuddered to a halt at the guardhouse barrier.

Patterson sighed, stood and shoved open the guardhouse door. A thick wall of subtropical humidity engulfed him.

The two privates sharing his shift hardly looked up from their card game, grateful their cantankerous sergeant had taken it on himself to leave the air-conditioned guardhouse to deal with the situation: lost tourists by the look of it.

The last off-duty personnel at Townsville's Lavarack Army Base, the country's biggest, had already checked in as close as they dared to midnight.

The twenty-year veteran sergeant trudged impatiently the few steps to the idling bus as its door hissed open. He sensed it had a full load.

A passenger jumped off. He seemed to be in some sort of uniform — and carrying a weapon.

An instant later Patterson froze as the cold barrel of a submachine-gun was jammed against his hot face. He stared uncomprehendingly at the bright red star on the passenger's cap. Then below it. What the hell? The man was Chinese.

In perfect English Patterson was ordered quietly to turn and retrace his steps to the guardhouse.

Other uniformed and heavily armed passengers swarmed off the Happy Tours Queensland bus.

They pushed in behind their leader and crammed the guardhouse before Patterson's lounging soldiers could spring from their chairs. The bewildered guards were instantly surrounded, their hands clasped behind them and locked together with plastic ties before they were shoved to the floor.

The takeover was rapid and disciplined. It took only seconds and was executed in near silence.

The guardhouse switchboard panel was wrenched open. The entrance floodlights and the guardhouse were plunged into near darkness. The remaining dim light shone mockingly from the guardhouse roof declaring the base's motto: "Guarding the North".

With a submachine-gun pressed painfully into his chest, Patterson was ordered to summon Brigadier Silvey.

The commandant was to be told there was an emergency at the guardhouse. Patterson was then to hang up with no further explanation. The sergeant did as he was ordered. He was then cuffed and joined his hapless squad members sprawled wide-eyed on the floor.

Brigadier Lesley Silvey reached the guardhouse on the run only to find himself surrounded by armed men. Manhandled briskly inside, he was ordered to make a call: to the duty officer, Australian Defence Headquarters, Canberra.

He was handed a written text to read. The grim faces surrounding him made it clear he had no option.

Minutes later a convoy of twenty-two more buses growled up to the entrance. The barrier was lifted. They rolled in taking different internal roads over the sprawling, 750-hectare base, home to more than three thousand Australian soldiers.

Small groups of the raiders were dropped at strategic locations, including each barracks block where they stormed in ordering groggy and baffled soldiers from their beds at gunpoint. Most of the Australians cursed, believing they were part of a surprise attack exercise.

* * *

With no official engagements, they had gone to bed early.

The Saturday dinner alone at The Lodge had been a tense affair. Already struggling with Australia's burgeoning economic crisis, Prime Minister Gary Stone faced a fresh one: he had been told that afternoon several arteries in his heart were more than ninety per cent blocked.

He was reminded of other, ignored physical niggles as the meal ended and he went to stand. The rush of pain in his left knee jolted him. It had taken four players to take him down. He had fallen awkwardly on the knee and been stretchered off.

Now the joints in his huge frame were reminding him of the toll he was paying for playing club rugby league well after his prime.

He had refused to acknowledge any ageing process as he reached his mid-thirties. He had been physically made for the game he loved.

The news about his heart condition had been a shock. He believed his burly, can-do political image would be at risk if it became public.

Australian prime ministers were expected to be fit. Their ridiculously long days and workload demanded it. He knew any health doubts would spark speculation on his fitness to lead, particularly from Jeremey Whittacker, the man he had narrowly beaten for the party leadership.

A fussy, over-ambitious, former merchant banker, Whittacker had married money and inherited a socialite wife who was even more determined to occupy The Lodge than he was.

Stone was determined not to become a lame duck leader after only two years in office and had questioned the doctor's prognosis, earning a fearsome scowl from Elaine for his childish attempts at denial.

The truth was, he was mortified at the prospect of having tiny, hollow steel rods pushed through his arteries to unblock them. Only old people had heart troubles. He was just fifty-two.

They had offered him a nitrate spray to relieve the chest pain symptoms pending the stent operation. When he hesitated Elaine had taken it, placing it determinedly in her handbag. She had no intention of going from First Lady to widowhood at forty-eight.

The doctor had warned against the dangers of sudden stress. Stone snorted at the advice, earning a second glare.

Rubbing away the pain in his knee joint, he followed Elaine upstairs to their private quarters. They had hardly spoken during the meal after he had waved away any discussion on possible dates for the stenting operation. He was still coming to terms with his new predicament.

Elaine dozed off first. Stone lay awake brooding.

The Lucky Country had not had a recession for more than a quarter of a century until he formed his government.

The great resources boom had busted. The country had gorged off its mining and energy wealth for years. When it ended, the average citizen was worth $260,000. An astonishing figure. The highest in the world.

With a population of only 23 million it had 1.2 million millionaires.

No stress? He was presiding over a slow-motion, economic train wreck. Earlier uncontrolled government spending had emptied the Treasury and piled up enormous, ongoing deficits.

But the voters resisted any thought of reining in their extraordinarily expensive welfare programmes. Full employment and comfortable lifestyles were essential ingredients for any government to remain in power.

Now the music had stopped. The prices of iron ore, coking coal and natural gas had crashed. It was a crisis most Australians didn't want to know about.

DAY ONE

3.42 a.m.

Private quarters, The Lodge, Canberra

It seemed he had been asleep only minutes when a rustling noise outside the door woke him.

He squinted at the bedside clock. Its dull-green digit flicked to 3.42.

A rap on the door sat him up. He heard a murmur of hushed voices. Then a second, firmer knock brought him to his full senses.

Elaine gave a start.

"What's happening?" she said.

The door to the private quarters half opened. A stab of light cut in to the room.

Stone tossed off bedclothes and swung his feet to the floor in a single move.

"Prime Minister. Are you awake?"

The urgent voice of John Able seemed incongruous in the pre-dawn bedroom setting.

"Yes, John." Stone stood up uncertainly. "What is it? What the hell's going on?"

Stone could see the tall backlit profile of the Prime Minister's Department's boss in the doorway. Able hesitated a long second.

"I'm sorry, sir, but we have been unable to find the Minister for Defence and General Thompson needs to talk to you — right now."

"At this hour? What's he want that's so bloody urgent?" Stone turned again to the clock. He hadn't been mistaken. It was only 3.42.

Able didn't reply.

"Come on, John, for God's sake." Stone felt a flush of impatience and the first serious stirrings of unease.

"I'll put the general on your secure line, sir," Able answered. He turned and left before Stone could respond. Stone heard several sets of footsteps retreating down the passageway.

Able had arrived with security guards in tow.

* * *

Stone sat on the bedside. Elaine anxiously hurried around to sit next to him. She unconsciously took his left hand, a habit of thirty-two years. They waited in silence for the shrill ring of the secure phone.

When it came, Stone leaned over to push the speaker button. His finger missed. He breathed in deeply, willed his shaking hand to stillness and stabbed a second time.

"General Thompson. What is it?"

"I have some pretty startling news I'm afraid, Prime Minister."

The sentence was left hanging. At sixty-four, General Alan Thompson had just nine months to run as the country's Chief of Defence. He struggled for words to describe his worst military nightmare. And the certain humiliation that would end his career.

Stone waited, slowing his breathing, hoping the general could not hear its raggedness.

"Defence Headquarters took a call from the base commandant at Lavarack, up in Townsville, early this morning," Thompson said. "Since then there's been a steady stream of calls from all our base commanders in northern Queensland, the Northern Territory and the far northwest of Western Australia."

He paused again and heard Stone mutter something indecipherable.

"Forces wearing the uniform of the Chinese People's Liberation Army have seized all our bases in the Top Half — army, air force and naval — the lot."

Stone said nothing, his mind spinning to grasp the news. He worried Elaine's fingers with one hand, twisting the bed covers with the other till his knuckles went white.

"I know it's a lot to take in, sir," Thompson offered in the silence.

Stone cleared his throat. "The Chinese have just seized all of our northern military bases in the last couple of hours and occupied half of our country?"

Before Thompson could answer, Stone went on: "How the fuck could that happen? It's not possible … are you absolutely sure, Alan?"

He tried to keep any trace of panic from his voice. He saw Elaine staring at him, one hand covering her mouth in shock.

Thompson named all the bases across the vast northern shores of the world's sixth-biggest country. Teams of lightly armed Chinese had simultaneously seized each one without a fight.

The modus operandi was identical. All base commanders reported their fate directly to Canberra as ordered. The Chinese had descended on their unsuspecting targets in anonymous civilian vehicles, mainly buses, four-wheel-drives and even the odd taxi.

The element of surprise was total. The enemy's strength was still unknown but its control in Queensland stretched south to Gladstone.

"There's more bad news I'm afraid," Thompson said. "Our base commanders say the Chinese regard all prisoners as hostages. If there is any counterattack they will be killed immediately. They are booby-trapping all barracks to guarantee that."

"How many of our people are up there?" Stone realised his voice was a hoarse whisper.

Thompson said there were approximately twelve thousand service personnel and a few hundred civilian contractors on the various bases.

Stone made an effort to collect his thoughts. "If they have Gladstone, are we likely to see them take a shot at Brisbane next?"

"They say not. The message relayed from our commanders claim the Chinese have no further territorial ambitions. This also leads us to believe the actual number of Chinese on the ground is small. I don't think they'd be able to handle a full-scale counterattack from us so the prisoners' lives are a chip they're playing, at least till they get reinforcements."

Before Stone could speak, Thompson said: "The Chinese also say their ambassador wants to meet you urgently this morning to discuss details of a peace settlement."

"A peace settlement?!" Stone exploded. He felt his pulse race.

He knew why the Chinese might possibly be content with the Top Half: it held most of Australia's mining and energy resources.

The most vulnerable frontier on earth had been protecting some of its most valuable energy riches. It had been breached without a shot fired in anger. It beggared belief.

But Australia had always been an impossible land to defend. A mass the size of the United States but with almost 26,000 kilometres of coastline.

Its resource wealth was scattered over enormous deserts with tiny populations. It was an empty land. It had been a sitting duck for determined invaders ever since Queen Victoria's Imperial forces had claimed it as a British colony more than two hundred years ago.

Stone heaved himself to his feet. "Well, what now? And where the hell is Bob Bradbury? Someone must be able to find him."

"Not so far, sir. I'll get the Defence Minister to call you as soon as we locate him," said Thompson. "Meanwhile we are mobilising and putting all our forces on full alert. I'll call you directly if there are any further developments."

He asked to be excused and Stone slowly leaned over to cancel the speaker button. He hit it on the second attempt.

* * *

Elaine watched the dawn light beginning to bleed around the edges of the heavy bedroom drapes.

"How could this have happened?" she said quietly. "This is madness."

Stone looked down and shrugged. "This madness happened to the Ukraine. Russia walked in and annexed Crimea," he said. "And got away with it."

Stone put his huge arm around her. They sat motionless, trying to absorb the enormity of the morning's events.

Elaine said, "Do you think the Chinese will get away with it too?"

Stone did not answer. He rubbed his chest and straightened his back.

Elaine shook him by the shoulder. They had to get up. He needed to take charge, she said.

Stone nodded in silent agreement.

He made for the en suite while she went downstairs to stir the rest of the household. But seconds after the shower was flowing the secure phone was ringing again. He trudged naked back to the bedroom while hot water drummed impatiently on the shower box floor.

It was Lindsay Noble who had insisted his call be connected immediately.

The Foreign Minister was in a panic. He had made the first call anyone in his position would after a military attack. To the US State Department in Washington. To invoke the ANZUS Treaty, the cornerstone of Australia's defence strategy since World War Two. Its ultimate security guarantee.

For its part in the alliance Australia had loyally gone off to war alongside America in its battles around the world, including Korea, Vietnam, Afghanistan and Iraq.

As he listened, Stone was alarmed his minister, a former strategic affairs professor with the prerequisite alphabet of degrees, had lost any vestige of his usual urbane manner. Noble had reached the US Secretary of State, Ben Strong.

"Christ, Gary, I got Strong on the line and he already knew what I was going to tell him!"

"For heaven's sake, Lindsay, calm down, man," Stone said, already fighting an icy shiver in his own stomach.

"He knew all about the Chinese. Everything. The Chinese briefed him as the bases were being seized, for God's sake," said Noble.

Stone said nothing.

"Do you realise what this means? They're going to hang us out to dry. We're on our own. We're fucked."

Noble paused to suck in a breath. "Strong said the Chinese had briefed him because they didn't want to risk the shock the Yanks would have if they'd turned on CNN and found out. The Chinese didn't want a macho jerk reaction. They wanted the cool heads in the White House to pacify the big dogs in the Pacific Fleet."

Noble stopped suddenly. There had been something America had offered. Slowly, imitating Strong's southern drawl, Noble said: "Lindsay, rest assured we will call immediately for an emergency session of the UN Security Council to condemn this flagrant act of aggression."

Stone grunted. "Lindsay, they're are not going to risk a war with China for us. Let's not kid ourselves. They never were. Not when it came down to the wire. All ANZUS ever entitled us to do was to 'consult' with America if we were attacked. There was never any guarantee they would gallop to our rescue in a war. Perhaps if we'd picked up some intelligence before the attacks they may have stationed a carrier force off Queensland but ..."

"Fuck, Gary. We're on our own. The Chinese ... I cannot believe we fell for all that hoopla and smiling photo ops with the new chairman. And their Pacific Fleet is off the Queensland coast on its way to Sydney for a goodwill visit, for God's sake."

"Lindsay, settle down, man. You're not helping matters. You're the Foreign Minister, you should know the Yanks and Chinese are the two most interdependent countries in the world. America runs on Chinese cash to fund its economy, China runs on its bullshit undervalued currency and cheap labour to rack up huge trading profits. Neither of them can afford a shooting war with each other."

Stone heard Noble take a slurp of something. He hoped it was only coffee.

Noble said: "The Chinese ambassador has called wanting a meeting. His name is Chen. He's only just been posted here. None of their embassy staff were expecting him. His wife is still in Beijing."

"So we're going to be meeting the next Governor of the Far North," said Stone.

"It's not funny, Gary. But it does look that way if they get away with his … this'… Christ … it's unbelievable …"

Stone told him they would meet the ambassador at The Lodge. Stone was determined not to confront a media pack outside his parliamentary office.

"Lindsay, I really have to go," Stone said.

"But we haven't even begun to discuss our strategy when we sit down with Chen. What's so urgent?"

"I hate cold showers," said Stone.

4.15 a.m.

Private quarters, The Lodge, Canberra

Elaine straightened his tie, brushed some imagined lint off his shoulder. He was good to go. She said John Able was in the dining room downstairs working on a timetable for the day. He should eat a good breakfast. It would be a long day.

Stone kissed her and looked around the private quarters. They were, like The Lodge, comfortable, not palatial. The building had never been intended as a prime minister's official residence when it was built back in 1926, let alone the 21st-century War Office he planned to make it.

Its small dining, lounge and reception rooms downstairs had been big enough for the state and royal occasions they had had to host, so they would be big enough for their new role.

The forty-room Georgian mansion was very close to Canberra City, Parliament and the Federal bureaucracy. Ministers and officials would come to him. He would preserve his precious energy. The media would be kept at bay till he was ready. His doctor would approve.

The Lodge had recently been renovated. It had bombproof windows and a state-of-the-art security system.

He went downstairs to find his department head fully suited at the dining table. Able's fingers were speeding across a laptop keyboard, a semicircle of notes and pads already surrounding it.

Able looked up. He was used to being at the crossroads of all government information.

"Prime Minister, it's getting light in Queensland. We don't have much time before all hell breaks loose," he said. "The news is already the big story of the day on the international news channels."

"And good morning to you, young man," Stone said pulling a chair from the table.

Able grinned and sat back. "Sorry about that, Prime Minister," he said. "Your breakfast is coming. Elaine ordered bacon and eggs. Says it's a special treat. Are you on a diet or something?"

"More like the condemned man's last meal," Stone said, and sat facing Able.

"Just joking," he added, a second too late to prevent a frown crossing Able's face.

Able held out a single sheet of paper. The proposed timetable for the morning. He had arranged a meeting with General Thompson and the Australian Security Intelligence Organisation (ASIO) chief Frank Church first off.

The Foreign Minister would be second cab off the rank and then Ambassador Chen of the People's Republic of China. An urgent televised address to the nation was scheduled and then a full Cabinet meeting.

Stone nodded his agreement as his breakfast arrived. Elaine joined the pair and ordered strong coffee.

"Where the hell is Bradbury? Has anyone found the bugger yet?" said Stone hacking into a large piece of bacon.

"Ah, no, sir. Not yet." Able broke eye contact and was suddenly occupied with his papers.

"Well, get someone to find him. Tell him there's a small invasion on. We've lost half the country before breakfast and it would be appreciated if, as the Minister for Defence, he might show up and take some interest."

Elaine raised her coffee cup. And her eyebrows. She took a mouthful and stared at her husband.

"For God's sake, Gary," she said with resignation. "Are you and Mrs Bradbury the only people who don't know?"

A forkful of bacon stopped halfway to Stone's mouth: "Know what?"

"He's been enjoying his lonely nights out in the suburbs for the last six months with a divorcee."

Stone slowly put his fork down, shaking his head.

"Fuck me. You mean the respectably married Minister for Defence is AWOL, out rooting his mistress, while the country is being raped by the Chinese army?"

"Watch your language, Gary. You're not at your trucking company's canteen any more," Elaine said.

"John." Able looked up from his keyboard. "Put Bradbury on your timetable. Before Cabinet meets. And I won't be requiring him at Thompson's briefing."

Stone glanced at the original timetable he was about to hand back for amendment.

"You didn't have Bradbury at Thompson's meeting."

"No, sir," said Able. "I didn't think he'd make the cut."

Stone picked up his fork again. "You're becoming a cynic, young man."

Elaine watched the exchange between the pair. Able was thirty-two, twenty years Stone's junior. But there was an instinctive osmosis between the pair. Able had been appointed to his position by the previous prime minister, an old foe of her husband's.

She knew the position was the most politically sensitive of any departmental job. The nerve centre of every government. Sifting, collating, coordinating and prioritising a flood of sensitive, secret, critical and occasionally embarrassing information.

After winning power, Stone had wanted a fresh face he could trust. A new broom for his new administration.

Amid his search Elaine heard rumours about Able on the cocktail circuit. She confirmed them. Able had told his colleagues he would resign if the next government was to be led by Jeremey Whittacker. She told Stone. He quietly shredded his potential candidates list.

Stone stood up to leave for his meeting with Thompson and Church.

"Well, tell me, before you go. What are you going to do with Bradbury? Sack him?" Elaine said.

Able squirmed at her bluntness.

Stone put his hands in his pockets and stretched backward.

"I'm going to do Defence myself, it'll make things much tidier," he said turning to leave without meeting her eye.

Able stopped him with a polite question: "Prime Minister, do you think I'd better call the Governor General then? He issues the ministerial warrants."

"Oh, shit. Yes, of course. Of course. Thanks, John. Put him on your timetable too."

"Of course, Prime Minister."

Able looked at Elaine. Her reaction following the Bradbury conversation had been a little odd. As though she were disappointed and upset at Stone taking Bradbury's portfolio. There was some strange, new dynamic between them. She sat silent, deep in thought. Then she finished her coffee and excused herself.

6.30 a.m.

The Lodge, Canberra

"Twenty-three million people will be waking up this morning to find their country has been invaded. Their grandfathers' worst nightmare has become a reality: the yellow peril has swarmed down on them."

Stone spoke slowly. Seated before him the Defence Chief, General Thompson, and Frank Church, the head of the Australian Security Intelligence Organisation, tension evident in their eyes. They found it impossible to hold his gaze. Instead they sat motionless in the lounge's big armchairs, bulging briefcases at their feet.

"And every one of those twenty-three million is going to ask the same question: How the hell did this happen?"

Thompson moved to speak but Stone's right hand shot up to cut him off.

"They will be in a state of shock when they learn that every single guard, at every single military base in the Far North, was derelict in their duty. Not a single shot was fired and the whole takeover was complete in less than an hour over three time zones and four thousand kilometres."

It was the greatest national military and intelligence debacle in the country's history.

"And you two are responsible for it. What am I going to tell them?"

Neither man spoke. Neither wanted to be first.

Stone stood up and removed his suit jacket. He crossed the lounge and stared out.

The tense silence grew heavy. Stone pivoted and leaned back on the windowsill crossing his big arms, his body language making its own statement and not inviting any response. Finally he strode back to his chair.

"Right. First business of the day. I'm sacking the Minister for Defence."

There was an involuntary intake of air from the young, pin-stripe-suited ASIO boss. He crossed his legs in a failed attempt to mask his surprise. Thompson remained still but his lined face began to flush.

"Church, for the sake of national morale and the outward appearance of government competence, you will arrange a cover-up to explain his resignation."

Church looked puzzled and wary.

"Bob Bradbury was AWOL, unreachable, in the early hours of this morning because he was out shagging his mistress when the invading hordes took over the country. Can you imagine the implications if this leaks out? The last thing we need right now is a sex scandal. What we do need right now is the full confidence and trust of the people to sort this Chinese shambles out. Find out who this woman is and send her on a long foreign holiday. The same goes for Bradbury's driver. Transfer him today to our Wellington embassy. A promotion. Remind him as forcibly as necessary about his confidentiality agreement."

The two men stared at him.

"Am I clear?"

Church nodded.

Thompson cleared his throat. "Who will be the new Defence Minister then, sir?"

"I will be," said Stone.

Both men nodded neutrally. Their worlds had somersaulted in less than four hours. Stone knew they were worrying about their own fates and was content to let them stew.

"First, I'd like to know what our military status is. Secondly, I'd like to know how it happened."

The old soldier exchanged a glance with Church and began.

It was a simple story of daring military planning, precision, speed and surprise. The current status was also simple: the Chinese had made a clean sweep and occupied all northern army, air force and navy bases. They had thousands of Australian service personnel locked in barracks.

Several patrol boats, three frigates and two Collins submarines were at sea when the attack took place.

One frigate was in the Indian Ocean, the other two off the New South Wales coast.

One submarine was in the Arafura Sea immediately to the north of the country where it had been monitoring scheduled Chinese naval exercises before the Chinese fleet sailed for the Sydney goodwill visit. The other submarine was in the Coral Sea, relatively close to Townsville.

The RAAF's thirty-six Super Hornets along with another seventy-eight, older fighters were at their bases in southern Queensland and New South Wales. The air force had no access to its emergency, defensive, standby airfields in Far North Queensland and the Northern Territory. The Chinese had seized the bases and their skeleton maintenance and security personnel.

Because of the distance from the conventional southern bases to the probable frontline, RAAF fighters would be unable to provide any worthwhile air cover for a land counterattack in the Far North.

Stone was unable to prevent a sigh as the litany of the disaster unfolded.

The Chinese had occupied most of Queensland north of Gladstone, which was 550 kilometres north of Brisbane, the state capital. They had apparently made Queensland's second biggest city, Townsville, with its population of almost 200,000, their administration headquarters. The captured Lavarack base was in one of its outer suburbs.

The Chinese had set up roadblocks along the Bruce Highway outside Cairns, Townsville, Rockhampton and Gladstone.

Service personnel not at Lavarack at the time of the raid had been called to their barracks in a general call-up alert in the early hours. In a clever ruse, hundreds of off-base personnel had subsequently been imprisoned as they hurriedly and unsuspectedly responded. An unknown number of regulars were still free in the city.

The Chinese had seized the rifles and automatic weapons

belonging to local police but had allowed them to retain their pistols and told them to maintain civilian law and order. The Townsville chief police inspector had been taken, presumably as a hostage, to Lavarack.

The Chinese were short of manpower, thought Stone.

Roadblocks were also set up on the desert highways leading west to the far-flung mining and outback townships.

The Chinese had mounted a mass cyber attack and created a communications blackout across the occupied areas. Landline and cellphone services had been terminated progressively since 3 a.m.

Internet service providers were disabled. Normal television and radio programmes had ceased and all stations in the north were simultaneously transmitting the same nonstop light music.

But the situation was about to worsen dramatically, Thompson said, gathering a folder from the briefcase he had ignored till then.

Chinese reinforcements were about to land. Satellite reconnaissance had picked up inbound flotillas of small craft packed with men. They had come from the Chinese aircraft carrier, *Liaoning*, and its four escort destroyers, which were cruising close to Townsville.

Previously the *Varyag*, the carrier had been purchased partially completed in a controversial deal from a penniless Ukraine in 1992. Refitted, she was a 67,000-tonne, 302-metre-long war machine bristling with thirty-six warplanes.

Stone rubbed his chin. "I can remember when they bought it and towed it to China. They said it was going to be a multi-purpose leisure facility."

He shook his head. Now it was sitting off Australia with enough firepower to sail south and create havoc in Brisbane, Sydney and Melbourne.

Thompson looked directly at Stone and said: "Don't forget, sir, we sold them our carrier for scrap too. They used the *Melbourne* to study how aircraft carrier hulls were constructed."

Stone stared back but made no reply. He knew the Chinese were already trialling their first home-built carrier.

Thompson looked back at his briefing papers. Satellite reconnaissance had revealed the movement of sixteen Chinese jet fighters from the carrier to Townsville's joint military-civilian airport at first light.

"The situation in a nutshell is we have lost our trained, ready, reactionary force, about seven hundred armoured fighting vehicles and a hundred artillery guns in one fell swoop with the takeover of Lavarack," said Thompson. "We have no other forces capable of mounting a counterattack immediately."

Thompson put his papers down and sat back stiffly. He knew his career was over.

He added, almost as an afterthought, "If we did have the forces for a counterattack, we'd have to deal with the Chinese promise to butcher all the prisoners they've taken."

No one spoke.

Stone stood again and walked back to the window. He attempted to calm his racing heart and steady the wheezy breathing he was afraid the others could hear.

Thompson broke the silence.

"It's an issue we'll have to face, sir, if the chips go down," he said quietly. "We cannot sit idly by while China brings in reinforcements. Our position would become militarily hopeless."

Stone stayed at the window, his back to the room.

His mind went back to the comforting Australian Strategic Policy Institute report on national military preparedness he had studied when he took office.

"Australia has the most capable air and naval forces in the South-East Asian region," it had said, "but while restricted by ageing equipment, the Australian Defence Force is highly capable of defeating direct attacks by conventional force. The ADF's intelligence-gathering capacities should allow it to detect any attacking force before it reaches Australia."

6.45 a.m.

The Lodge, Canberra

At thirty-nine, Frank Church was the youngest ever ASIO boss, controversially appointed three years earlier to clean out an agency that had stumbled about ineptly creating a string of politically embarrassing intelligence fiascos.

Pale-faced and worn thin by too many half-marathons, internal mutinies and the inability to delegate his overpowering workload, Church shuddered inwardly as Stone crossed the room to take his seat again.

Church had been awake since a panicked 3.24 a.m. call from an ASIO duty officer. He was stricken when he realised the catastrophic extent of the intelligence failure. He decided he would email his resignation to the Prime Minister's office.

His career was over and only a day of humiliating postmortems would lie ahead.

He explained the situation to Jocelyn. His wife had been startled and flung herself from their bed, tearing the sheets off him.

"We have two young babes fast asleep just down the passage. What will they think when they find out their dad threw a sickie when we were attacked? What will everyone else think?"

One of the children woke at the sound of her raised voice and began to cry.

"How can it be all your fault?" she demanded. "No one else saw them coming."

She had stood with hands on hips glaring at him. "Go to work, Frankie. We all need you to do your job."

She left him and he could hear her seconds later quietly soothing one of their sobbing twin daughters.

Stung and humiliated, he dialled his driver and made for the shower. She was right. How could it be all his fault?

In the following early morning hours he had roused officials nationwide and overseen a furious-paced investigation with the determination of a man with a day to live.

"We know how the Chinese arrived, Prime Minister," Church said.

"Pity you couldn't have told me yesterday," Stone said. "How? By submarine?"

Church tapped his gold pen nervously on the palm of one hand.

"Ah, um, no." He took a deep breath. "Not submarines, sir. They came as tourists and conference delegates."

Stone's dismayed reaction was as bad as Church had feared. Stone sat speechless for several seconds.

Finally, he asked, "And no one anywhere detected anything unusual with thousands of young Chinese men pouring into the country?"

Church straightened up defensively. "There was nothing to arouse any suspicion, Prime Minister. Some of the men were posing as tourists and others were pretending to be conference delegates — delegates attending the International Geological Institute conference. It was to be held over three weeks in several Top Half regions. The delegates used hotels and motels in Townsville, Cairns, Darwin and Broome."

He looked quickly down at his briefing notes to avoid the incredulous look on Stone's face. "They came by scheduled air-line and civilian charters, mainly through airports at Brisbane, Cairns and Perth. Our border control data shows about six thousand young Chinese males arrived in the three weeks before the attack."

"But where the hell did all these guys stay?" Stone demanded.

"They packed into every hotel and motel in the Top Half, by the look of it. The local businesses loved it. They were welcomed with open arms. And they were all polite and well behaved — not like most delegates to big corporate conferences," Church said.

"But surely there aren't that many places up there they could stay at. Not that number," said Stone.

"No, you're right, sir. But many of them were supposedly geol-ogists, so it attracted no attention when groups of them drove off with their tents and vanished into desert country on research and study trips."

Stone threw himself back in his chair. "Fuck me. The Chinese made the perfect invasion. So perfect we didn't even notice it."

Church nodded. "Prime Minister, it wasn't an invasion as anyone would understand it. What we've had is a terrorist attack on a grand scale. These people came disguised as civilians, armed themselves once they had infiltrated and then overran bases taking prisoners to use as hostages. Classic terrorist tactics. And done with speed and professionalism."

Stone grunted. Church was right. It was not the sort of attack any defence strategist would have prepared for. But it did not forgive the failure of the bases' guards. Even with peacetime mentality, their wholesale incompetence was scandalous.

Church opened another file. "Our investigations in the last few hours have uncovered the ring responsible for smuggling in the arms. Four Customs officers in Brisbane waved through a number of containers two months ago carrying a bill of lading for geological equipment. We're certain those containers were full of weapons, ammunition and uniforms. We've arrested the four. They were stupid enough to bank rather large sums transferred from Macau into their own or family bank accounts."

Church crossed his legs and went back to tapping his gold pen.

Stone nodded his head. "Thank you, that's good work. Good work. At least we know how they pulled this off. Not that it helps us a hell of lot at the moment."

Stone massaged his chest and squirmed in his chair. Church sat back in his chair with relief. It seemed he still had his job. So far.

"But surely six thousand men can't invade the entire Top Half?" said Stone.

The question hung in the air.

Thompson spoke up. "Prime Minister, I'm afraid six thousand is more than enough. There were only a dozen bases and they were taken completely by surprise. The enemy's lack of manpower wouldn't have been a factor — and they're not planning to have a full-on war. They are holding thousands of our people hostage to prevent any full-scale retaliation. If it looks like we'll call their bluff and risk a hostage massacre, they will have time to call up major reinforcements while we mobilise. They probably have half a dozen nuclear subs sitting off the coast right now to put a stop to any serious countermeasure."

Stone swallowed but said nothing. He felt a familiar tight pain in his chest. He checked his watch. It was time to go. Ambassador Chen was due in six minutes.

7 a.m.

Dean Street, Townsville

Brenda Patterson pulled the drapes back. It was going to be another beautiful, late-spring day. She looked at her watch and yawned. Her husband was late. He had landed the graveyard guard shift at the base last night but should have been home by now.

Johnny, her only son, had followed his father into the Australian Army and was with 2nd Battalion also at Lavarack. He was currently on a survival exercise somewhere out west but wasn't expected back with the rest of his platoon for another couple of days.

She padded barefoot to the kitchen, activated the coffee machine and switched on the radio. The DJ had a hangover, judging by the weird, soft music he was playing.

She gulped down a glass of water and turned off the air-conditioning. She and Keith could only afford to run it at night. It made sleep possible in the constant, humid heat of subtropical Townsville.

She checked the radio dial. It was still on their local commercial station. But the usual classic rock favourites were missing. There was light, orchestral music instead. Maybe someone very important had died.

There was a roar outside. The house shook. She recognised the sound of jet engines. But fighter jets weren't usually allowed to land with all that row over the city this early in the day. There were quite a few of them too. A big exercise must be brewing. There was always something happening in a military town.

She poured a cup of black coffee, lit a cigarette and sat at the kitchen table. The music suddenly stopped. There were several seconds of static.

Then a voice said, "This is the BBC World Service. Here is the news."

Brenda was puzzled. Keith didn't listen to the BBC. She didn't know if you could even get a BBC station in Townsville.

Her confusion turned to shock as the first words of the bulletin registered. She rattled her coffee cup back on its saucer.

"The Chinese Government announced today its military forces have occupied a large swathe of Australia, including the northern regions of Queensland, Western Australia and the Northern Territory."

Brenda stared at the radio. Keith was late. Where was he? Oh, my God. What was going on? And Johnny. In deliberate isolation somewhere out in the desert.

The BBC voice flowed on calmly: "An official statement from Beijing says the action has been taken to ensure China of long-term access to mining and energy resources vital to its national interests. The statement says China will annex a new autonomous economic zone in the regions it has occupied."

Brenda padded over to the kitchen bench where the radio sat, as though the news would somehow be easier to understand if the voice were closer.

"It is understood the Chinese takeover was the result of a lightning, pre-dawn invasion of surgical precision, which met no armed resistance."

She snatched a tissue with trembling hands and dabbed welling tears.

"The Chinese claim their forces now occupy all Australia's northern defence bases. Thousands of base personnel are being held prisoner."

Brenda slumped to the floor leaning back on the kitchen sink cupboards. Her sobs began to drown out the newsreader.

"The Politburo stressed China had no further territorial ambitions and wanted all Australian export operations to continue uninterrupted. It was seeking talks with the Australian Commonwealth Government to reach an agreement to formalise new borders and compensation for nationalised railways, ports and mining and energy resources in the new zone. The talks would also cover the eventual, orderly repatriation of the existing resource industries' workforce, which would be replaced by what it described as skilled Chinese workers. Meanwhile, all existing employees in the occupied zone were required to continue work as usual. The statement says it will be an offence under China's Economic Crimes Regulations for any worker to refuse lawful instructions."

With her knees pulled up to her chin, Brenda didn't hear the voice report the alarmed reactions in world capitals; or America's call for a Security Council resolution calling for China's immediate withdrawal.

Or the academic analysts opining Australia's Top Half had always been recognised as too vast and thinly populated to be defendable.

They noted China's military spending had increased by two hundred per cent since 2000 to more than $145 billion a year. Australia's defence spend was $26 billion, the lowest per capita since the 1930s.

China had an army of two and a quarter million and an air force of 2055 jet fighters. Australia had an army of 58,000 and ninety jet fighters.

Importantly, China had an aircraft carrier in the Coral Sea. It was the perfect platform for an invasion force. The Pacific superpower also boasted a substantial, long-range nuclear arsenal.

Oblivious to the one-sided statistics, Brenda ran to the front door and threw it open. Everything looked normal. Mrs Bagley's home was still right across the street. Her neighbours' houses were all there too, still and unchanged in the early-morning sun.

Coming toward her along the pavement she saw Pat Houlihan, out on his usual morning run.

"Pat!" she shouted at him. "Have you heard the news? The Chinese have invaded us!"

Houlihan stared with surprise at his barefoot neighbour but didn't break his stride.

"Don't be ridiculous, Brenda!" he shouted back. "Are you back on the meth?"

She watched him jog away. Another roar shook her home. She burst into tears again. They would all find out soon enough.

7 a.m.

The Lodge, Canberra

The gravel crackled under the limousine's tyres as Ambassador Chen arrived at a slow, dignified pace outside The Lodge's formal, loggia-styled reception area.

His official vehicle was flanked by four police motorcycles.

It was light but the vehicle's headlights were still on. Like a funeral procession, Chief Petty Officer Bill Solomon thought, as he prepared to meet the visitor. He was in full dress uniform as he had been for the last month on secondment to The Lodge.

Solomon opened the rear door and saluted. Armed guards around the entrance watched curiously as a nondescript, middle-aged Chinese man stepped out. He was wearing a perfectly tailored black suit and a red tie. His charcoal hair was combed straight back.

Perfectly in character, Solomon decided: Chen the undertaker. The diplomat's attempt at a calm demeanour was undermined by eyes that seemed to dart in all directions.

Hardly the warrior profile representing the terrorist hordes that had only hours before captured thousands of his fellow Australians in the Top Half, thought Solomon.

Chen felt unnerved by the silence surrounding him. The Lodge had the atmosphere of a graveyard. It felt chilly. Dangerous. Armed men were everywhere, staring at him.

He was alone. He carried a single thin folder. Diplomatic immunity was his only protection among these men with whom his country had just made enemies.

The grey-haired naval officer dropped his salute and without a word led Chen toward the main door.

Chen noted the Prime Minister was not waiting to formally greet him. Nor his fool of a Foreign Minister.

He effected a dignified air but as he reached the entrance there was a sharp crack. He jumped in fright, instinctively raising an arm to shield his face.

He looked fearfully around and saw the guards remained motionless. Except one, who slapped the butt of his weapon a second time and then slung it casually over his shoulder, ignoring him.

Chen felt his face reddening.

Solomon knew the guards would never shoot the Chink. But they were not beyond a little Aussie larrikinism. They'd all enjoy retelling the way they'd rattled the imperious ambassador.

It was a childish but timely reaction from men who knew Australia's best battle-ready troops were already languishing imprisoned at Lavarack.

In his father's day, the Australian Army had been the first to inflict a defeat on the Imperial Japanese forces in World War Two, in New Guinea. Now Australia faced another Asian invader.

Maybe the forces of history would finally overwhelm Australia? Who could beat China?

Solomon shook the thought from his head and escorted the ambassador inside. The reception area was brightly lit but deserted. Solomon turned right and led Chen down the wide passage to the lounge. It was empty. With exaggerated politeness he waved Chen to an armchair near the unlit fireplace. Chen sat and Solomon left.

Chen waited. And fumed. These Australian soldiers were the

descendants of the European armies that had humiliated his country for the last two hundred years. The British had forced their way into Hong Kong and coerced a treaty from China. The Portuguese had done the same in Macau.

They had demanded, and got by force, their "free ports". Then the Japanese had invaded and colonised all of Manchuria and Taiwan in the 1930s, butchering whole cities. Forty million Chinese had died in the conflict.

The wheel of history was turning full circle. Now his resurgent China, with its five thousand years of history, was to take its own "free ports" and the natural wealth it needed to safeguard its destiny.

And there was nothing America would do to stop it. It was no longer 1996 when China's demands for the return of Taiwan had led President Clinton to station two aircraft carrier forces in the Taiwanese Strait to deter a threatened invasion.

China had been forced to back down. It had been another humiliation. But it would be the last. The world had changed. China now owned the Pacific while it financed America's huge budget deficits.

7.10 a.m.

Private quarters, The Lodge, Canberra

Forced to take the high ball behind his try line, he would always attempt to crash through and take it back into the field of play as the other team stampeded to stop him.

With the Chinese ambassador waiting downstairs he was thinking of the alternative: taking the ball to ground, avoiding the hit-up and giving away possession.

Was it now better to ground it, stay down, feign an injury, tragically limp off hurt and be replaced? He had no answers and this Chinese chequers game had hardly begun. He felt nauseous. His chest felt tight.

He stretched his left leg to ease the knee pain and retreated to the en suite. The bottle of nitrate spray sat where Elaine had left it in plain sight. He squirted a dose beneath his tongue. Its mist went to his bloodstream and opened the arteries in his heart, immediately easing his chest pain.

Elaine came in silently behind him, saw the spray bottle in his hand and hugged him from the back.

"The children have been on the phone," she said softly. "They were wondering what's happening. If the news was true."

Stone stood still in his wife's embrace and sighed.

"They were coming for Christmas," she said. Christmas was only six weeks away. Well, it used to be, she thought.

Stone freed himself from her arms and turned around.

"Yes, and we're going to have roast turkey for Christmas dinner," he said. "With gravy."

"No, there wasn't going to be any gravy for you." She shook her head. "Not with your condition."

"It's Christmas," he said.

Elaine paused to consider the plea, then nodded her head slowly. "All right, you get rid of the Chinese and we'll think about the gravy situation."

Stone shook his head solemnly. "You're a hard woman, Elaine Stone."

He gave her a peck on the head and went downstairs to find Lindsay Noble. He was waiting anxiously in the dining room.

"Let's go and hear what the Ambassador for the People's Republic has to say," Stone said. "They might have taken Melbourne by now."

"No, they haven't," Noble said as he shook his head. "We'd have heard about it on the BBC."

* * *

Chen's slight figure was swallowed in the big armchair. He struggled to his feet when Stone strode into the lounge extending a large paw.

"Sorry to keep you waiting, Excellency," he said.

Chen bowed his head in the Chinese custom and the pair shook hands. Stone stood aside for the same formality to be exchanged with Noble.

The three sat down. The diplomat's features were partly obscured by the growing morning light from the big garden windows behind him. Stone offered him no coffee or drinks.

Chen opened his thin folder. It was bright red with an embossed yellow star on its cover. It contained a single sheet of paper.

Chen held it up and read: "The Politburo of the People's Republic of China wishes me to inform you that it has today annexed territory in the State of Queensland, Western Australia and the Northern Territory. My government is pleased that this action has been achieved without the loss of life."

China would guarantee the sovereign integrity of all lands to the south of its annexed areas upon Australia signing a settlement treaty in the next ten days accepting the new borders. China had no more territorial ambitions and no wish for bloodshed.

"However, any move by Australia to launch a counterattack will lead to an immediate annexation of more territory to the south, including Brisbane."

He looked up from the page and added, "And, you would appreciate, any aggression on your part would imperil the lives of the soldiers we have already captured."

Stone pushed his lips out and said nothing. Chen broke his gaze, looked down at his sole piece of paper and continued in a matter-of-fact style.

The treaty would outline the compensation to be paid to the Australian Government and resource companies for their assets; and arrangements for the repatriation of resource workers as their Chinese replacements arrived.

Captured military personnel would be released in twelve months, conditional on Australia agreeing to disband their units permanently.

Chen put the brief memorandum back in the folder and placed it carefully on the empty coffee table beside him.

He waited for the reaction. He had played out the next part of the meeting in his mind many times in the last month. The anger. The protests. The counter-demands. The threats. He knew he would relish it. He would relive these minutes, this highlight of his meteoric career, for the rest of his life.

There were sounds of busyness in the passageway. Vehicles could be heard arriving at the main entrance. Doors opening, closing. Muted conversations. But not a sound from the Australians he faced.

Stone seemed to be transfixed by the view of his gardens. Noble was studying an antique vase on the window table. Chen felt the first flicker of uncertainty.

They were in shock, he thought. They would get used to their new circumstances soon enough.

But suddenly the bear-like frame of the Australian Prime Minister rose from his chair and offered his hand.

Chen fought to control his surprise as he struggled to his feet from deep within the armchair.

Stone was dismissing him, he realised.

Matching the polite tone of his new nemesis, Stone said: "Mr Ambassador. Thank you for coming in. I'm sure my Foreign Minister will be in touch with you in due course."

Stunned, Chen bowed his head and shook hands with both men. Nothing further was said and he was left to make his way out unescorted.

As he reached the lounge door he knew he had revealed his fury and humiliation by walking too fast. Blood rushed to face. He had to open the door himself. He slowed his pace as he made his way to his waiting limousine.

In the lounge, Stone shrugged at Noble. They both sat down again. Stone felt his heart thudding. He had been unable to think of any immediate response to Chen's ultimatum so he had followed his instincts and kicked for touch.

There was a knock on the door. Able rushed in. "What happened, sir? Chen just went out the front door by himself with a face like thunder."

Stone looked at his department head and clasped his hands behind his head. "He told us we had ten days to sign a peace treaty giving away half the country. If we don't, they'll attack and occupy Brisbane. If we try to stop them, they'll kill all the prisoners they've taken."

Able waited.

"And?" he finally asked.

"We told him to fuck off."

Stone and Noble watched Able's horrified, uncomprehending expression and broke into laughter.

* * *

"How did the meeting go?"

Chen's chauffeur half-turned toward his passenger. Chen slowly massaged his forehead and stared out his window as the limousine pulled away, down The Lodge driveway. What to tell of the fiasco he had just endured? The Australians had given no indication of what they were thinking.

He prayed they would trade their empty northern deserts for their cities and not do anything stupid — like start an inconvenient war they couldn't win.

He had to compose himself. Beijing would be waiting urgently to hear. Probably the first to relay anything would be the man behind the wheel, the embassy's most senior intelligence operative tasked to spy on his every move.

Chen took a cigarette from a gold case and lit up. He exhaled a rush of blue smoke and said: "They were in a state of shock. They just sat there like beaten dogs."

The chauffeur nodded into the rear-vision mirror.

"I explained the basic points of the border treaty. There was nothing they could say really. They don't have any cards to play."

Chen's version of events cheered himself up. The chauffeur grinned. It was what everyone had expected.

"They do think we'll butcher their precious white soldiers. I could see it in their eyes," said Chen.

The chauffeur gave a short humourless snort. He would be reporting on the most stunning military victory in modern times.

7.15 a.m.

Breakers Inn, Surfers Paradise

Chris Sharp enjoyed a sleep-in when he was on holiday. But the middle-aged Sydney importer found it impossible to stay asleep as the sun scorched through the hotel's thin drapes.

Anna had no trouble. She worked shifts at all hours at an Air New Zealand check-in counter and could happily snooze off anywhere at any time.

It had been a late night. He and Anna had sampled several nightclubs along the Gold Coast's glitter strip.

He opened the balcony door and looked out on the surf crashing ashore along kilometres of white sands. Hot air rushed in, overwhelming the air-conditioning.

Squinting over the thirty-ninth floor's balustrade he saw a floating school of surfboarders waiting patiently for the next decent set.

He heard the sound of several horns disturbing the Sunday peace. Far below, a queue of cars was backing up along the main road from a service station.

He stretched his arms, yawned and went to look for some aspirin. On the way to the bathroom he picked up the television remote and sizzled the set to life.

He never made it to the aspirin supply. He forgot he even had a headache. He frowned at the screen at first unable to understand what he was seeing. And then he rushed to Anna.

She yelled at him angrily for waking her. He ignored her protests and explained what he had seen on the television. She watched the crazy man open their suitcases and begin to chuck in all their clothing, shoes and shirts.

She sat up, shielding her eyes from the light.

"Get out of bed quick," he ordered her. "We're going back to Sydney right now."

She stared at him.

"Go out and listen to the news if you don't believe me. But you've got two minutes and we're gone."

Sharp did not know it but he was already too late.

He decided there was no time to pay the account. He would settle it from Sydney.

The big Chrysler reached the hotel's underground garage exit and was halted by four other cars queuing to leave.

He glanced at the fuel gauge. It showed a smidgen over quarter full. He cursed. Looking pale and bedraggled, his wife reached for her cellphone. She had to tell the children they were coming back early.

She hit the favourites list and pressed the home number. The phone signalled busy. The kids were on the phone. The car finally moved forward but only after one of their queue drove down the footpath and forced its way into the crawling stream of traffic.

They waited. Sharp's fingers drummed the steering wheel. He reached for the radio and an excited voice flooded the car. They had had the volume seriously loud last night. He turned it down.

An angry woman was complaining servos were not rationing petrol. Two of her local ones were out already. She had a sick mother to pick up at Coolangatta.

Sharp glanced at Anna who was redialling. The busy dial tone repeated itself.

There was a loud crash as a big SUV tailgated an aged Toyota Corona. The old man driving the small Japanese car stopped and got out, yelling at the bearded driver behind him.

The altercation created a gap in the traffic. Sharp and his fellow hotel evacuees accelerated into it. A hundred metres on they caught up with the traffic tail crawling at twenty-three kilometres an hour.

They saw an old Holden shunted to the side of the road, steam billowing from its hood.

"Overheated," said Sharp.

"Christ, there's about a dozen people jammed in it," Anna said as they crawled past.

The temperature display on the dashboard already read 23°C.

Three kilometres further and the tail from a servo spilled out and blocked one of the two southern lanes. Staff were still pumping gas. Tense, impatient customers sounded their horns in vain for faster service.

As they crept closer, Sharp could see an elderly woman screaming and remonstrating with the servo cashier. There was a sudden flicker on the illuminated price board. A new dollar amount shone out. It was four times the normal rate.

The protesting woman screamed and attempted to strike the cashier. Frightened children belted into hot vehicles on the tarmac began crying. The hot, humid air stank of exhaust fumes. The woman marched defiantly to her car and drove off.

A servo staffer emerged holding a cardboard sheet. Handwritten on it, in large capitals: "CASH ONLY". He walked down the queue holding it above his head.

"Shit," said Sharp. "How much cash have you got on you?"

Anna dropped the phone in her lap and searched her handbag. She found twenty-three dollars. Sharp dug in his rear pocket and tossed her his wallet. She found another nineteen dollars. And four, now worthless, credit cards.

They decided to wait it out in the queue rather than risk driving on in hope of finding another servo. They now had the jitters. The general air of desperation was enveloping them.

Cashless people near the front of the queue argued with staff and grabbed the pump nozzles from them. Two fist fights broke out.

A large, potbellied, bald-headed man in oil-stained overalls appeared from behind the servo carrying a monstrous wrench. He smashed one brawling customer over the head. The man fell. The second scuffle froze.

Servo staff pushed both the non-cash customers' cars to the side. Others jumped forward to take their place. The bleeding man lay dazed and unattended on the side of the tarmac.

"Christ," Anna gasped, hands over her mouth. "What is happening? What is happening?"

Sharp said nothing. He switched off the air-conditioning. The cabin temperature rose almost immediately.

"Saving gas," he said. "This refuel isn't going to get us far."

They wound down the windows and edged another car space forward.

Anna redialled the home number.

As the tone bleeped busy again the car reached the pump. Sharp handed his notes over. The pump seemed to operate for only seconds.

The thug with the wrench watched as Sharp restarted the big V8 and eased toward the jammed highway. A beat-up Kombi, driven by a hippy with a greasy ponytail and a permanent, hazy grin, waved them in.

Gleefully returning the wave they rejoined the slow procession south. The radio was muttering. Anna turned up the volume.

"... have been overloaded. Emergency officials have appealed for people to use cellphones for life-threatening situations only. Mobile phone companies have also warned people not to add to the congestion by attempting to reach any areas north of Gladstone. All cell towers in central and northern Queensland have been shut down. All internet access in the region has also been cut."

Anna stared at the mobile in her hand.

"The police report the motorways south of Brisbane are choked and traffic is near standstill," said the radio. "A number of vehicles have overheated or broken down in the expressway centre lanes compounding the chaos. Passengers are trapped in the stranded cars. Tow trucks are unable to reach them in the gridlock. As reported earlier, there have been three deaths in road accidents confirmed on the expressway since four o'clock this morning. Ambulances have been unable to reach people injured in seven other crashes. Police are appealing for motorists to remain off the roads."

The Sharps looked at each other as they idled forward. What mess had they found themselves in?

"We also have unconfirmed reports of cars being hijacked near expressway exit ramps south of Brisbane. Witnesses claim families have been ordered from their vehicles at knife and gun point."

It was becoming a real-life nightmare. The Sharps held hands across the leather console. They were being swept up in a modern-day refugee exodus, the thin veneer of a civilised society already splintering.

The radio went on: "The Prime Minister, Gary Stone, is expected to address the nation shortly. Meanwhile, a Bankers' Association spokesman has confirmed most ATMs in the state were emptied shortly before six this morning in today's unprecedented panic run on them."

"It's going to be a hungry trip," said Anna.

"At least you don't need to worry about the diet today," said Sharp squeezing her hand.

Unbeknownst to them the traffic snarl ahead continued for more than 150 kilometres.

They did not see the barely edited panic scenes being broadcast on early Sunday television bulletins live from the overwhelmed Brisbane and Coolangatta airports.

Holiday-makers from the Sunshine and Gold Coast tourist meccas, north and south of Brisbane, had cut short their vacations and stormed the terminals desperate for seats home.

The Brisbane railway station had been mobbed while even bigger crowds jammed the Brisbane International Ship terminal. Huge sums changed hands for cruise ship tickets as the white liners readied to rush from Australian waters.

Anna finally switched off her phone. Better to save battery life.

They were nearly a thousand kilometres from home.

Their nightmare had just begun.

8.35 a.m.

Private study, The Lodge, Canberra

Gary Stone glanced nervously at his watch. He had twenty-five minutes left before his nationwide broadcast. A shocked and frightened nation was waiting to hear from him.

He knew Australians had become complacent about their privileged place in the world. Faced with the trauma of a foreign threat, they were reacting badly, some shamefully.

Police and news reports were painting a grim picture of fear and panic.

Hijackings, violence, profiteering and looting from mobs on the run south dominated the news.

Australia had been seriously attacked only once in its history. The Japanese had launched a big air raid on Darwin in World War Two — an even bigger one than they had launched against the Honolulu naval base, which brought the USA into World War Two. But Australia had never faced an actual invasion.

Stone had always believed Aussies under threat would be made of sterner stuff than they were displaying in the first few hours of this crisis.

The country's per capita spending on defence had sunk to the lowest relative level in more than eighty years, ignoring its isolated and fragile toehold at the bottom of Asia. His audience wouldn't want to be reminded of that but the voters had themselves created the problem, along with their weak political leaders.

The work for a real strategic defence force — a new fleet of submarines to properly protect its sea lanes against invasion — had constantly bogged down when governments confronted its huge cost versus voters' demands for more welfare spending.

Now a decision had been made at last to home-build a French designed submarine fleet but it would be decades before it was fully operational.

Meantime Australia had six weary old subs and was lucky to

have any three of them seaworthy at the same time. At least there were still two of them out there so far undetected.

The country he would address in the next few minutes had been the richest on earth twice in its short history — each time in commodity booms.

Stone knew from his high school history classes that in 1885, within a hundred years of the first Europeans settling in the colony, its prosperity was unequalled anywhere.

Colonial graziers exploited cheap land, a warm climate and open pastures to become the most efficient in the world, their sixteen million sheep supplying more than half the wool woven in the textile mills of Great Britain. Then the era of refrigerated cargo dawned and the boom rolled on.

That stellar prosperity had been welded to a gold rush reaching every state of the infant country. But the boom had ended and Australia fell from top to twenty-first in the wealth league. More than half a century passed before the resources boom of the mid-2000s drove it back to the top.

Until recently the only people richer per capita lived in tiny countries like Qatar, Norway and Luxembourg. But now the latest resources boom had collapsed too.

The Australia he governed was running broke, racking up huge deficits as a matter of course, its pampered and overfed citizens in denial. Now they faced a terrible war.

How could he rally them? Would it be possible if they knew the truth? A counterattack that would see twelve thousand POWs slaughtered. How keen would they be to fight knowing their cities could be obliterated by the nuclear weapons of the new Pacific superpower? Or that they were militarily on their own, without allies.

Some panic was understandable from people living in or near the Top End. But the vast majority of Australians lived in big cities clustered mainly around the southeastern fringe of the country — a world away from the mineral-rich northern deserts and in no immediate danger.

Clearly the people did not believe the Chinese would be content to stay put in the north. They feared a full-scale invasion was brewing.

The headlines on extra, early-morning editions of the metropolitan Sunday papers had reinforced this alarm:

CHINESE INVADE

DEFENCE FORCES SLEEP THROUGH ROUT

CHINA TAKES THE NORTH WITHOUT RESISTANCE

CHINESE FLEET SIGHTED OFF QUEENSLAND

TOWNSVILLE ARMY BASE SEIZED IN LIGHTNING RAID

12,000 POWs HOSTAGE IN QLD

US CONDEMNS BLATANT ACT OF WAR — UN SECURITY COUNCIL TO MEET

HIGHWAYS CLOG AS FAMILIES FLEE WAR ZONES

Stone glanced at his watch again. There was now only fifteen minutes to go. There was a knock and the door to the private, first-floor study swung open. John Able appeared.

"Oh, there you are, Prime Minister," he said. He was holding a small sheath of papers.

"How are you getting along with your speech notes, sir?"

Stone shrugged. "I've been trying to put some thoughts together but I got interrupted by Tommy Hutcheson."

"Oh?" said Able.

Stone told him the Police Minister was alarmed at the shambolic refugee situation in Queensland and northern New South Wales. There had been violent riots at petrol stations and three fatalities so far in road rage incidents and hijackings.

The minister had pleaded for armed troops to restore order by establishing roadblocks and forcibly halting the exodus.

Stone said he had warned Hutcheson roadblocks only worked if soldiers were able to shoot people who attempted to breach them.

Hutcheson had said as far as the police were concerned, people were already dying and it wouldn't be necessary to shoot too many at a roadblock to get the traffic to stop.

Able whistled. He sat down opposite Stone's desk. "So what have you decided to do, sir?"

"I told him I'd announce armed roadblocks in my speech."

Able looked at the ceiling and said nothing. Things were getting out of hand so quickly, he thought.

Stone broke the silence. "So that's one thing I'm going to say. But I haven't got very far with the rest, to be honest."

Able studied him. Stone's face was flushed. His tie was askew. He had a pad on his knee. There was almost nothing written on it.

"I've had a suggestion for your speech," he said.

"Have you put some thoughts down?"

"No, no. Jeremey Whittacker has, sir. He thought you might like a hand. His office has sent this over." Able held up the papers he was carrying.

"Whittacker! Thought he could help?" Stone's anger was instant. "What would that little wimp know?"

Able withdrew the papers. The Prime Minister would never know they were all blank.

Stone calmed himself and gave a small chuckle.

"Whittacker. The war leader," he muttered, mainly to himself. "Unbelievable."

Able felt a pang of guilt but his ruse to buck the Prime Minister from his growing indecisiveness had been an instant success.

Stone stood up. He tossed the pad aside before straightening his tie.

"Prime Minister, the people at the moment just want calm leadership. Reassurance the government is in control and exploring every option. Reassurance they face no immediate danger. The Chinese have said publicly they're camping in the north and satellite reconnaissance confirms there's no military activity near the border except at their roadblocks."

Stone rubbed his knee and straightened his tie a second time. He nodded his thanks for the summary.

"Don't worry, John, I won't fuck it up. I get gravy when I've sort this thing out."

He strode from the changing sheds, down the tunnel toward the field and the expectant fans. Able, pleased but mystified, followed. Gravy? Had he missed something in the strategic mix?

8.55 a.m.

The Lodge, Canberra

Bob Bradbury was waiting in the main lounge. He clasped his hands together to stop a small tremor that had persisted for the last few hours.

The Defence Minister knew Stone was about to broadcast live but Stone had asked to see him first. The PM probably wanted advice on what tone to set or some military analysis.

Still, he could not rid himself of some deep disquiet. The PM had not returned any of his calls before he had arrived at The Lodge. So he had turned up with the rest of the agitated posse of Cabinet ministers who were gathering in the dining room.

Bradbury bounced to his feet as Stone walked in. The Prime Minister was alone. He shut the door behind him and pointed Bradbury back to his chair. The pair sat down facing each other.

Bradbury sat forward. "This is a hell of a situation, Gary."

"Yes, Bob, it is," Stone said.

There was an awkward, two-second gap.

Bradbury went on: "I've got a few ideas about our options. Some thoughts on what our next move could be."

Stone said nothing. Bradbury was sure the silence reflected Stone's stress and confusion. He was here to help. He was needed.

He leaned forward confidently and said: "Gary, I know you're about to go on air in a few minutes but is there anything you want me to do right now while you're doing that?"

"Yes," said Stone. "Resign."

Bradbury's head jerked. His jaw dropped. His eyebrows jumped. He removed his glasses and stared at Stone.

"You know why," Stone said quietly to forestall any debate.

Bradbury swallowed.

"The fact is every senior figure in the military knows you were AWOL, uncontactable, with your mistress in the early hours of this morning.

"Those who don't soon will. Bob, it's only a matter of time before all the grubby details leak."

Bradbury sat stock still. Then his bottom lip developed a quiver.

"It's not a situation we can live with," Stone said. "The last thing I need now is a sex scandal and more allegations of government incompetency."

He took a notebook from an inside suit pocket and flipped it open.

"Mrs Gwen Bradbury cannot be allowed to know anything."

At the sound of his wife's name, Bradbury crumpled back in his chair.

"There will never be any need for her to know where you were busying yourself at two this morning when the balloon went up. The ministerial limousine parked outside the Dimmer Street residence of divorcee Anna Whiplestone last night in full view of passers-by had been driven there without authorisation by your driver, one Harry Cardwell, a single man. He and Whiplestone have been friends for some months but have decided to part ways. Later today he will begin a month's holiday in New Zealand before he takes up a long-term appointment at our Wellington embassy. His girlfriend will be flying to New York where she has decided to live."

Stone flipped a page of the notebook.

"You were at your Canberra flat all night. You suffered a reoccurrence of a formerly unannounced high blood pressure condition. The medications you took meant you didn't wake until five forty-five a.m. This morning you suffered a small stroke. In light of the seriousness of your condition and the undoubted stress you would face in this emergency, you have decided for the good of the country to retire."

Bradbury heaved a sigh. "Quite a cover-up you've managed."

He stood up slowly.

"I suppose you've got my resignation letter typed too?"

"Frank Church has. He's waiting next door."

Bradbury paused. "So, who's going to get Defence?"

"I am," said Stone.

Bradbury's eyes opened a fraction wider. He said nothing, turned and walked to the door. When he reached it the old philanderer pushed his head up and shoulders back.

He hadn't been sacked. He had resigned. In the national interest. His farm would not be divided in a messy divorce. And fuck Stone.

* * *

There was a knock on the lounge door. It opened and a bleary-eyed Joseph Martini stood staring in. He was the Trade Minister — and Stone's best friend.

"What have you done to old braggart Bradbury? Given him a good kick up the arse after this morning's shambles?"

"Christ, don't tell me you're hung over. Where have you been? At a Canberra Italian Club all-nighter?" said Stone.

"We're lucky there's a decent Italian club in the country's most boring city," said Martini. He walked in and helped himself to the chair Bradbury had just vacated.

Late to politics, the sixty-three-year-old widower, a South Australia vineyard owner, had been surprised when Stone put him in the Cabinet.

"Heard the news," said Martini rubbing both eyes.

"Shame Bradbury didn't. He was busy, shacked up with some

chick when the Chief of Defence was trying to find him in the early hours," said Stone.

"Oh, really? And?"

"I've just sacked him."

"Bloody good on you. We'll all be better off without that gasbag," said Martini. "How bad is it up north?"

"Couldn't be much worse. Lost everything in Queensland right down to Gladstone. In Western Australia they've taken from Port Hedland to the Pilbara iron ore mines and all the LPG gas installations in the Northern Territory."

Martini shook his head.

"I hope you're not thinking of me to replace Bradbury. I wouldn't know a tank from a bank."

Stone laughed. He leaned back and said, "No, I'm keeping the new glamour job for myself."

"Some glamour. You've only got half the bloody country left on day one," said Martini.

Stone ignored the comment. "I've got another job for you. I need you to use your delicate diplomatic skills on the Chinese. I want you to lead the Australian delegation to discuss China's demands."

Martini pulled a face and half stood, as though to sprint away somewhere. Anywhere.

"You must be joking. I'd be more likely to smack their lights out than talk to them," he said.

Stone stood up and walked to the coffee table. He fetched the single page of China's ultimatums and handed it to Martini.

Martini read it and whistled.

"What the hell do you want me to do about this?"

"I need you to buy me some time. As much as you can. We need to figure out what we can do to get out of this mess," said Stone.

"You want me to filibuster?"

"No, a bit more than that. You'll have to look defiant. Then conciliatory. And then defeated. Save the defeated bit till last. If they think we'll accept their border treaty they will be prepared to haggle longer. Right now, as you can see, they've given us just ten days to roll over."

Martini looked unconvinced. "Why don't you get Lindsay Noble to do it? He's the expert foreign affairs man?"

Stone paused.

"I can't. He's too polite and proper. He would have trouble being noisy and belligerent, not to mention lying outright. Which he would have to do because I'm not accepting this land grab. I need you to be the fox in the henhouse for the moment. Lindsay can be brought in later if need be. At present he's recovering from America telling him the cavalry won't be coming over the hill with an ANZUS flag flying."

"Shit, Gazza, you'll owe me for this hospital pass," said Martini. "Meantime you'd better get going. I hear you're about to make the speech of your life."

9 a.m.

Hazel's office, The Lodge, Canberra

The camera lights were blinding in the small office tucked away on the landing halfway up The Lodge's stairway. It had for years been the favourite workspace of Hazel Hawke during her husband's lengthy tenure.

Standing resolutely behind a hastily procured lectern bearing the country's coat of arms, Stone tried not to squint into the glare as he called for calm and order before several television cameras. He stressed there was no immediate danger to the country's state capitals.

The government was in talks with its allies and would be in direct negotiations with China demanding the immediate withdrawal of their forces.

He told a record television audience of sixteen million: "Australia has faced similar challenges in her history. And we have fought off others who would invade us. We are in an extremely dangerous situation, but we are unbowed. I ask you all to be patient while your government carefully considers what options it will adopt to resolve this latest challenge to our democracy."

He said it was critical the economy did not collapse. Everyone must return to their jobs when business opened at the start of the business week the next day.

To restore order, the government would establish army road-blocks on all highways south of Brisbane. There was no crisis to justify a refugee exodus. Only bona fide travellers would be permitted south.

He concluded with a message: the country's two million Asians had played no role in the events of the morning. They were as much victims as everyone else. There was to be no mindless, racist reprisals targeting a group of citizens whose loyalty was unquestioned by him.

The address ended. The cameras stopped. The lights went out. Members of the camera crews crossed the room spontaneously. They all shook hands with him. It was a silent tribute. No one said anything.

Stone turned and made for the dining room. His twenty-one-strong inner Cabinet were crammed around the table. They had watched his live telecast in the room on a monitor mounted temporarily on a coffee table.

There was a round of applause as he took his chair at the head of the table, next to his deputy. He leaned over and whispered to Jeremey Whittacker: "Thanks for sending your speech notes over, Jerry, but I didn't get time to look at them."

Whittacker gave a puzzled nod. He struggled to know if Stone was taking the piss or just disorganised and incompetent as usual.

The worst crisis an Australian Cabinet had ever convened to discuss was over in sixteen minutes. Stone reported Bradbury's stroke and resignation. There were murmurings of sympathy. Stone said in the interim he would act as Defence Minister.

He then outlined the military and diplomatic situation. Most of it was not new, a repeat of the information already reported in the media. He told them Martini would take charge in scoping out the detail of China's demands. Noble stared at his hands and said nothing.

There were gasps of surprise and grunts of anger when they learned America would take no direct action to help oust the Chinese. The ANZUS Treaty was a worthless document, Stone told them.

"What happened to the Pacific pivot?" one minister asked rhetorically.

There was little discussion around the table. The mood was subdued, sombre.

Stone had no opposition to the measures he sought to authorise: a state of emergency to give himself executive powers to govern by decree; the introduction of fuel and food rationing; control of air, road and rail systems.

The stock market would be closed till further notice but the currency would be left to float. When he sensed opposition to this, he said the Aussie dollar would tank but it was better to deal with that reality than try to overcome an inevitable currency black market if the government set an artificial, higher exchange rate. Heads nodded.

The exporters would be very happy, a minister said. Their goods would be some of the cheapest in the world.

Private account holders at the banks would have cash withdrawals limited to $1000 a day.

All airports, railways and bus terminals south of Gladstone would remain open. The government would underwrite all airlines' insurance cover.

There would be no censorship restrictions on the media. The government's messages would have more credibility if reported by a free press.

Whittacker stirred but said nothing. His supporters followed his lead. remaining mute.

Stone forewarned there could be reports of bloodshed as the army turned back desperate refugees at northern roadblocks.

As the meeting was concluding he insisted America's decision to abandon Australia militarily had to remain a strict secret for

as long as possible. Meantime the Americans' anti-China postur-
ing at the United Nations would give some Australians hope and
help prevent further needless panic.

The ministers filed out funereally. If caught outside their
offices by news cameras, they fought to look energetic and confident. They were professional politicians, after all. The government had the matter in hand, they would all say, and quickly
move on.

9.26 a.m.

Pitt Street, Sydney CBD

The Double Bay traffic from her daughters' private secondary
school had been light as usual on a Sunday morning. She had
dropped them off for their extra mathematics tutorials and
headed for her city office.

The civilised traffic was in marked contrast to the news from
southern Queensland that Lilly Yu was listening to as she edged
the Mercedes into the kerb to join a small queue to the underground garage she leased in Pitt Street.

The entry security barrier had jammed creating the back-up.
The other drivers playing weekend executive paperwork catch-
up sat impatiently as an attendant worked frantically to repair it.

Lilly tapped the steering wheel while her thoughts wandered
to the morning's sensational news of the Chinese terrorist attack
on the Top Half. Second-generation Chinese migrants, she and
her husband had watched the television reports with alarm.

But they decided not to allow the events in the north to disrupt
their Sunday plans as there was nothing they could do but sit
and wait for the government to assess its response. There was no
point in alarming their young daughters.

Peter Yu had been keen to have the penthouse to himself for
a few hours. He wanted to use his quiet time in the comfortable
home study. He was completing a ground-breaking medical

research paper for the Lucas Heights nuclear science centre. The paper was due in a week's time.

Lilly's thoughts were broken when two other shiny black limos appeared in the rear-vision mirror as they joined the growing queue to the garage. The CBD traffic on Sundays was always constant if not heavy.

Lilly knew her junior accounting assistant would already be waiting upstairs to brief her. Heather had spoken directly to the American clients who were demanding a greater, more urgent, effort to have their taxation liabilities reduced. Or eliminated.

They would be the first business of the day tomorrow at the accountancy firm where she had been a partner for the last seven years.

As she pondered the latest pressure on her accountancy skills, she heard a thud and felt her car rock slightly. The car behind must have nudged her. She pushed the unlock button on her door and opened it slightly to see what the problem was.

She found herself confronted by a young man with a shaved head. An ugly swastika was tattooed into his forehead.

Her hand shot to her mouth in shock as Shaved Head swore loudly and smashed his steel-capped boot into the rear passenger door. The heavy vehicle again reverberated slightly.

Shaved Head grabbed her door and yanked it open. She screamed and grabbed the leather armrest. She didn't have the strength to pull it closed again. She saw two other grinning, jean-clad, tattooed skinheads join Shaved Head.

One of them reached for her arm and tried to pull her out onto the roadway but her seatbelt was firmly attached. He swore, leaned across her tiny body, the steel buttons on his filthy jean jacket ripping across her face as he pressed the belt release.

A second later she was hauled out and landed on her hands and knees on the hard roadway. Screaming in terror, she tried to stand. She was silenced by a sharp blow to the face. She tumbled onto her back and one of the men kicked her viciously in the side.

In her peripheral vision Lilly saw the fracas was being wit-

nessed by a number of pedestrians who had stopped on the footpath.

Shaved Head spat at her, wrenched her to her feet and pushed
her behind the Mercedes.

Lilly realised in a panicked second none of the pedestrians
was moving to help her. Several of the men and a young couple
walked away. Others avoided the scene, peeling off the footpath
to cross the street.

"Fucking Chinks. We should never have let any of ya yellow
fuckers into the country!" screamed Shaved Head. She felt his
spittle on her face. "And now ya think you're gonna take over
Australia."

Lilly was shoved bodily over the boot of her Mercedes and
trapped.

"What ya got to say now, ya slope-faced bitch?"

His smirking mate slammed her in the face. She felt blood
trickling from her nose and into her mouth.

"Why don't ya fuck off back to where ya came from while ya
got a chance?"

Shocked and shaking uncontrollably, Lilly looked around
again desperately for help. Several white men in smart casual
wear appeared on the footpath beside the Mercedes. They
formed a small, indecisive huddle looking on silently. As she
watched she was mortified to see one of the group nodding his
head in approval.

But she saw another lift a cellphone to his ear. He turned away
as he spoke into it. Shaved Head turned to see what she was looking at.

"Who do ya think ya calling, mate?" he yelled. He leapt onto
the pavement and lunged at the back of the man. The cellphone
spilled to the ground. Shaved Head jumped on it with a heavy
boot.

"Ya was calling the cops, wasn't ya?" he snarled.

The shocked caller opened and shut his mouth wordlessly.

"Just fuck off before we deal to ya too!" he shouted. The man
fled.

He turned back to Lilly, still pinned against the back of the limousine by Shaved Head's accomplices.

Shaved Head lowered his voice. "Now, while ya little yellow fuckers are raping and looting up north, do ya think we could borrow your ride?"

Unable to move, Lilly stared back in silent, wide-eyed fear.

"That's very kind of ya," said Shaved Head. He lifted her free of the car and threw her bodily across the pavement into the stone wall of a bank. She screamed and slumped to the ground.

"Get in, boys," said Shaved Head. "These wheels are what ya call 'the spoils of war'."

They all laughed raucously and scrambled into the car. Shaved Head took the driver's seat. He put the limousine in gear and bolted from the kerb into the traffic heedless of the blasting horns and screeching brakes his flight created.

The Mercedes roared away. The skinhead in the back seat lowered the window to give a final single-finger salute to Lilly.

As the Mercedes disappeared, several women rushed to Lilly and helped her to her feet. In the distance she could hear the wail of a police siren.

The men who had been watching the fracas walked off. Some seemed sheepish; others unconcerned.

Lilly massaged her aching side and dabbed her bleeding nose. She was suddenly aware she was, now, a foreigner in her own land. No one had come to her rescue. Everyone had simply watched as she was battered and humiliated.

Amid the trauma her family's fate as Australians began to swirl through her concussed brain.

An uncertain young blonde woman offered her more tissues. She said an ambulance would arrive soon.

Lilly sat back down on the pavement and leaned on the grey stone wall trying to slow her breathing. She was looking down at the pavement when a pair of black boots appeared. They belonged to a police officer. He was standing over her.

After a few moments he said, "Be a good idea to make yourself scarce, lady."

His fellow patrolman strolled over to stand beside him. He nodded his head in agreement and they both turned away and went casually back to their police car.

Lilly's was the fifth such incident they had been directed to since their shift began. The policemen could hear the warble of an approaching ambulance siren. They wouldn't be waiting for it.

Lilly finally stood carefully as Heather walked up.

"Lilly, what's happened?" she said. "Who did this to you?"

Lilly quietly thanked the blonde woman for her tissues. Heather looked from one to the other. "I heard the garage barrier had broken and came down to find where you were. What on earth happened? Were you in an accident? Come on, I'll help you upstairs." She put an arm around her diminutive boss.

"There's no hurry. The Americans phoned. They've cancelled tomorrow's meeting."

As they began to walk slowly away, an ambulance swept to the kerb and killed its siren. Two paramedics jumped out, one carrying a first-aid kit. He asked if she needed help.

She shook her head. She had no broken bones and did not want to go to any hospital. They looked uncomfortable, took some details but did not press her.

Lilly limped to the foyer entrance where she stopped. She turned frowning. There was something amiss. She gave an inner shudder realising what it was. She was the only Asian person she could see anywhere on the street.

DAY TWO

The Lodge, Canberra

The phoney war began and a nervous calm settled on the country.

The refugee exodus had been stopped — if by use of force — and almost everybody went back to their jobs as the working week started.

Overseas, governments and the media had been agog at the sensational Chinese attack.

There had been spontaneous protest rallies. Some had ended in violence. There had been live coverage from Los Angeles and New York of Chinese businesses set alight by Molotov cocktail attacks.

The walls of Big Box retailers crammed with low-cost Chinese stock had been targets of abusive graffiti.

Chinese embassies everywhere had called for increased security protection as noisy, placard-waving mobs gathered. Activists demanded an international citizens' boycott on Chinese goods and services. They urged people to cancel their bookings on Chinese airlines.

The European Union and a score of other countries issued a formal travel advisory warning against travel to China. Insurance companies cancelled private insurance coverage for China-bound travellers.

Soon after, Chinese aviation officials hinted their airlines might withdraw from some routes for "safety reasons". They did not elaborate.

On the diplomatic front, several countries announced they were recalling their ambassadors from Beijing for consultations.

Global finance and share markets had been rocked by the long-term implications of China's shock expansionism. Trading on the Chinese stock exchanges was halted after prices began to tumble.

The value of the Australian dollar overnight had plummeted to a mere twenty-six cents to the American. The cost of all imports and the cost of living was poised to skyrocket.

Some economic forecasters predicted a forty per cent fall in gross domestic product. Others more than sixty per cent. They warned Australia's standard of living would fall drastically without the overseas earnings power of most of its mining and energy exports.

International rating agencies downgraded Australian bonds to junk level.

The big tourist market began a catastrophic collapse.

The first big labour lay-offs were reported.

Stone was glad Australia's plight was the major story of the day in the democracies even if their governments were paralysed by the military realities.

He feared the hungry, fickle, twenty-four-hour news cycle would soon relegate the Australian crisis to ongoing footnotes in a world beset with territorial and religious wars.

Stone noted the Chinese Military Commission had announced the successful testing of its latest long-range nuclear missile.

The Dongfend-41 could be hurled at targets more than twelve thousand kilometres away. The distance between Beijing and Los Angeles was ten thousand kilometres. The distance from the Chinese capital to Sydney was nine thousand kilometres. There was no subtlety in the message.

Stone knew he had to find a way out of the country's impasse. A way to reclaim the mineral- and energy-rich deserts in the north. But he didn't have a single, practical idea.

He was on the ground, crushed again by a four-man tackle.

He was winded and bruised. The mood of his traumatised team was oscillating between defiance and accepting the border peace treaty.

He looked at his watch. The second Cabinet meeting in two days since the invasion was about to start. He needed to have something to tell them. But he didn't.

* * *

Jeremey Whittacker arrived early and agitated. He sat alone at the temporary Cabinet table in The Lodge's dining room. He shucked a French cuffed sleeve from his pinstripe suit. He was a frustrated man.

He had made a conscious effort not to act superior before his colleagues. It was difficult — because he was superior. Smarter. More capable. More logical. Almost half his colleagues had already recognised that.

He was the Rhodes Scholar. The brilliant economics student who went on to a dazzling career in his father-in-law's merchant bank. With a fortune amassed, Joanna had pushed his attention to politics — and the prospect of real power and glamour.

He was parachuted into a safe Melbourne seat and eased into parliamentary life as an opposition MP. Joanna had been certain two years ago he would be the next prime minister when their party finally dumped its leader, a two-time election loser.

Whittacker knew he had persuaded many of his colleagues he was, in fact, the best candidate. Many, but not quite most.

He sat and opened his black leather pad feeling the agony of his defeat as though it were yesterday. He had lost by an exasperatingly small margin, five votes.

The leadership had gone instead to Gary Stone. A dropout law student who had inherited his father's rural transport business. A provincial who had become a local hero playing club rugby league in Lismore.

Whittacker got the powerless second prize of deputy leader. His party had gone on to win an historic victory sweeping both houses of the Australian Federal Parliament — a major achievement that should have delivered decisive government.

Instead, Stone had been too ineffectual and weak to make the tough decisions. Whittacker knew he would have delivered the strong economic medicine the country needed.

Stone had taken a more gradual — humane, he called it — approach to convince the masses the country's welfare budgets had to be cut and the deficits brought under control.

Stone was not the leader Australia needed facing its worst crisis. His Cabinet colleagues must recognise that now.

As 10 a.m. neared, Whittacker's fellow ministers began to arrive. They formed small groups as they waited. He joined one. The mood was depressed and restive. Fertile ground for him unless Stone came up with something decisive in the next nine days.

He couldn't control his obsession to discover which five MPs had not trusted him. Those five were the key to his future. The country's future. But they remained hidden behind encouraging platitudes. They were still in Stone's camp. As far as anyone knew.

The PM arrived, greeted everyone heartedly for his team talk. There was a long state-of-the-nation report, but no obvious strategy was revealed to deal with the crisis.

Joe Martini, rather than the Foreign Minister, was about to have his first formal meeting with the Chinese. Whittacker wondered how the old grape-grower would match it with the smartest the Chinese would have around the table. Stone needed to act logically, not emotionally.

Whittacker bit his tongue. The ministers asked plenty of questions but none voiced any criticism of Stone's actions so far. He had managed to calm the country with his emergency measures. They were responding to the captain's demands for unity in the face of the enemy.

The meeting wound up. Whittacker closed the leather pad and made his farewells. He would go home and talk to Joanna.

11.30 a.m.

The Lodge, Canberra

Stone racked his brain. The dream that had woken him momentarily last night eluded him.

In it he had solved the Chinese nightmare. But any real memory of it had gone when he fell back into an exhausted sleep.

He flexed his left leg, rubbed his knee and walked out onto the big lawns surrounding The Lodge. His ministers had left. While seeing them off, he had seen Elaine outside chatting with the head gardener.

As their discussion broke up he limped casually across to her, avoiding the two-man patrols crisscrossing the grounds.

Elaine looked up and spotted him. She smiled. He was looking very weary despite his efforts at being upbeat.

She had spoken perfunctorily with Jeremey Whittacker when he had arrived for the Cabinet meeting. He had attempted to dodge her but failed. She had greeted him a little too loudly to be ignored.

He was a strange, driven man. There had been rumours years ago about a hushed-up attempt he had made to take his own life when he failed a high school exam. It had been the last one he had ever failed, according to the story.

Whittacker was as tall as her husband but thin as a rake and perpetually as pale as a sheet. He loved his dark pinstripe bankers' suits. Stone hated ties. Whittacker had played hockey. Her man had played rugby league.

Played for a bit too long though, she knew, and it was catching up on him. The injuries, the drinking and smoking; the boys' camaraderie that was part of his sports life for so many years.

Stone had been frustrated when his father died of a sudden heart attack. He stepped in to take over the family transport business only two years into his law studies at Sydney University. He had done a remarkable job in growing the business state-wide and made more than a small pile along the way.

But his dream to be in law had been dashed. As a parliamentarian he was now in the business of making the law. It was one of life's ironies. Meanwhile their eldest son, Peter, was successfully running the business after Stone had been suddenly and unexpectedly pressed to contest the local Federal seat. He had won it handily.

Stone's laboured breathing broke into her thoughts as he came closer.

She leaned forward for a peck. He bent over and delivered.

"I hoped you'd still be out here," he said. "I had half an idea about this Chinese situation last night. Must have dreamed it. But I'm buggered if I can remember much of it."

She took his hand and they strolled toward the big swimming pool beside The Lodge.

"Was it a good idea?"

"Well, that's the problem, I think it was. But I can't remember any of the details. The old general was in it. The Chinese were in it."

Elaine stopped to look at a struggling piece of native fauna. All The Lodge's gardens were an array of different Australian natives.

"What you told me regarding the general's report wasn't pretty," she said.

Stone scratched his head: "No, none of it was pretty."

"I mean the part where he said our captured troops were hostages. They'd have to be sacrificed if we made a push north."

They walked on for a few moments in silence. Elaine broke it: "Oh, Gary, I wish we'd never had all this iron ore and the coal and gas and all the rest of it. It's brought us misery."

"What do you mean?"

"If we'd just been a country with plain old deserts of worthless sand, the Chinese would never have invaded. Our riches are turning out to be our ruin."

Stone shrugged.

Then he stopped suddenly. "What did you say about the fate of our prisoners? They'd be sacrificed."

"The general said they'd have to be sacrificed if there was a full-scale invasion," she said.

"Sacrificed. That's it. That's it. Sacrificed," he said. He hobbled quickly to the wooden poolside seat with Elaine in tow and they both sat down.

"I remember the dream. It's coming back to me. It was all about sacrifice. About a retaliation the Chinese would never expect. It would make their occupation meaningless."

"Gary, what are you talking about?" said Elaine.

He tapped the arm of the seat impatiently. "The Chinese were assuming Australia would not sacrifice its prisoners of war in order to liberate the Top Half. Their assumption had been right. Up till now."

A frown crossed Elaine's face. "What do you mean, up till now?"

"I think Australia *would* be willing to sacrifice lives to fight off the Chinese. But launching a full-on frontal attack with them holding hostages is not the way to do it. There's another way. An attack they'd never expect."

Elaine's frown deepened. "Gary, stop talking in riddles."

Stone sat back, crossed his legs and told her about his dream.

She sat in silence when he had finished. Stone moved on the hard wooden seat. "Well?"

"Gary, it's a repulsive idea. Thousands of innocent people could be killed or injured."

He said nothing. She turned and looked him in the eye. "Are the mines and gas fields worth it?"

Stone looked away from her gaze.

Elaine saw him tense. She began fiddling absently with an earring. "Gary, there is nothing I would like more than to send the Chinese packing — but they're here now. What if they're telling the truth, they don't want to come south, they're perfectly happy exploiting our resources from where they are? If we can get safeguards, a border agreement with them, surely that would make more sense than risking your idea?"

Stone shook his head in exasperation and pursed his lips.

Elaine went on: "What do you think would happen to morale if the Chinese respond and their rockets take out Brisbane's power supply, for instance? We've seen the sort of mob panic that happened with just the threat of an attack. Suddenly there's no more hot lattes in the cafes? No more light? No more television? No more lifts in apartment buildings? No more traffic lights? No more petrol pumps? And no more running water?"

Stone folded his arms. "Don't you at least want to try? My idea is to stop a full-scale shooting war, not start one. I'm trying to show them any victory they think they might have would be a Pyrrhic one."

Stone took her hand. He softened his tone: "Darling, our casualties would not necessarily have to be very high. Any deaths would be a small sacrifice if the idea works."

He heard her take a deep breath.

A pair of guards strolled past. Birds began screeching in a territorial dispute. The sun glared off the pool. A weedeater roared into life somewhere in the distance.

Stone let her hand go and put his arms behind his head. "We can't give the show away without a fight. We'd become a Third World vassal state. We'd be under the threat of a complete Chinese takeover at any time. We'd be giving away our children's heritage. We can't do it."

Elaine felt her eyes welling up.

"We have to try," Stone said softly. "Australia is too big a prize to hand over without a shot fired."

Elaine nodded reluctantly. She found a tissue in her sleeve and blew her nose.

She leaned across on his shoulder. "I know. I know."

She gave a deep sigh. "But remember what mother used to say. 'You can't get a little bit pregnant.' Once you start on this idea, you're committed — and you have no idea how the Chinese might retaliate."

"But you do think we should try?"

She nodded against his shoulder. She patted a tissue against her face as a new tear ran down one cheek.

"Yes, I think we should try."

Then she stood up quickly. "Come on. There's work to do."

Stone pushed himself to his feet. She looked up at him. "You know, I'm glad you're the Prime Minister."

Noon

The International Conference Centre, Canberra

The room was clinically neutral. Not a bright colour anywhere. The décor was matched by the Chinese delegation.

All three wore black suits, white shirts and dark-red ties. Their delegation leader, a Mr Wu Seng, sat between his other two delegates for the first session of the Australia-Sino Peace and Border Settlement Talks.

It was a posh title for a meeting to confiscate most of Australia's energy resources, thought Martini. He wore a tweed coat, light-brown shirt and tie. The tie design displayed a colourful bunch of grapes.

The parties introduced themselves. Martini had no idea how he would remember any of the Chinese delegates' names, except Wu Seng. He stamped on his memory he was there to 'woo Seng' — into talking too much and believing Australia would settle a border deal while he bought the time Stone needed.

Australia had one other delegate, Mark Roberts, a Foreign Affairs Department official, whose dress code pretty much matched the Chinese diplomats'.

"Mr Martini, you will be aware of the outline of our offer to prevent a full-scale war and takeover of Australia," Wu began quietly. "We have the full details here."

Martini blanched as Wu shoved a ten-centimetre-thick bound dossier across the table. It was a little more than the one page he'd been shown by Stone.

Martini deflected the dossier to Roberts, who opened the first pages as though it were an unexploded bomb.

It was a couple of thousand pages: the details of Australia's required capitulation and where its new borders would run.

"Well, just before we go into that," said Martini loudly, "there are a couple of things I'd like to clear up with you blokes."

The three Chinese jolted to attention. They had all met Lindsay Noble but none had come across the Trade Minister.

"You haven't got a show of getting anywhere with these talks unless we get the cities back."

Wu looked stung. He looked to the man on his right, cleared his throat and said: "I beg your pardon, Mr Martini."

"You heard," said Martini. "We might as well get off on the right foot. We won't be letting you have a dozen of our cities."

Wu stared and fiddled with the front page of his mammoth dossier.

He made another attempt. "We are not offering to return any of the cities we've occupied, Mr Martini. But we are offering to repatriate your troops and energy workers in the next twelve months and leave Brisbane safe and untouched on your side of the border. The people living in the occupied cities can elect in due course whether or not they want to resettle in the south."

Martini shoved his chair back and crossed his legs. The move revealed red socks above his brown shoes.

"I don't know how you think you'll get away with this little escapade of yours. Has someone told you Aussies don't like a good fight?"

Wu looked confused. "What would be the point in fighting? You would lose. Millions would be killed and your cities destroyed. It would take only a matter of days. We are making you a very generous offer. Our air force and navy would cripple your cities in a matter of hours. I don't think you understand the seriousness of the situation you are in."

"You're right, Mr Wu, there are a couple of things I don't understand."

Wu nodded. A look of relief began to appear. It lasted only a second.

"Why the hell would you want to invade Australia to get its iron ore and coal mines? Or its natural gas fields?" said Martini.

He pulled his chair back into the table, placed both elbows on it and clasped his gnarled hands together.

"Haven't you noticed the price of iron ore is half what it was? Same with coal and natural gas? You guys are getting this stuff cheap. It won't be much cheaper when you're running things yourselves."

Martini laughed and reached for the glass of water before him.

"And what are you going to do with it all anyway? Your own economy is in slow-mo. You've done all the big build. You don't need zillions of tonnes of iron ore any more. That's why the prices tanked in the first place."

Wu whispered something to his right-hand man, who nodded and frowned.

Right Hand coughed and said slowly as though explaining something to a small child: "The annexation is about the long-term strategic demands of our homeland. We are securing essential strategic resources for the next two hundred years."

Martini shook his head.

"You're a bunch of economic drongos," he said. The Chinese looked more confused.

As they started to whisper among themselves, Martini thudded his water glass on the table. They jumped.

"Anyway, let's deal with this border proposal of yours. It's a non-starter like it is now. Talk to your Politburo guys and tell them all the energy resources are in the middle of the deserts. Not in the cities. They don't need the cities," said Martini.

He stood up.

"Let me know what they say. Come on, Mark, we'll go next door."

Roberts stumbled to his feet and followed Martini.

"What's next door?" he said as they reached the door. He looked behind him. The Chinese sat perplexed, staring after them.

"One of my downtown offices," said Martini. "It's disguised as a wine bar."

Martini held the door open for him and waved at the immobile Chinese delegation. "See you all tomorrow then. Cheers."

5 p.m.

Lavarack Barracks, Townsville

The humiliation was the worst part of it.

Brigadier Lesley Silvey had had a ready-to-go force of highly trained soldiers under his command. Specifically to defend the north. Now he commanded nothing. He and his force were impotent prisoners in their own barracks. It was more than a humiliation. It was a national tragedy.

He had been allowed by the Chinese commander to visit all the barracks on the huge base. His men were on short rations, bored, angry and restless, but there had been no mistreatment.

The young captives got an hour's exercise a day in the scorching heat of the base's heavily guarded sports field. The rest of the time they were confined to their barracks.

They filled the interminable hours with games, reading and watching videos.

A mass break-out was on everyone's mind but the Chinese were adamant they would execute ten Australians for every one that attempted to bust out.

Silvey had subsequently told his men he alone would make the call and take the responsibility if there were to be an organised escape effort. There were to be no solo attempts.

On the first day of the takeover, he had been taken to his old office to hear the BBC World Service reporting the Australian Government was in peace talks with officials of the People's Republic of China.

The talks concerned the new border the Chinese were proposing for an annexed Top Half.

The Chinese commander, Major Hu, urged Silvey to continue

to restrain his men. There was no need for lives to be lost needlessly. He was certain the border talks would end the crisis and Silvey's men would be repatriated very soon.

Silvey listened to the broadcast with disbelief. When it ended he was depressed and gobsmacked. His government was giving up without a fight. And he was to blame.

Lavarack should have been guarded with the respect it deserved. Not handed over to a bus full of terrorists without a shot fired in its defence.

Silvey had taken the opportunity of his meeting with the Chinese commander to warn him the killing of any prisoners in retaliation for an escape attempt would be a war crime. The commander listened attentively but then chuckled and shook his head.

He had his orders. The People's Liberation Army would not be subject to any war crimes.

DAY THREE

Guest bathroom, The Lodge, Canberra

Joe Martini felt he had drawn the short straw being sent off to filibuster the arrogant Chinese. He had no cards to play. His demand for the return of all the Queensland cities as a precondition to a treaty was certain to be refused but the haggling would occupy time. Every day mattered, Stone had told him.

Arriving at The Lodge for the third Cabinet meeting since the crisis, his ageing bladder sent a message. He bypassed the dining room and made for the guest toilets.

He found Stone there washing his hands. Stone looked up and greeted him cheerfully. Martini returned the greeting and made his way to one of the urinals.

"Were you having a nervous one, Gazza?" he said.

"Not really. I've had a few nerves lately but I'm feeling a lot better now. I've made a decision on how we should handle this Chinese problem."

"What is it you've decided?" Martini asked, unzipping himself and stepping up to the urinal.

Stone told him in a single sentence.

Martini swivelled sharply to look at Stone, who was busy towelling his hands.

"Christ, Gazza. What are you talking about?"

"Joe, you're pissing on your shoes."

Martini swore and swung back toward the urinal. He was disbelieving. He zipped up and shook his wet shoes.

He turned to speak but the toilet door opened and another minister entered.

"Good morning, gentlemen," he said. "Joe, you've pissed on your shoes. Are the Chinks making you nervous?"

Martini looked down.

"No," he said, "the Chinks are no trouble. They've pulled their big surprise."

* * *

Jeremey Whittacker again had arrived first, in a foul mood. He had not been consulted by Stone on any strategic matters since the crisis began. He was being kept isolated, completely in the dark.

Stone had been acting dictatorially, grabbing the role of Defence Minister to consolidate his power. Whittacker knew he should have objected to that when it was announced. He had missed a vital opportunity.

Whittacker worried that Stone and Thompson were hatching some half-baked combat idea that would lead to a full Chinese invasion.

He was no coward, he thought. He was pragmatic. Accepting the Chinese boundary offer would save millions of lives. It would save Australia. The Chinese had what they wanted. Australia would learn to live within its reduced means.

8.36 a.m.

The dining room, The Lodge, Canberra

"I want to be on record as condemning this madness. The Chinese will come down on us and destroy everything we've built. They will not fall for some amateur bluff like this."

Whittacker shoved himself back into his seat, daring anyone to challenge his logic.

Sitting beside him, Stone was slack-jawed at the intensity of his deputy's instant rejection of the concept he had code named END. The letters stood for Emergency Nuclear Deterrent.

Stone felt his heart pounding and his face colour. Whittacker had stilled the room.

The ministers around the temporary Cabinet table squirmed uncomfortably in the tense silence while trying to digest the implications of the idea themselves.

The Agriculture Minister eventually asked quietly: "Is there no hope of the army marching north and knocking them out? Before big numbers of reinforcements arrive? There can't be that many of them up there at this stage?"

"No," said Stone. "There is no hope of us being able to do that. They hold twelve thousand hostages. Even if we were to sacrifice them we would almost certainly lose in a full-frontal assault. Because of the distance we have no close air support. The Chinese have more than thirty fighter bombers at hand. Some are already on standby at the Townsville airport and others are just offshore on their aircraft carrier. It would be a massacre."

"Shit," said the minister. Looking around the table he saw his colleagues avoiding his eyes.

"So we're pretty stuffed," he said. "It's surrendering and accepting their terms or trying to bluff them out."

Whittacker jumped forward in his seat. "It would not be surrendering. Under their treaty we retain almost all our populated territory."

Martini gave a loud sigh. "For God's sake, Jerry, we'd be handing the country over to them. They'll choose when they take the rest of us. This terrorist attack is just to get a foothold. Even if they never attack in force, our long-term economic viability will be stuffed without the north and its resources. With their economic power they'll be running the show without firing a shot. Our standard of living would collapse. The country would stagnate. There'd be no growth or new jobs. We can't all go back and live on farms and milk cows and shear sheep. It would be the end of Australia."

The Education Minister nodded. "Anyone with half an education would be hightailing overseas to get a decent job and make some money. Our standard of living is dropping fast enough now with the slump in commodity prices."

Whittacker pursed his lips at the minister but said nothing.

The Foreign Minister coughed for attention.

"I'm the first to try to avert a war. And I don't like the END idea at all but I can't see any other option that will allow us to fight back," said Noble. "I can assure you, I've made calls on all our allies and there's not a country that's going to help us in a war against the Chinese."

The room went silent again for a minute.

The Welfare Minister asked, "Can we threaten them with the idea? They may see sense and agree to leave."

Several heads nodded hopefully.

"Joe, what do you think? You're the one talking to the Chinese," said Stone.

Martini stared at the ceiling.

"The Chinese just won't believe us," he said. "They'd laugh me out of the room. They're certain they've got us beat."

Stone looked at the Welfare Minister. "Well, that's your answer. Because they are in such an arrogant state of mind, everyone should know that once we start this we would have to act fast to keep them off balance. For END to work they have to believe it has always existed and been our top-secret, ultimate defence strategy. And they may well think it is a logical strategy given our unique geographical circumstances."

Stone saw a number of ministers nod their heads for the first time.

"It'll be the bloody END all right if they don't buy it," said the Health Minister.

There were murmurs around the table.

Stone took a deep breath. "The fact is, signing a border treaty is just putting off the inevitable. Joe's right, they'll be free to take the rest of the country in their own good time."

"That's right," several ministers said simultaneously.

Stone felt Whittacker straighten beside him. The momentum of the debate was ebbing away from his frantic deputy.

But Whittacker was not without support. Several ministers argued Australia's only practical future lay in cooperating with China.

Martini's anger at the appeasers finally broke: "We need to show some balls. And act like men. END is the only idea that gives us some hope. And kicks the Chinks in the slats."

Whittacker gave a disgusted snort but as he began to reply, Martini slapped a hand on the table. "I'm not telling my sons I agreed to sign a surrender treaty with the Chinese when there was a hope of beating them."

Whittacker shrugged. There was no point in arguing with an imbecile. He smirked and rolled his eyes at two of his most loyal supporters.

Stone was feeling hot and nauseous. The debate had to be closed down. It was in danger of getting out of hand. Fear and indecision were feeding old animosities.

He called for order.

"Most of our decisions are made on a consensus basis but on this, everyone is going to have to make a call," he said.

Whittacker nodded agreement and sat upright, confident. He thought the mere suggestion of END as a practical option was ridiculous.

Stone took a look around the table at his twenty-one sombre ministers. He decided he would resign if he lost the vote. Whittacker could be the appeaser. It was not a job he could do.

He cleared his throat and asked everyone in favour of adopting END to raise their right hand. Several hands shot up immediately. Others paused for a few seconds.

Thirteen hands eventually went up. He had won.

Whittacker sat red-faced, humiliated.

He got to his feet instantly the meeting formally ended. He was unable to meet Stone's eye as he turned to leave.

For Stone, the vote was the most important in his career. It had been a critical test and most of his team had backed him when it mattered. But he felt drained. He had won a healthy thirteen-to-eight majority.

But there was another interpretation that could be put on the result: it would take only three ministers to have second thoughts and his majority would vanish. He understood the reality. His grip on power was tenuous.

He was already pondering a second string in his military strategy. He would not risk another Cabinet row. He would make the call himself. He was the Defence Minister, after all.

2 p.m.

Bangalow, northern New South Wales

Caught on holiday in Surfers Paradise on the morning of the invasion, Chris Sharp and his wife, Anna, had joined the chaotic rush south, away from the Chinese front but into an ongoing nightmare.

Caught with little cash for petrol, they had made it only about an hour's journey south over the Queensland border, to the small town of Bangalow, before their fuel ran out.

Sharp had been forced to take a mere $500 for his cherished Chrysler. It would enable them to buy food while they hitchhiked the hundreds of kilometres home to Sydney and their teenage children.

Ominously, there was little traffic as they waited for a ride. Vehicles going south were often overloaded. Other, similarly overloaded, vehicles were heading north. They had apparently been turned back at a roadblock.

After an hour's wait on the roadside outside Bangalow, a hippy with a ponytail and a stupid smile stopped his battered Kombi van and waved them aboard. He wasn't sure where he was going, he said happily, but he was going somewhere south.

The Sharps gratefully piled in, moving a large, open sack of marijuana to the tattered rear seat. Sharp was certain he had seen that smile before. Weird things were happening.

He pretended he hadn't smoked pot before but he and Anna soon gave in and accepted the hippy's second offer, sitting back to puff and let the world drift by in a mellow haze.

Sharp thought of the smirking buyer who had virtually stolen their car. He had towed the big V8 behind his service station where Sharp was certain petrol was being hoarded in the underground tanks.

With nowhere to sleep on their final night in Bangalow, they had pleaded with him to let them doss down in the car one last time. He eventually agreed, for fifty dollars.

At daybreak Sharp poured a full bucket of fine Bangalow gravel into the petrol tank and another into the engine's oil sump. That made the five-hundred-dollar deal fair, he reckoned.

The Kombi rattled its way steadily south on the winding, coastal highway.

Five kilometres north of the New South Wales town of Ballina they rounded a bend and the hippy jammed on the brakes. They were at a tail of idle cars stretching kilometres ahead.

A distant sign said FEDERAL CHECKPOINT.

Sharp and Anna got out of the Kombi and walked toward it with growing trepidation.

When they were close enough they saw the smaller print: EMERGENCY POWERS ACT IN FORCE. PROOF OF IDENTITY ESSENTIAL FOR BONA FIDE SOUTHBOUND TRAVELLERS.

They retraced their steps relieved and in high spirits.

The Kombi was gone. So was any documentation of their identities and Sydney residence.

They stood looking dumbly around. Confused and then angry.

They turned and walked back toward the sign. Ahead, beyond the line of cars, they could see crowds of people.

Off the road to one side there were tents, smoke rising from outside many of them.

As they reached the edge of the crowd, Sharp asked a woman holding the hands of two young children what was happening.

"This is one of the roadblocks to stop people leaving Queens land," she said. "I'm from Sydney. I've been waiting in this queue for the last couple of hours. They're letting people through if they can prove they've got homes down south but it's a very slow process."

"Good God!" Anna cried. "Our luggage has all been stolen. My handbag's gone and all our wallets and credit cards and driver's licences were in it."

Sharp remembered throwing his wallet across to his wife when she was searching for cash to buy their last petrol at a Surfers Paradise servo.

Anna turned to Sharp. "What are we going to do? What are we going to do? We've got no ID, we could be from anywhere. How are we going to get home?"

Sharp pulled his frantic wife to him. She was on the verge of tears and despair. He wasn't far away.

"We'll wait in the queue and explain the situation," he said.

The queue shuffled forward at a snail's pace in the heat of the day. Grim people walked back past them to their cars and drove off. Some were angry, some in tears.

The checkpoint structure finally came into view. Ahead of them Sharp could see coils of barbed wire and a makeshift road-block consisting of orange marker cones, some trestle tables and several concrete barriers forming a narrow S-bend south.

Very young soldiers and a number of older Military Police officers were manning the checkpoint.

Arguments broke out continually. Most of the travellers were turned away. Some were in tears. But some returned for their cars and were waved through.

The roadside tents Sharp had seen earlier were crowded. They formed a refugee camp, he realised. On Australian soil. There were many children running between the tents and adults cooking over gas barbecues.

"What's going to happen with these people?" Sharp asked the woman.

"They're from up north. They're refusing to go back," she said.

"The Army doesn't know what to do with them, so they're just camping here."

Anna was gripping Sharp's arm with a new intensity as they edged forward. Now there was just the woman and the two kids before them.

They were allowed through. A young soldier with two stripes on his arm looked up and waved Sharp forward impatiently.

"We are on our way home, to Sydney," Sharp said.

"ID?" he said, barely looking up.

"Our luggage and all our papers have been stolen," said Sharp.

"Well, you can't come through without ID and proof of residence."

The soldier took a deep breath. He was clearly weary from his thankless duty. He must have been standing there for hours, Sharp thought.

Anna pushed forward. "We can't give you any identification. It's all just been stolen. We hitchhiked here and the hippy who brought us just did a runner when we got out of his van."

Her voice was shrill and panicked. The soldier hardly reacted.

"You can't come through without ID and proof of residence," he repeated, and looked over Anna's shoulder to the next person in the queue.

"We have nowhere to go. Nowhere. Our home's in Sydney. We've lost our car, our money and all our luggage. You have to let us through, for the love of God!" screamed Anna.

Hearing the fracas a heavy-looking MP strode toward them. The impatient crowd behind began shouting for them to move on.

In the midst of the row, with the guards distracted, a young couple with backpacks pushed past the soldier and the Sharps and ran through the checkpoint.

The MP turned and drew his pistol. He shouted at them to stop. The pair raced on. He fired into the air. The crowd gave a spontaneous gasp.

Other soldiers appeared from the roadside ahead of the

escapees. Blocked, the pair suddenly pulled up and leaned forward, hands on knees, panting.

The soldiers grabbed them roughly and manhandled them further down the road and into a large, covered Army truck. The soldiers returned to the road bank, sat and began smoking again.

The MP turned back to the Sharps.

"What's going on here?" he said.

Sharp began to explain but the corporal said, "They have no ID or proof of residence, sir."

"*We live in Sydney — our ID has been stolen!*" Anna shouted.

"And I think they're druggies," said the corporal. "They stink of weed."

Someone behind them in the queue yelled: "Get them outta here, we've got to get home." There was a loud chorus backing the demand.

Anna turned to them. "We have to get home too."

"All right, that's enough," said the MP. "You can either join those last two in the paddy wagon or go back the way you've come. Up to you."

Sharp took Anna by the arm and led her away back through the muttering crowd.

Anna began crying. "What are we going to do now? We've nowhere to go."

"We're refugees. Let's go over to the refugee camp and say hello. They look like nice people."

They walked over to the encampment and soon discovered there wasn't an inch anywhere to spare. One of the campers took pity on them and offered them his SUV to sleep in.

They awoke the next morning and stretched their stiff bodies. Sharp talked to the SUV owner. The man accepted Sharp's promise to repay him in Sydney for any food he would share.

The day dragged past. Nearby at the checkpoint tempers flared periodically as newcomers continued to be turned back. Many pitched tents along the road rather than take their children back north into the danger zone.

Some residents from nearby Ballina brought fresh fish to sell to the refugees and others gave away bread and large bottles of desperately needed water. An Army mobile kitchen arrived late in the day and handed out meals and more drinking water.

Sharp was reading a four-day-old newspaper in the fading light when Anna came running.

"Chris! Chris! I've just seen Bill Snell. He's here. With the Army," she said. Snell was a Sydney neighbour and a major in the regular force.

Sharp jumped to his feet and they hurried to the checkpoint. The young soldier saw them coming and waved them away. Beyond him they saw Major Snell.

They both yelled at the top of their lungs. Snell swung around, recognised them and waved. Minutes later he had confirmed they were Sydneysiders and the Sharps were through the checkpoint.

Anna hugged Snell so hard he grunted and feared for his ribs. He offered them a ride to Ballina in his Army Jeep. It was as far as he could take them but it was all they would need. Ballina had a small airport and its feeder airline service accepted credit cards. Snell provided the credit card.

Anna called the children. They were frantic and burst into tears when they heard her voice. They would use the last of their petrol rations to be at Sydney Airport to meet them.

Their aircraft took off and made a wide circle. Below, Anna could see the roadblock and smoke from scores of fires scattered along the highway. She sat shaking as the scene disappeared from view.

DAY FOUR

7.30 a.m.

The Lodge, Canberra

Frank Church sat in the front of the limo beside his chauffeur. There were fewer cars on the road. The short trip from Canberra City to The Lodge was now several minutes quicker.

The ASIO boss knew the skyrocketing price of rationed petrol was partly responsible. But there were also a lot fewer people in Canberra. Departmental heads were reporting a growing number of empty desks.

Public servants were leaving for their home towns and families across Australia with or without permission. He had lost several junior staff himself.

Church looked out at the quiet suburbs. He fidgeted nervously, still worried each trip to The Lodge would be his last.

The Prime Minister had said nothing of his fate since making it clear he and General Thompson were the pair he blamed for the horrific intelligence lapse that had sparked the crisis.

Church's car pulled up at the main entrance. He put a hand on the driver's arm.

"Can you wait, please? I don't think I'll be long."

The driver looked at him. "Don't worry, I'll be here. We're not all leaving."

"Good," said Church. "There's no bus service out here." The driver laughed.

Church let himself out and the driver took the vehicle to a

small car park beside The Lodge where he lowered the windows and lit a cigarette.

He switched on the radio and heard New Zealanders had raised five million dollars in a day to fly their expatriates' children to safety. The youngsters would be told it was a special, pre-Christmas holiday trip.

Church made his way past the entrance guards to the now familiar but unlikely nerve centre that was The Lodge's dining room. He saw Thompson ahead of him in the passage. Maybe they were both being sacked at the same time? Was Stone learning about time management?

The PM was sitting with John Able. They stopped talking when the pair arrived. Stone told them to sit opposite him. He had something to tell them. They both nodded, girding themselves for the worst.

Stone spoke for less than a minute.

When he had finished, Church felt a mix of fear and relief. He still had his job. But he was now involved in a radical new plan. He could scarcely believe either. He saw Thompson unfold his arms and sit back restively in his chair.

"The poison pill option," Church said tentatively.

"That's what the Chinese must think. They must believe that we'll make sure that if we can't have our resources, no one can," said Stone.

Church said nothing, the full grotesque nature of the proposal forming in his mind.

Stone had somehow got the Cabinet to agree to his Emergency Nuclear Deterrent concept. It called for the urgent assembly of a number of radiation dispersal bombs. The bombs would be detonated beside mines, natural gas installations and export ports in the occupied territories.

They would shower a layer of radioactive fallout over them. The poisoned, irradiated areas would be uninhabitable for decades, maybe generations.

The resource workers would have no warning of their plight. The communication blackout in the north ensured the Australian population would also be unaware a dirty-bomb counterattack was under way. Thousands in the north could perish in the immediate blasts or die later of radiation poisoning.

The Chinese would be told scores of the bombs had been secretly embedded throughout the north more than twenty years earlier.

Australia's strategic plan was always to reveal their presence as the ultimate deterrent in the event of an imminent invasion. The deterrent had not been revealed because the Australian Government had had no opportunity to. The Chinese terrorist invasion had caught it totally off guard.

Stone's bluff called for his bombs to be detonated rapidly over a few days as though they were only part of a big stockpile of the national deterrent.

Church's immediate practical reaction was, if the bombs could be made, with the necessary physicists rounded up somehow, they would almost certainly need more than the seven days left till the Chinese deadline expired.

"What if I can make more time?" said Stone standing and glancing at Able.

"It depends on how much more time," said Church.

"I can make more but it would be days, not weeks."

Church nodded uncertainly. "You realise what you're talking about would have to be some kind of suitcase bombs?"

Stone cocked his head. Thompson turned to Stone. "They'd have to be small enough for our commandos to carry onto the sites. The irradiation bomb doesn't have the big mushroom cloud and the force to knock down whole cities. It's a dirty bomb. It kills people and contaminates the earth it settles on for years, maybe decades. We don't know for how long. There's a lot of controversy on this point."

Church nodded. "The bombs' radiation clouds are particularly effective on dry desert lands. Humidity and damp lessens its impact considerably. So pretty perfect for your outback targets."

They were known as RDDs, radioactive dispersal devices. Church knew about them because he had spent years thwarting terrorists from building one in Australia. Their critical advantage was they did not need enriched uranium. The radioactive core would be detonated by a massive dynamite charge. It would make them quicker to build in the limited time available — if they could find the people and facilities to manufacture them.

"These will be isolated blasts but an RDD will have the Chinese army's Geiger counters going off the clock."

Thompson said: "Once the bombs are built, the job of penetrating enemy lines and manually positioning them will take time as well. It's a tall order, sir, and there's no figuring what the Chinese might do in retaliation. They have real nuclear weapons at their disposal. And they have our POWs. What you're suggesting is a very high-risk option."

Church agreed. He was worried the Chinese might have deployed a large part of their huge submarine fleet to encircle Australia. The Chinese fleet had sixty-nine submarines of various sizes and capability in service — only three fewer than the American navy. It had many more than required to target each major Australian city.

Without the need for another Liberation Army soldier landing in Australia they could level the state capitals firing conventional or nuclear missiles while submerged offshore.

The Royal Australian Navy's three destroyers and dozen frigates would be sunk in relatively short order against such overwhelming odds. It was a grim picture, he said, but to date the RAAF's Orion sub-hunters had detected nothing sinister off the coast.

"Maybe the Chinese thought they wouldn't need any subs," said Stone.

"Maybe not, Prime Minister, but if you implement this plan you would have to weigh up the option of losing all our big cities, and losing them within a few hours," Church said. "There are still options for securing a peaceful border settlement that may avoid any further Chinese advance."

Church withered under the glare Stone gave him.

"That's a political decision for you, of course," Church said.

Stone sat forward. "Yes, it is a political decision for me. And I've made it. The Chinese think we're too soft to take them on — too squeamish to sacrifice our own people to protect the country. They're wrong. Can you get me the bombs?"

Church looked at Thompson, turned back to Stone and said: "How many do you need?"

Stone said to pull off the biggest bluff in military history he would need half a dozen. If the bluff didn't work quickly, it wouldn't work at all, so there was need for more than six.

"We won't detonate all of them at once. We'll do two or three attacks quickly over a few days. The Chinese have to believe these bombs are only the tip of the iceberg. That we have a whole stockpile of them hidden and lined up and we'll keep letting them off rapidly until they leave."

"That's a big bluff all right," Church said.

Stone changed the course of the conversation. "No one will even know about these dirty bombs, that's one of the reasons we can attempt this. No one in the south will believe the Chinese if they tried to reveal what we were doing. We place a different value on the lives of individuals. We are civilised. We would never dream of killing our own people — would we?"

No one answered.

"This means the whole project must remain absolutely top secret. We cannot afford a public backlash while we're staring down the Chinese. Once we've fired all six of them the game will be up. It won't matter what people find out after that. But it's critical in the meantime there is no hard evidence of what we are doing. None of the suitcase bombs can fall into enemy hands. If things go badly and the commandos are threatened with capture while positioning them, they'll have to detonate them manually."

Thompson said: "That would make it a suicide mission if the chips go down."

Stone nodded. "Yes, it would."

Thompson made no comment. He turned his attention back to the near-impossible time frame.

Thompson: "How much time do you really think you can buy us, sir?"

Stone looked at Able, who pondered the question.

"We have Joe Martini filibustering the Chinese," said Able. "I think he would be able to keep them talking for a few extra days beyond their deadline if they get the sense we are beginning to accept defeat. Let's not forget they don't want a full-scale war themselves. Right now they want to take what they've grabbed with no further fuss. World opinion hasn't exactly been kind to them. They will be more patient if Martini plays his cards right and gives the impression we're facing reality and surrendering."

"Christ, he's going to hate this," Stone said almost to himself. He looked at the men around him and said: "Okay, I'll leave the three of you to get this thing going. John will make sure you have every government resource at your disposal. END is our top war priority."

Stone left and the three men were left in a tense silence with their own thoughts.

Church was not sure the project was practical. Thompson was not sure a proud, nuclear-armed China could be bluffed into military defeat. Able was certain the objectives were noble but its ghastly human toll would destroy the Stone government, win or lose.

Finally, Able said, "Well, there's only one place I know in the country that has any nuclear know-how and radioactive waste material."

Thompson nodded. "Yes, Lucas Heights."

Lucas Heights was the home of the country's only nuclear reactor and the Australian Nuclear Science and Technology Organisation, a world-rated research complex. It boasted a staff of one thousand.

"How are we going to keep the lid on this once we start recruiting physicists?" said Church.

"We'll lock them up in their research centre till the job's done," said Thompson. "It's only forty kilometres from the heart of Sydney but it's a perfect spot to work in secrecy. It covers seventy hectares and it's surrounded by bushland. It has its own accommodation facilities."

"There is one small problem," said Able. "We need to put an international net out to recruit weapon physicists — all the Lucas Heights ones are engaged in medical and environmental research. How are they going to react when they're told their outfit is going to be building dirty bombs and they can help if they choose to?"

Thompson stared off in the middle distance, folding his arms.

"I don't know the answer to that," he said after a few moments.

"Well, we won't know till we ask," said Church. "Let's check now which scientists here and abroad would have the expertise and be prepared to help build some dirty bombs. This means we'll have to risk getting the support of the research director at Lucas Heights, whoever he is."

They all agreed. Able would arrange for the director to fly to Canberra on an air force VIP jet immediately. Thompson would have him escorted to the jet by two of his Military Police officers — just in case there was any reluctance to travel at a minute's notice.

Church found his chauffeur stubbing out his sixth cigarette in the car park. It had been a long wait. His boss clearly still had a job but he was tight-lipped and preoccupied.

From the rear seat of the limousine the ASIO head googled the Lucas Heights research staff list. He searched till he found the research director.

His name was Chinese: Dr Peter Yu.

10.30 p.m.

Wall Street, New York

He put down the phone and exhaled. He looked out at the lights from his thirty-eighth-floor Wall Street office.

He had done a lot of business, made a number of big calls on less information than he had today.

Yesterday Zak Eisner watched the rolling sales figures from America's biggest retailer, Mal Mart, on his trading screens all day.

There had been a decline.

Nothing major.

But a decline.

Paid for his trading instinct as much as his talent for following hard statistics, he had ordered the sale of his pension fund's whopping $9.3 billion holding in Mal Mart shares.

It was a big call.

The retailer and its share price had previously enjoyed more than three decades of solid growth.

This morning his fund's shares began flowing quietly and largely unnoticed onto the New York Stock Market.

But Eisner had known the sheer volume of his sales would begin to depress Mal Mart's stock value before the day was up.

If they fell too far too fast his sell call would be questioned upstairs. At least until the wisdom of his hunch became a reality.

Eisner was in his tenth year as a Wall Street trader.

His undisputed success — reflected by his salary and bonuses topping $21 million last year — had bought him the power and confidence to make these calls.

At twenty-nine he knew he was nearing the peak, and end, of his career. Soon it would be time to cash up and leave. Career spans in his profession were short.

He knew one big, wrong call abruptly ended most traders' careers. He was determined it would not happen to him. He had watched the events in Australia with a keen interest and sensed a deep alarm among Americans.

The inevitable had happened after years of warnings about the Pacific superpower's arms race. The dragon was breathing fire. Eisner was gambling that Mal Mart would become a natural anti-Chinese victim after the invasion. Australia was a friendly ally and democracy.

Mal Mart epitomised the choke-hold Chinese manufacturers had on American retailers and manufacturers.

It had been one of the first chains to embrace the sea change that global trading had created. It quickly exploited the vast array of cheap Chinese imports on offer.

While Mal Mart and other big retailers sucked in the low-cost Chinese goods, American manufacturers had shuttered, their prices uncompetitive.

This week the retailer was one of the first to be targeted with angry graffiti.

Without any formal organisation or national coordination — but assisted by millions of social media messages — American shoppers were already being urged to leave "Made in China" goods on the shelf.

It was in some ways a feeble and humiliating response from a superpower like America. But still a response that reflected the anger of ordinary citizens, ordinary consumers.

Eisner, a hawk permanently circling the market, believed the citizens' boycott would gather an unprecedented momentum and affect the value of any corporate closely linked to the Middle Kingdom.

Eisner had heard rumours Mal Mart bosses were becoming quietly frantic and that morning had sent Chinese suppliers their first "cancel" message for new orders.

They feared billions of dollars of goods could be left on their shelves if the traditional Christmas sales boom did not eventuate.

Trading days to Christmas were running out.

Eisner had hit the sell button.

His staff had asked: All of it?

All of it, he assured them.

Mal Mart's shares becoming penny-dreadfuls? Eisner knew the unthinkable had already happened several times in the last few years.

Several of the country's biggest banks had collapsed and most credit facilities had evaporated overnight in one crisis.

The once mighty symbol of American world dominance, the car industry, had been resuscitated only by an infusion of hundreds of millions in cash from the Federal Government's money printing machine.

Eisner knew past boycotts based on national anger with another country were typically short-lived: marketplace reality and pricing quickly restored the status quo when emotions calmed.

But he was confident his sell call was good business.

At the market close, his online trading screen showed Mal Mart shares had come off by eighteen per cent. Sellers were already outnumbering buyers.

By the end of the following day an orderly retreat would become a stampede.

He had moved early and saved his fund several billions.

There would be no call from upstairs.

6.31 p.m.

Double Bay, Sydney

Lilly Yu snatched up the phone. Peter had been due home more than an hour ago.

She sighed in relief when she heard his voice.

"Oh, I've been so worried about you. Where are you?" she said.

"Lilly, I'm in Canberra. Actually, I'm at The Lodge."

"What are you doing at The Lodge? The girls and I need you at home. We're frightened. We don't know what's going to happen next …"

Lilly moved on her chair to ease the bruise on her thigh. She had stayed home in their Double Bay penthouse, too afraid to venture into the city again after Sunday's attack. She had been counting the hours till Peter got home — safely. Her imagination had run riot all day.

Peter had been appalled and in a state of disbelief when she had limped from the lift into the apartment. But he had insisted on going to work at Lucas Heights the following day as normal.

He had dropped the girls at their private school on the way and arranged for a limo service to collect them after the last class.

But Lilly was traumatised. She had huddled alone in her favourite lounge chair all day indifferent to one of the world's most expensive views before her.

She was one of two million Asians in Australia. One of a million of Chinese descent. Asians made up eight per cent of the country's population but latent white Australian racism had never been far from the surface as she and Peter worked their way through university and into professional careers.

They had done well. Not unusual for second-generation migrants whose parents had sacrificed much to ensure they were well educated. And integrated.

"I'm sorry. I don't know when I'll be back. I don't know what's going on," said Peter. He heard a sharp intake of breath from Lilly and regretted his ill-chosen words.

"I was picked up by a couple of Military Police officers and flown here today by myself in an air force jet. The Prime Minister's head man met me and said Mr Stone wanted to speak to me personally."

"Oh, no. Are you under arrest or something?" said Lilly. "What have you done?"

Yu tried to calm his frightened wife. He had done nothing wrong. He was perfectly safe. He'd be able to tell her everything soon — when he found out himself. He would be home as soon as he could.

"How are the girls?" he asked.

"They're fine. There was no problem getting home from school. They have a lot of friends there, so their day has been pretty ordinary. They're doing homework at the moment as though things are normal," said Lilly.

"Well, they're not normal. Make sure they don't go anywhere but school until I get back," said Peter.

He looked up and saw Able had entered the room. He knew Able had heard the last of his conversation.

"I have to go. I'll call you as soon as I can. Don't cry. It'll upset the girls. I love you," he said.

6.32 p.m.

Private study, The Lodge, Canberra

Stone swore. "Unbelievable. The guy's Chinese and his wife's just been beaten up in the street — and we want his help with a dirty bomb."

Able nodded. "That's why we've told him nothing. Unfortunately, he's the head honcho scientist. And there's a fair few Chinese among his staff, more than I would have thought. That's why I brought him straight here. I'm not sure he's feeling very patriotic about Australia at the moment. I think you need to handle this situation personally. I think an explanation, a briefing, directly from the Prime Minister might be needed to carry the day."

Stone said nothing. He took a deep breath to ease a flash of chest pain.

"His name is Dr Peter Yu and he's in the lounge downstairs," said Able. "Born here, educated here, brilliant academic record. Rose through the ranks very fast. Internationally respected. He made the top research job at forty-two. I'm not sure we'd get many of the Lucas Heights scientists to cooperate if he turns us down."

Stone sighed. "The perfect man ..."

He leaned back in his chair. "How do we know about the wife?"

"Church had ASIO vet the family. They did a big electronic surveillance scoop and her name came up on a Sydney ambulance database."

"Not a police accident report?" said Stone.

"No. A squad car attended when she was attacked but the cops did nothing. Asked no questions. Took no details and left when the ambulance was arriving. She was beaten about and traumatised but there were no broken bones. She refused to be taken to hospital for a check-up."

Stone said: "Has there been much of this? Chinese being bashed up on the streets?"

"Yes but most of this sort of harassment is going unreported. The Chinese are keeping themselves to themselves. Keeping their heads down and keeping off the streets," said Able.

Stone nodded slowly. Australia: another great melting pot of people where the temperature had never been hot enough to dissolve racism and prejudice.

It wasn't his fault. But he had to deal with the here and now. He needed all the help he could get.

"Okay. Give me a minute and I'll be down," said Stone.

He fished in his suit pocket as soon as Able closed the door and shot another spray of nitrate under his tongue. He found his tie and carefully put it back on.

Getting top team players was always easier if your side was winning. His side wasn't winning. What was worse, if his side failed, his new prospective Chinese recruit would face a very uncertain fate at the hands of his ancestral homeland team.

Yu stood respectfully as the Prime Minister came in. He was a big, heavily built Aussie but his suit seemed loose on his frame. He looked taller than on the television but his hair was a great shock of grey. He looked exhausted.

He crossed the room and put out his right hand.

"Dr Yu. Welcome to The Lodge. I'm sorry you've been brought here in such a rush but there is a war on and the matter I want to discuss with you is rather urgent," he said as he pumped Yu's hand.

Yu nodded his understanding and sat again as the Prime Minister landed heavily in an armchair and began rubbing his left knee.

Able introduced him to a third man who followed Stone in: Mr Frank Church, the head of ASIO. The four of them sat down.

"I was sorry to hear about your wife," said Stone.

Yu found it impossible to disguise his surprise.

"I hope she's recovering all right. It would have been a dreadful experience," said Stone.

Yu was lost for words. Eventually he said: "Thank you for your concern. She was very shocked. We all were. She was too frightened to leave the apartment today. I had to take my children to school before work."

"Yes, I know," said Stone.

"You know?" said Yu.

Stone nodded. ASIO had acted quickly investigating the Yu family once Peter Yu's potential role had been raised earlier in the day.

"Have you been spying on me?" said Yu. "My family has done nothing wrong. What's this all about?"

"It's about saving Australia," said Stone. "And I know your family has done nothing wrong. That's why I want you to do a job for me. Unfortunately, if you agree you won't see your family again for a little while. But I will make certain nothing further happens to your wife or daughters. They will be given twenty-four-hour protection."

Yu felt a growing alarm as he stared at Stone.

"You do want to help save Australia, don't you?" said Stone.

"What do you mean? Why wouldn't I? I'm an Australian." Yu felt his face flush.

Stone leaned forward and met Yu's indignant stare. "Yes, your wife is an Australian Chinese too. That's why she was attacked. Just because she was of Chinese descent. That's the uncomfortable truth. When a country like Australia is attacked, people get scared and tribal. They get racist. The worst in some people comes out. In America in the last world war, all the Japanese Americans were interred in concentration camps."

Yu gripped the side of the chair. "Are you telling me you are going to put all Chinese Australians in concentration camps?"

Stone suddenly laughed.

"God, no. No way. Relax. I'm telling you I'm aware that there is a seam of racism in every country and Australia is no exception."

Yu said: "I can't believe you would ever have any doubts that I would want to help. Australian Chinese are as committed to the country as everyone else. We have no loyalty to mainland China or its politics."

Stone nodded. "And that's why I've brought you here. I want you to do a very special, very secret job for Australia."

"Any job," said Yu. "I'd be happy to do any job for Australia. Particularly if my family is kept safe."

"Thank you but you don't know what the task is yet."

"It doesn't matter. I will do it," said Yu.

Stone turned to Church.

"Frank, you'd better tell Peter what he's just let himself in for."

Church sat up. "Dr Yu, we want you to use Lucas Heights to build half a dozen dirty bombs. We are right now locating nuclear weapon physicists capable of doing this work but we need your help and cooperation. Your facility is the easiest to secure. It's surrounded by bushland but close to Sydney with its own accommodation. It already has laboratories and equipment — and, of course, a modest stockpile of residual radioactive waste from your nuclear reactor that we'll need for the actual bomb building."

Yu folded his legs and sat back. "I understand. You don't need enriched uranium which is just as well because we don't have any. Our facility is dedicated to nuclear and environmental research. What you are after is more like a mini neutron bomb. Only local destruction but lots of radiation fallout."

Church said, "Yes, but a lot simpler than a neutron bomb. We'll be making a simple device with a radiation core which will be detonated by a big slab of dynamite."

The scientist rubbed his chin. "What are you going to use such bombs for?"

Church explained the poison pill bluff.

Yu looked at Stone. "My God. Killing the people and poisoning the land you're trying to save. That's one hell of a strategy. I can see why you need top secrecy about a deal like this. Do you really think it will work?"

Stone raised both hands palms out and said: "We are in a desperate situation. We can't launch a frontal attack without risking the thousands of prisoners the Chinese are holding as hostages. I believe fewer lives will be lost this way if it works out. The Chinese will be dumbfounded when these bombs start detonating and I'm hoping they will believe us when we tell them we've had this as a secret strategic defence system for the last few decades. After all, END is a logical concept for a rich but isolated country like ours. Like everyone else, China knows our coastline is indefensible. END makes sense. It adds to the credibility of the bluff."

Yu sat quietly absorbing Stone's rationale.

Fearful of losing him, Stone said: "Only a small number of bombs are involved in the bluff. Believe me, Cabinet has agonised over this. They only approved it this morning because it offers our best hope of breaking the military impasse."

Yu ran a hand over his closely cropped hair.

Stone asked: "Do you have any better idea?"

Yu raised his eyebrows. "No. No, I haven't ... but I'm glad it's not my decision."

Yu seemed to resolve his own doubts. He turned to Church. "We would have to find a way of getting most of our staff out of the facility. They are a pretty smart crew. They'd suss out something's up. I think the government should announce a partial closure of Lucas Heights as a safety precaution. You could say there was a danger of the reactor becoming a Chinese bombing target."

"Good idea," said Church.

"Who are the weapon boffins you're talking to?"

"I can't give you any details but we have six physicists who have worked at American nuclear weapons plants. Three of them are New Zealanders who didn't take much encouraging. Two are ours and one is British," said Church.

"They'll need a team of assistants," said Yu. "Let me come up with a list of suitable people. I take it they're all going to be kept locked up at Lucas Heights for the duration?"

"Well, comfortably locked up. We can't let them go home every night," said Church.

"Okay. How much time have they got?"

Church paused and looked at Stone before answering: "Ten days."

Yu laughed. "No way," he said. "You're kidding me."

"It's the only time we've got till the Chinese march south," said Stone. "That's why we need your help — right now."

"I thought they said they're happy to stay in the north?"

"Don't believe everything you hear in the media," said Stone. "They're planning to come south in the next seven days taking Brisbane first unless we sign over the Top Half of the country.

"Ten days is how much time we think we can spin out our negotiations with them."

"Oh, boy." Yu removed his glasses for an impromptu clean.

"I'd better get back then," he said. "By the way, does this mean I'll be comfortably locked away at Lucas as well?"

"I'm afraid so. But don't worry. Your family will be safe. Our people will drive your children to and from school, and your wife to her office if she wants to go," said Stone.

He stood and the others followed his lead. "For what it's worth, I think she should go back to work. She won't have any more louts to worry her. And anything's better than sitting around home alone and worrying."

Yu nodded his agreement.

"I'll have a word with her. She's not going to be too keen on me being away."

Then his face lightened. "But it'll only be ten days, won't it?"

Stone grinned. "That's right. Only ten days. She won't want to be kept waiting."

8.46 p.m.

156 Griffith Road, Canberra

Church flung his briefcase on the couch and let Jocelyn give him a big hug. He felt he deserved a big hug. It had been a big day. A big successful day. Maybe the most successful of his career.

"Why are you looking so pleased with yourself?" she asked. The children were in bed and she had Frankie to herself for a grown-ups conversation.

"Today we had a great start in recruiting physicists to build a bomb for us," Church said.

"Oh. A bomb?"

Church nodded.

"What sort of a bomb?" She turned to the coffee table, took a bottle and poured two large glasses of chardonnay.

She was handing one to her husband when he answered: "A radioactive one."

Her hand paused in midair. "Radioactive?"

He took his glass from her hand.

"What do we want a radioactive bomb for?" she said.

He clinked her glass, took a sip and sat in the comfort of the couch. Jocelyn remained standing with a frown wrinkling her face.

"It's all top secret. You can't tell a single soul," said Church.

"I know the rules, Frankie," she sighed. "But what the devil do we want with a radioactive bomb?"

Church explained END — the radioactive poison pill strategy. When he finished she slumped down on the couch and stared at him. He felt the atmosphere cool.

"We never seem to learn anything," she said. "Even if this END thing works, do you know how long it took to try to clean up the Maralinga site in South Australia after the British finished letting off their nuclear test bombs?"

He went to reply but she went on: "Fifty years. Fifty years. They've had two goes at it and the radioactivity is still trapped in the soil. They've tried bulldozing the contaminated ground into pits but even now it's impossible for anyone to live in the place. Aboriginals from there have gone blind, got cancer. They've tried to keep them off the area but it's been impossible. They say it's ancestral land. And now we're going to contaminate the resource areas and kill off whole mining families — men, women and children — without any warning. It's insane."

She stopped. Her eyes drilled into him. "I hope it wasn't your idea."

Church's happy glow had rapidly dissipated. Her hostility was a shock.

"No, it wasn't my idea," he said.

"But you're still happy to help carry it out," she said.

He grew defensive and began arguing the logic, the greater good behind the END strategy. Civilian deaths happened in any war. There was always collateral damage. The future of Australia was at stake, for heaven's sake. The country faced certain defeat unless it acted boldly.

Jocelyn became increasingly angry.

"You're talking rubbish. I bet the real reason you're not going to tell anyone about this great idea is because you know the public outcry would topple Stone before he pulled the trigger," she said.

"It has to stay secret. We have to take the Chinese by surprise. We can't give them any warning. We need to shock them into believing they've gone a line too far."

"That's bullshit, Frankie. You know full well if people found out about this plan there'd be no nukes detonated killing off Australians. And what's more repulsive is that this sort of bomb doesn't knock down whole towns or anything, it mainly just kills off people and ruins land with its radiation poisoning."

Church downed the last of his wine.

"You just don't understand the strategy that's in play."

"Don't tell me what I don't understand," Jocelyn said. "What happened to using troops and jets and things to fight a war?"

"Because we wouldn't win with troops and jets and things. Can I have another glass, please?"

She ignored him. "How many people do you think we'll kill?"

Church ignored the question. He stood to get the wine bottle from the coffee table. He wished he had never mentioned a word about END.

Jocelyn declined his offer of a refill. She began a new tirade insisting no governments could be trusted. They had lied about the dangers at Maralinga. They had lied about making Aussie troops crawl through the desert sands as human guinea pigs and then denied any of their sickness was from radiation.

"The Aboriginal tribes at Maralinga got a whole thirteen million dollars for their wasted land and sickness. It's just disgusting. And we're meant to be a democracy. What a laugh," she said.

Church stood. "We are a democracy. That's what we're fighting to defend. I'm too tired to argue. Don't worry about any dinner for me, I'm going to bed."

DAY FIVE

1 p.m.

The Lodge gardens, Canberra

Admiral Brian Robson had no idea what to expect when he was summoned to The Lodge. As his official car drove through the gates he saw the Prime Minister strolling slowly by himself on the big front lawn. He seemed to be limping slightly.

The Navy chief had heard nothing from the new Minister for Defence since a message on the first day of the crisis. It said China had demanded both Australian Collins submarines, patrolling at the time of the attack, return immediately to their Garden Island base near Perth.

The call was being ignored but the submarines were to surface and surrender if they were detected. The government did not want a sudden, unplanned escalation of the confrontation.

A Chief Petty Officer opened his door, saluted and said Stone would like a private word with him. Mystified, Robson left his briefcase with an aide, walked over to Stone and saluted.

Stone shook his hand. "Come for a walk with me. I want to clear something up before we join the others."

He turned to wave an arm across the sweeping lawn. "This garden is made up entirely of Australian natives, you know."

"I trust that includes all these guys around here with guns," Robson said.

"As far as I know. I've banned tour buses, so we should be okay."

The admiral laughed.

After a thirty-six-year naval career he didn't have a high opinion of politicians. Over the years governments had promised much, usually around election cycles, but produced little.

The Navy should always have had a fleet of at least a dozen submarines to patrol the enormous oceans surrounding Australia and the east-Asian shipping lanes. Instead it had six. The same number Singapore had to guard its tiny island nation. It was a joke.

And the half-sized fleet they operated had made things worse by traditionally being the Defence Department's most expensive single item and its worst performing.

Finally, the Navy had been promised its minimum fleet of twelve killer subs. But he would be well retired before even the first of the new French-designed Shortfin Barracuda subs became operational in the early 2030s — if it was completed in time in Adelaide, which it wouldn't be.

He had worked with previous Defence Minister Bradbury but had never dealt directly with Stone, who had sent shockwaves through the Defence establishment when he summarily sacked his minister for being AWOL the morning of the shock invasion.

Robson was almost certain he had been called for high-level strategic talks at The Lodge because his last two submarines were about to be ordered home as part of a border agreement.

There had certainly been no sign the government was powering up the Navy for a combat role in the north.

He was, like most of the Defence Force brass, depressed at the success of China's lightning raid of the north. Australia's pants were around its knees and the government seemed to be waffling toward a treaty of appeasement.

When Stone posed his question almost casually as they walked along, Robson was taken by surprise. He was uncertain what Stone had actually said and wondered momentarily if he had heard correctly.

"We need to sink the *Liaoning*. Is there any real chance your

Collins could blow a couple of holes in her, send her to the bottom? Or would it be a suicide job?"

Robson recovered quickly. The best defence was offence. "Prime Minister, I thought you'd never ask," he said.

Stone chuckled.

"Prime Minister, they're hunter killers. They are made for this type of mission," Robson said. "You can forget all that business about them being 'dub subs'."

Every defence planner knew the Chinese aircraft carrier and its three dozen fighters cruising off the Queensland coast would spearhead any invasion force.

Stone's question had been rude, disrespectful, but the Collins had been a nightmare since the first one was launched in 1993. They had suffered never-ending technical and mechanical problems. Their "dub subs" nickname had been justified in the early years.

Frequently, the Navy had struggled to keep a single one operational. It had been impossible to find enough submariners to crew them.

"You know the background on those subs," Robson said.

"Yes, I do," said Stone, "that's why I got you out here, away from the others. I need to know if these old bloody things can be of any real use to us."

Robson sighed. "We've done a lot of work on them in recent years. Our crews are very professional. They'll do the job. The Collins aren't as fast as the big American nuke subs, but they're quieter and that's a huge advantage. They're silent deadly weapons. That's what they were designed to be."

Stone raised a sceptical eyebrow.

Robson said: "They've done some exceptional kills in exercises against the Americans."

During one they had slipped undetected through all air and surface anti-submarine screens around an eight-ship American amphibious assault force. There had been a succession of similar successes.

"With the Chinese we'd be up against detection sonars that

aren't as powerful or as sophisticated as the American ones —
and the Collins would have the element of surprise," said Robson.

"The Yanks were expecting us and we got through. I don't
think the Chinese will be expecting anything. They think they've
got us for dead."

"Well, we're not dead," said Stone looking at his watch. The
Joint Chiefs of Staff meeting was due to start.

"I know you are being confident but I'm worried about
whether the subs are in a condition to attack. As I understand it,
one of them is very low on fuel, and everything else — its crew's
been out there for almost seventy days."

Robson moved his cap back slightly on his head. "On the
Rankin they'll all be pretty weary all right and their diesel situation will get critical in the next few days but they're close to the
carrier so the job can be done if you give the order sooner rather
than later. We don't have the time to bugger about, sir. And the
longer they're shadowing the Chinese the greater chance they'll
be detected — and then the game will be over."

Stone nodded that he understood.

They stopped at the high-security fence at the southern end
of the grounds and waited for a pair of guards to walk out of
earshot.

"I've been thinking how important the element of surprise is,"
Stone said. "I've spoken to Martini. He's been foxing the Chinese
and dragging out their bloody peace negotiations. I've told him
to tell the Chinese tomorrow we've agreed to order the missing
Collins back home to Garden Island. And the day after tomorrow
one will appear. Two days later the second one will. We want the
Chinese to believe we are going to give them the Top Half."

Robson grimaced. "How do we attack the carrier and be tied
up at Garden Island?"

"You build two decoys," said Stone. "The Chinese will be convinced we're beat and the dub subs have gone home."

Robson frowned. He shook his head. "Prime Minister, these
subs are huge. They're the biggest conventional subs in the world.

They're almost eighty metres long. How am I going to build two replicas of these monsters in the next seventy-two hours?"

Stone placed a big mitt on the admiral's braided shoulder. "Very quickly. The same way we're building six radioactive bombs."

Stone smiled and winked. He enjoyed Robson's gobsmacked reaction and started off again toward The Lodge. Robson shook his head. What radioactive bombs? What the hell was going on?

He quickly caught up with Stone, who seemed to be favouring his left knee and wheezing slightly. The man had no idea of the feat he was asking. The decoy task was one of nightmare proportions.

Stone seemed to read his mind. "You only have to build the top of a sub out of wood with a conning tower sticking out of it, paint it jet black and float it off its wharf. Moor it tightly and it won't go anywhere. It'll look like a sub from a recon satellite, won't it?"

Robson found himself nodding.

"And it's what the Chinese will be expecting to see. That's more than half the battle. They'll be tickled pink. Their ego will be more than satisfied and they won't look any closer. It's the same decoy trick we use when we're duck shooting."

They trudged on. Stone said: "So can you do it?"

"Of course, sir," said Robson. "Sink one aircraft carrier surrounded by four escorts and God knows how many subs, and build two decoys."

The pair continued on to the official entrance. Robson realised he was outpacing Stone.

"Prime Minister, is everything okay? You sound like you're a little out of breath."

"No, no. I'm fine. Had a lung infection for the last couple of days."

Thompson and Church were waiting on them in the dining room.

Stone pulled up his chair. "Sorry to keep you. I've had a chat to Brian about the *Liaoning*. He's sure his boys can send it to the bottom."

Thompson nodded. Church folded his arms. "Oh no, not the Collins. It's Sweden we should declare war on."

Robson was forced to smile with the others. The Collins design had been a stretched version of the Swedish Västergötland class. Its selection had been the first of many controversies and corruption allegations that mired the Australian submarine project.

The legendary botch-ups in construction, the huge overruns in time and money and the submarines' unreliability had followed.

Stone outlined his decoy plan. Then explained the END project to Robson. If the Chinese called his bluff and retaliated after the first bombs were detonated, he wanted the *Liaoning* and its fighter jets sunk. It would give Australia some glimmer of hope in a full-scale confrontation.

11.47 a.m.

International Airport, Sydney

Anna Sharp struggled to hold back her tears.

Nothing in her nine years at Air New Zealand's Sydney check-in prepared her for the queue of traumatised children and parents stretched before her counter. Not even her own dramatic escape from Queensland among the refugee panic only days before.

Anna made herself stare fixedly at her computer screen in a vain effort to blot out the heart-wrenching scenes: toddlers sobbing inconsolably, clinging desperately to their parents. Mothers fighting back tears, convinced their children would be safer in New Zealand.

The infants knew it wasn't a real Christmas holiday they were going on. Normal school holidays hadn't begun, and their mums and dads weren't coming.

Instead, for most, it was an uncle or granny meeting them at the Auckland International Airport terminal.

Anna could see they didn't really understand why they had to go. But their parents feared Australia would soon be a war zone as it faced off against the Chinese.

New Zealanders had raised millions in a matter of hours to fund charter aircraft and ferry the children of their expatriate workforce from the Australian state capitals.

Anna was heart-torn as the elder brothers in a family typically put on a brave face, brushing aside tears and taking the hands of their younger siblings on the final stretch to board.

Most of the children would dawdle uncertainly, stopping and turning repeatedly at the departure gate for one last wave good-bye.

Some tore themselves free and sprinted back to their parents. Their distress created more consternation among those still mustering the courage for their own final farewells.

The babies were quiet until they were prised from their mothers' arms by the volunteer stewardesses and carried through the Customs aisles. Their cries for mum would begin long before they were out of sight.

It seemed as though the whole terminal was awash in tears and fear.

Overwrought and exhausted, Anna looked at her watch. She knew the plane would miss its flight schedule. The emotional effort to load the reluctant young human cargo was a time-consuming nightmare.

Clinging to stoic-faced teddy bears and ragged pink pandas, the parade of infant refugees from Australia was a one-hundred-thousand-strong evacuation.

With its previously booming economy, Australia had provided high-paid work for Kiwis. Before the crisis, six hundred thousand had settled in Australia. Fifteen per cent of New Zealand's population. Most had children. Most wanted them well away from any danger.

Anna had watched in dismay when television news crews arrived earlier to capture the emotional chaos. Their bright lights and cameras had triggered off more alarm and commotion among the children.

Scuffles broke out as angry fathers attempted to drive off the camera crews. Anna never saw what they filmed because none of the television channels ran any footage. It was judged too raw for public viewing and too damaging for morale.

As the computer spat out the last boarding ticket, Anna heaved a sigh of relief. Her scheduled shift was about to begin. It had been an amazing few days in the aviation business.

Incoming flights were almost empty. But outgoing ones, like the one she would be processing shortly, were packed.

She cringed at the prospect of more shouted confrontations with desperate people jostling for position in the queues.

The price of a ticket to Los Angeles was now five times more than a week ago. It had not deterred demand.

The rule allowing a single piece of hand luggage was strictly enforced. The aircraft were at maximum allowable passenger weight. Travellers eager to escape made last-minute gifts of their excess cabin bags to counter staff. Sarah had so far collected eleven. A "war bonus", she rationalised.

While the airlines' ticket prices had leapt, Anna knew the corporate charter companies on the other side of the airport were exploiting a panic-driven bonanza among the rich and famous.

Seats to Los Angeles on the corporate jets were selling for $60,000 each. The price had been $25,000 two days ago.

The black market price being offered for tomorrow was $100,000.

Her friends among the charter company staff had been startled yesterday when a cabin full of well-heeled passengers were herded from one jet by their pilot at gunpoint. He rushed his own family on board and, using his filed flight plan, flew out of the country.

Anna's thoughts were broken as her last mother customer kneeled to kiss her six-year-old daughter goodbye and readjust the big name tag around her tiny neck.

The little girl asked if they had ice cream in New Zealand. Assured they did, she nodded and took the hand of her escorting stewardess. The pair walked slowly down the departures passage. As they disappeared from sight the mother broke down.

A police officer bristling with weaponry appeared from the crowd to comfort her. He put an arm around her and carried her handbag as they joined the sad procession of parents making for the exit.

Anna kicked shoes from her aching feet and looked up at her first LA-bound customer. No, he couldn't take two pieces on board. Sorry. Where had he purchased his ticket? Sorry. It was a forgery. There was no such flight as NZ202.

5.55 p.m.

Ernie's Bar and Grill, Surfers Paradise

Florence Bartlett was bone weary. Worn out by life really. Long before the Chinese rushed to claim all that dreadful, hot desert a few days ago.

Now she surveyed her bar in downtown Surfers Paradise. Seven drinkers. Six of them local barflies and one a hapless, stranded Melbourne tourist. The six always drifted in about ten minutes before the evening news.

There were greetings all round. They ordered beers. The tourist had gin and tonic. A week ago she and Ernie, her boss, would have been bustling to serve thirty to forty thirsty drinkers at the end of a hot day of holidaying.

"Florrie, another one, love," ordered Stan.

She turned to reach for a new glass and caught her reflection in the bar's mirror. Her ageing, Sunshine State face was a mass of deep wrinkled lines, her hair swept back in a tight bun. She knew if she smiled it would reveal a new chipped tooth. It would stay chipped. She didn't have the money for a dental repair.

The small crowd of patrons began to fall silent as Ernie raised the television volume. The beginning of the news was sometimes the best part. The national anthem played against a backdrop of World War Two black and white Movietone clips. They depicted

Diggers fighting the hated Japanese Imperial Army to a standstill in the jungles of New Guinea.

The news last night had been good. The Prime Minister had outlawed any mortgagee sales or evictions of Queensland businesses unable to meet their lease payments. Ernie would have had to shut the doors without that protection.

If Florence lost her job she would be in a hopeless position. The tourists had all fled the city and it was now full of idle hotel workers and tradespeople. There were more than a hundred thousand of them.

She was now literally on her own. Her husband had died twelve years ago, one of her sons was trapped in Cairns, the other had made it out in the first mad exodus to Sydney.

Tonight's news began with the peace talks. They were continuing behind closed doors, the reporter said. Again, there were no details of what was happening. Florence shrugged. It had been the same story every day.

At least the little yellow buggers were staying put. She had been brought up on World War Two stories about the "Brisbane Line".

It was the officially denied story of how military planners had drawn a line on a map of Queensland just north of Brisbane. The state capital was to be the first mainland line of defence against the invading Japanese. The Far North was to have been abandoned as indefensible. Every Queenslander believed the Line story was true. Florence's father certainly had.

Florence poured another beer as the newsreader reported several deaths at marinas in Sydney, Melbourne and Perth. Ocean-going yachts were being stolen and sailed away by people joining the "chicken run".

The police were treating the deaths as homicides. The victims had been stabbed or shot attempting to resist the "chickens".

A growing number of vessels were ignoring customs clearance and heading directly to sea.

Everybody had a drink, so Florence was able to give her full attention to the next item. Fifteen environmentalists had been beaten by workers firing up an old coal power station in New South Wales.

Greenies had attempted to blockade the road to the station. The workers had swiftly and brutally cleared it before the police had shown up. Oil was now too scarce and expensive to use as a fuel for power generation.

Several of the drinkers cheered. The bloody greenies had got what they deserved.

It was just more needless violence, Florence thought. People were in a turmoil. Many wanted the government to settle with the Chinese so life could get back to some sort of normalcy. Others wanted to form volunteer battalions to fight.

It was impossible to know what the government was doing. It had just been talks, talks, talks.

An outback cattleman appeared in the next item. Wearing a sweat-stained hat and dusty brown clothes, he had managed to elude the roadblocks and escape south.

He had cheery news of a five-kilometre-long iron ore train being derailed. The rail lines had been dynamited. There were tonnes of explosives around every mining site. Miners had helped themselves. In the national interest, of course, he said with a wide smile.

He had other tales of mine workers sabotaging their machinery and the inhumane shortage of beer they were suffering.

There was a shortage of food and fuel but morale in the occupied regions was good. Everyone up there was expecting the Aussie army to turn up any day, guns blazing, to rescue them.

The final item was greeted with fits of laughter. There had been an official protest from the Chinese Embassy regarding a comedy programme.

Unhampered by censorship or political correctness, the programme had featured a skit of Aboriginals teaching Chinese infantrymen how to wade into shallow waters to fish for crocodiles. Another gave lessons on moving ant hills.

The Chinese had complained the report was racist and unhelpful while peace talks were continuing.

The news ended with more of the national anthem and Diggers parading at some unidentified barracks. The current affairs report was next. The anchorman said it would cover the slump in house prices.

Ernie turned the volume down. The drinkers huddled. Nothing much was going on, they agreed.

In a few days their bar wouldn't exist.

11 p.m.

Dean Street, Townsville

Six kilometres from the Lavarack base in the suburbs of Townsville, life was on hold for Brenda Patterson.

Her husband was locked away at the base and she had heard nothing from her son. Johnny had been on a survival exercise in the desert somewhere when the Chinese struck.

Like everyone else, Brenda lived in a vacuum. There were no television or internet communications. The radio continued to carry light music and was interrupted occasionally if the Chinese wanted to issue new instructions or warnings to the public.

Food was being rationed while peace talks were under way. Petrol was available for essential services only. The population had to walk in the tropical heat if they needed to leave their homes.

All non-urgent surgery at the Townsville Hospital had been halted. Chinese border guards manning the roadblocks had orders to shoot to kill if anyone attempted to escape south.

The Chinese broadcasts promised normal life would resume in a matter of days with the completion of the border treaty talks.

Brenda felt depressed and helpless.

She was startled by a tapping on her bedroom window. She parted the curtains but could see nothing in the dark backyard.

"Mum. It's me. Let me in the back door."

She ran for the door in a rush of joy at the sound of Johnny's voice.

She went to wrap her arms around him but was pushed back inside.

"Quiet. Quiet. There are Chink patrols everywhere," he hissed.

He crossed the floor to part the front window curtains slightly and peep outside. Satisfied, he returned and embraced his mother. She seemed to have aged somehow in just days.

Johnny told her his five-man squad was returning from the ten-day survival exercise when a farmer had waved their army truck down and broke the news.

His sergeant had immediately decided to hide the truck. They had made the final part of their way back to Townsville on foot, dodging Chinese patrols and roadblocks.

Brenda's elation quickly turned to despair when Johnny rummaged in his bedroom and returned to the kitchen with his scoped hunting rifle. He saw the anguish on her face.

"Mum, my sergeant and I have decided we're going back out. We're going to do some hit-and-run raids on these Chinks to make sure they don't think they've beaten all of us," he said.

"But what can a few of you do?" Brenda said. "You'll be caught and shot. There must be thousands of them."

"We won't get caught, Mum. This is our home territory." He laughed. "We've just been proving we can live off the land."

Johnny held up his rifle and peered down the scope. "And this little beauty is just the thing for hunting Chinks. They won't know what hit 'em. It's as good as a sniper rifle."

He held his mother's gaze. "And anyway, what would the old man say if he found out I was on the loose with the lads and did nothing?"

Brenda sat at the kitchen table quietly sobbing as her son collected canned food from the cupboards and took a bottle of water from the fridge. She was proud of him. But the prospect of both the men in her life being in danger was too much.

He kissed the top of her head and slipped silently out the back door and into the darkness.

Sergeant Guy Waters was waiting in the shadows. He and Patterson had decided they would trek south toward Bowen. He had worked at the big Port Abbot coal export facility nearby. The pair were convinced with their local knowledge they could sabotage it.

They had chosen it because of its strategic value to the Chinese. It was a rare deep-water port on the Queensland coast. It could take bulk carriers with draughts of up to fifteen metres. Almost two hundred called every year.

To reach the huge ships, the port's trestle jetty and coal conveyor ran kilometres out to sea. And each year fifteen million tonnes of Queensland's Galilee Basin coal was dumped off the conveyor and into the cavernous holds of the bulk carriers.

Patterson was particularly excited about the mission. He was an activist greenie absolutely opposed to the port's operations and its planned expansion.

The port intruded into a corner of the Great Barrier Reef World Heritage Area. Patterson and other environmentalists claimed the dredging operation needed for the expansion would endanger the surrounding ecosystem.

DAY SIX

8.10 p.m.

Elizabeth Bay Marina, Sydney

Jeff Bolt was breathing hard. He had bustled his wife, Jenny, and their two children on board and started the big diesel engine below.

Now he was easing off the aft mooring line holding the *Pacific Queen* to her marina berth. In the half dark, he could make out the silhouette of Jenny near the bow, as she stood ready to cast off the forward lines.

He heard the aft lines splash into the water before scampering back to the cockpit to put the vessel into gear.

"Okay, let go forward," he called as loudly as he dared.

There was no reply from Jenny who was staring at the bright lights of the Sydney skyline. She had not wanted to come. He had to wear her down over several days. They had to escape while they could.

Australia was stuffed. They were among a few of the lucky ones who had the means to get out, get to sea and away from all the bloody panic and the Chinese.

Supplies of petrol and food were already becoming short and the rationing system was a shambles.

Jenny had argued about the dangers to their young sons. Argued about everything really.

The only part of his plan that had not upset her was the theft of his boss's yacht. Thirty metres of seagoing luxury, she was worth more than thirty million dollars on a bad day. Jenny loathed Charles Murphy. To her he was a rich, arrogant bastard who paid lousy crew wages.

Jeff looked back up the marina wharf. A figure had appeared in the distance.

He cupped his hands over his mouth and called again more urgently: "Let go forward! Jenny! For Christ's sake, let go forward!"

She broke from her trance and rushed to pull the mooring line over its bow cleat. She threw it on the wharf. The heavy rope landed with a loud clap.

Jeff rolled his eyes and, under his breath, cursed the noise she had made as he eased the throttle forward and into gear. The yacht slid along beside its berth, the engine's waterline exhausts chugging gently.

The *Pacific Queen* had everything his family needed to flee and survive. Crucially it had its own water makers. He had just overhauled them and replaced their filters. They could choose safe destinations thousands of kilometres from Sydney.

It had all the comforts of a luxury apartment. The kids would be happy with the stack of video games, satellite television and their own oversized staterooms. The Master's Cabin was bigger than his bedroom at home. Jenny would revel in its plushness once she settled down and could see he had made the right call for the family.

The galley's freezers were packed with fine foods. All on account from Murphy's providore whose manager knew the tall, strapping skipper of the *Pacific Queen* from previous visits.

Jeff had not sought any customs clearance. The risk of his plans being discovered was too great. In a few more months there would be no Australian Customs. He would make for the Sydney Heads and lay a course for Fiji.

He heard footsteps running down the marina wharf. He turned and saw Murphy only metres behind. The yacht was idling cautiously parallel and only half a metre from the wharf.

Murphy came abreast of the *Pacific Queen* and shouted: "What the hell is going on here?!"

Jenny gave a short scream and stumbled back from the bow toward the cockpit.

Jeff turned the bow further from the wharf but the marina berth was too narrow to open up a sizeable gap.

Murphy leapt from the wharf and landed heavily beside the cockpit. He scrambled to his feet and screamed: "Where the fuck do you think you're off to, Bolt?!"

"Jenny, go down below with the boys. I'll sort this out," Jeff said. He turned to Murphy and raised both his hands.

"Boss, there's nothing to get excited about. I can explain everything."

"Fuck that, just reverse and tie up to the wharf. Was that Jenny I saw? What the hell do you think you're pulling?"

Jeff put the yacht into reverse gear. Its stern swung back toward the wharf. Murphy waited on the duckboard ready to make his yacht fast again.

Jeff opened a side hatch and fished in his toolbox. He located a heavy spanner. As the yacht reached the wharf, he stepped out of the cockpit behind Murphy and struck him on the back of the head.

Murphy gave a grunt, collapsed and fell into the black, oily marina waters. Jeff looked down on the corpulent, lifeless figure floating face down.

He checked the jetty. It was deserted as far as he could make out in the fading light. He stepped back into the cockpit and for the second time pushed the engine into forward gear.

As he guided the vessel out into the harbour Jenny came through the cockpit hatch, eyes wide, her body shaking.

"What happened? Where is he?"

Jeff waved a thumb over his shoulder. "We had a little chat. Told him we had to borrow his yacht."

"Fuck, Jeff. What did you do?"

"Nothing, calm down. We're getting out of here before the Chinese arrive, all right?"

She broke into sobs and fled back into the huge saloon.

Jeff could make out two more yachts ahead of him making for the heads. There were a few other sensible buggers, he thought.

DAY SEVEN

3 p.m.

The Lodge, Canberra

Jeff Bolt's murderous exit triggered a political storm in its wake. The body of Charles Murphy was dragged from Elizabeth Bay surrounded by news cameras.

Unbeknownst to Bolt, Murphy's wife had seen the attack on her husband from the marina car park. The media portrayed Bolt as a cowardly killer deserting his country.

The murder morphed into a rash of stories in the mass circulation tabloids claiming the rich were using their luxury boats and private jets to flee to safety overseas. Ordinary strugglers were being left to face the Chinese.

The stories were largely untrue. A check the following day showed almost all of Australia's rich listers were still in the country.

But, like any Prime Minister, Stone appreciated the fragile, tense boundary between the rich and poor in Australian society. Electoral victory was a delicate balancing act.

Ongoing front-page stories were exposing society's fault lines as fears of a full invasion grew. Each story carried photographs of luxury craft streaming out to sea from marinas all around the country.

Some owners insisted their pre-Christmas voyages had been planned for months. Others hid below decks from media helicopters and their cameras.

One tabloid photo spread captured a fashionably dressed family walking toward a glistening private jet waiting on the tarmac for them. A Rolls-Royce in the background completed the elite scene.

The story claimed they had paid thirty-five million dollars for the jet — ten million more than its asking price the previous week.

Stone wondered what had become of the million-dollar Rolls when the jet roared away. He was angry the jet-setters had not been identified correctly. They were wealthy, vacationing Americans caught up in the Chinese crisis.

The extortionate price for airline tickets was also causing widespread dismay. There were frequent reports of unruly scenes at international terminals among those desperate to flee.

But it was the lawlessness in the wealthiest suburbs that worried Stone the most.

Empty harbourside mansions were being looted and set on fire. They were targets because their owners had allegedly joined the "chicken run".

Fire trucks were showing an unusual tardiness in reaching these multi-million-dollar infernos. The firemen had caught the public mood and had little interest in saving the shuttered "castles of the rich", as one tabloid described them.

Exploiting the mayhem, professional criminals could not believe their good fortune as they burgled and burned.

Stone sat at his desk staring at the headlines. A society of fat, happy and smug people was disintegrating as it faced a world of uncertainty and subjugation.

The value of homes and old-age superannuation funds were collapsing. A leap in inflation was speedily chewing up any cash savings.

Australians' lifestyle and affluence was vanishing before their eyes. Rumours of the country's fate ran wild, the lack of any apparent government action to deal with the crisis compounding their fears.

Protest marches were being organised demanding the government agree to a border settlement and avoid war.

Stone held his head in his hands and closed his eyes. Chaos and more chaos. He felt helpless. He could not announce the measures he had under way to tackle the Chinese. But he had to restore order and hope.

He lifted his head and sighed. It must be near half-time. His team had to know victory was possible. Its best players were being held in reserve but some action was needed before the scoreboard became too lopsided and morale slumped fatally. A stern team talk was needed. And quickly.

He dug in his pocket for the nitrate spray and, with his free hand, reached for the phone. He decided he would give a state-of-the-nation address. Urgently. Tonight.

John Able come on the line. Stone told him he wanted an invitation issued to Ellen Jacobs. She was the anchor at Australia's highest rating current affairs programme.

"You want the blonde Rottweiler, Prime Minister?" said John Able.

"Yes, John."

"Okay. What time?"

"At six o'clock."

"Prime news time."

"Yes."

"Are you going to the studio, sir?"

"No. Our lounge will be fine."

"Okay. I'll call her."

Stone smiled as he replaced the phone. He understood Able's surprise. Jacobs, a glamorous and seemingly polite interviewer, was, for politicians, a media dilemma.

Many self-important and over-confident politicians over the years had sought exposure to her millions of viewers only to be seduced by a smiling assassin capable of quietly exposing nasty, career-ending truths.

Stone knew he had chosen well. He had to reach the biggest

audience he could. He had to perform as a leader and he was doing this by eschewing the soft interview.

His gamble was keeping control of it. Choosing the Prime Ministerial mansion as the venue was part of that. To calm a shaken country he needed to be seen as a leader they could trust. Someone in control.

If he lost control and Jacobs became the junkyard dog … the prospect didn't bear thinking about.

* * *

Stone ordered most of the armed guards at the main entrance out of sight before Ellen Jacobs' entourage arrived with their cameras and sound equipment. He didn't want footage of The Lodge looking like it was under siege.

He took several big breaths and flexed his left knee before entering the lounge with its oversized armchairs. They weren't oversized for his bulk. They would be for Jacobs' willowy body.

The camera crew was waiting patiently. He sat down opposite Jacobs. After some small talk the jean-clad, long-haired producer attached their lapel microphones.

The producer counted down the final seconds with the fingers of one hand. Jacobs tossed her long blonde hair back and cleared her throat.

"Prime Minister, thank you for being with us tonight," she began pleasantly.

"You're with me actually, Ellen. Welcome to The Lodge."

Thrown off her stride momentarily, Jacobs took refuge by peering down at the clipboard holding her prepared questions.

"Prime Minister, we have seen some shocking scenes in recent days of some of our fat cats abandoning the country in their jets and gin palaces. Clearly these people don't feel safe or that the government has any answers to the Chinese crisis. How do you feel about that?"

He answered with a shrug of his big shoulders. She looked

puzzled. He waited a long second, deliberately building audience attention.

"It's not how I feel about it that matters, Ellen," he said. "It's how the Chinese feel about it that matters."

Jacobs' eyebrows rose above the famous bright blue eyes. She lowered the clipboard to her lap. "How do you mean?" she said.

"I mean it's how the Chinese feel about these events that matters. I believe the chaos and cowardly actions by some people will be giving the invaders heart," Stone replied.

He looked directly down the barrel of the camera. "They will have seen some of our people in panic. This is exactly the response terrorists want to see. They'd have been elated at this. Overjoyed. They'll feel emboldened and more certain their reckless adventure to annex northern Australia, and our most valuable resources, will pay off."

Jacobs said: "So you don't see these people as refugees but as cowards?"

"They are cowards," Stone said. "Their homes are not under any immediate threat. There has been no full-blown invasion.

"Instead Joe Martini is in ongoing negotiations with the Chinese to resolve the crisis. These cowards are making his job harder. They are weakening his leverage."

Crossing her long legs, she asked what he, as the Prime Minister, was going to do about the "exodus of the cowards".

Stone shook his head casually. "I'm not going to do anything. We don't need these sort of lily-livered traitors on our team. They have chosen to leave when we most need to show a united front. They can go but they can't expect to be allowed to come back and carry on as usual once we've resolved this crisis."

Pushing a stray blonde hair from her face, Jacobs shook her head. "But do you have the power to revoke anyone's citizenship?"

"Yes, I do. And I'm saying anyone returning after this crisis will have to provide bona fide reasons for their departure."

Before she could find a follow-up question, he went on: "But there'll be some people we'll be insisting come back. In fact, we'll hunt them down — and they'll be tried for murder, theft, assault, arson and hijackings."

Jacobs squirmed forward to the edge of the wide chair. "Prime Minister, I asked you earlier why people felt the need to panic. They have no apparent faith your government is doing anything to resolve our situation. What is it exactly the government plans to do?"

Stone broke eye contact with her and looked down the camera barrel again. He could sense millions of eyes fixed on him.

He could feel the heat of the camera lights through his suit. There was probably some perspiration gleaming on his forehead. He sat upright, speaking calmly and deliberately.

It was time. The fans needed to know the game was still winnable.

"What I can tell you tonight is that there are a number of actions under way that will lead to an end of this Chinese state terrorism we face. I will be able to tell you about them in detail in a few days. In the meantime we need to stand together and not to allow fear to take over. We will want to look back on this time as one in which we all faced down a crisis with courage and determination. Not panic and profiteering."

He sat back and gave a decisive nod to the camera. "Good night. Stand firm."

Before Jacobs could react he unclipped his lapel microphone and handed it to her with a quiet thanks, stood and walked from the room.

He had sent his message. To Australia and China. He did not want it diluted or sidetracked with further questions.

The cameras were still recording and showing viewers a disconcerted Jacobs holding the Prime Minister's microphone in one hand as she turned in search of her producer.

He signalled something and she turned back to the camera. "Well … I think we'll be crossing back to the studio … that was Prime Minister Stone … yes … this is Ellen Jacobs at The Lodge, we are returning you to the studio. Good night."

The brilliant glare of the camera lights faded quickly.

The producer crossed the room in the sudden gloom to take Stone's microphone from Jacobs as she stood. He said: "Bloody hell, what'd you make of that? Sounds like the old bugger's giving up on the peace talks and going to war."

From the corner of his eye he saw members of the camera crew frantically waving their arms. They were too late. He looked at the mike switch in horror. It was on. Millions had just heard him.

DAY EIGHT

The Lodge, Canberra

The Prime Minister's call for the nation to stiffen its back was the main story the following day. As he sipped an early-morning coffee, Stone looked in grim satisfaction at the country's newspaper and online headlines.

FLEEING COWARDS STONED

ACTION PROMISED TO END TERRORIST INVASION

STONE USES WAR POWERS TO STRIP REFUGEES OF CITIZENSHIP

PM DRAWS RECORD 17.5 MILLION VIEWERS

DICTATOR STONE ABUSING EMERGENCY POWERS — CIVIL RIGHTS UNION

PRODUCER SUSPENDED FOR UNPROFESSIONAL CONDUCT

5.54 p.m.

On board HMAS Rankin, *Coral Sea*

John Scott knew what every other crew member knew. The fuel on their stinking oven of a submarine was fast running out.

When news of the Chinese strike broke, the Chief Acoustic Warfare Analyst and the fifty-eight weary crew on HMAS *Rankin* had been at sea just four days short of their official, maximum endurance time of sixty-eight days.

They were ordered to stay on patrol. It had begun routinely, covertly monitoring the Chinese naval vessels exercising in the Timor Sea.

They tracked the People's Liberation Army's Navy flotilla across the Arafura Sea eastward to the Coral Sea where it began to head south toward its ultimate destination: a goodwill visit to Sydney.

When it reached the Coral Sea the *Rankin*'s original orders were to break off and head for Perth and home. Their sister submarine, the HMAS *Sheean*, stationed in the Coral Sea, would take over the surveillance role.

Now Scott was praying the *Rankin* — one of a fleet of the world's most trouble-prone submarines — would not falter. It was sneaking along silently, its battery-powered electric engines delivering a minimum four-knot speed.

The four hundred tonnes of batteries had to be recharged by its three diesel generators and they needed to "snort" fresh air on the surface. And that was a big problem: besides the risk of being spotted while semi-submerged so close to the enemy, the generators were on the last of their diesel reserves.

He adjusted his headphones and stared at the sonar screen as he had each patrol for the last ten years. The cushioned headphones were clamped over a perpetually damp head. The overheated atmosphere of the submarine was another routine ordeal they all had to live with.

He listened to the faint ping and watched the passive sonar

screen flare as it reflected the Chinese ships. They were only thirty-three kilometres away to the east.

Rankin had been able stay in touch at such a low speed because the enemy vessels were cruising in a leisurely, wide, holding circle.

Divorced eight years, Scott was the longest-serving submariner on board — four years longer than his current skipper.

Crew turnover in the submarine fleet was notoriously high. He knew most members of his young sonar team would be gone with the rest of the current crew within two or three years.

Working conditions on a Collins were arduous for even the hardiest souls — more stressful for longer periods than SAS soldiers had to tolerate.

Scott accepted life on a sub was one of stifling claustrophobia and sometimes hideous smells from oil, diesel and body odour.

In the first few days at sea he had suffered the usual dry mouth, sore throat and constipation created by the dryness of the artificial air they all breathed.

In a no-sunrise-no-sunset life the worst thing on patrol were the coffin dreams. He knew they were the most common dream of submariners but he'd had more than usual recently.

In normal conditions, time often flew. Everyone worked, slept, ate, watched movies and played games in the confined spaces with their low ceilings and narrow passageways. Everyone had two jobs and the essential team spirit in such crowded quarters built strong bonds.

This was now no normal patrol. Scott had watched the fearful expressions of young crew members when they learned of the Chinese crisis and their orders to remain on station.

The *Sheean* was exactly sixty-nine kilometres to the east on the far side of the enemy convoy. Its presence was an odd comfort. They were not completely alone hiding out here.

He felt the presence of the skipper behind him. He turned his swivel seat and gave a thumbs up. The skipper nodded and moved on.

Scott's six-hour shift was ending. He spotted his replacement,

Michael Muir, chatting to a weapons officer in the control room. They would be trading rumours.

The sonar man would be wanting to know if they had received any new orders from Admiral Robson. Scott knew they hadn't. But they would have to come soon.

Beside the fuel issue, they all lived in fear the *Rankin* would be detected in their long-running cat and mouse game with the Chinese fleet. So far they had been lucky.

As the oldest crew member, he was frequently allaying the worst fears and wilder rumours among the juniors.

The previous night he had got a smile from one of the five female submariners on board, recounting how Aussie ingenuity had made it so difficult for enemy sonar to detect them.

The British and American navies had created a tile coating for their nuclear subs to make them almost invisible to enemy sonar. But they refused to share their knowledge.

So Aussie boffins had invented their own tiles from scratch. They had almost eliminated the sonar signature on the Collins. It was a matter of pride British and American subs had been seen since with tiles missing. This had never happened on a Collins.

She laughed when he told her the Aussie tiles were held on by an off-the-shelf commercial glue used for things like sticking cat's eyes to the road.

His shift over, he stood, stretched and stifled a yawn, avoiding a lungful of dead air with its dry, diesel flavour. He imagined the joy of breathing real, fresh air. No one appreciated fresh air like submariners.

The brass accepted the *Rankin's* cooling system was overloaded. Temperatures were permanently too hot for the crew and the high-tech equipment. But there was little they could do about it. It was another result of the many design problems of the home-built subs.

Scott handed off to Muir and made his way to the small mess. He collected a tray and was dished up a meal. At least the food was outstanding on a sub. Particularly the first days of each patrol before they dug into the frozen stuff.

He sat opposite Robbie Peters, a young midshipman pushing food about with a fork but eating little. The midshipman still had traces of acne on his face. His hair was a grease ball and his eyes a reddish smudge.

"I hear we're having trouble again with the radios," Peters said without looking up. Much of their communication equipment was near obsolete.

"I bet the Link 11 is working," Scott said.

Peters sighed and nodded. "Yeah, that bloody thing is working no problem."

The Link 11 was the receive-only system for combat orders and data.

"There was another big leak in the periscope," he added. "It sucked in half the bloody ocean. Well, it seemed like it."

"Again?" Scott said. He caught himself and added: "Don't worry, all subs have leaks from time to time, son."

"Hah, they didn't tell us that when we joined."

Peters wearily put his fork down and bent across the table. "Is it true a hose in the *Dechaineux*'s engine room burst and she nearly sank?"

Scott raised his eyebrows but said nothing. All the old hands knew about the near disaster on board HMAS *Dechaineux* — another of the Collins fleet.

Peters stared at Scott. "Is it true they finally managed to shut the leak off only twenty seconds before she got too heavy to resurface?"

Scott said nothing.

Then Peters shook his head and picked up his fork again.

Scott shovelled another mouthful of food toward his mouth. "But they did fix it, son. That's what mattered."

He remembered the incident well. Every sub in the fleet was recalled for an emergency inspection. The freaky thing was, the engineers couldn't explain the hose failure. Afterwards the brass decided to reduce the safe maximum dive depth.

"Twenty bloody seconds." Peters exhaled a lungful of air and began gathering up his plate and utensils.

Scott reached across and put a hand on the teenager's arm.

"Son, you need to stop worrying. Remember, you're on a sub that right now is running fine, and very quietly. The Chinks don't even know we're here, do they?"

Peters shrugged impatiently.

"*Rankin* and *Sheean* have both sneaked through air and surface screens around American aircraft carriers. In war games we've sunk two of their nuclear subs," Scott said.

"Gave the Yanks a helluva fright. They couldn't believe how quiet we were. And that was in an exercise when they were expecting an attack."

Then Peters gave a slight nod and met Scott's eye.

"But this isn't a war game," he said. "This is different."

Scott gripped the arm tighter. "No, this isn't different. If we're sent in we'll be doing exactly what we do in training. It'll be just like an exercise. We'll slip through the cordon and blast these bastards. We'll be gone before they know what's struck them."

Scott saw Peters' unconscious nod, his confidence rise, at least for the moment. "Yes, I know *Sheean* hit two of those big Yankee Los Angeles nuke subs in an exercise."

Scott said: "And we've got those big fucker torpedoes we made with the Yanks. The Mark 48s, they'll take anything out."

Scott released his grip. He told Peters the biggest worry was *Sheean* might be tasked to the glory role, taking out the carrier, while the *Rankin* got left to smack the escort destroyers.

He sat back and pointed his fork at the midshipman. "Robbie, these subs of ours can be bastards of things, but they're very potent weapons. We just have to keep them working properly. They're never as bad or as good as everyone thinks. You know, there are a lot of people out there depending on us right now. Now, go and get some sleep. You look like you need it."

"I do. We were working for ten hours straight after that last bloody leak," he yawned. As he made to stand up, Scott gave him a comradely punch on the shoulder. "Well, I hope you fixed it good, son."

"No worries. She's good now, bloody thing. What's happening with your lot? Do we still have contact?"

"Don't worry. We won't lose them."

"Okay, I'll see you later." Peters left, turning side on to pass another crewman in the narrow passageway from the mess.

Scott sat by himself and finished the last of his meal. He knew the real problem with the Collins was the effect their ageing dynamics had on their weight: they were gradually becoming heavier, hotter and noisier as they got older.

The *Rankin* was gaining one and a half tonnes every year. Her firepower — designed to be twenty-two torpedoes — had been cut back to overcome the weight gain.

It was a vicious circle, he thought.

Her radiated noise would eventually become so loud she would be easily detected by foreign navies.

The Navy was getting new French subs but that was a lifetime away. Meanwhile the Collins had to do with the promised upgrades in sonars and sensors and comms.

He doubted whether most of the old fleet would last until the replacements arrived, no matter what the politicians were saying.

He finished his meal. The servings were noticeably smaller as the cooks rationed the remaining food supplies. He made his way down the narrow passage to his rack and, hopefully, some sleep.

It was hot and airless as he removed his rubber shoes and lay down fully clothed. He knew he stank. But so did most of the others. One got used to it. It was just the way it was on subs. He might have a shower tomorrow. He'd see.

As he lay down he sensed a tiny vibration change.

The *Rankin* would be at its most vulnerable as he tried to doze off. She had begun discharging her ballast tanks, coming to shallow periscope depth as she had to every twenty-four hours to snort the fresh air essential to run the diesel engines.

The brass had decided many years ago an air-independent propulsion system was too expensive.

He rolled over and hoped he wouldn't sink into another coffin dream.

DAY NINE

Parliament Buildings, Wellington

Trevor Stanaway shook his head as he watched the television news coverage of the protest marchers. They were trudging and chanting their way up Auckland's Queen Street, banners held high.

There were more of them than the New Zealand Prime Minister had expected. But he had no regrets. He had made the right decision. He knew it would create an uproar among the lefties, pacifists and other spineless wonders.

Unfortunately, it had also raised consternation among a few of his own shaky Members of Parliament.

The Chinese Ambassador had had plenty to say already. He had left Stanaway's Beehive office in Wellington only minutes before the 6 p.m. news, warning the People's Republic was "saddened" by New Zealand's "interventionist" policy. It would "seriously damage" relations between the two nations.

Stanaway's image flashed onto the screen. He was announcing his decision to order the RNZAF's five Hercules transports to Brisbane, the expected flash point if full-scale war was to break out.

Their enormous cargo holds would ferry in medical supplies. They would then stand by in Australia to evacuate any overflow of wounded troops and civilians the looming confrontation with China would create.

Stanaway had ordered New Zealand hospitals meantime to halt all non-urgent surgery in preparation for the expected influx. The Australians were anticipating thousands of casualties if the balloon went up. He couldn't see how that wouldn't happen.

He had chosen the steps of the old Parliamentary Buildings to hold the press conference. It had added gravitas and authority to his message.

His podium was flanked by members of his Cabinet in a false display of unity. He knew some were dreading China's response.

But they had all turned up when ordered. Either that or they had to resign. There was no point in being in charge if you didn't take charge, he always said. No point in buggering about.

The television coverage switched back to the protesters. He scanned their banners: "NOT NZ'S WAR", "GOVT ACT IS SUICIDE", "THE PEOPLE WANT PEACE", "KEEP NZ NEUTRAL".

Watching the demonstrators he thought it was just as well the buggers didn't know about the other order he had issued.

The RNZAF's sub-hunting Orions had also been dispatched to Australia where they would quietly join the RAAF in its desperate search to locate possible Chinese nuclear submarines off the capital cities. None had been detected so far.

New Zealand's move was the first and only military assistance offered to Australia by any country since the crisis had begun. It would cause a political and diplomatic storm when the full extent of it eventually became public.

Stanaway was unable to send any jet fighters. The RNZAF had none. Their fighter squadrons had been scrapped years ago. The South Pacific had then been judged by the government of the day as a benign region militarily.

The reality of the crisis had come home to New Zealanders when its naval vessels began to mine the approaches to Auckland and Wellington harbours earlier in the week.

The flood of children pouring across the Tasman Sea to safety had already shaken the country, the airport scenes providing a stark and emotional reminder of New Zealand's precarious position.

Stanaway had made his fortune in property before entering politics, and diplomatic niceties were not his strong suit. He hoped he hadn't been too offhand with the Chinese Ambassador.

He'd played golf with him in better days but the guy was bloody hopeless. Couldn't hit straight and missed half-metre putts.

A waste of space really. Anyway, Stanaway knew there was no polite way to tell the New China to piss off.

So he thanked him for coming and said it was up to the Politburo to come to its senses and call off its dogs of war. His advice had not gone down too well.

But what had China expected? New Zealand was only two thousand kilometres from Australia. The two countries had fought alongside each other in every world war and most regional conflicts.

They were the world's most identical countries. They were both former British colonies. They spoke the same language. They were First World countries with independent justice systems and democratically elected parliaments.

New Zealand had once been part of the state of New South Wales. There was still a provision in the Australian Constitution to allow it to become a state.

Stanaway's domestic critics had spent all day furiously condemning his so-called humanitarian assistance as a "suicide policy" that would lead New Zealand needlessly into a war it could not win.

Some even said China's claim to the mineral and gas riches in Australia's Top Half were inevitable and logical moves for the Pacific's new superpower.

Stanaway looked up as a secretary entered to tell him his RNZAF VIP jet was ready.

"Sue, did you pack the important stuff?" he asked.

She grinned. "If you mean the golf clubs, yes. They're on board. And no, nobody saw them being loaded."

Outside the Beehive, his driver opened the rear door to the Rolls-Royce and Stanaway made his bulky frame comfortable in its lush leather upholstery.

The government had supplied a vehicle but he wasn't going to be driven around in a bloody diesel Beemer with his knees around his ears. So he used his own car.

Powered by the world's biggest twelve-cylinder production engine, it set the Greenies off something terrible. It was well worth it. The tree huggers were never going to vote for him anyway.

The big limousine wafted its way silently through another Wellington rainstorm to the aircraft that would fly him to meet Stone in Canberra.

Australia was New Zealand's front line and both countries had always been ultimately dependent on America for protection. In an irony not lost on New Zealanders, Australia had determinedly remained a member of the ANZUS alliance and a loyal ally of America.

But its steadfast, good buddy policy toward America had failed spectacularly when put to the test.

Even the small, two-thousand-strong force of US Marines, stationed in the Far North as part of America's much vaunted Pacific pivot, had unwittingly rotated home days before the Chinese arrived.

New Zealand's socialist-leaning, anti-American electorate had gone the opposite way to Australia in its relations with America. US Navy visits were banned unless their ships were declared to be nuclear free. The US Navy refused to do that as a matter of long-standing policy. The standoff had soured relationships between the two countries and the naval visits had halted.

Away from the noise of politics, however, New Zealand remained an active member of the Five Eyes electronic spy network with America, Australia, Canada and Britain.

Another irony in the current crisis was New Zealand's mineral and energy wealth. Per head of population it was greater than Australia's. This bounty had been locked up by entrenched environmental groups who had successfully fought any large-scale developments. But the Chinese knew the treasure was there for the taking.

With only four million people, New Zealand had its own vast, indefensible coastlines around two main islands. It was another empty land ripe for colonising.

6.30 p.m.

Higginsbottom Travel Centre, Kensington, London

Charles Higginsbottom was sure he was no worse than anyone else. When there was bad news about other people, in other countries, one's immediate thought was: how does this affect me?

The news China had grabbed a big chunk of Australia was a shock, of course. But not that much different to the one he felt when Russia had seized Crimea or Isis had chopped up another group of Christians. It was all so far away, my darlings. Someone else's crisis.

So his first, guilty, thought on news of the Australian crisis was: I need to hurry and switch my clients to travel far away from Asia-Pacific. There were plenty of other safe, and expensive, destinations for his well-off Kensington clientele.

He determined the shenanigans in Australia were unlikely to unsettle his prosperous little business. Well, not so little, really. He had established his travel agency twenty-eight years ago and things had gone tickety-boo.

Of course there had been the hijacking scares and the odd recession and things like that, but generally he had adroitly ducked and dived his way through.

Lately, business had been very good. The older darlings were again flush with cash and had bucket lists for exotic places he was well placed to guide them to.

Then the Australia thing suddenly changed everything. The cyber nasties had targeted China Southern Airlines' reservations system and collapsed it. And China Southern was the world's fourth-biggest airline. The impact was, simply, frightfully enormous.

There were dreadful scenes and chaos at Heathrow Airport. The airline suffered the same unbelievable bedlam at every airport it flew to. And they flew to quite a few, as he well knew: eight hundred and ninety-eight, to be exact.

The poor sods at the Taiwan-based China Airlines went into a total spin. They launched a huge, hurried television and internet advertising campaign pleading their case: they were not, bless them, the horrible China Southern Airline.

They were China Airlines, the Taiwan China airline. Taiwan was the democratic, freedom-loving China, across the Taiwan Strait from the bad communist China.

China Airlines' desperate campaign was doomed, of course. Few outside Higginsbottom's game would bother to distinguish between the two. The good chaps in Taiwan just had the wrong name at the wrong time.

Their eighty-one aircraft were still struggling on with emergency subsidies from their government but they were defying economic gravity as ticket sales fell like a stone.

After the scenes on telly, everyone seemed to panic. They phoned and emailed him by the hundred, cancelling their bookings. And most of them were not the slightest interested in rebooking.

They'd had their little pants scared off them and the annual sojourn to escape Britain's chilly winter had been put on the back burner, so to speak. Even the busy, busy corporate clients, always in such a hurry, off to Beijing on another deal, had found other uses for their time.

Most had been very apologetic. "Charlie, we don't know which reservation system could be next. The Chinese might start attacking our ones. We'll come back when things settle down, old boy."

Higginsbottom sat at his desk staring at the ceiling. His world was coming to a standstill.

Now airlines everywhere were cancelling flights as passenger loads tumbled in a suddenly frightened world.

Things hadn't been going too well for China Southern even before the cyber attack. They had faced big fines at airports for missing their scheduled takeoff and landing windows.

The Chinese blamed refuellers for taking twice the normal amount of time in filling their thirsty aircraft. Their planes were always the last in any queue at any Western airport.

Others had been forced to take off with their toilet systems unflushed. It was all just too much. The stench and stretched bladders on the long hauls was simply intolerable. Well, just imagine.

He couldn't blame anyone for cancelling.

Then Vietnam caused a real fuss. It refused China permission to fly over its airspace. The Chinese had ignored the no-fly ban and gone all macho, sending up squadrons of fighter jets to escort its passenger planes.

Now other countries were considering their own airspace bans.

The last straw snapped an hour ago. China Southern grounded its massive fleet of three hundred and fifty aircraft. They cited safety reasons for the decision.

Overnight a fifth of the world's airliners were out of action. Forty thousand travellers a day were grounded along with them. And sixty-five thousand airline staff were jobless. The numbers were simply mind-blowing.

The Aussies must have something very valuable for the Chinese to put up with all this fuss, Higginsbottom thought.

The phone rang. It was Lord Thornburn. He had a daughter stuck down in Sydney. Charlotte. Seemed to find herself in a spot of bother wherever she went.

Could Charlie arrange a charter jet to get her home as soon as, please, before the whole show went up in smoke?

Of course he could, Higginsbottom assured him. He could do it right away. He was having quiet day.

DAY TEN

The Lodge, Canberra

Stanaway could see a smiling Gary Stone waiting at the official entrance to welcome him. His old buddy had lost a ton of weight and looked drawn and worried.

Stanaway decided he wouldn't add to his problems by complaining about being jammed into an official Holden the Aussies kidded themselves was a limousine.

Late the night before there had been spontaneous applause among staff and travellers when he made his way through the Canberra airport terminal.

Stanaway unscrambled his legs to exit the vehicle and caused a ripple of surprise among the crowd of journalists when he emerged wearing an open-neck shirt and a casual blue sports jacket.

Slightly taller than Stone and another former rugby player, Stanaway dodged Stone's handshake and gave him a bear hug instead, sparking a firestorm of flashlights.

"Working from home, Gazza?"

"The coffee's better."

"I had a nice reception at the airport — a lot better than the farewell I got back home. The Chinese Ambassador was a bit lukewarm as well."

"Oh. Unhappy, was he?"

"You could say that. He wanted to know what the hell we're up to getting involved in a scrap China was going to win. Asked if we had a secret nuclear missile system."

Stone's smile suddenly disappeared.

"What? What's the matter?" said Stanaway.

"There's something you need to know, not out here. Come inside. Now you've decided to poke the dragon in the eye, there are a couple of things I've got under way I should tell you about."

Stanaway followed Stone into The Lodge. They turned into the dining room where half a dozen big-screen computers crowded its formal, highly polished table.

"When are they going to get a decent place for you?" he asked. "You can hardly swing a cat in here."

"It's always been as tight as a fish's," said Stone. "We spent a bloody fortune getting the possums out of the roof and a decent air-conditioning system not long ago but we couldn't touch the size of the rooms — it's a listed historic building."

"Comfortable place to run a war from, is it?"

Stone waved him to a seat. "The war. That's what I want to have a chat to you about. What exactly did the ambassador say to you about nuclear weapons?"

Stanaway frowned and hunched his big body forward. The dining room chair creaked in protest. "Well, nothing really. I thought he was trying to be a funny bugger."

Stone said nothing for several seconds.

"It's an odd thing for a diplomat to say, wouldn't you think?"

"I suppose it is. Clearly you think there was more to it. What are you up to, Gazza? Have you got a secret nuke up your sleeve?" He gave a half laugh.

In a reflex motion, Stone looked behind him although he was certain they were alone.

"As a matter of fact, I'll have six of them up my sleeve."

He enjoyed Stanaway's shock. "Fuck me. Who knows this?"

"No one. Well, no one's meant to. Did your Chinese mate elaborate in any way? Do you think they could know?"

Stanaway sat back. The chair again protested.

"I don't know, Gazza. It was an odd question. I'm certain from my reaction he wouldn't have any reason to believe I'd have known anything about it. I was too busy telling him he'd regret trying to barge his way into our backyard."

Stone pushed a hand through his hair. "Well, we'll just have to hope my surprise is intact. The balloon's about to go up. Three days from now, if we can get all the bloody things built and keep the Chinese talking while we're doing it. It'll be at two o'clock in the morning when the first one detonates. The same time of the day the Chinese grabbed all our bases. I want the Chinks to get as much of a surprise as I got at that hour of the morning."

Stone explained the END concept. Stanaway listened in incredulous silence.

Stone said if the Chinese didn't buy the bluff and open war broke out, he had two Collins submarines set to attack China's aircraft carrier off Townsville.

If they could sink it, China's full-scale invasion plans could be delayed. Their forces would be robbed of essential air support.

When he had finished, Stanaway gave a low whistle. "Gazza, my son, you're rolling the dice with that plan."

"Yes, I am, but it might be our only chance of getting the country back."

A steward arrived with coffee.

"I know what a risk you've taken sending us those Orions. Do you want us to paint out the RNZAF logos? I could say we bought them off you," said Stone.

"Fuck no," said Stanaway. "Our people will want to fly under their own colours. Let's face it, the Chinks will deal with us how and when they like anyway if you go down to them."

Stanaway stood, swallowed his coffee in one gulp. "Enough of this war talk. I've brought my clubs."

"I know," said Stone.

"How? Do you have spies on my jet?"

"No. You turned up in a sports jacket. You're a stirrer. You want the Chinks to see us playing golf rather than panicking about them."

"I'll be the one panicking if you try to use your Bill Clinton scoring skills."

"I don't need to cheat if I'm playing you. But we'll get a caddy to score if it makes you happy."

"I hope he can count to more than four then."

They walked toward the door. Stone said he could only manage nine holes. He was recovering from a slight lung infection.

"Is that why you've lost a bit of weight? Are you okay now, old son?"

"Fit enough to beat you," said Stone.

Outside, the media scrambled to their vehicles. They were as disbelieving of the destination as Stone knew the Chinese would be.

On the course, Stone hooked his first tee shot.

"I take it that's your practice shot, Bill," said Stanaway leaning patiently on his number two wood.

"No, I've decided to take it easy on you," said Stone.

"If you're going to make shots like that in front of the media, you'd better start news censorship this afternoon."

Stone straightened his game up by the second hole and the pair played as cameras flashed and whirred.

By the time the shortened game finished, Stanaway could see Stone's lung infection was giving him trouble.

"Who won?" a television reporter yelled at them as they walked back to their limousines.

"He did," both Prime Ministers chorused.

The caddie folded the scorecard and pocketed it — another state secret for his retirement bestseller.

Stanaway was driven directly to Canberra Airport to fly home to a country in a silent panic. Stone went back to The Lodge only to walk into a fresh personal crisis.

12.30 p.m.

Private quarters, The Lodge, Canberra

"I'm back," said Stone thumping down on the ottoman at the bed's end. He pulled both shoes off and began wriggling his toes. He arched his back and relaxed it. It had been too long since he'd been on a course.

"Don't you want to know who won?" he called. He could hear Elaine moving in the en suite and a tap running.

There was no reply. He rose and walked to the window. The guards patrolling the grounds were now an everyday sight. The November sun was scorching the lawns already. A hot, dry summer was forecast.

He tapped his suit pocket and felt the ever-present spray. He had sneaked a shot shortly after the game. He felt fine right now.

The room was still empty when he turned. The tap in the en suite had stopped running.

"Don't you want to know who won?" he tried again in a slightly louder voice.

Elaine appeared in the doorway. She held a tissue and her eyes were red.

"Darling, what's the matter? What's happened?" he said.

Elaine walked quietly over to the ottoman and sat, looking at the floor. She blew her nose and blinked back tears.

"Gary, there's something I have to tell you," she said.

Stone stared. He felt his pulse surge, his chest tighten.

"I had a call from Peter just before you went on television with Ellen Jacobs. I didn't tell you. I thought you had enough on your plate but …"

"Peter?" He hadn't spoken to his eldest son since the crisis had enveloped them.

"He wants to leave and take Margaret and the two boys out of the country, out of danger."

Stone leaned back against the windowsill.

Elaine pulled another tissue from her sleeve and wiped away more tears.

"Gary, they have two young children. They're all very frightened … they want to do what's best for the kids … some of their friends have already booked flights to leave."

She took a deep breath and met her husband's gaze. "I didn't know what to say to him. He didn't ask me. He just said he was sorry but he was taking his family and going as soon as possible."

Her shoulders sank. She looked down at the floor again.

"No one really thinks we have a chance to win this. Not even my own son," Stone said.

He could not have his son running away. Not after the Jacobs broadcast. It would be a political calamity for him and national morale. Peter had to stay. So did his family.

He pushed himself off the windowsill. "He can't go. Call him back and tell him to grow a spine."

He was angry and hurt.

"And tell him whatever happens, he won't be leaving the country. If he tries I'll have him arrested. Tell him his passport is invalid as of now. Tell him he has a public duty to stand with the rest of us — and me in particular."

"You tell him," choked Elaine.

"No. He didn't dare call me. He called you. He won't take a call from me. It has to be you. I just cannot …"

He suddenly realised his anger was being vented at the wrong person. He walked across the room to where she was sitting, sobbing, and knelt down. He put a hand on each of her knees.

"I'm sorry. I know they're scared," he said softly, "everyone is scared. But I'll have this Chinese mess sorted out soon."

Elaine looked up. He saw surprise and disbelief on her face.

"Darling, I have things in hand that will turn the situation around. You need to trust me. And so do Peter and Margaret."

Elaine gave a slight nod and blew her nose again.

"Please call Peter. Just say we're having roast turkey for Christmas dinner at The Lodge and I expect the whole family to be here."

Elaine gave another small nod. His hands were still resting on her knees. She put her hands on them and coughed to clear her throat.

"That would be the turkey roast *with* the gravy, I take it," she said slowly.

"That's the one," he whispered with half a smile.

There was a knock on the door. They both stood. He gave her a silent peck on the lips.

As he moved to the door, Elaine asked: "Who did win?"

"Bill Clinton," he said and opened the door to Able waiting impatiently with a handful of papers.

DAY ELEVEN

Lucas Heights, Sydney

He hadn't been on a possible suicide mission since he had fought his way into the ranks of the Special Air Service Regiment six years ago.

A walking bulk of super-fit muscle, sinew and determination, Blackie Johnson lived for his career among the super-elite of Australia's military.

It was as if the regiment's motto — Who Dares Wins — had been written just for him. A hard-drinking, rebellious teenager with a love for guns and hunting, he joined the Australian Army at eighteen.

It had been an inauspicious start.

Within two weeks he faced insubordination charges and thought his army life was over before it had started. But the Army thrived on tough raw material like the Blackie Johnsons.

Blackie had taken his punishment and gone on to spend the next five years with 3rd Battalion, Royal Australian Regiment at Lavarack. He then took on what he regarded as a soldier's ultimate challenge: to join the legendary SAS troopers.

The ruggedness of the induction training was infamous. As he kitted up for his first day, Blackie knew three-quarters of all the men around him would fail to cope with the tremendous physical and mental barriers they would face.

But he had made it and went on for even more intense training at the SAS headquarters at Campbell Barracks in Perth. The satisfaction he felt was worth the grinding, never-give-up effort needed.

Money was never a major incentive but Blackie took pride in being among the most highly paid soldiers in Australia. His wages and allowances took his income to $100,000 a year.

He felt he had made it on every level he dreamed of.

Then the Chinese had arrived. The squad he led was one of five chosen to deliver and conceal a suitcase dirty bomb behind enemy lines.

They were warned the mission could turn into a suicide one. The existence of the bombs had to remain top secret and none was to fall into enemy hands. The bombs were to be detonated manually if that risk arose. That would be lights out.

Like every squad, his was trained in the art of survival for long-range, intelligence reconnaissance in enemy-held territory. It was skilled in sabotage techniques, handling explosives and creating havoc when required — but never on this scale.

Blackie never considered the possibility of capture. He wasn't going to be the first SAS trooper ever to fall into enemy hands.

The troopers had been told it would be a volunteer-only operation. They had all burst into laughter.

The Prime Minister's radical plan, to bluff the Chinese from Australia by exploding portable bombs and irradiating areas around strategic energy sites, was right from the SAS's Who Dares Wins playbook.

With the four other squad leaders, he had today been spirited from Perth to the outskirts of Sydney and the Lucas Heights nuclear research centre.

The place chosen for the bomb assembly was more like a recreational facility surrounded by hectares of pristine bushland.

It was its isolation on the edge of a major city that provided the project with its ideal security. The government had poured every resource it had into the bomb build. It had been a top-priority, no-expenses-spared project.

As they arrived it was clear the research centre was heavily guarded.

They had to pass through two lengthy security checks to reach a bland conference room where they were to meet the chief physicist in charge of the bomb assembly — and receive last-minute instructions.

They sat patiently. They were all good at waiting. They would wait for hours or days during covert reconnaissance missions.

They had been greeted with curious stares from the few staff they encountered on the way to the conference room. The troopers did look incongruous in this clinical, scrubbed-clean environment.

They wore scruffy civvies and were unshaven. Their hair was long and straggly. They would have possibly been spotted by military people as commando types but the staff had obviously never seen anything remotely as untidy or intimidating in their midst.

After fifteen minutes the door opened and Frank Church, the ASIO bossman, walked in. He was followed by a second man in a white laboratory coat. He was thin, lanky and bespectacled. He was Chinese, for God's sake.

Blackie saw the squad leaders exchange glances.

Church seated himself at the head of the table and indicated the Chinese man to sit beside him.

"Gentlemen, this is Dr Peter Yu. Dr Yu has headed up our Emergency Nuclear Deterrent project here," Church said.

He looked around the room. He was encircled by a bunch of scary, scowling, hard men.

"Dr Yu's team has worked every hour God made for the last eight days to assemble the radioactive bombs you will be taking to the enemy."

There was no response from the soldiers.

"He will show you the device and explain how to set its firing mechanism. Don't worry, it's been designed to be detonated remotely, by satellite signal, not manually — for obvious reasons."

Church's effort to lighten the mood fell flat. The soldiers remained impassive.

"But it can be manually detonated in the highly unlikely case that it becomes necessary."

Blackie saw the purple patches beneath the boffin's eyes. Yu looked like he'd been in the bush on recon for a couple of weeks.

"A couple of things before you start showing us these dirty bombs." It was Dirty Dawson. He'd been bawled out once early in his training. There had been a spec of dust inside the barrel of his rifle.

"Yes, sergeant," said Church, grateful for any response.

Dirty pointed at Yu. "I'm not being racist or anything but can I ask why you have a Chinese guy in charge of this? We'll be going out there to scorch his mob out of the country."

Before Church could respond another sergeant said: "Yeah, how do we know these things won't blow us to kingdom come?"

A third sergeant stood up shaking his head as though he were about to leave. "Why couldn't you get an Aussie boffin to put these things together?"

Yu leaned forward and touched Church's arm. He removed his glasses and looked up.

A tense silence stretched as he began to clean them with a tissue, ignoring his audience. He lifted the spectacles to the light. Satisfied they were perfectly clear, he put them back on his nose.

The sergeants followed his every move. Yu slowly folded his arms and sat forward to rest them on the table.

"Before we start, I have a couple of questions for you too," he said.

He looked directly at Dirty. "Can you tell me how you let a force of communist Chinese terrorists take over half my country while your army, navy and air force were all asleep in bed?"

Dirty opened his mouth and closed it. The third sergeant took his seat again.

"I'm a very busy man. Doing important nuclear research, creating radioisotopes to treat cancer. In the last eight days I have had to leave that and work twenty hours a day because you guardians of Australia couldn't defend a single one of your northern bases."

Yu sat back. "Now, I'd like my country back. This is why I have helped to assemble these bombs. To give you a second chance to do your job."

The sergeants looked at each other. No one spoke. Church looked on the edge of a smile.

Yu stood. "Now, if there are no further questions, follow me — I'll try to show you how to prime these bombs without blowing yourselves up."

The troopers all stood obediently.

"Fuck me," whispered Dirty. "I walked into that." The others nodded and shrugged.

Yu led them to what looked like a laboratory with a number of big benches. Black backpacks lay on six of them. Yu lifted the flap of one to reveal a shiny steel box crisscrossed with a number of leads. He turned a dial on the top of the box and two red lights blinked alternatively.

"This dial activates the bomb. Once it's switched on it can be detonated remotely by satellite signal from Defence Headquarters in Canberra or from your own radios if necessary. If the device fails to detonate on the remote signal …" Yu leaned over the pack and took hold of a buckle on a second flap. He turned it over. They could see a small keypad.

"You put in the correct code and the buckle will open. This is to prevent any accidental opening of this flap because the button inside it will detonate the bomb manually."

He looked at Dirty. "We don't want any accidents, do we?"

The troopers surrounded the pack as Yu pressed numbers into the keypad. The flap opened to reveal a large, red plastic dial.

"The satellite signal will be tested shortly before detonation time. If it fails you will have to return to the pack and use your field radio signal to detonate it. To make the radio signal active you turn this dial hard right. But your radio signal must be sent no more than one kilometre from the bomb to be sure it will detonate. If this is necessary, I'd advise you to hunker down real well and keep out of the direct blast. Don't hide behind a wall. It would probably get flattened. Get into a deep hole, that's what I'd recommend."

"What do we do when it blows? Run like hell?" said Blackie.

"Yes," said Yu. "Into the wind preferably, for at least three kilometres. The bomb will shower radioactive fallout over anything downwind."

Church stepped in and pointed back at the red button. "Now, this is the nasty part. If you still have the device with you and it is in danger of falling into enemy hands, turn the dial hard right, as before, but press it firmly in."

Yu looked around the men. "In that instance you don't have to worry about the running bit."

The troopers grunted and smiled at the black humour. It broke the lingering tension in the room.

Yu turned to face Dirty. "This device has been put together by me and two other Aussies. There were four others in the team, three from New Zealand and one from Britain. They were all regular Anglo Saxons, though. I think we can trust them."

Yu smiled at their discomfort.

"Sorry, doc," said Dirty looking at the floor, "it was nothing personal."

Yu nodded.

"We have designed this pack to weigh only twenty-five kilos so it can be carried like a backpack. A lot of the weight is the dynamite. The dynamite will explode the radioactive core over a wide area. The core heat in the ..."

"Okay, doc. No need to get all technical on us. We get the picture," said Blackie.

Yu nodded. "Okay, well, good luck."

Blackie turned to the others. "All right, guys. All very simple, yeah?"

The troopers grunted their agreement. Blackie looked at Yu. "Thanks, doc, you can leave it with us. We'll do our best to get your country back."

Blackie shook Yu's hand. The other sergeants followed his lead.

The backpacks were loaded from a covered bay at the rear of the complex. The troopers headed for the transport aircraft, which would fly one group north and the other west to rendezvous with their Black Hawk helicopters.

The ground-hugging helicopters would ultimately take them for daring night drops close to their ground zero targets in Western Australia and Queensland.

Blackie had been assigned to the destruction of two strategic Queensland export ports. It would involve an unexpected challenge: Private Jabril Allunga.

Yu watched them drive off. Church shook his hand and thanked him. Yu exhaled a weary sigh and felt in his pocket for the Mercedes keys. Lilly would be excited to see him home a day ahead of schedule. It would be a great surprise.

5.35 p.m.

Double Bay, Sydney

Peter Yu stopped off at the small florist shop only a kilometre from his penthouse apartment. The elderly shop owner was doing a last tidy-up before she closed the doors for the day.

She smiled when Yu walked in. He had been a good spender the few times he had visited.

There was a huge bunch of roses out the back, she told him. They had been ordered by an excited gentleman who never arrived to pick them up. The romance of the moment must have petered out sometime during the day.

She handed them to Yu and said he could have them for half price. He declined the offer. It was a special evening, he said. Anything discounted would be inappropriate.

She laughed and processed his credit card. Yu left beaming, clutching his prize. Roses were Lilly's favourite flowers.

He parked the Mercedes in the underground garage. He left his suitcase in the boot. He wanted to arrive carrying only the big bouquet.

Lilly's Merc was in her bay but with a dust cover over it. She must have decided she would only venture out in the company of her government security detail.

Yu punched the button for the top floor and the big lift sprang to silent life, delivering him to the penthouse's spacious, private lobby.

There were three red suitcases lined up on the floor. Puzzled, he called out: "Lilly, it's me. I'm home. At last. Where are you? Where are the girls?"

He walked through to the lounge. Through the huge plate-glass windows he could see the sun setting over the harbour, creating a rippling orange carpet.

Lilly was standing beside the couch, a telephone in her hand.

"Peter ... what are you doing here?" she said.

Her eyes fell to the huge bunch of red roses. She looked up and stared at him. Her feet felt glued to the carpet.

"We've finished the job," he said. "It's all done. And a day ahead of schedule."

She said nothing.

"Isn't that marvellous? I didn't call. I thought I'd come home and surprise you and the girls. Where are the girls?"

Lilly slumped down on the big white couch.

"What's the matter? What's happening? I thought you'd be rapt to see me," he said. "I bought you these." He held the roses up, felt foolish at her unresponsiveness and lowered them to his side.

Lilly looked down at her hands and then placed the phone back on its cradle.

"Peter, I'm not staying in this country a day longer," she said.

He looked at her blankly. The roses fell from his hands and scattered on the floor.

"I'm going to Toronto, Peter. There's no war there and they welcome people like us."

"Toronto? What are you talking about?"

"I haven't been able to talk to you so I had to make the decision on my own. What I felt was best for me and the girls," she said.

"You're going to Toronto? Why Toronto?" He felt a wave of confusion and exhaustion. He fell into the armchair opposite her.

Lilly played with her necklace as tears filled her eyes.

"There are three quarters of a million Chinese in Toronto. Mandarin and Cantonese are common languages there. There are more Chinese in the city than native-born Canadians. The Canadians are different, friendly people."

Peter shook his head, unable to grasp the enormity of what he was being told.

"When were you going to tell me?" he asked.

"As soon as you were finished with the big, secret project," she said, her voice tinged with anger and resentment.

"I've been dumped here, a prisoner in my home, driven around with my girls by bodyguards. It's been frightening. You decided your project was more important than us."

Peter shook his head. "Where are the girls in all this?"

They were already at Sydney Airport, Lilly said. Air tickets were so scarce she had been unable to buy three together. The girls were on a flight an hour ahead of her. Her aircraft left in two and a half hours. She was about to leave when he walked in.

"This is unbelievable." Peter sat with his head in his hands.

"I don't want to leave you. But I have to get out of this racist dump," said Lilly. "I can't stay another day. I hate this city. I'm not hanging around to get beaten up again by ignorant, white skinheads. And I'm not going to spend my life hiding and apologising for being who I am."

She began sobbing. He went over to her. He tried to explain the events of the last few days had been critical to Australia's survival. He knew after a few seconds he was wasting his words.

The penthouse intercom buzzed.

Lilly dabbed her eyes and strode to it. She pressed the speaker button. A tinny voice rasped: "Mrs Yu. Your taxi is waiting." She said she would be right down.

"I have to go, Peter. I'll call as soon as I arrive. You decide where you want to be. I'm sorry ... but ..."

She hoisted two of the three suitcases into the lift and stepped back to take the third. Peter watched in silence.

The lift door closed with a quiet whoosh.

8 p.m.

Departure Gate 10, International Airport, Sydney

Captain Duncan Bridgeman was ready for the pullback when the message came.

There was a security issue, he was told. The big Qantas A380 was to wait at Gate 10. He would be updated on the flight's status shortly.

Bridgeman cursed. The co-pilot beside him had heard the radio message and shook his head in sympathy. He called the ground crew on the low-slung pullback tractor and told them there would be a delay.

Bridgeman was annoyed. He had been on time despite a capacity passenger load and the big task the cargo handlers had faced.

Business and first-class seats had been ripped out and replaced by economy ones allowing eight hundred and fifty-three people to fly. The biggest number he had ever flown in his twenty-three-year career.

The fuel tanks on the world's biggest airliner were brimful. It was at its maximum takeoff weight. It would use every metre of runway to get airborne. He was anxious to get it up there. Australia was a powder keg. His jet was a petrol bomb.

The monstrous, wide-bodied jet would hurtle from Sydney to Los Angeles nonstop at Mach .85 — almost the speed of sound. It wouldn't be fast enough for some of his human cargo fleeing Australia.

He feared the wait would lose him his tight departure window. The A380 already needed a wider window than other airliners. It created such a wake turbulence, following aircraft had to wait on the tarmac till it was at least seven kilometres ahead of them.

Sydney air traffic was heavy and the time slots precious, even with the scrapping of the night curfew regulations.

Every outbound aircraft he had flown for the last eleven days had been packed but cabin crew numbers had been quietly reduced to a minimum. The airline wanted every seat it could muster for the outrageous ticket prices it was charging.

There would be no dinner service. It would be biscuits, nuts and small plastic bottles of water. The usual bar service had been eliminated. He knew not a soul would complain. They wanted out of Australia more than they wanted a drink or an airline meal on a plastic tray.

He knew passenger tension would edge up as soon as he announced the delay. He had seen the rows of worried faces back there hardly believing they had scored a ticket and were headed to safety.

He did his practised, calm patter over the PA: "Good evening. This is your captain, Duncan Bridgeman, speaking. Our flight has been delayed but we don't expect the delay to be long. Please remain in your seats with your belts fastened."

Forty rows away in the upper section of the airliner, Lilly Yu sat back in a newly installed economy-class seat. She had forgotten how small they were. She held her Kindle but was too fraught to read.

A police officer walked down the aisle. He stopped at her row and politely asked the man in the aisle seat beside her to accompany him. There was something they had to check. Just to be on the safe side.

The policeman asked the passenger if he would bring his personal luggage with him. Surrounding passengers stared and whispered as the policeman led him away. Lilly got the shivers. Had she been sitting next to a terrorist or some criminal trying to escape Sydney?

She thought of her daughters already on their way to Los Angeles. And her husband, Peter, who had been devastated by her decision. But she had to get away.

Bridgeman checked his watch. Seven minutes had passed. He saw a black government limo led on to the busy tarmac by an escort vehicle with its red and blue emergency lights flashing.

His radio crackled and he was told he would be cleared to taxi within five minutes. His flight plan had been altered but he had been given a priority place in the queue.

Well, that was something, he thought.

Perched in the small cockpit fourteen metres above the ground, Bridgeman turned and watched the two vehicles stop beside the plane. They were dwarfed by the bulk of the airliner. Two men got out of the limo.

Bridgeman wiped the window with a sleeve and peered out. He saw a tall, bespectacled man in an open-collar shirt. His clothing looked dishevelled.

His fellow traveller was a big bear of a man with a shock of grey hair wearing a dark suit, tie and shiny black shoes.

Bridgeman frowned and did a double take. He poked his co-pilot in the side. "Do you know who's down there? Who's holding up the flight?"

The co-pilot leaned across. The instrument console was so wide he could see very little below the side window.

"Dunno, skip, can't see much from here. Does he look familiar?"

"Familiar? That's the bloody Prime Minister. I'm sure of it."

Bridgeman turned back and swept an eye over his instruments. The co-pilot unbuckled and squeezed over to the left-hand window.

"Christ, I hope Gary Stone isn't leaving the country," Bridgeman said, mostly to himself. "What would that mean?"

Trying to make out the figures, the co-pilot shook his head: "No. No way. He wouldn't be quitting. It must be someone who looks like him. Have you ever seen him in real life? Or just on the telly?"

Bridgeman swivelled to look again. "I'm telling you, it's Stone. He's shaking the other guy's hand goodbye. He must be coming with us."

Both pilots craned to watch the scene.

The co-pilot said: "Fuck. The guy he's shaking hands with is Chinese."

"What the hell is going on?" said Bridgeman. "Why's he shaking hands goodbye with a Chink? He's not giving the game away, surely? And after all his big talk?"

"I don't believe it," said the co-pilot.

"We should push back and leave the bugger behind," said Bridgeman.

The co-pilot squirmed for a better view. "Yeah, maybe you're right, it does look like Gary Stone."

"I'd love to know what they're talking about," said Bridgeman.

They both stared at the extraordinary scene they were witnessing.

"Oh, boy. Now Stone's giving him a bear hug," said Bridgeman.

"And patting him on the back," said the co-pilot shaking his head.

They both fell silent. The embrace ended.

Stone got back in the limo.

They watched in confusion as the Chinese man was led to the rear door and up a hastily arranged gangway.

"You're right. He's not quitting," said Bridgeman. "Thank God for that."

"I told you he wouldn't be," said the co-pilot leveraging himself back into his seat.

"Who's the bigwig Chinaman then?" said Bridgeman.

The co-pilot shrugged and put his headphones back on.

They waited in silence for another two minutes and then the control tower told them to taxi to runway two.

"Tower, any identity details on that last passenger?" said Bridgeman.

"Negative," said the tower. "ASIO requested your aircraft be held for security reasons. You are now cleared for immediate departure."

Lilly felt the slow pullback. Six hundred and fifty tonnes began to ease gradually away from the terminal. The man that had sat beside her had disappeared. He must have been a crim or terrorist. She put her head back and closed her eyes. What a day.

Then she heard and felt the man plonk himself down beside her again. He couldn't have been a crim or a terrorist.

She squirmed down in her narrow seat and took a deep breath keeping her eyes shut. Relaxing as best she could and hoping he wouldn't want to start a conversation.

Suddenly, the man firmly pushed against her elbow on their shared seat rest. The territory war had started, she thought. She had consciously steadied her breathing when he shoved her elbow a second time, more roughly.

She turned to glare at him in annoyance. The man said: "Do you have any idea of how cold it is in Toronto at this time of the year?"

"Peter!" she shouted. Heads everywhere turned in alarm.

"I'll bet you one week of four degrees Celsius will change your mind," he said. "And the girls will hate it."

She couldn't understand a word he was saying. She tried to hug him but the seats were too crammed. She settled for clutching his arm and wiped away tears of joy with her other sleeve. "What are you doing here? How the devil did you get on this plane?"

Peter sat back in his seat, a grin widening over his weary face. "I have friends in high places."

She still didn't understand — but she was too happy to care.

His friend had been in a very high place, Peter thought. Twelve kilometres up, in fact, heading for an unscheduled meeting with his RAAF's chiefs at Richmond air force base outside Sydney when Yu's phone call was patched through.

Stone had listened to the distraught scientist, diverted his VIP flight to Sydney International Airport while calling Frank Church. Yu got his seat. Next to Lilly. The hapless and bewildered traveller bumped off was guaranteed a seat on the next Los Angeles flight. If there was going to be another one.

After a few moments Lilly whispered: "Will it really be four degrees Celsius when we get there?"

"No, darling. That's what it is now. It will be night when we finally arrive. The temperature will be minus seven degrees."

"Oh," said Lilly.

Her cousin hadn't mentioned that to her when she called looking for a temporary home. Peter looked very relaxed, she thought. He knew the girls would side with him.

Sydney did have the best climate in the world. And all their friends were there. Oh dear. What had she done? There were plenty of seats to be had flying back, she consoled herself. Dirt cheap.

DAY TWELVE

The International Conference Centre, Canberra

Martini sensed things were finally heading for an angry show-down.

The size of the Chinese delegation to the Australia-Sino Peace and Border Settlement Talks had doubled to six.

The Chinese diplomats had filed in quietly and taken their places across the conference table, their black suits, white shirts and dark-red ties reflecting on its gleaming surface.

They reminded him of a row of constipated penguins.

On the Australian side he sat alone with his Foreign Affairs minder, Mark Roberts. Poor bugger. But he was learning.

Martini believed the new show of force by the Chinese revealed their delegation was under enormous pressure from Beijing. Reinforcements had been sent in to find out what the hell was going on.

The deadline to complete a settlement had been ten days. That had been two days ago. The talks had hit continual brick walls, constructed deliberately and at random by him. He enjoyed feigning bad temper when he had no logical reply to their arguments.

He had filibustered and ducked and weaved until the Chinese were confused and near their wits' end.

When his reservoir of ideas to sidetrack the talks ran low, he would call for a halt to take advice from the Prime Minister. The

Chinese soon learned he rarely went anywhere near The Lodge but decamped in the early afternoons to a nearby wine bar dragging Roberts along.

The Chinese had been conceited knowing they held all four aces in the card game. But their confidence and Oriental inscrutability began cracking badly by the end of the seventh day when there had been little hard progress in reaching an agreement.

Martini had successfully burned up precious time pressing for a demilitarised corridor along the Bruce Highway, the main Queensland route north.

He had argued it could carry badly needed food and other supplies to the northern cities, a concession the Chinese were initially keen to explore. The proposal would also have allowed the Chinese to maintain control of the export ports and mines on either side of the highway.

Beijing had dithered for days, finally insisting there would be no need for the corridor if their delegates got on with the job of signing a formal border agreement.

Today the Chinese had wheeled in their top constipated penguin in Australia, Ambassador Chen — the diplomat who had delivered the original surrender ultimatum to Stone.

He sat pink-faced on the right hand of the official delegation head, Wu Seng. It looked like the Politburo had shoved a red-hot poker up his backside.

He could hardly sit still as the talks began with Wu asking whether Prime Minister Stone had come to a final decision to sign the border agreement following yesterday's round of talks.

It was Roberts who replied. He gave a theatrical sigh and pushed his upturned hands out on the table.

"He is a very stubborn man," Roberts said.

Chen's complexion went from pink to red. Wu frowned and said: "Does he fully understand the situation Australia is in? That it is being offered a generous settlement? Does he want another demonstration of what he's up against?"

Roberts looked at his hands and gave a small shake of the head.

He had become quite the expert at playing the good cop, thought Martini.

"What sort of demonstration did you have in mind?" said Roberts.

Chen broke in: "Maybe a rocket into The Lodge?"

Roberts seemed to consider the idea.

"No ... I think that would make him even more stubborn. I think you would end up with a full-scale war — and you don't want that, do you? Not with the rest of the world isolating your country and shutting down your factories."

Martini suppressed a grin as Chen's complexion changed up a gear, from red to crimson. Chen gave a furious glance at Wu, who was clearly being lined up as the scapegoat for the stalled talks.

Martini felt a fatherly pride about Roberts' development. The stiff, buttoned-up official had almost packed it in after the first day.

Martini had abruptly called off the talks to take advice and took an astonished Roberts off to the wine bar almost before opening time.

Roberts' various academic degrees in international relations had not prepared him for Martini Diplomacy. But now he was getting the hang of it.

Stone had been delighted at their successful stalling tactics. He personally heaped praise on Roberts. He knew the official was the reserve player on the field, terrified he would drop a key pass.

Stone treated each day's delay as a critical bonus. He was buoyed as his poison pill idea edged forward. He laughed at Martini's unalloyed accounts of the Chinese delegate's confusion and impatience.

After the second day, Stone had sat them both down and asked Roberts the question that had troubled him from the first shock news of the Chinese strike: Why Australia?

Roberts was in his element. "Any superpower will do whatever it needs to, to protect what it believes is in its best interests, its security. Australia is an empty country. The least able to defend itself but with the most energy resources within China's sphere of influence, the Pacific."

There had been no practical alternative, so far as the new Politburo was concerned.

"If they had had a go at their near neighbours they'd have bought a fierce fight with the Vietnamese, who they've been at war with on and off for centuries, and who don't have our natural resources anyway. North Korea does have natural resources but it has nuclear weapons and would use them. South Korea has almost no natural resources, just a capitalist system that works wonders. The Philippines is an overpopulated, corruption-ridden Latin American-type country with nothing to offer. Japan has no natural resources and would fight to the death against the Chinese, whom they hate and regard as inferior. Indonesia has great resources but it has a huge population, two hundred and fifty million people, mainly Muslim, to overcome. New Guinea is also rich in resources but a mountainous, logistical nightmare of a place and half occupied by Indonesia anyway."

Stone said: "That leaves us as a no-brainer, I guess."

Roberts nodded. "From the perspective of a superpower bent on securing permanent resource supplies, yes."

"Why the hell wasn't all this explained years ago? How come we thought we were far away and safe?"

Martini said: "Because we've got bloody short memories."

Roberts folded his legs. "We were warned. In the last war the Japanese were on top of us. If it hadn't been for the Yanks we'd all be talking Japanese now."

Stone rubbed his left knee and tried to straighten his leg.

"Well, the Yanks are nowhere to be seen this time," he said.

"America is no longer the dominant power in the Pacific. And it's sick of its failed wars," Roberts said.

"Australia's problem is the fact nobody has ever been interested in living in the Top Half. In the 1930s, when there was a wave of anti-Semitism throughout Europe, we even considered making the Northern Territory a Jewish homeland."

Martini had never heard of this. He said: "Like the Unpromised Land, you mean?"

Roberts politely ignored him. "During this latest mining boom there were only two hundred and forty thousand people in the territory, half a person for every square kilometre."

Stone looked up from his knee massage. "And the bloody Western Australians didn't even want to be part of Australia. Most of them voted to be a separate territory of the British Empire."

Roberts laughed. "That's right. They never liked the Federal government idea. A third of them today weren't born in Australia. If you'd had that vote a couple of weeks ago you might have got the same result."

The sound of a chair moving back from the conference table snapped Martini back to the present. He looked up. Chen had got to his feet and reached for his briefcase.

"Mr Martini, you can tell your Prime Minister his time is up," said Chen.

Martini leaned forward. "Are you walking out of your own peace talks?"

Chen stood still, suddenly uncertain.

"What is the world going to think if you do that? What is the Politburo going to think?" said Martini.

"I think you'd better sit back down. You bugger off now and you've got a sure-fire shooting war. We all know you don't want that."

The Chinese delegates averted their eyes from Chen. His were riveted on Martini. The barbarian, sent to try to intimidate the might of China.

"I have nothing more to say to you. The time for words is over," Chen said.

"So you want a war?" Martini said.

Chen threw himself down again and jabbed a finger across the table. "That has always been your choice."

"If you get up and leave, then it will have been your choice," said Martini.

Roberts said: "Mr Ambassador, I'm sure the Prime Minister

appreciates the gravity of the situation but you have offered no face-saving way for him to agree."

Chen switched his attention to Roberts, the intelligent, educated man who should have led the Australian delegation.

"We have offered to save the rest of your country from certain destruction," Chen said. His tone was placatory and calm. A reasonable man spurned.

"Yes, you have offered that," Roberts agreed. "We appreciate that. But the Prime Minister made a major concession when he agreed to call home all our submarines. And you rejected the demilitarisation of the highway corridor after telling us you thought the idea had merit."

Chen swivelled in his chair and said nothing.

"You can understand the problem we have dealing with our Prime Minister," Roberts added.

Chen looked wary. The rest of his delegation was sitting motionless, afraid to draw any attention to themselves in the highly charged atmosphere.

"Perhaps you should give us one last chance to discuss things with the Prime Minister?" said Roberts.

Martini huffed a bad cop noise.

Chen waved a hand casually. "Agreed. One more day."

"No." Roberts shook his head. "Two. And we will guarantee he calls you — with a final decision."

"You guarantee? Huh?" said Chen.

Wu cleared his throat and said: "Mr Ambassador, we have nothing to lose."

And everything to gain, he thought. They would, at last, have a final decision to report to Beijing. And a very good chance to avoid a war.

After all, the Australians had done nothing to mobilise their forces. They knew they had to come to a border agreement sooner or later, however reluctantly.

Chen nodded. "All right. Two days then. You guarantee that, Mr Roberts?"

"Of course. You have my word," Roberts replied.

Martini shrugged and nodded. Chen smiled. The delegations rose from the table.

Chen took the last shot. "You will be late for your wine bar, Mr Martini, if you don't hurry."

As the Chinese drove away in their black Mercedes, Martini made for the bar. The staff immediately delivered his favourite pinot noir and poured a glass of water for Roberts.

Martini put out his hand. "Well done, Mark. That's two more days you've delivered. Gazza will be very happy."

Roberts beamed.

He bent over the counter pushing the water glass away. "Excuse me, I think I'll have a pinot noir too, thanks."

7.35 p.m.

The Lodge, Canberra

Joe Martini stopped in the lounge doorway and turned to Elaine.

"Good God. What's happened to Gazza?" he whispered.

The Prime Minister was slumped in one of the lounge chairs, head back, snoring quietly. Several files were spilled at his feet.

Martini was fatigued himself. It was now twelve days since the lightning takeover of the Top Half. The Chinese had now lost patience waiting for their coveted border settlement treaty.

Martini had attended his last round of negotiations. He never had to see the penguins again.

Martini's efforts to prolong the talks had been undermined by the total absence of any military support for Australia, apart from New Zealand's small but brave sub-hunting contribution.

China's certainty it would get its border treaty never dimmed. Their arrogance never abated until the very end when they realised they were being played for fools.

The panicked flight of Australian refugees had not helped. Nor had the two Prime Ministers incongruously playing a relaxed round of golf before the world's media. It had all made his job harder as it confused and annoyed the Chinese.

But he had brought Stone precious time. The ball was now in the Prime Minister's court. But Stone looked too beat to play it.

"He's lost a lot of weight and he's not sleeping well," Elaine said, "but he's in good spirits."

Elaine fell easily into her patter. It had become routine. But being sworn to secrecy about her husband's deteriorating condition was a burden.

He seemed to be losing weight rapidly. His suits were becoming baggy and hung on him loosely. The pallor of his face grew to match his grey hair. His quick stride now reduced to more of a steady limp.

As the physicists worked frantically on the END bombs and the Collins submarines dodged detection in the Coral Sea, he was retiring each day to the bedroom for afternoon naps.

She knew Able was alarmed at his weight loss and lack of energy. Earlier that day he had taken her aside and asked if Stone was suffering from something more serious than a lung infection.

She assured him he was not. His doctor was treating him with antibiotics.

Martini remained uncertainly in the doorway.

"Shall we let him sleep?" he asked.

"Absolutely not," said Elaine, "he's been waiting here to see you. He's just nodded off."

She walked over and shook his shoulder lightly. Stone blinked his eyes open and a smile broke across his drawn face.

"Sit down, Joe," he said, "you look tired, mate."

Martini almost laughed. He sat down and accepted coffee from a steward who had materialised beside him.

"Mark and I've got the pricks stretched to fourteen days but that's it, I'm afraid. Are you ready to go?"

Stone nodded. He told Martini the first detonation was set for the early hours of the next morning. They discussed the possible Chinese reaction for the umpteenth time.

Fifteen minutes later they both wished each other well and the meeting broke up with one of Martini's bear hugs. There was no air of excitement as the final moves in the drama were about to play out.

* * *

When Elaine arrived, Stone was sitting on the bed tugging his tie off.

An hour earlier she had finally mustered the courage to phone her son. But, unexpectedly, it was her daughter-in-law Margaret who answered.

Elaine's prepared speech for Peter was abruptly redundant.

"Hi, Elaine," Margaret greeted her quietly. "I know what you're calling about."

Neither spoke for a moment.

"It's all right," Margaret sighed finally. "We've had a long talk. We've decided to stay here. Peter is very sorry. It wasn't all his idea, you know. I thought it would be better to get away while we could. Now we can both see what a selfish idea that was ... Elaine, are you crying? Don't cry. Tell Gary we'll be there for Christmas dinner."

"Thanks, love," whispered Elaine. "Thank you. And tell Peter we love him and we're really looking forward to seeing you all."

Elaine hung up quickly before she completely lost her composure.

Now she took her husband's discarded tie and kissed him on the head.

"Peter says he's sorry. Margaret says they'll all be here for Christmas dinner and turkey," she said.

Stone looked up. "Well, that's great. Thank you for that, darling. You've done a very important thing. For everyone."

As Elaine turned to hang the tie in the closest, Stone said: "I knew that turkey-with-gravy thing would bring him to his senses."

She turned back swiping him with the tie. She couldn't decide whether to laugh or cry.

10.35 p.m.

Port Abbot, Queensland

Johnny Patterson and his sergeant, Guy Waters, were on the outskirts of Port Abbot walking carefully down an unsealed secondary road, skirting a cane field, when they were suddenly blinded.

A Chinese voice behind the searchlight shouted something at them.

Patterson dived off the road and into a ditch full of dead weeds. A shot rang out and there was more shouting in Chinese. He looked back and saw Waters motionless and exposed on the road, a hand shielding his eyes.

Three Chinese soldiers appeared running from the darkness behind the searchlight. One screamed in English: "Down on road! Down on road!"

As Patterson unshouldered his rifle, Waters lay down with his hands behind his head.

The English speaker wore an officer's epaulettes and aimed a pistol in the general direction of Patterson's hiding place.

"Come out. Come out. Or we kill your comrade!" the officer shouted.

The Chink was rattled, thought Patterson. They shouldn't have missed him while they could see him. Now they weren't sure where he was.

The officer bent over Waters and kicked his rifle away. The other two soldiers moved gingerly forward as a fourth remained in the ute sweeping the powerful searchlight along the roadside.

Patterson waited till the light had passed over on one of its swings and leapt from the ditch, bolting into the edge of the thick sugar-cane stand for better cover. The Chinese heard the movement but saw nothing.

The searchlight swung wildly in response.

The officer walked over to Waters' sprawled body.

"Come out now or we kill your comrade!" he shouted. He fired his pistol into the air.

Patterson lay down. He was hidden on the edge of the field but had a clear view. He looked down his scope. The officer had dropped his pistol down again, aiming at Waters' head.

Patterson unbuckled one of his hand grenades. He put it down at his side and raised his rifle to sight the officer.

"I count to three. After that your comrade dead!" the officer shouted.

Patterson let him get to two and squeezed the trigger. Half the officer's head vanished and his body crashed heavily to the ground.

Patterson sprung to his feet, hurled the hand grenade as hard as he could toward the vehicle. As the deadly missile flew through the air he quickly fired a round from his hip. A second Chink soldier fell screaming.

The hand grenade exploded with a roar in the silent countryside. The searchlight went out. The vehicle's engine roared to life. The soldier remaining on the road shouted and Patterson could hear his pounding boots as he ran for the vehicle. They were little yellow bastards in more ways than one.

"Sergeant, get over here!" Patterson yelled. Waters got shakily to his feet, found his rifle and ran to where he had seen the barrel flash.

The Chinese had a small ute by the sound of the motor, thought Patterson. It reversed away at high speed, its headlights switched off or blown out by the grenade.

The Australians waited, crouched beside the cane field.

After several minutes they heard the ute. It was coming back. Fast. It was only twenty metres away from them when its surviving headlight lit up the roadway. It screeched to a halt close to the dead officer and the wounded Chink, who was still writhing on the ground.

Suddenly, a machine-gun opened up cutting a swathe through the cane above their heads. It splintered and crashed down around them.

Waters dived for deeper cover. Patterson lay down following the muzzle flash through his scope. When he was ready he fired. The machine-gun died.

There was a ghastly metallic clash of gears as the driver fought to find reverse. Patterson shot out both tyres on his side.

The Chinese driver began yelling hysterically. They had no idea what he was saying. He got out of the ute with his hands above his head and walked toward them.

Patterson turned to Waters. "Do you want him?"

"Whaddya mean?" said Waters.

"They were about to blow your head off. Do you want him?"

Waters shook his head. The Chinese driver walked toward the dead officer and the soldier who lay moaning from the shot he'd taken in the stomach.

Patterson strode out of the cane field. He pointed the driver toward the dead officer and mimed instructions for him to pull the body to the ditch. The driver did as he was ordered and Patterson waved him back to the wounded Chinese.

Again, he mimed the same instructions and the wounded man was carried over and put gently in the ditch. Finally, the driver was marched back to the ute to retrieve the dead machine-gunner and add him to the body pile.

Patterson shoved the driver to the edge of the ditch. He waved his arm indicating the driver should face the cane field. The soldier, instead, stood still and shook his head. He began a terrified wailing and crying while yabbering incoherently in whatever language he was speaking.

"Whaddya doing, Johnny?" Waters called.

"Just finishing off the job." Patterson raised his rifle and fired. It was his second head shot of the night but this time at close range. He felt some of the driver's blood wet on his face. He wiped it off with a sleeve. He'd stood too close.

"Johnny, what the hell are you doing? He was a prisoner. You shot him in cold blood, for Christ's sake," said Waters.

"Sarge, that officer was about to shoot you through the head."

Patterson went to the side of the road and looked down on the injured man. He was writhing, one hand holding in his innards and the other frantically waving Patterson away. Patterson fired his third head shot of the night, standing well back to avoid any further blood spatter.

Patterson walked over to the ute. Its front was splattered from grenade shrapnel. Its remaining headlight was still on.

"Come on, sarge. This ute will ride its wheel rims. We've got a ride to the port. If that Chink hasn't entirely fucked up the gear-box."

Waters got in the passenger seat in a state of silent shock. His private was a killing machine. He began to wonder if he'd picked the right man to be with on a sabotage job.

Patterson's quick action had saved his life. Or had it? He believed the Chinese would have taken them to Lavarack as prisoners, not murdered them. Or would they have?

Waters sat and stared ahead. Patterson turned the ute around. There were protesting, grinding noises but the gears still meshed.

It helped if you knew which way to push the gear lever, Patterson thought. Maybe the Chinks didn't get to drive a lot. He nursed the ute steadily along the road he had travelled many times in his youth, toward the port.

They hid the ute in another cane field and walked the last two kilometres to the huge coal mountain and the port administration offices. There were lights on in the night watchman's shed. It was the same one they'd snuck past many times as kids.

He didn't know what had happened to old Jock Stanley, the night watchman, since the invasion but someone was moving about in the shed.

They skirted around it and crept toward the long jetty that held the enormous conveyor belt. They climbed on it and moved for the few first metres on their hands and knees to stay out of sight.

* * *

Jock Stanley was leaning over the coffee pot. Since the little yellow bastards had arrived he had become their chief coffee maker and general dogsbody.

He'd had a good, cushy job for his last year before retiring, as the port's night security officer.

He made sure there were no trespassers and nothing went missing from the big site. Slippage, the bosses called it. There was none when he was in charge.

Now the Chinks were the biggest thieves out. They'd help themselves to anything not nailed down. They were meant to be guarding the place. He was meant to be helping them.

Mainly this involved yelling in English if any of the Bowen brats turned up to play silly buggers on the jetty.

If the loading was stopped, they'd jog for bloody miles out along the conveyor belt if he didn't see them first. They'd fling themselves into the sea and swim back. The sheilas didn't. They reckoned there were sharks down there. They screamed each time the boys jumped. It was all a big game. The boys were always going to show their bravado.

He took two coffees to the guards sitting at the small table. They were yabbering in their language. Some guards. They'd only moved outside once tonight.

Stanley shuffled back to the pot and stared out the grimy window as he took a sip of the hot coffee. He almost choked on it. There were two uniformed white men outside only metres away.

They were partly bent over and moving silently, painstakingly.

"You right, old man?"

He turned and realised his near choking had attracted the guards' attention.

"Yeah, yeah. I'm fine," he nodded his head. He turned his back to the window casually continuing to block their view from it.

"You have weak coffee. Not China coffee," the guard said.

Stanley nodded again and gave a rare smile of agreement. "Yeah, it's crap, all right."

He raised his cup and turned back to the pot and the view outside. The area was lit but not well lit. What light there was threw up a forest of shadows. It never worried him. His eyesight was twenty/twenty. He could smell intruders on his jetty even if he couldn't see them. Jock Stanley was a pro.

He took a second sip and stared into the shadows. One of the two figures darted into a sliver of light as he reached to pull himself up on the jetty. The figure was wearing an Australian Army uniform. There were three stripes on his arm.

The second figure followed, hoisting himself onto the conveyor. He had no stripes but he was definitely wearing an Australian Army uniform. Both of them had rifles.

He had to get away from the terminal. And soon. Something was going to happen. He didn't want to be around when it did.

He looked at his watch. It was 11.47 p.m. He hoped the two out there didn't do anything in the next thirteen minutes. Fortunately, it was a very long walk out to the end of the jetty where the conveyor met the various loading chutes.

The Diggers didn't do much of a job hiding themselves. Their crawling bodies were in plain sight had the Chinese guards ever bothered to stand and look outside. But in another few minutes they would be far enough away from the guardhouse lights to be lost in darkness.

He sighed with relief when they were finally swallowed up in the night.

At midnight Stanley pointed to his watch and said: "Well, I'll be off now."

The senior guard frowned. "No, no. You stay. We wait for patrol come back."

Stanley felt a shiver run down his creaking body. He sat down slowly on one of the hard wooden chairs and said a little prayer.

DAY THIRTEEN

12.02 a.m.

Port Abbot, Queensland

Adjusting his night goggles, Blackie peered landward down the enormous length of the trestle jetty. He could see no movement in the pitch black, though he could not be certain there was none because the structure stretched almost three kilometres before reaching the shore.

He was alone with his chook, Jabril Allunga. The Aboriginal had been a bit uppity about the nickname, until he discovered all SAS signalsmen were called chooks.

Blackie had ordered the other three squad members back to their inflatable and out of harm's way. He and the chook would use the second craft to rendezvous with them twenty kilometres south.

He and Jabril had almost another hour to wait, till within sixty minutes of the detonation time to allow the bomb the best chance of remaining undiscovered by any Chinese guards.

They had only seen a single, two-man patrol in the three hours since they had clambered silently up the jetty and positioned the bomb at the sea end where the conveyor belt system split to load several ships simultaneously.

The guards appeared bored and had walked, chatting quietly, past them, overhead on the conveyor belt. They had been too lazy to walk to the far end of the jetty.

They were slack buggers for reputed special forces troops.

Probably lulled into a false sense of security by Australia's apparent failure to take them on. Boy, were they in for the daddy of all shocks at 2 a.m. Not that they would be alive for more than a nanosecond after the bomb went bang.

Jabril was lying lengthwise behind him on the narrow deck space between the overhead conveyor belt structure and the jetty's spindly-looking sides.

The jetty's conveyor spewed millions of tonnes of Queensland's Galilee Basin coal into the holds of an armada of almost two hundred bulk carriers a year. Business since the invasion had slowed. Fortunately, tonight there were no ships in the loading bays. The jetty was a desolate place.

But it was a strategic deep-water port asset the Chinese wanted.

Blackie suddenly felt Jabril prod his leg. He turned to look back at the man from Darwin's Norforce territorial surveillance unit. He had been seconded to the squad only days ago. The man was almost invisible in the night.

"Someone's on the jetty," he whispered.

Blackie cocked his head. He could hear nothing but the slight lapping of the waters below.

Jabril had been treated with some initial suspicion by the hardened troopers he had been sent to join temporarily.

None of them had ever served with an Aboriginal. Norforce recruited mostly Northern Territory and Western Australian indigenous territorials for their surveillance skills with little regard to the Army's standard educational entry qualifications.

Blackie admired the Army for it breaking its own rules when it was necessary but he knew the recruitment policy was a cause of resentment among his troopers. They had been pushed to their limits just to get a foot in the SAS door.

Jabril had parachuted in, so to speak, to one of the most dangerous, critical front-line assignments the SAS had been given for years.

He had trained as a wireless operator and his record showed he had outstanding reconnaissance skills. He had worked in cities along the Queensland coast. He knew the Abbot Point-Bowen and the Gladstone regions intimately. It was the reason he was with them.

Despite their reservations, the squad had quickly warmed to him. They found him confident and stroppy and not a man to be trifled with. They respected his stamina. He came from Northern Territory desert country where training SAS reconnaissance teams regularly roasted in 45°C summers and froze in their sub-zero winters.

After being dropped by the Black Hawk chopper twenty kilometres from ground zero, Jabril had taken his share of the load as they took turns carrying the twenty-five kilo bomb in its waterproof backpack on the dangerous journey north.

They had detected and skirted around constant enemy patrols. Blackie had no idea how the reservist chook would react in a combat situation but there was nothing he could do about that now.

"I can't hear anything," he whispered.

"There are two people and they're coming this way," Jabril insisted in a tone that left no room for dispute.

Jabril was in danger of pissing him off. Blackie regarded his own hearing as first rate.

He strained his ears and again raised his night goggles. He couldn't hear or see anything. The intruders must be a long, long way away. Or Jabril had a case of nerves and was imagining things.

The chook's name, Jabril, in his Aboriginal dialect was similar to his nickname. It meant owl. It probably meant the bugger could see and hear in the night while being naturally as black as your hat and impossible to see.

The pair lay dead still on the jetty's deck, one behind the other, squeezed uncomfortably into the cramped space below the conveyor. Occasionally, Blackie could sense Jabril squirming to stretch his limbs and keep the blood flowing.

Minutes passed. Then Jabril whispered: "They're still coming this way. They're going very slowly. Too slow to be Chinese, I think."

"Okay, if you say so," Blackie muttered. He still couldn't hear a thing.

A minute later a movement sparked in the greenish haze of his night goggles.

"I see them," he said. He still couldn't hear them though.

Another minute dragged past. The two figures came closer but they were still at least three hundred metres away.

He tensed as he began to hear faint footsteps for the first time. He couldn't leave the jetty while the two intruders were anywhere near the bomb.

He turned back to Jabril and said: "Get your knife out. No gun. There can't be any shooting."

"Sure, no problem, sarge," said Jabril.

He was a casual bugger for a new boy, Blackie thought.

On the pair came toward them. They moved carefully but steadily. About a hundred metres away they paused for a whispered conversation, looking around, then continued to move forward again.

Jabril chuckled. "They're not Chinese. They're white fellas."

"What?" said Blackie. "White fellas?"

"Yes. Can't you see anything?"

Blackie bit his tongue.

The intruders were walking along the top of the conveyor belt. They would pass about a metre above them if they went unchallenged.

Jabril made a singsong, almost inaudible, whisper: "I dunno what they're doing out here, but they're shark tucker if they come too near."

Blackie did an inward moan. No, no. This was the problem if you worked with amateurs.

He turned his head again and breathed. "Maybe, maybe not. Let them get alongside us and then we'll grab them. If they're not Chinese we may not have to kill them. Follow my lead."

Jabril sighed. "Sure, sure, sarge. No probs."

The two figures were less than twenty metres away when Blackie winced as Jabril dug his fingers sharply into his leg.

"They're in Aussie Army uniform. And they have rifles on their shoulders."

For fuck's sake, thought Blackie. What next?

Lifting his head he could see with the night-vision glasses Jabril was right. They were wearing infantry fatigues. One had a sergeant's stripes on his sleeve. They both had rifles. One was non-army issue.

Blackie's mind raced. If they were Aussie soldiers they would speak English. It made things easier. Hopefully. Whatever happened he couldn't let them retrace their steps and risk the operation.

Blackie moved to a kneeling position. Jabril copied him. When the pair were directly above them on the conveyor belt Blackie stood and said politely: "Good evening, gentlemen, please stand perfectly still and don't make a sound."

Both the conveyor walkers gave a gasp of shock. Both stopped and looked around in the darkness.

"Keep your rifles on your shoulders. Kneel down slowly. Keep absolutely silent," Blackie commanded.

"Okay, okay," said the sergeant. "Where are you?"

"We're just below you," said Blackie.

"Oh, I see you. You said we. Where's your mate?"

Jabril gave a short chuckle.

"I'm part of the dark," he said but moved a fraction so they could make out his silhouette.

The sergeant dropped to his knees. "Christ, you scared the shit out of me. Who are you guys? What the hell are you doing out here?"

Blackie noticed the second soldier had been slower, more reluctant to kneel.

"You go first," said Blackie. "Who and why?"

The sergeant said his name was Guy Waters. He and private Johnny Patterson were with the Royal Australian Infantry Regiment, 2nd Battalion, based at Lavarack. They had been on a desert survival exercise when the balloon went up. They had since dodged Chinese patrols and made it to Port Abbot.

"What for?" said Blackie.

"We plan to wreck the conveyor system. We've got hand grenades to do the job. I worked here. I know its weak points, out at the far end where the loading system is," said Waters.

"If we can sabotage that we'll fuck up the whole place for months."

Patterson suddenly interrupted: "And let the Chinks know we're not giving up without a bloody good fight."

Blackie ignored him and said to Waters: "You're going to use hand grenades?"

"We have to use what we've got. We'll improvise. It's not perfect but they'll make a bloody great mess of the system," said Waters.

"Fuck. You'll end up killing yourselves trying a stupid stunt like that," Blackie said. "And how were you going to get off the jetty again if you hadn't fragged yourselves?"

Patterson patted the rifle on his shoulder. "We'll kill off any Chinks who try to stop us. This is my own hunting rifle. It's got a sniper scope or as good as. I'll take out any slant-eye who gets in our road. Anyway, you haven't told us what the hell you're doing out here."

Waters raised his hand. "Sorry, sergeant. Johnny's a bit passionate. His old man is locked up in Lavarack. He's hot to trot but he's a good boy."

Jabril gave another quiet chuckle. "He'll be a dead, good boy shortly."

The other three switched their attention to his near-invisible face.

"Who the fuck are you, Abo?" said Patterson and began to stand again.

In a split second he was wrenched feet first from the conveyor by Blackie. He crumbled with a dull thud at the trooper's feet and felt Blackie's heavy boot stomp his face to the deck.

"I told you to kneel, private. And to keep quiet."

Blackie looked up at Waters. "You're a brave bugger, mate, and I appreciate your intentions but there's no way I can let you go any further. Or go back the way you came, for that matter."

As he spoke Patterson gurgled and squirmed to free himself. Blackie pushed his boot harder into Patterson's contorted face. "What is it, private, you don't understand about the words keep quiet?"

Waters looked down at Patterson's squirming figure. "Would you mind, sergeant, telling me what it is you're up to and what unit you're with?"

There was a pause. Blackie took a deep breath. "Sorry, we're operating on a strictly need-to-know basis. But we are both with One Sabre Squadron, SASR."

Waters remained silent, digesting the reply. "What do you plan to do with us if we're unable to go back?"

Blackie saw him cast an eye at the sea below.

"You want us to go swimming? With the sharks?"

"No, we'll take you back with us. We have an inflatable hidden below," said Blackie. "I'm sorry but we can't allow you to be discovered anywhere around here tonight. Particularly with an army uniform on."

He lifted his foot off Patterson's face and told him to stand up. He took Patterson's rifle from his shoulder and gave it to Jabril, telling him to unload it.

He knew Patterson was seething and humiliated. He didn't want to kill the boy. He just wanted him under control.

"In another hour, everything going according to plan, we'll be out of here," said Blackie. "But if we get discovered by the Chinks, no one will get off alive. Am I making myself clear?"

Waters cleared his throat. "No. You're not making a lot of sense. I don't know what your orders are but if you're only on a recon exercise and you're not going to blow this conveyor, the Chinks will be free to go on loading from it."

Blackie said: "I'm sorry. Your freelance operation is over. Now please step down off the conveyor. You're too easy to spot up there."

Waters didn't move. "Why can't we go back the way we came? We got here without being seen. And we can make things uncomfortable for the Chinks in other areas around here after you've gone."

Waters' question was perfectly reasonable, thought Blackie. Except in this case if he stayed around Port Abbot he would be toast. Radiated toast at that.

"I'm afraid we can't risk leaving you on the loose," Blackie said.

Waters sighed and slid noiselessly off the conveyor. As he did, Patterson found his voice: "How the hell are we going to climb down this in the dark? We're not all commandos, you know. We're not part of the $100,000-a-year elite cowboy show. We're just infantry. The cannon fodder. I'd rather die shooting Chinks than drowning down there."

"You can die right here if you want," said Jabril.

"Who's speaking to you, Abo?" Patterson said.

There was a heavy silence.

Blackie turned to Patterson and jerked his thumb at Jabril. "I'm afraid he's right, Johnny. You can die right here if you want to be a stupid prick. Either way you're not walking back and you're not shooting anybody tonight."

"Bullshit. I'm on the same side as you. What are you going to do when I tell you to get fucked? Shoot me?" Patterson said.

"Are you disobeying an order, private?"

"I'm blowin' up this conveyor terminal and shootin' any Chink that comes along. You and your Abo mate can have a look around and run along. Someone's gotta start fightin' back."

Blackie looked at Waters. "I need you stay perfectly still. Okay?"

Waters nodded.

Blackie looked over Patterson's shoulder and said quietly to Jabril: "No noise, chookie."

Patterson was frowning at Blackie in angry confusion. He started to turn toward Jabril when the signalman's hands darted out. Patterson found his mouth and nose covered and crushed closed.

Patterson tried to lash out with his legs. The signalman snapped his head viciously to the right. There was a crack.

Patterson slumped to the narrow deck and lay lifeless. Waters gave out a stifled cry. "What the hell …?"

"Sorry about that, Waters," Blackie said. "There's too much at stake here to have an extended debate with Johnny boy. I take it you have decided to come with us when we leave?"

Waters stared in shocked disbelief.

"You didn't have to do that," he said.

He knelt down by Patterson feeling for any pulse. There was none.

"You've murdered him. All hell will break loose when this comes out," he said.

"I don't think so. He'll be a hero when all this comes out. We'll both recommend him for his bravery and a medal for valour for his rearguard actions against the Chinese tonight," said Blackie.

He turned to Jabril. "Tie him up. We'll have to lower him down. We can't leave any trace up here in case another patrol does show up just after we've left. Nice job by the way, for a chook."

Jabril smiled. A moment later he said: "Do you guys really get a hundred grand a year?"

Blackie punched him lightly on the shoulder. "Don't be getting any thoughts above your station, son."

* * *

At precisely 1 a.m. Jabril received the coded signal. The remote detonation test had been successful. The bomb would be detonated at 2 a.m. Satisfied there was little chance the bomb would be found, they prepared to make for the safety of their rendezvous down coast.

Jabril went down the side of the jetty first. Blackie lowered Patterson's body over the side to him. Waters went over next, terrified as his feet felt for the crossbars of the trestle wharf. Jabril helped him into the inflatable.

Blackie joined them after one final sweep of the jetty with his night-vision goggles. There had been no further Chinese patrols. Time was running short.

If they were going to go, they had to go now because they had to row the first two kilometres. The powerful outboard engines couldn't be started until they were out of sight around the nearest headland.

Blackie concentrated on rowing the bouncing rubber craft into an incoming tide. His powerful arms began to ache with the exertion. He watched Jabril pulling on his oar uncomplainingly. Did Aboriginals do boats as well as deserts?

He finally started the outboard after almost thirty minutes and they chugged steadily out to sea over the World Heritage waters of the Great Barrier Reef. He felt a flood of relief to be out of immediate danger for the first time that night.

Fifteen minutes on he placed the engine in neutral. As the small craft bobbed about he lifted Patterson's body from the floor and sat him upright. His head dangled at an odd angle.

He began to strip his uniform from him.

Waters watched in silence, his hands trembling slightly. Blackie passed the dead soldier's dog tags to him.

"He was your boy. Stuff his tags down the inside your shirt," he said.

Waters nodded uncertainly.

Blackie yanked Patterson's boots free and threw them over the side with his uniform. They sank quickly. As Waters' eyes widened, Blackie lifted the body and pushed it head first into the black sea. It was swallowed up in an instant.

Blackie looked at Waters. "The boy had a broken neck. We wouldn't be able to explain that. Not when he was shot by a Chink and fell off the wharf in a brave rearguard action covering our escape. His dad in Lavarack will be proud of him."

Waters stared dumbly into the sea.

"It's for the best. You'll understand soon enough why you weren't allowed to stay or walk off that jetty. In twenty-five minutes it won't exist. Nor will anyone within three kilometres of it."

"What the fuck are you people up to?"

"The same thing as you were. Just on a bigger scale. And a lot more permanent."

Jabril laughed. "Yeah. A lot bigger. Your private was a dead man walking. You're lucky you came along when you did without the Chinks seeing you."

"I've got no idea what you people are talking about," Waters shook his head.

"Sergeant Waters. I do have your word, don't I, that the sequence of tonight's events is as we've agreed?" said Blackie.

Waters closed his eyes and nodded.

At exactly 2 a.m., Waters flinched. A thunderous explosion rolled out over the sea kilometres behind them. It was preceded by a searing white flash.

"What the hell was that?" he said.

Blackie ignored the question and turned to Jabril. "What's for dinner tonight? Not more snake?"

"I thought you liked snake. Isn't that why they call you guys snakeheads?"

"I thought maybe you could rustle us a decent goanna."

Jabril laughed.

"Are all your jobs this dangerous?" said Jabril.

"No, no. It's the training that's dangerous. Most of our fatalities happen when we're training."

"You're kidding."

"Nah. We lost twelve guys in a night exercise when two Black Hawks collided. That was pretty tragic. Poor bastards. They were just thirty seconds from their drop point and bam!"

Jabril shook his head. It was a Black Hawk that had whisked them here just above sea level. Another would shortly leapfrog them to a new hideout near Gladstone for what would be their second target.

"Our first fatality in a war zone wasn't even caused by the enemy. One of our guys out on patrol in Borneo was gored by an elephant. But what about dinner? How about you get us some chicken?"

"I'm a black fella in surveillance signals, what would I know about stealing chickens?" Jabril let out a high-pitched laugh. "You're good at the stealth stuff, steal and strangle your own."

"No, no. You're our man at strangling. I saw you in action tonight."

Waters shot from his seat in the bouncing boat. "For Christ's sake. That was a young man you killed tonight. It's no laughing matter," he yelled. "What would happen if the truth ever came out?"

Blackie sighed. "I thought you didn't want to go swimming."

Waters paused and sank into his seat. He knew Patterson's death was murder. Now he'd seen five murders in one night, four of them Chinese. He had almost been a murder victim himself.

Now, one murderer was going get a medal.

As the squad waited at its coastal rendezvous for the Black Hawk to pluck them from under the enemy's nose, a new drama was about to play out at The Lodge.

1.57 a.m.

Private quarters, The Lodge, Canberra

Stone woke and checked his bedside clock. He hadn't set the alarm. There had been no need. He had waited thirteen days to make this 2 a.m. call.

Elaine stirred and saw him sitting up. She got out of bed and padded quietly round to sit next to him. They silently watched the seconds tick off.

The security phone finally shrilled at 2.01 a.m. Stone picked it up. Able said: "General Thompson has just confirmed the detonation went as planned. Are you ready to go, Prime Minister?"

"Yes, John. Let's see how Ambassador Chen likes an early-morning call."

Stone had approved each of the six irradiation targets himself. The first this morning had been at Port Abbot. The second tomorrow morning would be near a big Hopes Down iron ore mine on the Pilbara, in Western Australia's Hamersley Range.

Geologists had estimated the mine's life span at thirty years. Soon some of it would be nil.

The Hamersley Range had more than a dozen mines and eighty per cent of all Australia's identified iron ore reserves. He wanted the opening bets of the bluff to be big, symbolic ones on each side of the country. As he waited to talk to Chen he refused to let himself think of the collateral damage the bombs would wreak.

Able left Stone's line open and he and Elaine heard the embassy's number ring for almost thirty seconds before it was answered.

Able identified himself and asked to speak to Chen on a matter of gravest urgency.

Stone could make out a small hubbub as the embassy's graveyard shift was stirred to life.

A second person came on the line asking Able to again identify himself. An interminable two minutes passed before they finally heard an extension line connect and ring once.

Chen grunted his name.

"Your Excellency, this is John Able, Prime Minister's Department. The Prime Minister wishes to speak to you. Can you hold the line, please?"

Chen gave a second grunt.

Stone took a deep breath, bracing himself.

"Your Excellency, I'm sorry to bother you at this hour but my treaty negotiators promised I would call you about our final decision regarding the border. My government has reached a decision, which needs to be passed on to Beijing immediately."

Stone could hear coughing and rustling.

"My government finds it is unable to accept your border treaty proposals and has, instead, begun to implement Australia's Emergency Nuclear Deterrent defence plan," said Stone.

"To this end, a radioactive device was detonated a few minutes ago at the Abbot Point bulk loading terminal in Queensland. The port's infrastructure has been destroyed and the region surrounding it coated in radioactive fallout."

Chen said nothing.

"You need to take urgent measures to evacuate any of your troops and port workers who have survived. Otherwise it's a no-go area."

Chen suddenly interrupted in a high-pitched voice: "What are you talking about? What is going on? What is this nonsense?"

"I would appreciate it if I could continue my message, Excellency," Stone replied.

Chen fell silent but Stone could hear him breathing hard.

"Australia's Emergency Nuclear Deterrent strategy ensures no foreign country can seize our natural resources. Radioactive devices are hidden beside all our strategic assets. We are now activating them as we are unable to accept the terms of your border treaty."

If necessary, the government would render all its resource sites unusable for the next hundred years. Any gain China had hoped for from its invasion was now null and void.

Chen whispered: "This is nonsense. This is impossible."

"Excellency, please call your military commander in the Port Abbot area. He will confirm what I'm saying. It's urgent you evacuate the area immediately," Stone said.

Chen began a coughing fit. Stone could now hear other, urgent voices in the background.

He pressed on: "Now I want to come to the most important part of my message."

The coughing stopped. Chen must have raised his hand for silence, as the background commotion suddenly subsided.

"My government is giving China ten days to remove all its forces from Australia."

Several seconds passed before Chen replied, slowly, carefully. He was choosing his diplomatic response, Stone thought, the one being recorded for his masters.

"Prime Minister, I fear you have made a tragic mistake. We will not be intimidated into a retreat from our new economic zones by any threats. We are prepared to make whatever sacrifices are necessary for the good of our people."

Chen cleared his throat. The high pitch was gone. "You will

appreciate we cannot let this attack stand. We have been negoti-ating in good faith and have been deceived."

Before Stone could respond, Chen added: "I will relay your message to my government immediately."

The line went dead. Stone looked at his wife. "He didn't say goodbye."

Elaine shook her head. "Maybe he doesn't like you."

"But he really doesn't know me."

Able's voice broke in over the banter: "Will there be anything else, sir?"

"No. Thanks, John," Stone replied. "Get some sleep. I don't think anything will happen till the morning. We've given them a lot to think about."

Stone put a big arm around Elaine's shoulders. "There's no going back now. We're pregnant."

Elaine nodded and shivered. She went back to her side of the bed, glancing at the illuminated alarm clock: 2.06. Everything had happened so fast.

6.30 a.m.

The Lodge, Canberra

Australians woke to a bright sunny day unaware their govern-ment had pulled the dragon's tail.

Stone checked the early-morning news on his iPad. It had been a normal night of scattered crimes, more calls for a Chinese border settlement, unemployment numbers climbing and several bush fires around Adelaide.

The attack in occupied territory had gone unreported. As he desperately hoped it would. His luck was holding. His Cabinet members had been advised and secrecy was again emphasised.

By mid-morning Thompson confirmed none of the defence or intelligence agencies had any Chinese reaction to report. The next hour dragged by and then the next.

By 1 p.m. Stone had his nerves sufficiently under control to eat a good lunch.

He filled the tense hours in the cat and mouse "no-man's-land" created by the counter ultimatums to busy himself with the small mountain of routine government paperwork that had been set aside since the crisis erupted.

Whittacker pestered him demanding updates. By early afternoon he stopped taking the calls. Able was left to assure him they would be in touch if there was a development.

1.15 p.m.

The Lodge, Canberra

Shortly after lunch Elaine took a call from Jocelyn Church. Elaine had met the wife of the ASIO director only briefly at official government receptions. She knew Jocelyn had twin baby daughters but little else about her.

Jocelyn was apologetic. She knew how busy Elaine was but wanted to see her urgently.

Since the Chinese crisis Elaine had, ironically, more spare time than she was happy with. All routine government entertainment, diplomatic and political events had been cancelled.

Elaine invited her to afternoon tea.

She took her to the private upstairs lounge for tea. Jocelyn appeared timid and nervous.

They sat down opposite each other in the armchairs. Jocelyn sat forward with her knees together, her hands struggling to find somewhere to settle.

Elaine found herself growing anxious and ill at ease. When the usual, polite small talk about the décor, the view and the weather was dispensed with, Jocelyn cleared her throat and said: "You know what happened last night, don't you?"

Elaine was taken aback. "I don't know what you mean, my dear. What particular thing are you referring to that happened last night?"

Jocelyn looked down at her clasped hands. "You know — the bomb thing."

Elaine said nothing. She reached for her tea as calmly as possible. She looked over the cup as she took a sip and raised her eyebrows.

"I'm not supposed to know anything about it, of course," said Jocelyn.

Elaine took another sip.

"What is it you're not supposed to know?"

"Please don't treat me like a child," Jocelyn said. She felt her face turning crimson.

"I'm talking about the nuclear bomb that your husband set off … up north … that's killed God knows how many people."

It was out.

Jocelyn sat back and stared at the Prime Minister's wife. Maybe she didn't know. What have I just done? Probably lost Frankie his job for a start, she thought in a panic. The visit had been a mad idea. She should stay out of matters that didn't concern her. But they did.

Lengthy seconds passed.

Elaine fought to remain outwardly calm but knew she was losing the battle. She could deny all knowledge and call security. That was the easy way out. She did not have to engage in any soul-searching with this young woman about strategic matters of state.

She had already fought her own doubts and fears about END. She had decided to accept Gary's rationale. But she had done it with huge misgivings.

She had sat beside him in the early hours of this morning when he revealed the detonation to the Chinese and ordered them to leave the country in ten days.

Now she was sitting with the highly emotional wife of the country's intelligence chief wanting to discuss top-secret operational matters that would almost certainly compromise Australia's only chance of victory if they became public.

"Of course I know about the bomb," she said finally. "The same way I presume you do. Our husbands told us."

Jocelyn gave a slight nod. She was abruptly lost for words. For direction. What had she hoped to achieve with the wife of the Prime Minister? She felt a little stupid. Naïve. Frustrated.

"Well, I think it's wrong," she said. "I can't believe we could carry out this sort of madness against our own people."

Elaine took a deep breath.

"Maybe it is wrong. What suggestions do you have that would force the Chinese out?"

Jocelyn looked down at her hands again.

Elaine turned to pick up the teapot. She topped up her cup. She held the pot out to Jocelyn who shook her head absently.

Elaine raised the cup to her lips again. "Anyway, what is it you want me to do about it?"

Jocelyn reached for her cup and shrugged. "I don't know really. Maybe I was just hoping this bombing campaign could be stopped somehow. Someone must be able to do something. It's unconscionable. I know the men won't stop it. I had a huge row with Frankie when he told me about it. There is no way he's going to argue against it with your husband. He's in favour of it, for God's sake."

"So you think the wives should stop it?" Elaine gave a slight grin. "Oh, that the world was that simple. Maybe you should be talking to the wife of the Politburo chairman."

Jocelyn said nothing.

Elaine finished her tea and sat on the edge of her armchair.

"Young lady, you do realise you've put me in an impossible position?"

Jocelyn gave a start, her eyes widened.

"What do you mean?"

"You have been discussing top-secret information you are not allowed access to. You weren't even certain that the person you raised it with had knowledge of it."

"I know. I know. But I had to discuss it with someone. You

were the only person I thought would know and have the slightest possible chance of getting the bombing stopped."

"Well, what you've done is totally wrong. You have arrogantly assumed everyone involved in the decision, including your husband, disregarded the human toll, the risks and the outcry that will come eventually. For the record I happen to share your concerns. I think the option of spreading radioactive waste is a dreadful one. But it's the one that's been chosen. Australia is in a desperate situation, it has its back to the wall."

"Oh, my God," said Jocelyn putting her hands over her mouth. "What are you saying?"

"I'm saying I should have you arrested."

Jocelyn shuddered. Tears began to run down her cheeks.

"How do I know you won't go out and start talking to other people? What sort of a position will I be in if you do? Do I tell my husband that I was aware you knew and did nothing about it while you sabotaged the whole campaign?"

"No, no. I swear I won't tell another soul." Jocelyn began crying. "I have two babies at home."

Elaine knew what she should do. But she knew she wouldn't do it. She would let Jocelyn leave The Lodge.

Jocelyn blew her nose on a tissue and said quietly: "Frankie wouldn't even be in the job today if it weren't for me."

Elaine lowered her cup. "What?"

"He decided to resign the morning of the invasion. I made him get out of bed and go to work." She began sobbing again.

Elaine stood.

"Go home," she said.

Jocelyn got up from the chair and dried her eyes.

Elaine said: "Go home but tell your husband you came to see me. I'll be telling mine. Gary trusts Frank. If your husband trusts you, nothing more will happen."

Jocelyn nodded silently and Elaine showed her to the door and down the staircase, through the empty lobby, past the guards and to her car. She watched her drive slowly away.

She went inside to find her husband. She feared if she hesitated she might not do the right thing. He was relaxed, signing documents in the dining room.

Elaine gently took his pen from him and told him his bomb secret was loose. She told him the reason for Jocelyn's visit. He nodded and sighed.

"But you let her drive off?" he said.

Elaine shrugged.

"Okay. Can I have my pen back, please?"

She passed it back. "Okay what?"

"Okay, decision made. I trust your instincts, darling."

4.14 p.m.

The dining room, The Lodge, Canberra

Ambassador Chen spoke to Able when China formally responded to the Port Abbot attack and the ten-day ultimatum to quit Australia. He declined Able's offer to put Stone on the line.

He told Able Australia's action was regarded as a serious and dangerous development.

The Chinese wanted to restart the peace talks the next day but at a new venue — in Queensland's big resort city, the Gold Coast, eighty kilometres southeast of Brisbane.

Stone called Martini.

"Why the hell do they want to restart on the Gold Coast?" Martini said.

"I don't know but it's better than them sending a missile into Brisbane," said Stone. "The worst scenario is they may be preparing to try to take Brisbane and they want you near the frontline to see it."

"That means they haven't bought your bluff," said Martini. "Why do we need to go and talk to them at all? You've told them they've got ten days to pack up and get their yellow butts out of the country. Just let off another nuke to nudge them along."

"I think we should accept the invitation," Stone said. "It's just possible they've realised they can't afford to start a full-scale war.

If that's the case, they may be searching for a face-saving way out. What's important is what they haven't done. They haven't started shooting the prisoners, which they promised to if we counterattacked."

"Well, I think it's a waste of time. The buggers will be up to something," Martini said.

"Joe," said Stone, "stop being so grumpy. You have to go even if it's to get the new lay of the land. We've given them a bloody big shock. Go and see where their heads are. You might enjoy it. The Surfers Paradise beaches are beautiful — and there won't be any crowds on them."

"Enjoy it?" Martini said. "Not bloody likely. You've got an apartment up there so you know how hot it is at this time of the year."

Martini gave a sigh of resignation. "At least I'll have plenty of hotel rooms to choose from."

"That's the spirit." Stone laughed. "I'll have Able get an RAAF VIP flight to take you up right away."

Their discussion ended. He sent a brief email update to Whittacker.

The evening's intelligence meeting heard there were no indications of any build-up of Chinese land forces on the closest border, near Gladstone. Admiral Robson joined them briefly and warned again diesel and food supplies on *Rankin* were dangerously low.

Stone apologised but said they were stuck in a waiting game. The *Rankin* had to hold on. Robson left in a grim mood.

Martini was back on the phone soon after his touchdown at Coolangatta Airport, the nearest airport to the Gold Coast. His voice sounded hoarse and tired.

"Gazza, these buggers are playing games already," he began. Stone could hear ice clinking against the side of a glass.

"Their delegation boss apologised profusely but said some bigwig Politburo guy wants to change the meeting venue. They want it moved to Q1. It's a high-rise right on the Surfers Paradise beach."

"Yeah, I know it. It was the tallest residential tower in the world when they built it. It's not known as a conference venue," said Stone.

"No. I know. I have a bad feeling in my bones," Martini said.

"You will if you drink too much of that scotch."

Martini ignored the comment.

"Well, there's something strange going on. They're being so bloody polite. Not like we've just let a nuke off under their bum."

Martini said the bigwig was a Vice Premier by the name of Chang Leng. He was one of the newer Politburo members appointed following the death of the old chairman.

"Well, you'll be talking to the top rung," said Stone. "I hope that's a good thing. Look on the bright side. Their reaction to being bombed is to want to talk."

"Those antibiotics of yours must be starting to work, Mr Positive," said Martini. "I'll call you tomorrow."

DAY FOURTEEN

Q1 Apartments, Surfers Paradise

He hadn't slept well. The huge bed was too soft. The air-conditioning too cold. The day ahead would be a bloody waste of time.

The lift hurtled Joe Martini seventy-nine floors up the Q1 so fast his ears popped. He swore softly as it came to a halt at the observation deck, which was still some way below its full 348 metres height.

The blue glass tower soared over every high-rise stacked around it along the Surfers Paradise "glitter strip".

The elevator doors hissed open. He put his head up, shoulders back and braced himself. He could see Wu Seng, China's chief negotiator, sitting with two aides at the small conference table they had set up in the observatory.

He crossed for the perfunctory handshake and looked up. He felt himself suddenly transfixed by the spectacle outside.

Before him a sweeping panorama of foaming waves tumbling onto golden beaches stretched north as far as the eye could see before vanishing into a haze brewed by the surf.

The observatory floor was 235 metres up. It was awe-inspiring, he thought. No wonder millions of holiday-makers were seduced by the place.

It was a far cry from the flat, dry wine country in South Australia where he had lived and worked for most of his life.

He looked at his watch. It was exactly 10 a.m. The Chinese delegation had arrived before him but he had beaten the Vice Premier to the meeting. The Chinese were sitting along the table with their backs to the stunning view.

They seemed very casual, sitting back, relaxed, drinking coffee. They offered him one. He accepted.

These were the people he had suckered, led along for days with assurances a border settlement was about to be approved. Then they got nuked. They must be pissed. But this morning they were polite and charming.

He looked along the table. Wu was the only delegate with a file in front of him. His spirits, lifted by the spectacle of the Gold Coast, began to deflate. Something was wrong, just as he had warned Stone. The buggers were up to something.

He had always trusted his instincts. If his sixth sense told him something bad was going to happen, it did.

He had overcome droughts, grape disease, collapsing prices and heaven knows what other tribulations over the years — because he sensed when bad things were coming and acted on his instinct. He was certain something bad was coming this morning.

He lifted his coffee and nodded thanks to Wu. He took a sip and tapped his watch. It was now 10.03 a.m. and time to start.

"Where's the Vice Premier?" he asked.

Wu shook his head. He was sorry. Mr Chang's aircraft had been further delayed.

"It's a bit late to tell me that," Martini said. He shoved his chair back.

Wu leaned forward shaking his head. "No, no. Mr Chang is very sorry, very sorry. But he has told me this meeting should go ahead."

Martini was half standing.

"Please sit down again, Mr Martini."

Stone had told him not to be grumpy. He begrudgingly pulled his chair in again and drummed his fingers on the table.

Looking relieved, Wu tried to check his watch without being obvious.

Martini wagged a finger at Wu. "You know my government has decided not to sign a border treaty with you and has implemented its Emergency Nuclear Deterrent policy."

Wu waved a hand carelessly. "You mean the poison pill strategy?"

"Everything you came for will be poisoned. It will be radioactive for the next century. Useless to you," Martini replied.

Wu opened his file and began tapping a pen on it. "We have considered your actions and I have been instructed to advise you, Australia has until this time tomorrow to the sign the treaty — the one you told us two days ago you would get your Prime Minister to agree to."

He glanced at his watch again. It was 10.05.

Martini was shaking his head and about to reply when the building shuddered.

With a thunderous roar a jet fighter flashed before his eyes. It seemed to be at touching distance. The star on the Chinese Shenyang's fuselage was a blur of red. The observatory windows flexed in protest as it howled away at supersonic speed.

It startled Martini who leapt to his feet. Seconds later the glass tower shook again as a second and then third fighter swooped past terrifyingly close.

Martini was deafened by the ear-splitting roar of the jet engines. The three Chinese delegates sat motionless, staring at him, their faces expressionless in an ostentatious display of cool.

He saw the jets head several kilometres out to sea, turn sharply and sweep back toward the line of high-rise apartment blocks and hotels lining the beachfront.

They reached the shoreline and the leading Shenyang jerked slightly as a missile shot from under a wing. A fireball exploded halfway up an elegant, white tower. The other two jets began attacking separate towers.

Glass and concrete erupted from the buildings as the rockets tore into them and smoke began billowing from gaping black wounds.

All three jets swung back to sea forming up to return at almost sea level. He could understand why Shenyang meant Flying Shark in Chinese. Screaming at wave height and then weaving between the resort's high-rises at the speed of sound, they shattered the sound barrier with a thunderclap.

The boom rocked the coast. The sonic blast shattered windows for kilometres.

It was a terror message the Chinese wanted everyone to hear. Particularly him. He saw in his shock he had knocked over his coffee. Its contents had spilled across the table and soaked Wu's file before he could move it.

Meanwhile the three raiders rejoined in a formation and headed north. He was still standing when he saw a single jet break off and turn toward the coast again about twelve kilometres north of Q1.

It appeared to slow, almost to stall speed. It was only metres above the sea when it unleashed a single missile. He watched puzzled. The target was clearly a low-rise complex some distance from the main centre of the attack.

Then the state-of-the-art jet turned and dramatically demonstrated its enormous, 325 metres a second climbing power and vanished with the others northward.

A strange silence enveloped the observatory. Then, through the towering wall of glass, Martini could hear the muted wail of sirens.

Wind fanned tongues of flame within the trio of high-rise targets before him, the strong sea breeze pushing clouds of black smoke out horizontally.

In the still atmosphere Wu coughed for attention as one of his staff used a tissue to mop up the coffee spill.

None of the Chinese had turned to look at the destruction outside. It was an amazing feat of self-discipline, Martini thought. All that theatre for him.

"I think we have demonstrated that our patience is at an end," Wu was saying. "Your government's senseless attack at Abbot Point has destroyed an important port and caused us considerable casualties."

Martini's eyes flicked between the flaming buildings and Wu.

He studied the windows. No, he couldn't toss him down seventy-nine floors because the bloody things didn't open.

Wu said: "If there is no peace treaty signed by ten tomorrow morning we will be in a state of war. The time for talking is over, Mr Martini. Please tell that to your Prime Minister."

Wu gathered up his soggy file and stood. "I suggest we adjourn."

Martini suddenly strode around the table with a beaming smile. He held out a hand to Wu. Disarmed, Wu took it hesitatingly.

Martini shook it vigorously and then slapped the surprised Chinese diplomat sharply on the back several times.

"That was one helluva aerobatic show you put on. Thanks for letting me sit on the side with the view."

Wu's two Chinese aides watched nervously, their eyes darting warily from their boss to the crazy Australian Minister.

Dropping Wu's half-crushed hand, Martini continued to smile happily. Wu stared at him nervously, then nodded to his staff and made for the refuge of the lift.

"Oh, and thanks for the coffee," he called after them cheerfully. "Sorry I spilled it all over you."

There was no reply. The lift doors shushed shut.

"Pricks," he muttered to the empty observatory.

He walked slowly across the room and rested his forehead against a cool observatory glass. A chaotic scene was playing out far below. He inhaled deeply in an effort to slow his racing pulse.

The phoney war was over.

There were times when he hated his sixth sense.

10.44 a.m.

The Lodge, Canberra

"Gary, this has gone far enough. You have tried your bluff strategy and it's failed. And it's cost lives. We have to go back to the negotiating table."

Stone rolled his eyes and held the phone away from his ear. Jeremey Whittacker was obviously watching the live television feed from Surfers Paradise. Stone could hear the television presenter's voice on Whittacker's phone echo his own set.

If anyone should be whingeing or panicking, it should be Martini who had just had a Shenyang jet blast past a metre away from his window seat at the speed of sound.

"Oh, God. I hope we aren't too late to get a deal," Whittacker was saying. "Did the Chinese have anything to say before the bombing started?"

"As a matter of fact they did," said Stone.

"What was it? What was it?"

"They said there would be no war," Stone replied.

"That's wonderful, just wonderful."

"Well, not till after ten a.m. tomorrow."

"Christ, Gary. What the hell is going on? What is happening at ten tomorrow?"

"That's the new deadline to sign their treaty."

"Oh, my God. We have to act fast. Gary, you know preventing a full-scale war is the right thing to do," said Whittacker.

The line went silent apart from the distant voice of the Gold Coast television reporter.

He heard Whittacker sigh. "You need to call Cabinet together. We need to review this whole END idea of yours."

Stone yawned. "No, Jeremey. There's no need for another meeting. The Cabinet has already decided on this course of action. I'm just implementing it."

"God in heaven," said Whittacker.

"Did you ever consider, Jeremey, that it's the Chinese who are in the weaker position?"

"How the hell could they be in a weaker position?" Whittacker said.

"Well, they played their hand. We raised them. They said if we attacked them they'd start to kill prisoners and send their army south to take Brisbane. But they didn't. Now they've extended their deadline for another day."

"Gary, this is not a poker game. This is deadly serious. Millions of lives are at stake," Whittacker said, almost shouting.

"What will everyone say when they find out we've been killing our own people?"

Stone paused and thought about the question.

"If we win, they'll say it was worth the sacrifice. If we lose, it won't matter. None of us will be here. I'm sorry, Jeremey, but I have to go. I'll tell Able to keep you updated."

Stone put the phone down, cutting off any further, pointless argument. The worrying thing about the conversation was that his deputy was quite right. Millions could die.

He looked up at the television to see stretcher bearers carrying the crumpled body of a middle-aged woman to a waiting ambulance. The bottle blonde reporter in the foreground looked traumatised.

She was saying Florence Bartlett had arrived to open a downtown bar when a missile hit the upper floor of her building. Huge slabs of concrete and masonry had crashed to the footpath, killing her instantly.

Stone sucked down a spray of nitrate as he looked at the crushed body and thought of the many more innocent Florences who could die in the coming days.

The reporter said the death toll of twenty-seven had been light because most of the hotel towers had been near empty.

Some of the worst injuries were among pedestrians who were badly sliced by razor-sharp shards of glass raining down from windows thirty or forty floors above. Many of the windows on buildings not directly attacked had been splintered by the jets' sonic boom.

Sprinkler systems had eventually doused the hotel fires, she said.

The acute fuel shortage had halved the number of ambulances available to ferry injured people to Gold Coast hospitals. I should do something about that, Stone thought.

The reporter added the hospitals were fully staffed. No medical personnel had joined the earlier panicked exodus. He would definitely do something about that, Stone decided.

The ambulance doors closed on Florence Bartlett's body. She was the first victim he had seen for himself in his high-stakes bluff. She probably wouldn't be the last because the game was not over.

A successful bluffer moved boldly to ultimately shake the other player's confidence. It was the only way to make them fold.

Stone was certain he was creating serious doubts about any instant success the Chinese leadership had hoped for. But how serious, he had no way of knowing.

He reached for the phone and asked the operator to find him Thompson. He put the receiver down to wait for the call back when Elaine walked into the lounge.

As she sat down the phone rang and the general came on the line. Stone told him he wanted to double up. Two bombs were to be detonated at two the next morning.

Elaine listened, raising her eyebrows. Then, much to Stone's relief, she gave a slight nod.

2.15 p.m.

The Lodge, Canberra

While all the attention had been on the Surfers Paradise attack, Church added another helping of gloom at the early-afternoon briefing.

Stone left the dining table, where Church had been doing most of the national status update, to stretch his left leg, ease the pain gripping his buggered knee and hobble to the coffee urn.

Church was warning a national fuel shortage was threatening to paralyse what was left of the economy.

Australia's standard three-month supply of petrol and oil had vanished. The widespread panic buying and black-market hoarding had left most pumps dry in the capital cities.

Stone's attempts to introduce rationing had been widely ignored and come to nothing.

The state capitals reported half their public transport bus fleets were at a standstill, while Sydney's electric commuter trains were dangerously overcrowded. The economy was being strangled and jobless people were joining the pro-treaty protests.

Stone poured himself a cup of black coffee. Elaine had now placed milk on his banned list. He looked at the others around the table. Church and Thompson appeared to be as weary as he was. Able just looked like Able always did.

Stone said: "And while the petrol pumps are empty, we have two supertankers full to the brim sitting off Sydney Harbour?"

Church nodded his head.

"Have they said why?"

Church pursed his lips. ASIO had been intercepting all communication traffic with the ships for several days.

"The ships have been ordered to heave to until further instructions, sir," said Church. "The captains haven't been given any reason for this but one of them has a pregnant wife. He's been chattering on the phone trying to explain why he won't be home as he promised in time for the birth of his second son. The wife's been giving him a hard time. One of the things he's told her is he believes the owners are waiting for the price of oil to go even higher. He says his company is thinking of demanding gold for payment — they don't trust Australia's currency or chances of beating off China."

Nobody said anything. The general flipped over some paperwork in front of him. Church moved in his chair and tapped his gold pen to no discernible rhythm.

Able watched Stone staring silently at the floor.

"Prime Minister, why don't we go and get the oil?" he asked.

Stone's head shot up. "What do you mean, John?"

"I mean seize the ships and bring them into Botany Bay. It would only need a tip-off that they're carrying a big cargo of drugs, which those ships often are, and we could board them, take them over," he said.

Thompson laughed. "Get Frank's ASIO spooks involved and you could be certain to find whatever drugs you like on board."

Stone limped back to the table. "Bloody good idea, John. How could we do this?"

Thompson answered: "We can take the Federal Police out in a couple of Navy patrol boats. The Navy'll have the equipment and skill to board it. They'll even have someone who can dock them if it comes to that."

"Okay, let's grab them. And do it today. I don't want them sailing off somewhere else and leaving us with our happy band of profiteers," said Stone.

He looked at Church. "What's the next little crisis you've got on the agenda, Frank?"

Church looked at his notes. There was only one other thing.

"There's a peace rally being organised on the lawns of Parliament this afternoon," he said. "They're demanding the government sign the Chinese border treaty immediately. They say every city will be bombed like the Gold Coast if we don't."

Church said his agency was monitoring the rally's ringleaders. The television news channels would be broadcasting the proceedings live.

"The rally's illegal, Prime Minister. You could send in the cops and close the whole thing down," said Thompson.

"Well, you could," said Able, "except there are already two or three hundred people there and you'd risk a riot happening in front of the cameras."

"He's right, of course," Stone told Thompson.

Speaking to himself, he said: "If people aren't profiteering and hoarding, they're out trying to give the whole bloody country away."

He lifted a hand unconsciously to a pain in his chest. He pulled it away quickly when he saw the others watching him.

"Let them do their protest thing," he said. "Tomorrow morning's bombs will give the Chinese the real message."

They gathered up their papers. Thompson and Able were the first to hurry out.

Elaine arrived cup in hand looking for the dining room's faith-ful coffee pot when one of Church's aides strode briskly in. He walked directly over to his boss ignoring her and Stone, holding out a cellphone.

The aide bent over Church and said something in his ear.

The news clearly rocked Church and he grabbed the phone, snapping his name. The aide stood back while Church remained at the table.

Elaine went to the coffee urn. The aide looked undecided on where he should be and opted to wait outside. He quietly closed the door behind him.

After several seconds Church's eyes swept around the room and found Elaine and Stone watching him.

"Are you sure? Are you sure there's no mistake?" he asked as he stood and turned to the wall behind him.

Fearing another crisis of some sort, Stone and Elaine waited till the hushed conversation ended.

Church turned and went back to his seat. He looked ashen. He said nothing and stared at the table.

"What's happened, Frank?" said Stone.

Church continued to stare at the table. Elaine took her fresh coffee and went to sit opposite him, next to her husband.

Finally, Church looked up. His voice was almost a whisper: "That was one of my agents. He's monitoring the rally outside Parliament."

He paused.

"So?" said Stone.

"My wife is listed as the third speaker at the rally."

Church looked down again and heard Elaine say: "Gary, I'm sorry."

Church lifted his head in surprise and confusion, which mounted when he saw Stone take her hand and say quietly: "It's okay. It's not your fault."

"I was sure I could trust her," said Elaine.

Church sat back, his mouth open in growing dismay.

"Your wife came to see Elaine," said Stone. "She said you had told her about END. She said she was appalled by the idea and wanted Elaine to help her stop it."

Church seemed paralysed. He stared at each of them in turn.

"Oh, Christ," he finally muttered. "What's she up to?"

"I think we can guess that pretty easily," said Elaine.

Church look mortified and went to stand but sat down again.

"What is her mobile number?" said Elaine. Church told her.

Elaine took her mobile from a pocket and dialled it. She pressed it to her ear. After a moment she lowered it and pushed the speaker button.

A tinny voice was saying: "... please leave a number and I'll call you back. Have a happy day."

"Frank, how long have we got?" said Elaine. "I saw Sky Channel upstairs and they're already showing quite a crowd there. From what your agent's told you, when would you think the third speaker would begin their address?"

Church looked at the ceiling and said: "They usually rave on for about twenty or thirty minutes each at these sort of things, sometimes longer."

"That gives us enough time to get to the rally," said Elaine. She stood up, gave Stone a peck on the head.

"You're going to the rally?" said Church.

"Yes," said Stone. "She's going. If you're going too, you'd better stay out of sight."

Church stood up gathering his papers and said: "Prime Minister, I'm very sorry about ... about this whole ..."

Stone used his jaw to point him after Elaine and said nothing.

2.45 p.m.

Parliament Buildings, Canberra

Elaine had Able bring around an unmarked car. She directed her two close protection officers to the back seat. Church sat silently beside her as she drove.

When they reached Parliament's front lawn there were big

banners and a large crowd gathering around a tent that had a speaker's platform in it.

Church stayed in the car half a kilometre from the throng while Elaine walked to the edge of the protesters' ranks and looked carefully around her. There was no sign of Jocelyn. She was handed a pamphlet by a man with a "Peace Now" badge.

The pamphlet listed the third and final speaker of the day as Ms Jocelyn Church. She was described as the chair of the Women for Peace Forum in Canberra.

Elaine pressed recall and Jocelyn's number lit up. The call again went to message service. With her guards close behind looking overdressed for the occasion, she dived into the crowd.

After ten minutes of searching there was no sign of Ms Church and the first of the speakers took the stage. The crowd applauded wildly. She spoke only briefly and an aged peacenik took over the microphone. He was apparently also well known to the crowd, which welcomed him with loud cheers.

Elaine felt more frantic as the man wound down his speech. She moved closer to the stage. The crowd was packed in. Her guards struggled to keep close to her.

Peacenik then began to introduce Jocelyn Church. She appeared abruptly on stairs leading to the stage. She moved to the rear of it and sat, waiting for her glowing introduction to finish.

Elaine was now jammed tight in the front rows of the mob. She got her mobile free from her pocket. Using Jocelyn's mobile number, she switched to text.

Her fingers ran urgently over the keys: "Your twins in accident. Frank on way to hospital. Call me urgently. Elaine Stone."

She pushed send and prayed. Seconds later she saw Jocelyn pull her vibrating mobile from a coat pocket. It was a spontaneous action based on habit and reflex. She had been concentrating on Peacenik's words of introduction, her speech notes clasped in her free hand.

Elaine watched as Jocelyn read the message. The hand with the speech notes went involuntarily to her mouth. She replied instantly.

Elaine's mobile ring was almost drowned in the crowd noise.

"Hello, Jocelyn."

"Oh, thank God I got you. What's happened to the twins? Have they been hurt?"

"Listen very carefully, Jocelyn. Nothing has happened to the twins. But if you ever want to see them again, you will do exactly as I say."

Elaine heard a large intake of air in response.

"I'm standing in the crowd only a few metres from you, Jocelyn. I can see you quite clearly."

Jocelyn looked up, sweeping the sea of faces before her.

"The punishment for treason and the disclosure of state secrets is life, Jocelyn. And I know spending the rest of your life in prison while your girls grow up isn't something you'd want."

There was another shocked gasp.

"This is what I want you to do. Go to the microphone and tell everyone that you hate wars and death — but Australia is a great country and worth fighting for. This is not the time to sign a treaty and capitulate."

There was no answer.

"Do you understand or would you like me to repeat that?"

"I ... I ... um ... I understand."

"Good girl. Now go ahead, you're on, the crowd are applauding you."

Elaine broke the connection. Ms Church made her way to the centre stage. She had no smile to reflect her boisterous welcome.

Moments later the peace lovers became confused and then angry as she began to speak. Boos began to ring out. She continued to talk over the top of the din. Then Peacenik came forward. To roars of approval he took the microphone from her.

Tears streaming down her face, she turned and walked down the stage stairs and into the arms of two casually dressed ASIO agents.

They told her quietly she was under arrest on suspicion of breaching the Official Secrets Act. They would not handcuff her if she came peacefully. They took her speech notes.

She was led to an unmarked car. Further down the road she could see her husband in a second unmarked car. He was staring at her. He made no move to leave the vehicle as she was driven away.

4 p.m.

The Lodge, Canberra

"How'd you get her say that stuff?"

Stone was beaming when Elaine walked into The Lodge.

He had watched the television coverage. The rally had ended in disarray and confusion. Several of the crowd told television reporters Ms Church had showed a lot of guts and her speech had made valid points. Australia was too great a country to give away.

But most were angry at her and said Australia was on the brink of disaster and needed to sign the border agreement and avoid a war.

"I managed to have a little chat with Jocelyn just before she spoke," said Elaine. "More importantly, what happens now, to her — and Frank?"

They left the lounge and walked up to their private quarters.

"I can't sack Frank for doing what you and I do all the time, discuss all sorts of state matters, secret and public," said Stone. "So I've told him he'll keep his job but his wife and children are to be held at Campbell Barracks until this crisis is over."

"Campbell Barracks, near Perth? Where the SAS are based?" said Elaine.

"Yes. I want her well out of the way. Somewhere she's completely isolated."

Elaine nodded uneasily.

"Once the END thing becomes public at the end of all this business, you will let her go, won't you?" she said.

"Yes, I will," said Stone. "But it's all over for them as a family. Frank has been humiliated, he wants nothing more to do with her."

Stone removed his tie, sat down and rubbed his knee. "It's been quite a successful day. The cops claimed they found a dozen or so kilos of cocaine on a couple of tankers, which they've ordered to port. The tankers are discharging their oil and as we speak the price of black-market petrol is falling."

He looked up at Elaine. "And my wife has singlehandedly disrupted a public rally of my enemies. What happened that Jocelyn changed her mind at the last minute?"

Elaine walked over and kissed him gently.

"I nuked her," she said.

9.56 p.m.

The Lodge, Canberra

The bedside phone woke Stone. He rolled over and lifted the receiver. He had dozed off fully clothed reading an intelligence report speculating America was considering freezing China's US Treasury bonds.

He had long ago despaired of any meaningful help from the Yanks. The freezing of Chinese funds would not exactly help Australia by ten o'clock in the morning.

"Stone here," he croaked. He coughed to clear his throat. "Sorry. Stone here," he repeated.

"Oh, Gary, it's Lindsay here. I'm sorry to bother you at this hour. Actually, I wasn't sure whether to call you or not."

The Foreign Minister's voice was distant and hesitant. Stone pressed the phone harder to his ear.

"No problem, Lindsay," Stone said. "What's up?"

Stone was aware he had virtually sidelined Noble since the start of the crisis. The professor had become a nervous wreck when he first learned of the Chinese raid and the Yanks' impotence.

Stone had let Martini front the Chinese while Noble had busied himself lobbying United Nations delegates to support Australia's demand for the withdrawal of Chinese forces.

"Ah, well, I've had a call from Jeremey. A couple of hours ago," Noble said.

Stone felt his hand tighten on the phone.

"And what did the Deputy Prime Minister want?" he asked.

"Well, I wasn't quite sure. I'm still not quite sure," Noble said. "He was very casual … wanted to know how I thought things were going."

"What did you tell him?"

"I said I thought it was too early to tell how our strategy might play out. The Chinese response was predictable but it may have been driven because time is against them — the international pressure they're under is growing by the day."

Stone said nothing.

"Whittacker said he was wondering if lives were being lost for no purpose."

Noble paused again.

"Then he said he felt the attack on Surfers meant the Chinese weren't buying our END bluff and any further nukes being set off would ruin our chances of getting a peace deal."

"How many others has he phoned? Did he say?"

"Um, he gave the impression he'd had conversations with some of the others. The 'thinking members' of Cabinet, was the way he put it," Noble said.

"Christ, what the hell's a 'thinking member'?"

Noble didn't answer.

Stone was shaking his head. He stopped himself from swearing aloud.

"Lindsay, thank you for letting me know this. We're at a crucial point. I can't afford to have anyone second guessing me right now."

He coughed again to clear his throat. "Will you do something for me? Can you make some calls yourself and see what you can find out?"

There was no immediate reply. Stone knew that in the next few seconds Noble would have to weigh his own political future. If he agreed to make the calls he could easily get caught on the wrong side of any Whittacker coup.

"I don't know, Gary. I'm not much good at this sort of intrigue."

Stone fought to remain calm. "I appreciate that but ..."

"Look, let me think about it," Lindsay said, "there may not be anything to worry about."

"There will be plenty to worry about if Whittacker surrenders our country," Stone said.

"Gary, it is quite possible they could just stay where they are. They want our energy resources. I don't think they want a full-scale war for the rest of the country. The risks versus any extra rewards for them are too great."

Stone said: "Yes, but we know the Chinese have been caught completely off guard. They don't want a big war here. They can't get the resources they want if they are radioactive so sane heads may come to bear in the Politburo."

Stone knew it would be a mistake to push too hard. But Noble was a player he wanted on the field for the second half.

"Lindsay, you're the country's top diplomat. It would be totally in order for you to make a few calls to brief some of the senior ministers. If you do that you will get a sense of where they stand," said Stone.

"It would be difficult for Whittacker to accuse you of lobbying if you're bringing key ministers up to date."

"That's true ... that's true," Noble said. "Oh dear. What a mess. Gary, let me have a think about it ... let me sleep on it."

"Okay, no problems," said Stone. "One other thing, Lindsay. You should know I've had Martini fronting the Chinese because he's been ordered to lie about our true intentions. I didn't want you to be in that position. When this madness comes to an end, I'll need you to negotiate the face-saving solution that'll allow the Chinese to leave peacefully. Martini would never be able to do that now. He's been the front rower punching up the centre. They hate him. They'll never trust him again."

"Okay, okay. I accept you've had to play the game the way you see it," said Noble. "Let me sleep on it. I'll give you a call tomorrow."

He said good night and put the receiver down.

Stone sat still, his mind spinning, the dial tone droning on.

Whittacker had to turn only three votes to overcome the five-vote Cabinet majority backing the END policy. The Gold Coast bombing outrage would have unnerved some of his ministers. People were scared. The economy was grinding to a halt.

And the SIGN THE TREATY rallies had picked up steam.

He was in a race against time on two fronts. Politically and militarily.

At least Whittacker had no time to act in the four hours before the Chinese got the answer to their latest ultimatum.

DAY FIFTEEN

6.30 a.m.

The Lodge, Canberra

Gary Stone slept through the two overnight detonations.

He smelled the fresh coffee when he walked into the dining room where Thompson, Able and Church were already waiting for him.

"Still no reaction from the Chinese?" he asked, sitting at the head of the table.

"There's no sign of any increased activity," Thompson said. "And the aircraft carrier is still in its holding circle."

"Phew," said Stone lifting a cup of coffee to his lips. "So far so good then?"

The other three nodded.

Stone looked at the wall clock. "And still three and a half hours to go to the Chinese deadline."

He sat at the table. "Any reaction from Chen at the embassy?"

"No — and there won't be," said Church.

Stone almost spilled the coffee he was holding.

"What?"

"He's been recalled. He left Canberra late last night."

"What does that mean?" Stone asked.

Church pursed his lips. "The embassy staff say he's returning to Beijing for consultations. We think there's a chance he may have been sacked because he's been played for a fool. He'd been negotiating with an enemy that he told the Politburo was defeated. Our battle-ready troops were all locked away as hostages. Our submarines all meekly back at base. No obvious mobilisation of our forces. The treaty was a formality. Now look what's happened. Their army will be reporting casualties and radiation sickness and burns among its troops. The Chinese have been told nuclear bombs are located near every major energy resource but they can't find them. And they're still going off. His achievement record will not be looking flash. And don't forget they've been told the region around each explosion is contaminated for another hundred years. What will be even more disturbing for them is the Australian Government killing its own people as part of its determination to leave nothing for the enemy."

Church opened a file on the table. There had been a number of other positive developments.

"Really, like what?" Stone asked.

"Let me go quickly through them. Item one, by far the most important we think," Church nodded toward Thompson, "concerns the convoys of Chinese troop ships and their supply vessels. We've been tracking them by satellite and they seem to have come to a virtual standstill. Item two, the CIA tells us the Chinese President has cancelled all public engagements. They think there may be a rift in the new Politburo but they're only guessing. Item three, what we know for sure is the stream of cancel orders from the West to Chinese manufacturers has turned into a flood. When the global financial crisis struck China in 2008, for instance, fifteen thousand factories closed down in the Shanghai region alone. The number in this crisis is double that. This has all happened very quickly. The Politburo will have been taken by surprise, they wouldn't have foreseen this. Item four, the Politburo has a new headache. Dissidents in Tibet have taken advantage of China's preoccupation with us and there's been widespread, violent protests demanding independence."

Flipping over the page before him, Church continued down his list. Item five, America had announced its Pacific Fleet had put to sea from Hawaii on what it said was a routine deployment. Its destination was classified as normal.

Item six, more Chinese embassies and businesses had been attacked by angry mobs in the US and parts of Western Europe. Chinese airlines had cancelled all scheduled flights to America and Europe.

Church looked up at Stone and smiled. "You will like item seven: the Zambian and Congolese governments have announced the re-nationalising of their copper and zinc mines."

"Re-nationalising them? The Chinese paid billions for them only a few years ago," said Stone.

"They've decided to take the moral high ground," Church said. "They're keeping the money and taking back the mines to protest against ...," he leaned forward to read the fine print, "the criminal, illegal invasion of Australia."

Laughter broke out around the table. It had been a long time since that had happened, Stone thought.

"The Chinese are suffering the torture of a thousand cuts," he said, moving his weight on the chair.

"Prime Minister, don't read too much into any of this," Thompson said. "The enemy here will be angry at our response to their last ultimatum."

Folding both arms over his chest he said the ostensibly peaceful situation could well be because the Chinese commanders had not had the time to plan a major strike south.

"Well, why have the troop ships come to a standstill?" said Stone.

"They're not at a standstill, we said a virtual standstill. They're idling along at minimal speed. They haven't turned around," said Thompson.

"How much notice will we get if they decide to strike?"

"The first thing we'll see before any big campaign is their aircraft carrier come south."

Unfolding his arms and sitting forward the general sighed. "Our priority would be to defend Sydney."

Stone pushed his empty cup and saucer away on the table. "So Brisbane would be sacrificed?"

"It would have to be, Prime Minister." Thompson held his eye.

"About a third of our population lives around Sydney. We'll fight a rearguard action with what's left of our troops in Queensland but our firepower will have to be concentrated around Sydney to have any chance of holding off a Chinese invasion. Your END strategy and the hostage threat hasn't allowed us to mobilise. There wouldn't be time to move big troop numbers north, and I wouldn't recommend it anyway."

Opening a map, Thompson turned it toward Stone.

Standing up for a clearer view of it, Stone could see the infamous Brisbane Line of World War Two had been replaced by a Sydney Line. The plan would abandon a huge slice of the country.

The meeting had begun so cheerfully, he thought.

"A lot of their strategic moves depend on them managing to get the *Liaoning* south," Stone said.

Thompson gave Stone a tired look and shook his head slowly. "I don't think we can rely on the Collins in our planning, sir. *Rankin* is almost out of fuel. The *Sheean* would be on her own. The carrier has a screen of at least four destroyers and possibly a sub lurking around it. They're not good odds, I'm afraid."

All eyes turned to Stone. He stood and straightened his back. He remembered other tough times in his fifty-two years. He turned his chair around and sat with his arms resting over its back.

"Gentlemen, this is what I see. We've called their bluff on the hostages with a dirty bomb. They've attacked three high-rises in Surfers Paradise — but still nothing's happened to the prisoners. We've detonated another two bombs among them — and still they're silent. There's no sign of them mobilising, their leader has disappeared from sight, their ambassador has been recalled, their troop ships are on go-slow, the *Liaoning* is still cruising in circles up north, their economy is being crippled as we speak, and the Tibetans are in open revolt. So you tell me who's winning?"

They all looked at him guardedly. No one volunteered a comment.

"Unless the Chinese call at ten and say they've decided to leave,

I intend to detonate all three of the remaining bombs in our arsenal tomorrow."

7.30 a.m.

International Airport, Sydney

Anna Sharp booted up her Air New Zealand check-in computer. Water dripped onto the keyboard. She brushed her hair back again. She should have towelled it dry properly in the cloakroom.

She walked in the rain the last three kilometres to Sydney Airport. Any buses still running were jam-packed. The rest were awaiting a fuel shipment. The wait would be long. Shipping companies were refusing to risk their tankers in a war zone.

The Prime Minister's undertaking to insure the vessels had made no difference. The Australian dollar was now worth a mere twenty-three cents to the American dollar. The fuel's cost, if it ever arrived, would be prohibitive.

That morning she had watched an amateur video showing Chinese jets zooming between Gold Coast towers, unloading streaks of smoke that splattered into bright red-orange explosions on the side of the tall, white buildings.

Anna had come to work because the only other option was sitting at home. But now she looked up and saw the new queues before her check-in station and began to regret the decision. The bombings had created more panic for air tickets.

Airlines were scheduling more flights. Before her was a sea of anxious faces clutching air tickets worth a small fortune.

Her current customers were checking in to fly to Auckland. But they would take any plane, anywhere, so long as it was away from Australia.

Thousands were overcrowding resorts in Fiji, Tonga, Rarotonga, Norfolk Island and Hawaii. A few lucky ones made it to Los Angeles but usually only the really wealthy.

The private jet flights had stopped. Their owners and crew had

hightailed it after the rash of hijackings and violence on the tar-
macs.

She had escaped Queensland but was now trapped like millions of others in the southern states. Last night there had been
a noisy rally outside her apartment. The neighbouring park had
been crowded by protesters chanting *"Sign the treaty!"*.

She couldn't understand what the government was doing. Or
not doing. Then the Gold Coast had been raided and all those
people were carted away in ambulances. Some of them all cut up.
It was horrible.

She finally turned the television news off only to be reminded
of the crisis by the loudspeakers still blaring from protest leaders
in the park.

She looked up and took reservation forms from the bejewelled
hand of her first customer. She was envious. Chris's business had
been a good earner but turnover had now plummeted and their
combined savings wouldn't pay for half of one of these tickets,
even if they were allowed to withdraw more than a thousand dollars a day from their bank account.

Her car was locked permanently in the garage. Not because of
its value, which was very little, but because its petrol tank was
still half full.

Despite his age, Chris talked about volunteering for some role
in the army. She had burst into tears at the thought. And then felt
ashamed.

It was hard to believe life had been so good only a fortnight
ago.

She clicked at the keyboard. She noticed the woman with the
jewels was also wearing a fur coat and beaming as the boarding
tickets were punched out.

Her husband was fretting whether to abandon his briefcase or
the clothes in his carry-on. He decided to keep the briefcase. He
asked Anna what he should do with the expensive-looking carry-
on.

She suggested he give it to the poorest porter he could find. She
already had a sizeable collection of abandoned carry-ons. She

didn't want any more. These days she felt depressed every time she looked at them.

The wife took umbrage.

"The poorest porter?" she snorted.

She took her husband's bag and walked off toward the guest lounge. She was hoping to find an airport staffer more grateful for the goods. Good luck with that sweetheart, Anna thought.

The next couple had a single ticket. The woman was brushing back tears. She said they only had enough money for her to fly. Her husband was staying.

"Andrew says it'll be all right. Gary Stone will sort everything out but ... I don't know how he can." Her voice faded out.

Her itinerary document with the booking number was damp and smudged. She must have cried a lot of tears over it.

Anna focused firmly on her screen. She had gotten better — but not much — at blotting out the emotional drama confronting her routinely. She was at the coalface of the refugee panic every day. She tapped in the particulars. One economy-class seat to Auckland.

The boarding pass clicked from the printer. She pushed it toward the weeping woman, who shook her head as if repelled by it.

She backed away a few steps. Her husband stepped forward, thanked Anna quietly and took it. Holding his wife by the hand he led her gently toward the departure gate and Customs.

Anna pushed the COUNTER CLOSED sign and rushed to the cloakroom. She would go home. Anything was better than being trapped, helpless amid the unfolding desperation and fear swamping her check-in.

7.30 a.m.

The Lodge, Canberra

The early-morning briefing was rounding up when there was a

short rap on the door and Elaine appeared. Ignoring the others she said: "Gary, come with me — quickly."

Stone heaved himself from his chair and followed his wife. She led him along the corridor into the downstairs lounge and closed the door.

"What's going on?" said Stone, staring at Elaine's back as she stood before the television set, bringing it to life with the remote pad. She found the news channel she wanted and stood aside.

The image showed a Flying Doctor aircraft, the Brisbane International Airport terminal in the distant background. Someone in a white coat, presumably a doctor, was bending over a patient on a stretcher near the plane.

Two Flying Doctor paramedics watched anxiously from each end of the stretcher.

"They started showing this clip a few minutes ago. They've been repeating it since," said Elaine.

"But what's it showing? It's very fuzzy," said Stone.

Elaine turned and said: "I'm afraid the radioactive cat might be getting out of the bag again."

Stone moved closer to the television and its wobbly, blurry image.

The twenty-four-hour news channel anchor appeared: "We will be back shortly. Stay tuned for more on this breaking story."

A cartoon character advertising cheap car insurance replaced him.

"What's going on?" Stone repeated.

Elaine sat in one of the armchairs. "I had the television on upstairs. The Breaking News logo had flashed up, so I stopped to watch it."

The channel had received an amateur iPhone video from an airport worker that claimed to show a Flying Doctor aircraft landing on a mercy flight from within enemy territory. The worker claimed the flight was from a central Queensland airstrip near Port Abbot.

An ambulance and a doctor were sent to meet it.

The anchor reappeared, the Breaking News banner flashing

behind him. A skinny guy in a tight suit holding a microphone was standing outside Brisbane Hospital's emergency ambulance bay, sharing half the screen with the building.

Skinny was asked for an update. He complained he had little new information from the hospital authorities since a man in his mid-sixties had been admitted about an hour earlier.

He had been taken to the burns unit initially but had almost immediately been transferred to an isolation ward. No reason had been given for the transfer but clearly the authorities were keen to keep the man away from other patients and staff.

Ambulance staff had been more forthcoming. They told Skinny the man was charred down one side, his head hairless. They had not come across anything like it. They said their patient was alive but in a critical condition when they landed at a strip near Bowen, about six kilometres west of the port.

They had been surprised when the Chinese had called them in and asked them to take a patient to Brisbane for medical treatment. They had not been allowed to fly south of the Gladstone border since the invasion.

The Chinese had not given them any explanation for the patient's condition but had identified him as a Mr Jock Stanley, a night watchman at Port Abbot. Their English was poor and they seemed anxious to leave the scene and for the aircraft to get back in the air.

"I'll get the others," said Stone. He returned moments later and they all watched a repeat of the clips.

Twenty-four-hour news was really repeat news, thought Stone, something that could work in their favour. Skinny appeared exasperated at being once again asked for an update on a story that was hitting a brick wall.

Elaine remained seated and silent. The men stood in a small circle.

"We have to shut this down, and quickly. The patient is obviously a victim of the Port Abbot attack," said Stone.

"We could but you are the only Prime Minister to run a war

with no media censorship," said Thompson. "This is the sort of mess you get into."

Stone glared at the general. Both men were reaching the end of their tether. Able intervened: "Well, we can't introduce it now, suddenly. The story would grow legs quicker than you could say END," he said.

Elaine touched the mute button.

"Can you see what's going on here, Gary?" she said. "The Chinese won't lift their communications blackout, so they've flown in some live evidence of our attacks. They'll let the media do the rest of the job of exposing the Emergency Nuclear Deterrent for them. They're certain public outrage will force you to sign the border treaty."

Stone nodded. "I know. If the patient is confirmed publicly as a radiation victim, Whittacker will step in, claim he was opposed to END and have all he needs to pull off his coup."

A wave of exhaustion and depression gripped him. Only minutes ago he had been on top of the world. The tide had seemed to be with him at last. Now his feet were being whipped from under him. He shook with the feeling of self-pity and turned to Elaine.

She moved in her armchair and folded her arms. "There's no point in arguing over spilt milk. Give the news channels something else to talk about and it will go on the back burner pretty smartly."

The others glanced at her.

"You're right," said Able. "Feed the chooks."

"But what can we feed them?" said Stone.

There was a long silence.

"Why don't we just feed them the story they've already half got? The Chinese have arranged medical treatment for a port worker badly burned in an industrial accident. Meanwhile we'll keep the real cause of his condition away from the media by sending some medics to ferry him away to a military hospital. The army does have some specialist burns units."

"It might work," said Able. "I'll get the media team to work.

While I'm arranging that I think General Thompson ought to call the hospital and make them an offer they can't refuse."

"Okay, let's do that," said Stone.

"Stay here, Frank," he added as Able and Thompson left.

"While they're busy with that, can you have someone from your dark arts gang pull the electric plug on that television station for the next hour?"

"No point, Prime Minister. All the television stations have back-up electricity generators," said Church.

"But they do suffer bomb scares, don't they? Occasionally, they have to evacuate their staff if there's a genuine threat," said Stone.

Elaine turned her head to listen, a scowl clouding her face.

"Yes, sir, they do suffer bomb scares and need to evacuate," Church nodded his head. "Particularly if the police tell them there is a real and present threat."

He turned and left the room.

Elaine stood up. "Oh, how quickly power can go to the head when plans start to go awry."

"Don't lecture me," Stone said. "It's essential the END business remains secret."

He stood in front of her, putting his hands on his hips. "I'm on the verge of winning this war, which everyone else thinks is an impossibility. We just have to hold our nerve for the next few days."

"You really think we're winning?" said Elaine.

Stone looked stunned at the question.

"Yes, really," he said. "Don't you?"

Elaine leaned back in the lounge chair, looking up at him. "You know I'll support you, and whatever you think is best. But you need to keep your feet on the ground. The last thing we need is a desperate dictator abusing his power. That won't help anyone or save Australia."

She got up, kissed him on the cheek and left. On the television screen Skinny had been replaced by a Blondie.

Stone sat down. His wife's comments hung in the air. He watched the channel's latest attempt for a fresh angle. They interviewed a few more airport workers but none could add a skerrick of new information to the story. The Breaking News banner continued to flash in hope.

Elaine's comments had surprised and disturbed him. He was no desperate dictator. Was he? No. He was more like a desperate gambler. He had to appear in control, confident. The Chinese had to blink.

The door opened and Church returned. He nodded to Stone and pointed to the television set. Stone saw Blondie sign off and the news channel logo fill the screen. A recorded voice began repeating a message. The station was experiencing a technical fault with its satellite and would resume normal broadcasts shortly.

"The police bomb squad are on their way, sir. ASIO intercepted a credible terrorist threat to the station. The station has agreed to evacuate the building while the police conduct a thorough search," said Church.

Stone thanked him. His action had been a bit dictatorial. But it was a good feeling, snapping one's fingers and having television stations shut down and oil tankers hijacked for their cargo.

He had the entire apparatus of the state at his fingertips. Perhaps no other Australian Prime Minister had ever had the power he was able to wield right now.

He massaged his left knee and was about to stand when Thompson and Able reappeared.

"Sorry, Prime Minister, the hospital won't let him out," said Thompson. "They say he is in a critical condition and can't be moved."

"Jesus," said Stone. "So much for the dictator ..."

"Pardon?" said Thompson.

"Oh, sorry, nothing."

Thompson said: "One of their doctors is ex-Army. He's speculating from his training that the burns are consistent with being caught in a nuclear blast. He's wanting an explanation from the Chinese. He thinks the Chinese may be using tactical nuclear weapons against locals who've formed guerrilla bands and started a serious fight with them up north."

"Good God," said Stone.

"And he's calling in a specialist to confirm the patient has radiation sickness."

"Fuck," said Stone.

Able began shaking his head. Another drama to overcome, somehow.

"At least none of the media knows this doctor's suspicions yet, sir," he said.

The four men stood in a familiar circle.

"Prime Minister, this doctor is a national security risk," Church said. "He's not qualified to make these assertions and create widespread, unfounded public concern."

"You mean we should arrest him?" said Stone. "Get him out of the way quick?"

Church nodded.

Thompson said: "Okay. Let's kill two birds with one stone. We'll use a chopper and the hospital's landing pad. It's on the roof. We'll grab the doctor and stretcher the patient out. There will be nothing for the television crews to film from the ground."

"Well, the next thing we better do is announce the injured man has recently returned from Africa and has a contagious disease," said Able.

He tore up the media release he was holding.

"You're a devious bugger, John," said Stone grinning.

"Yes, Prime Minister. I'll organise a new media statement. We can have it out there before that station comes back on their air. That won't be till we tell the police to pack in their bomb search."

"That means its rival stations will actually have the contagious disease story before they do," said Stone.

"That's the breaks in newsland," said Able. "The new angle sabotages their story completely. They'll follow the new scent."

"What about the poor bugger that's half melted? What happens with his medical treatment while we're whisking him about the place like a piece of baggage?" said Stone.

"Prime Minister, the guy is toast. There's nothing anyone will be able to do for him," said Thompson. "Even if he was able to survive the burns, which is highly unlikely, the radiation sickness will kill him in the next thirty days at the latest."

"And he won't be the only bomb victim, sir," said Church.

Thompson nodded. "No, he won't, but there won't be very many, sir. Our boys said the port was basically deserted when the detonation occurred. Just a few night-shift staff and Chinese guards. There were no ships loading. The nearest town is Bowen. The wind was a southeasterly as usual, and the radioactive cloud was blown away from the city."

Stone said: "Okay, let's get busy. Make sure the doctor and his specialist burns mate don't speak to any media. Get them both out of the way for the next few days and take the hospital manager with you for good measure. He knows too much."

An hour later, back on air, the news channel learned it would cost them $20,000 a time if it wanted to re-broadcast the iPhone video clip. The grainy clip was never seen again.

ASIO had quietly gone into the media business. The airport worker who had taken the film had signed a copyright deal with an overseas news agency no one had ever heard of and pocketed $50,000.

Blondie was now back in the studio where she broke the latest, sensational news in the Flying Doctor story. She had a much bigger story to tell, she said.

The evil Chinese had apparently used a so-called mercy flight only to offload a victim suffering a highly contagious African disease. They were probably hoping it would spread rapidly through southern Queensland. It was a sick form of germ warfare, she concluded gravely.

The victim had now been flown to a special isolation centre for treatment. There was no threat to public health. No further details were currently available.

Meanwhile bushfires were sweeping through more than three hundred hectares west of Brisbane. More of this Breaking News would follow shortly.

There was a brief sighting of Skinny standing patiently against a background of blackened, smoking farmland ready to deliver an update after the commercials. The Breaking News banner was flashing triumphantly.

The chooks had been fed.

1.30 p.m.

The Lodge, Canberra

The message came just as Stone had finished a good lunch. The latest Chinese deadline had come and gone three and a half hours ago. Nothing had happened, giving The Lodge's routine a surreal edge as the SAS was far away busy positioning the last three bombs.

The message was handed to him by one of the secretaries. Stone thanked her and unfolded it. His heart rate jumped. It was from the Foreign Minister. It contained only four words. "Call me ASAP. Lindsay."

Clutching it tightly in one fist, Stone walked in dread slowly up the stairs to his private office on the first floor and closed the door. He straightened out the note on the desk and tapped it slowly with one finger. He saw his hand was trembling.

He lifted the phone to his ear. The dial tone droned ominously. He put it back in the cradle.

Did ASAP mean good news or bad news? Had Whittacker rounded up the numbers he needed? Or did Noble have good news he wanted to tell him as soon as possible?

Outside it was another hot, cloudless day. Christmas was fast approaching. He had planned the family's Christmas dinner for so long he couldn't imagine it not being held at The Lodge.

He knew he wouldn't be spending it at his luxury, waterfront apartment on the Gold Coast.

After the Surfers Paradise attack, Joe Martini had discovered what the final target of the raid had been. A Chinese jet had veered away from its two companions just north of the main resort and launched a single missile.

The missile had torn into the luxury, low-rise Allisee Apartments. He had emailed Stone a private message with several photos before flying back to Canberra.

"Hi, Gazza. The Chairman of the People's Republic has left u a personal calling card. After the main raid today, one jet went up the coast and put a missile through your front window. Precision bombing. No casualties in the bldg. Missile had no warhead but it has wrecked your pad. Media still unaware u r owner. Maybe u should take yr personal listing and address out of the local phone book!! C u tomorrow. Regards from Paradise, Joe. PS Luv to Elaine. Tell her charcoal is the in colour."

The photographs showed the blackened interior walls of the apartment. Smoke was still rising from the ruins of smashed furniture. His favourite painting was miraculously still hanging from the lounge wall but lopsided and scorched.

The attack had left a gaping black hole in the front of the building where the big plate-glass window had been blasted to smithereens.

He had shown the email and photos to Elaine last night. She looked through them, shaking her head sadly.

"They want you to know you're in a war," she said. "Imagine if any of the family had been there? God, what'll it be next?"

What would it be next? He hadn't told her about Noble's call and Whittacker's manoeuvrings.

Stone lifted the phone again and slowly punched in the numbers for the Foreign Minister's direct line. It rang several times and when it was answered he could hear voices in the background. Noble was evidently in a meeting.

He must have seen Stone's name come up on the phone's call identity screen and answered it immediately.

Stone heard the background voices fade away while his heartbeat ratcheted up. A few seconds later Noble said: "Good morning, Gary."

"Well, it's started off very well," Stone said. "Those intelligence reports are the best news we've had since this whole business started. Particularly the troop carriers virtually becalmed."

"Yes, I saw them. It was good news," Noble said.

"Better than good, wouldn't you say? More like great news."

Noble didn't reply. Stone's receiver vibrated against his ear. He realised his hand was still trembling badly.

He kept his voice as light as he could: "You left a message, Lindsay."

"Gary, I didn't want to be the one to tell you this."

"Tell me what?"

Stone heard Noble draw a deep breath and a door shut.

"It's over, I'm afraid. You've been rolled."

"Oh no." Stone slumped in his chair.

"Whittacker's got the numbers. I'm sorry, Gary."

Stone felt like he'd been hit by a truck.

"He's going to convene a special Cabinet meeting tomorrow afternoon at four and table a motion of no confidence if you don't resign."

Stone then heard a second voice in the background. He heard Noble telling the person to come back later.

"The word is he's going to call you shortly and ask you to announce your resignation today," Noble said. "Gary ... are you still there?"

Stone muttered a reply.

"Gary, I can't hear you," Noble said.

"Just when things are starting to go our way," Stone repeated. His voice was rasping, sticking in his dry throat.

He pushed his chair away to stand. "You know the world will never be the same if China gets away with this. There are so many people depending on us to stand up to them."

"I'm afraid Whittacker is hell bent on coming to an agreement with them. He asked me to formally contact Chang Leng and invite him to Canberra tomorrow morning to resume the border talks. Chang is the Vice Premier, who was meant to be at yesterday's meeting with Martini. Of course, I had to decline his request. I told him there was nothing I could do officially through the ministry until he is the Prime Minister."

"Quite right. Good for you," said Stone.

"But he is going ahead with a private invitation anyway. He's even trying to organise a guard of honour for the arrival. I don't know what the legalities are on that sort of thing."

Stone didn't know either. "Will you stay on in Cabinet?" he asked.

"Well, I don't think I'll be very welcome after today's little squabble," Noble said.

Stone sighed. "Lindsay, I appreciate your call. And all your efforts. I'll speak to you later. Right now I'd better go and tell Elaine what's happened."

Stone ended the call and reached for his pocket. He gasped down a measure of nitrate spray and went to find his wife.

He would be too late.

* * *

Desolate and breathless, Stone walked slowly down the passage toward their private quarters. As he reached them, the door flew open and Elaine appeared, distraught.

"Gary, what's going on?"

Stone looked at her, startled.

"I've just had Joanna Whittacker on the phone," she said.

Stone felt his body stiffen.

"She said she called to chat, now the news was out."

Stone shook his head. "Oh, dear God."

"She asked if we have any personal furniture here. She's having all the government furniture removed. She's bringing her own. I had no idea what she was talking about. I feel so humiliated."

Stone was dumbfounded. He stood speechless and then took her arm and guided her back inside the bedroom. They sat together on the big ottoman.

"I have just put the phone down from Lindsay Noble. I was

coming to tell you. Darling, I'm out. Whittacker has the numbers."

She leaned against his shoulder. He heard her muffled voice: "How could this happen? Why has the Cabinet suddenly decided to back Whittacker?"

He hugged her and sighed. "They're very scared. They want an end to this whole business."

Elaine sat up. "We're all scared. So what?"

Turning fully to face him, she said: "So does this mean we've lost the Top Half? The Chinese win?"

Stone avoided her stare and shrugged.

"What a little weasel Whittacker is. He got his wife to make the first call. He hasn't got the balls to do it himself."

Stone laughed at her indignation. "Language, my dear, language. You are still the First Lady till four tomorrow afternoon. A little decorum, please."

"Bugger that," she said.

She fluttered a hand in front of her. "No, no. No government furniture, thank you. What a snooty bitch. That call would have made her day."

Elaine paused for moment, collecting her thoughts.

She stood up. "Well, the good news is you can now go and have that heart procedure done, and get fit again."

Before he could speak, the security phone warbled. Stone struggled up to answer it. He recognised Thompson's voice immediately.

He was about to face another mutiny.

* * *

"The city is a mass of rumours you're resigning," the general said with no preamble.

"I'm afraid it's true, Alan."

"Christ," Thompson said.

"Whittacker's got his little coup all organised," said Stone. "He has the numbers to roll me. I've just had Noble on the phone confirming it. There will be a Cabinet meeting at four tomorrow afternoon."

"I see," Thompson said.

"He's terrified of the Chinese. He's privately invited their Vice Premier to Canberra tomorrow for a chat about peace and harmony."

Neither man said anything for several seconds. Thompson broke the silence: "Prime Minister, what does this mean for the orders you gave me this morning?"

"The orders stand. I'm still the PM and the Defence Minister, and the Cabinet has authorised me to carry out the END policy and that's what I'll be doing until they remove me."

Thompson cleared his throat. "With all due respect, Prime Minister, this places me in a very awkward position."

Stone said nothing.

Thompson said: "This gives me an ethical dilemma. I know the government is about to sue for peace. It will abandon the nuclear strategy and the plans to attack the *Liaoning*."

"No, no, Alan. You're wrong. It's me who has the ethical dilemma. You have your orders."

There was another silence between them. Finally, Thompson said: "You know it's not as simple as that."

Pinpricks of sharp pain swarmed over Stone's chest. He said: "Yes, it is as simple as that. General, what would you have me do? Give up now? Surrender the country?"

There was no reply.

"You've heard the latest intelligence reports. We are not beaten. They're the ones in disarray."

The general said nothing. Christ, I'm in another bluffing game, thought Stone.

"General, are you asking me to blink at this late hour?"

"No, sir, I'm not asking you to blink. I'm just clarifying my orders."

Stone stabbed the nitrate bottle under his tongue and fired a new shot of spray. How many was that today?

"Thank you, General. About those orders, I've decided we'll detonate the last three bombs later than we planned.

"I want them to go off at ten thirty tomorrow morning and not two o'clock. And I want the Collins to attack the *Liaoning* and her escorts as soon as possible after that."

In the pause that followed, Stone could sense the general computing the change of plan.

"Ten thirty in the morning, yes, sir. You realise the bombs will probably detonate while the Chinese Vice Premier is still in the air en route to Canberra to see Whittacker?"

"Yes, exactly."

"What is it you're hoping to achieve at the eleventh hour, sir?"

Stone pulled his chair back and put both feet on his desk. It was something he rarely did. As a kid he'd seen photographs of President Nixon doing it.

He had always regarded it as an arrogant posture. Today he had to feel a little arrogant. He refused to feel the game was lost.

"General, when you're bluffing with a weak hand you never know till the very last second whether the other guy is going to fold. You're trying to make sure he's under as much pressure as you are," said Stone.

He chuckled. "I'm going to put a bomb up Chang as he's flying in for peace talks. What do you think Beijing will make of that?"

Stone waited.

"I don't know, sir," Thompson said.

Stone crossed his legs on the desk and stretched comfortably back in the chair. He should have tried this position before. Then he remembered what happened to Nixon. He was impeached and booted out of office.

He put one leg back on the floor. "I'm not folding my hand until four p.m. tomorrow when Cabinet meets. I'm playing out every last second."

Thompson murmured something as though he understood and Stone was ending the conversation when the general abruptly interrupted him: "Prime Minister, I would just like to say it's been a privilege to serve under you, sir. I'll be resigning myself tomorrow afternoon. If you'll excuse me, sir, I have to go now. I have Admiral Robson on the other line."

He ended the call before Stone could respond. He looked around. Elaine had left the room. He decided it was time to talk to Able.

As he went downstairs he reflected on Whittacker's failure to call him. He realised he was already suffering the inevitable fate of all lame-duck leaders: irrelevance.

* * *

Stone could see from Able's face news of the coup had spread fast. Able stood up as he entered.

"I'm sorry, sir," he said. "This is a sad day for Australia."

Stone gave him a small smile.

Able was unable to return it.

Stone briefed him on the new attack orders and their timing. Able couldn't hide the expression of surprise on his face.

"I know," Stone said, "but I'm not blinking — and I'm still the Prime Minister."

Able studied his boss. "Yes. Yes, you are, sir."

His eyes dropped to messages on the desk. The Deputy Prime Minister's Office had called seeking an appointment for Whittacker early tomorrow morning.

Whittacker's private secretary said Stone would be asked at the meeting to resign before Cabinet convened. He felt it would make things less messy.

"Less messy," repeated Stone.

"Yes, Prime Minister, less messy. Mr Whittacker would also like to take the opportunity after the meeting to show his wife around The Lodge — to refresh her memory on its décor."

"That'll be the bloody day," said Stone. "Tell his office I have too many commitments to schedule a meeting tomorrow morning."

Able nodded and said there had also been a call from Admiral Robson. He had asked in a roundabout way about the Whittacker situation.

"Did he say if his beloved subs are still holding together?"

"Yes, he did, sir. The subs are holding together but the crews are exhausted from playing hide and seek with the Chinese Navy."

"I know, I know. A few more hours and it'll be over," said Stone. "He's getting his attack orders as we speak. Meanwhile get Whittacker on the line; he's clearly in no hurry to ring me. I'll take the call upstairs."

As he turned to leave, Able handed him an envelope.

"That's my resignation, sir, effective at four tomorrow afternoon."

Stone stopped in his tracks. He looked at the envelope and his emotions threatened to overwhelm him. He took it without a word, reaching across the desk to shake Able's hand. He turned abruptly and left.

* * *

The phone jangled four minutes later. Sitting back in his chair Stone lifted the receiver: "Stone."

"Oh, Gary. I was just going to call you."

Whittacker's voice was casual and friendly.

"You seemed to have found time to call everyone else," said Stone.

"Now, Gary. There is no point in the two of us arguing."

"I'm not arguing, Jeremey."

"Gary, you have lost the support of your Cabinet. I'm very sorry it has come to this."

"I'm sure you are."

"We all know you did what you thought was best but most of us can no longer go along with your scorched earth policy."

"It wasn't my policy, Jeremey," said Stone. "It was the policy of the majority of Cabinet."

Whittacker ignored the remark. "We also think we will lose the support of the public when they discover what is occurring with these dirty bombs in the north. The backlash could destroy our party."

"Destroy our party?" Stone said, "Are you seriously worried about party politics right now?"

"Gary, we are acting to save the country as well as the party. We don't believe the Chinese will succumb to the sort of pressure you're trying to assert. They'll simply decontaminate the bombed areas and rebuild the infrastructure themselves. I think if we don't reach an accommodation with the Chinese immediately they'll take the rest of the country and we'll all end up as coolies."

Stone sighed. "Jeremey, I have a proposition for you. If it becomes public knowledge — and it will — that you plotted against me to become Prime Minister in the middle of this crisis, you will be regarded as a quisling, even in the vassal state we will become. But I will resign willingly if you give me one more week in office. If nothing changes I will plead ill health and resign. You will become the Prime Minister and go ahead with your peace treaty talks. I believe we are reaching a tipping point and the prospect of a full Chinese invasion is fading. Whatever the out-come, I will plead ill health and resign in a week and you will be the new PM."

Whittacker was silent. His mind raced. This was out of left field. He would become Prime Minister without rancour. But, he thought, he was going to anyway. He had the numbers. The lead-ership was his in a day's time.

Joanna would be a wonderful First Lady. It was what she had always wanted. Now he could give it to her. People would under-stand his need to halt Stone's brutal poison pill strategy when they learned of it.

And if Stone, by some miracle, turned the tide on the Chinese, there would be no guarantee he wouldn't renege on the deal.

This could be his only chance of being Prime Minister. He couldn't hesitate. He was too close to his prize.

"I'm sorry, Gary. It's too late. The die is cast," he said.

Stone felt the last vestiges of his power slipping away. "All right, Jerry, but you know you're giving the country away and our respite from the Chinese will be temporary. They will come for the rest of us when it suits them."

"Oh, it's Jerry now, is it — Gazza?" said Whittacker. There was anger in his voice.

"Yes, Jerry. My wife was right. You really are a little weasel," said Stone. "And if your wife dares to set one foot inside The Lodge before tomorrow night I'll have her arrested."

He paused, then added: "And, Jerry, warn her not to get too comfortable. The Chinese will want the place soon enough for themselves — and they'll probably keep your furniture."

Whittacker scoffed: "Well, I think it was my wife who was right. She said you were a buffoon whose only talent has been to run a trucking company in the provinces. And you can plead ill health right now and resign, Gazza. Everyone has seen you panting after taking six steps. Who do you think you've been fooling? You're not fit for the job physically or mentally."

Whittacker drew breath. "You're just hanging on trying to be a hero figure and killing thousands of innocents while you're doing it."

Stone moved to replace the receiver. "Whittacker, this conversation is over, but you should know this: I'd rather be a hero trying to win than a gutless coward giving in."

He hung up. Elaine's head peered around the door. "Who were you arguing with?"

"Whittacker," he said.

"Oh, him," she said and closed the door again.

6.15 p.m.

Lavarack Barracks, Townsville

"There's a Private Alan Morris asking to see you, sir. He says it's urgent."

Brigadier Lesley Silvey slumped lower in his chair and checked his watch. He had never heard of the man. If a soldier wanted to speak to someone in authority there were channels. One just didn't knock on the boss's door in the Army.

Silvey felt worn down. The last fifteen days had been the worst of his career.

He had finally authorised the mass break-out attempt most of his men had been urging on him. It was timed for 5.30 p.m. tomorrow. To maintain absolute secrecy, the rank and file would not be told of the plan until the last minute.

Lavarack, with three thousand personnel living on base, had been the biggest military installation seized in the Chinese terrorist raid.

He had been the man in charge. The man responsible. The loss of the base had neutralised the Army's only big, battle-ready force. He had been depressed and racked with guilt since.

Until today he had steadfastly refused to consider a break-out — and for good reason. Or reasons. None of which had pacified his restless men.

The morning after the takeover he had been escorted to his old office to visit the Chinese Commandant, Major Hu. He heard first-hand the BBC radio news: the Australian Government was negotiating a new border north of Brisbane.

The report hinted an agreement was imminent. Major Hu had taken the opportunity to warn him he would shoot ten prisoners for every one that attempted to go over the fence. Silvey had subsequently insisted there was to be no maverick, individual escape bids.

He knew most of his men were sure he had lost his bottle. His two medals for valour were counting for nothing in the raging debates in the barracks.

Time had dragged by without any further news of the promised border settlement, or surrender, as he thought of it. He now believed the talks had gone off the rails somehow. It had been too long.

Then two days ago one of the base's doctors had been taken under guard to the Townsville Hospital where a number of people were being treated for severe burns.

The patients were beyond any meaningful medical help. On his return the doctor said it appeared they were victims of a violent blast or firestorm.

The news blackout in the occupied area seemed to be complete. The cyber attacks on the communications infrastructure had clearly been devastating.

The only news from the outside world reaching Lavarack came from rumours spread by the civilian truck drivers delivering their meagre rations. The drivers had all heard of the big explosion at Port Abbot but the reason remained a mystery. They hoped it had been the work of saboteurs.

His soldiers tomorrow night would be armed with only clubs of broken furniture when they attempted to surprise and overrun their guards. The guard posts, the Chinese barracks and the armoury would be attacked simultaneously.

Silvey would then mobilise quickly to attack the enemy garrison in Townsville and recapture the airport, destroying any Chinese fighter jets there.

A polite cough broke into his thoughts. The steward stood awkwardly by the door where he had been patiently waiting for a response.

He saw the brigadier had, again, drifted off in his own thoughts. He had become a different man since his capture.

From his position in the doorway, the steward could see Morris waiting outside in the corridor, impatiently moving his weight from one leg to the other.

Morris had used his initiative to get this far, the steward thought. He had told the Chinese guard posted at the entrance he was rostered to serve in the mess that night. The indifferent guard had let him through without checking the story.

"Any idea what he wants?" said Silvey.

"No, sir. Just that it was urgent and he had to speak to you directly."

Silvery raised his eyebrows. "Who is this Private Morris, do you know?"

"He's with Sergeant Keith Patterson's platoon, sir. You know, the mob on guard the night the Chinese showed up."

Silvey nodded. The platoon was now infamous.

"All right. Ask him to come in."

The steward turned and left. Moments later Morris strode purposefully in and stood to attention. He looked nervous.

Silvey stood wearily and the private saluted.

"Private, I understand you have something urgent you need to tell me?"

"Yes, sir."

"Well, let's hear it."

Morris broke out in a sweat.

"Sir, my sergeant got some very bad news today. His son is in 2nd Battalion. He was one of the guys outside the camp on a survival exercise when the Chinese hit us. One of the local delivery drivers told him the body of his son, Johnny's his name, has been found washed ashore near Bowen."

Silvey nodded.

Morris coughed, struggling to find the words he needed.

"Johnny had had his neck broken, sir."

"Well, private, I'm very sad to hear that," said Silvey.

"Thank you, sir. But the thing is … the sarge heard all the rumours about the big blast near Bowen and is sure Johnny was involved — he's sure the Chinese have murdered him. The sarge is very upset, sir. He broke down completely when he heard the news. He's completely distraught. He's been quite out of it since the Chinks surprised us in the guardhouse. Now he's just …"

"Private, I'm sorry to hear that as well. Any father would be grief-stricken," said Silvey. "Could you not have told your own platoon leader about his state?"

Beads of sweat ran down Morris's face even as he paled. He began to reply but only a stutter of words came out.

"What is it, private?"

"Sir, the sarge, he's a good man … one of the best … I don't want to do anything that would get him in trouble … but the thing is, he's talking of breaking out tonight, sir."

Silvey groaned. "Oh no."

"He wants revenge. He wants to kill some Chinks. Johnny was his only son. He wants me and a couple of the other squad members to go with him. He says he's tired of waiting for the brass to get the balls to take the Chinks on."

Silvey slowly folded his arms and stared at Morris.

"You know what would happen if he, or any of you, makes an attempt to scarper, don't you?"

"Yes, sir … the Chinks will kill ten of us for every one that tries to get over the fence."

Silvey nodded. "Private Morris, I know it hasn't been easy for you to come here but you've done the right thing." He saw a wave of relief cross Morris's clammy face.

Silvey returned to his chair. He stroked his leathery face and looked at the table in front of him for long seconds.

He knew an attempt to grab Patterson physically in his current mental state would be dangerous. A loud fracas would draw the attention of the guards who were already a jittery mob.

Somehow he had to quietly neutralise Patterson.

"Private, as you know there are a lot of lives at stake here," Silvey said. "I want you to keep that in mind when I tell you what I've decided."

Morris looked stricken.

"Do you understand, private?"

"Yes, sir … I think, sir."

"Where has Patterson chosen to attempt his escape?"

Morris told him.

"Okay. I want you to tell Patterson he will have a much greater chance of getting away if only you and he go alone."

"You want us to have a go, sir?" Morris looked perplexed.

"Yes, I do, private. But you won't get very far," said Silvey.

"Sir, I don't understand."

"You will be caught as soon as you leave the barracks you're in."

"Who will catch us that quick, sir? We know our way round this base like the back of our hand. They'd have trouble catching us straight away."

"No, private, they won't have any trouble catching you straight away."

Morris shook his head. "How can you be so sure of that, sir?"

"I'll be tipping off the Chinese."

Morris stared at his commander. "But we'd be shot, sir."

Silvey said: "No, there's no chance of that, private. I'll be speaking to the Chinese commandant myself. I'll do a deal that no harm will come to either of you. I'll tell him I am honouring an agreement with him that no one will attempt an escape."

Morris looked through half-closed eyes. Had Patterson been right? Were the brass too gutless to have a go?

"Private, I need to tell you a couple of things. First, I have no such agreement with Commandant Hu but he'd like to think I have. Secondly, I promise you, your stay in the detention block will be a very short one."

Morris stood up straight. "How can you guarantee that, sir?"

"Do you trust me, private?"

There was a very long silence. Morris looked at the floor.

"Well, private?"

"Yes, sir … I think so, sir."

"Well, know so, son. Nothing will happen to you. Your sergeant will just think you've been unlucky when you walk straight into the Chinese. Don't resist capture. You will be back with all of us in a very short space of time."

Morris nodded unhappily: "A very short space of time …"

"Yes. A very short space of time," said Silvey.

The look in Morris's eyes softened and he slowly nodded. Silvey saw a glimmer of understanding on the soldier's face.

Morris came to attention and saluted. "Understood, sir. Permission to leave, sir."

Silvey returned the salute with a sharp nod and the slightest of smiles. "Permission granted."

"Yes, sir. Thank you, sir." He did a parade ground perfect about turn and left.

The steward reappeared and announced the evening meal was about to be served in the Officers' Mess.

Silvey said: "All right. I'll be right along but I've got to make a friendly call on Commandant Hu first."

DAY SIXTEEN

Brigadier

9.08 a.m.

Gladstone Harbour, Queensland

"We're going to have to go back in."

SAS squad leader Sergeant Blackie Johnson swore under his breath. The newly seconded Private Jabril Allunga had a bad habit of stating the obvious.

The Aboriginal signals man — their chook — was tapping his watch. He could be an annoying bugger.

"I can tell the bloody time, Jabril," Blackie said. "Check comms again and ask if they know what's up."

The 9 a.m. satellite test signal to their second bomb had failed.

Jabril lay still, hidden among the scrub. "Waste of time. The satellite signal or the bomb's aerial isn't working. Something's gone wrong."

"Just do the check, will you?"

The test signal failure meant they would have to dig up the bomb they had carefully concealed the night before. It was beneath a metre of coal. It would need to be manually primed.

This would allow it to be detonated by their own wireless. The catch was their wireless had to be within a kilometre of the device when the signal was sent. They would need to find somewhere safe to shelter close by.

Meanwhile they would have to re-enter the Tanna Coal Export

terminal in broad daylight. They had little time left to accomplish the mission. The detonation timing had been changed from 2 a.m. to 10.30 a.m. — less than ninety minutes away.

They were perched on a small rise overlooking both the big coal export terminals in Gladstone Harbour. Their three fellow squad members had moved last night, as planned, twelve kilometres south of the blast area once the bomb was in position.

He and Jabril had waited to watch for any sign of the bomb being discovered. It was not allowed to fall into enemy hands at any cost.

The bomb would obliterate the terminal and its radioactive fallout would spread over the nearby Wiggins Island terminal as well, fanned by the steady, prevailing southeasterly winds. The winds that would blow the deadly fallout cloud away from the thirty-two thousand unsuspecting residents of Gladstone and their three comrades.

The two terminals represented the world's fourth-biggest export complex. It was about to be made worthless to the Chinese. Two terminals for the price of one. It had been an excellent plan. Now it wasn't.

It had become overcomplicated the minute they arrived and surveyed the scene. Jabril had sighted a collection of shacks only five kilometres to the northwest, in the immediate path of the fallout.

The ramshackle settlement was the current home of the tiny Durumbai Aboriginal clan sitting, ignored, outside bustling Gladstone city. Through their binoculars they could see people and young children moving about the dusty, forlorn camp. Jabril recognised friends and extended family among them.

Any attempt to reach and warn the inhabitants would jeopardise the mission. Blackie pointed out the Gladstone population would face the same risks if the wind suddenly swung about. No one would be allowed to warn them either.

The Aboriginal settlement would have to take its chances.

Jabril looked stricken. What chances? The Aboriginals had no chance, he argued. Their mission had been planned so Gladstone's population was unlikely to be in any real danger.

The squad members looked to Blackie for their lead. He was trying to look resolute. But he was torn.

The squad medic, Glen Selby, said: "Well, Jabril, I think we would be able to get over there and back without too much bother but that's not the real problem. How the hell would we get a hundred people to pick up sticks and move? We would have to give them a compelling reason. It can't be the real reason. They might not want to go. And if they did, their movement would have the Chinks swarming all over the place."

No one said anything. Jabril sat and took a long swig from his water bottle. He stared at the settlement.

"If we can get over there, I'll get them to move," he said finally.

"How?" said Blackie.

Jabril crossed his long skinny legs and sat upright. "They'll 'go walkabout'. They will move when I tell them bad spirits are about to descend on their homes. And I'll be telling them the truth."

Selby shook his head. "Look, we'd all like to save them but their sudden mass movement would be seen by the Chinks. They've never heard of whole villages going walkabout."

Jabril said: "Don't worry, the Chinks won't see them — they'll disappear. None of them will move until it's dark."

Selby frowned. "But how far would they get before the bomb's detonated?"

Jabril waved one leg in the air. "We were given long, skinny legs for moving far and fast when we had to hunt. And, anyway, I'll tell them they must walk south, away from the fallout. They will be well clear of danger."

Blackie had agonised as he listened to the exchange. He was on a top-secret mission to detonate a radioactive blast. It would destroy a huge chunk of important infrastructure and cause casualties.

Bloody Jabril was now making the civilian collateral damage real. He was definitely an annoying bugger.

"All right, chookie, this is what we'll do," he said.

Jabril turned a fearful gaze at him.

"Jabril, you're the owl. You fly over there and warn them. But you'll have to fly on your own. If you don't come back, the rest of us will take care of the bomb."

Jabril nodded excitedly, tears of relief ran down his face.

Blackie turned back to face the terminal. "You'll have to lose your uniform. And you'll have to go unarmed. Look like you're one of them."

"Yes, yes. I can do that."

"If you get stopped, your best defence will be to act drunk," said Blackie.

Jabril pulled a face. "It would be a struggle — but I think I could probably pull it off."

He laughed and slapped his side. The troopers shook their heads.

They made him drink the last drop from his army water flask before they confiscated it. They stripped him to his underwear. The underwear was non-Army issue. Territorial soldiers supplied their own.

As he was about to leave, Blackie pulled him aside. "Drunk or not, keep well clear of the Chinks. They're very jittery and trigger-happy at the moment. People like you keep blowing up their new real estate assets."

Jabril had shaken his hand and vanished down the hillside.

As night fell after the quick-death Queensland sunset, he silently reappeared.

The Aboriginal settlement had been quietly abandoned.

At midnight the squad moved out toward the terminal. Their infiltration went perfectly. They went undetected and the bomb was hidden.

* * *

"It's not going to blow."

"Christ, Jabril. Can you change the tune?"

The signalman crawled up beside Blackie, who was scanning

the terminal through his binoculars. There were no ships loading and the terminal appeared deserted except for a few guards sporadically wandering its perimeter.

"Comms say it's a technical glitch," said Jabril.

"Fuck," said Blackie. "We'll have to trigger the bloody thing ourselves. The sort of exercise Dr Yu had warned would be detrimental to the health unless you were very close to a very deep hole. Get Selby on the wireless."

Selby answered the radio instantly. Blackie took the mike: "Selley? The bomb's broke. The test transmission failed."

Selby laughed. "I hope Dirty Dawson doesn't hear about it. Round two with Dr Yu would be entertaining."

"It would be but Yu's made sure it will still go bang, we just have to reset it so our wireless signal will light it up."

Selby said: "This means another visit to the terminal in broad daylight."

"That's right. Get back here as fast as you can. Time is running out. We'll meet near the southern entrance where we went in last night."

"Boss, I hope you can remember how to reset it manually."

"I remember the bit about running like hell for three kilometres into the wind before we detonate it."

Selby laughed. "That's helpful. Okay. We'll make our way back to hold your hand."

"Okay. And keep your heads down for Chrissakes."

"Roger that," said Selby, "don't start without us." He clicked off.

Blackie worried that the three had some distance to cover in a hurry.

He passed the radio handset back to Jabril. "Chookie? Which way do we turn that emergency detonator button?"

"To the right. Don't you remember? How come they pay you fellas a hundred grand a year?"

"I was just checking if you knew," said Blackie.

Jabil rolled his eyes.

They crawled down the hill toward the terminal and their rendezvous point.

Selby and the others were waiting.

Selby said: "Thought you weren't coming. Did you get held up?"

Blackie looked at his watch. "How the fuck did you get here this quick? You were twelve clicks away."

"We got a taxi," said Selby.

"What? You got a taxi? No, no, spare me the details."

"Okay, but I had to pay with my own money," said Selby. "Just remember that when I put in my fifteen-dollar claim."

Jabril, anxious at the task ahead, grunted impatiently.

Blackie briefed them as they lay hidden in the scrubby land near the entrance. He and Jabril would locate, uncover and reset the bomb while the other three ran interference if any guards should show up.

Guard patrols they had observed from their lookout on the hill had been few and far between.

There was no mention of the order forbidding the device to fall into enemy hands. Their lives depended on the mission being completed without being seen.

Blackie had everyone remove their hats. Their dirty, straggly hair and unshaven faces would help them look like terminal day labourers at a first, distant glance. Everyone would need to conceal their weapons as best they could, by holding them close to their sides.

"If it stays all clear, we'll make a run for it as soon as the signal's reset."

Selby said: "We won't have to run far."

Blackie half closed his eyes. "Why?"

"I told the cabbie he'd get the return fare. I paid him the fifteen dollars and tied him up nice and tight. He can't move. He's in the boot and the cab's around the first corner outside to the right."

Blackie shook his head and swore under his breath. He led the motley-looking squad across the road.

They walked casually. No guards were in sight along the southern perimeter. The entrance was a large gap in the high wire fence. Big enough for heavy machinery to enter. No effort had been made to close it off.

Inside the terminal they crept between the rows of stockpiled coal destined for the conveyor loaders and the bulk carriers.

The place looked different in the daytime. Blackie hadn't expected he'd have to come back; he looked about trying to orient himself.

He walked to the left and looked down the gap between the coal piles. They were all identical.

"I think we walked two rows to the left last night," said Blackie.

Jabril had been walking close behind him. Blackie heard him stop.

"We walked three rows to the left when we came in last night."

Blackie swore again and walked on another two rows. There was coal scattered on the floor between the steep hillocks of the black rock. It crunched noisily under their rubber-soled boots.

Three of the squad walked backwards sweeping the rear. Their ears strained for any sound above their footsteps. Jabril led them quickly about fifty metres down the third coal aisle. He pointed to a spot.

Blackie raised an eyebrow. He reached into his pockets for the thick leather gloves he carried and began to dig as fast and as quietly as he could.

About a metre down he uncovered the backpack. Blackie looked at Jabril. "What are you smiling at?"

"Nothing. I'll take the other end," said Jabril. They heaved the twenty-five-kilo pack to the surface.

Jabril turned it over to access the emergency button.

Blackie peered over the chook's back and whispered: "Turn right you reckon?"

Jabril straightened up and shrugged. "Dunno. Let's see what happens."

"Getting a sense of humour now, are we?"

Jabril leaned forward again and punched the code into the keypad that protected access to the large red button beneath it.

"Dr Yu said turn it to the right, it'll be all right. Turn it to the right, and push in tight — an' it's good night."

Blackie heard Jabril click the button into its new position.

It was now armed for the radio signal the chook would send, once they had got out of the place. At least a kilometre out of the place.

Blackie grabbed the pack to lower it back into its hiding place when they heard footsteps and froze. Someone was walking near one of the neighbouring coal rows. Blackie looked back down the aisle. The other three troopers were nowhere in sight.

"Get down and I'll push some coal over you and the pack," Blackie whispered.

Jabril lay down and Blackie dug into the coal and spread it over him and his weapon. It would provide no close-up concealment. But someone standing at the far end of the aisle might miss them.

Blackie squirmed his way into the filthy pile of black rocks, using his hands to sweep some of it over his legs, body and head.

The steps came closer. They stopped. Blackie could almost imagine someone breathing. He lay face down in the filthy coal. He felt coal dust clogging his nose. He fought to slow his breathing and not to choke. He failed.

His sneeze was like an explosion. Instantly he was kicked viciously in the thigh. As he recoiled from the blow he heard Jabril shake coal off himself as he stood.

Then a Chinese voice said: "Ah ... Abos again."

Coal grit obscured Blackie's sight. He could make out a very short Chink guard standing in front of Jabril unconcernedly putting his automatic weapon back over his shoulder. Aboriginal trespassers were clearly not regarded as dangerous or uncommon around the terminal.

He heard Jabril: "Sorry, man. We just came in to hide so we could drink our scotch without the cops hassling us. We weren't nicking anything."

Shorty stood with his hands on his hips, ignoring Blackie whose face and hands were coated black with coal dust. He resisted the urge to brush it away.

"What scotch?" Shorty asked.

"In my backpack." Jabril pointed to the backpack laying half buried in the coal.

The guard bent over and grabbed the top strap. He grunted at the unexpected weight and let it fall back on the ground.

"That very heavy lot of scotch."

"It's two dozen of the best," said Jabril.

The guard paused. "You pick it up and come with me — and your friend. He come too."

Jabril picked the backpack up and Blackie stood carefully. He had still hardly earned a glance from the guard. Shorty strode off in front of them.

The trio walked to the end of the row and turned toward a small hut on the edge of the coal hills but inside the fence. Jabril walked between Shorty and Blackie.

As they came close to the hut Blackie could see two other guards through a filthy window. They were sitting on a tatty couch drinking something from mugs.

They got up and came outside as Shorty waved to Jabril to put the backpack down on a rickety table beside the hut. Blackie squatted beside the table to reduce his height.

Shorty said something in Chinese to his comrades. One nodded and replied. Blackie could make out the word "Abos" amid what he supposed was Mandarin. He looked about but could see no sign of his other three squad members.

Shorty moved to the pack and tried to open the main strap. After several attempts he stepped back, unshouldered his rifle and aimed it at Jabril.

"How this open?"

"I'll show you how it opens — but you've got to let us keep two bottles."

Shorty rounded on Jabril. In a single vicious thrust he smashed the butt of his weapon into the Aboriginal's nose. Jabril was unconscious before he hit the ground.

Shorty turned to Blackie.

"You. Open this."

When Blackie reached full height Shorty raised his gun again, aware for the first time the second Aboriginal was a larger sort of black fella. Must be a half-caste, he thought.

But clearly a fearful one who appeared confused.

"Open, open," Shorty demanded.

Blackie began to nod his head furiously and move nervously toward the table, his head bowed low and submissive.

The other two guards on his left came forward for a better view of the pack. Shorty remained on his right. Jabril moaned and moved a hand over his smashed and bloodied face. The guards ignored him.

Blackie turned the outer strap clasp upside down. The guards saw a miniature keypad. Blackie keyed in the four-number code and opened the flap.

The two hut guards immediately shouldered him aside to get to it. They lowered their heads together to peer inside.

Behind them, Blackie straightened and in a quick clapping motion smashed their heads together. As they were falling, he jabbed to the right with an elbow catching Shorty on his left ear. Shorty shuddered, fell and lay still in the coal dust. He hadn't seen what hit him.

Blackie pulled his knife from its sheath. In three sharp moves he stabbed each of the guards in the throat. He stood, listening intently.

He could only hear Jabril's laborious attempts to breathe. He pulled all three bodies into the hut, pulled a soiled set of curtains across the window and closed the door.

He relocked the backpack and pushed it under the table.

Hefting the Aboriginal across his shoulders he walked quietly toward the entry gap in the fence. His three troopers emerged silently from the coal hills before him, weapons at the ready.

"We had a spot of bother. The chook's had his nose smashed. He's been out cold, probably concussed. Selley, you take him and hide near the entrance."

He looked at the others. "We still have a job to do. The bomb's primed but we have to re-bury it, pronto."

Blackie turned and the three walked as quietly as they could back to the hut. A trooper broke off at the end of each coal row, their weapons raised for instant action. Blackie shouldered the open pack and carried it down the nearest row.

He hastily re-buried it in a shallow grave. The terminal remained as quiet as a graveyard.

They picked their way to the original bomb position and retrieved the scarcely concealed weapons and radio that had been abandoned when they were discovered. They had been in the plant about fifteen hair-raising minutes. Ten minutes longer than they had planned.

At the entrance, Jabril was conscious and refused to be carried. They hid in the long, roadside grass as a ute carrying two guards drove past.

It disappeared from sight and they walked out onto the road. It was deserted. There were no shouts behind them. No shots rang out.

Selby began stage whispering something. Blackie turned toward him and realised he was grinning and silently mouthing: "Taxi, taxi."

Exposed, they walked casually for an eternity toward the nearest intersection. Then the first shot rang out from behind them. Then they heard shouting. Guards came running toward the southern fence line from all directions.

"Run!" Selby yelled. "We need to get just around the corner."

The five sprinted the remaining hundred and fifty metres to the intersection. Jabril struggled to keep up, almost tripping several times. Blackie grabbed his arm to keep him upright and moving.

They heard more shots fired and several bullets whistle over their heads.

They turned the corner. They could see the rear of an old white Holden taxi standing empty beside the roadway only twenty metres ahead. They raced for it amid the sound of Chinese boots pounding the sealed road out of sight behind them.

When the first half dozen came into view they were in the middle of the road and without cover. The troopers were crouching behind the Holden.

Each routinely selected a single target. On an unspoken command they fired a salvo simultaneously. Four of the Chinese went down. The remaining pair dived for cover on the roadside. Neither made it.

Blackie heard the roar of ute engines racing toward them from the direction of the terminal.

He saw Selby struggling with a key he'd inserted into the driver's door. Finally it opened. Seconds later there was the sweet, familiar music of an old Holden starter motor grinding. After several nervous coughs the engine wheezed into life. The troopers piled it.

Selby put the taxi in gear and roared off.

"Loop back to the other side of the hill we were watching from," Blackie ordered.

They squad members looked at each other.

"That slope is too low to protect us from the blast," said Selby.

They all stared at Blackie. He ignored the question. "We'll go back to the summit and wait."

"Wait? For what?" Selby said.

"Our next taxi," said Blackie. "Jabril, call up the Black Hawk. Tell them where we are and get them here pronto."

Jabril, crammed in the rear seat, muttered something and wrestled to position his radio set in the speeding car. Comms answered immediately. He relayed Blackie's request and their grid map position. His nose was blocked with dried blood and his voice sounded odd.

Comms asked him to repeat the message. He did. There was a tense pause. The seconds dragged. Then Comms repeated the squad's grid position.

Comms said the Black Hawk ETA would be seven minutes from its camouflaged hiding place in a deep, bush-clad gully outside Gladstone.

"Shall I tell them they'll probably be under fire?" Jabril asked Blackie.

"No point. They'll know we're in the shit. There'd be no other reason we'd have whistled them back in daylight."

Selby looked over his shoulder at Blackie. "Never bloody satisfied. Got you a perfectly good taxi and now you want to fly."

"It's too expensive by cab. You've already clocked up fifteen bucks," said Blackie twisting around to peer out the back window. The Chinese were still not in sight.

"Anyway, I figure the chopper can get us closer to the terminal and the hell away a bit faster than your cab."

He saw Jabril looking at him. "No, chookie. Going on a nuclear bombing run is another thing we won't be telling the pilots. They'll be cool."

At the base of the small hill, Selby pulled the taxi up with a lurch and the troopers sprang out.

"Get the driver, Selley," said Blackie.

Selby went to the boot, unlocked it and hauled the driver out. He was soaked in sweat. He blinked furiously in the sunshine. He was gagged but made no effort to make any sound.

Blackie said: "Selley, cut the guy loose and bring him with you. If we leave him here the Chinks will kill him."

He turned and led the others in a race up the hill.

Selby's razor-sharp knife sliced through the plastic restraints around the driver's hands and legs. He pulled the gag from his mouth.

The driver stretched his aching limbs, shook his head and rubbed watering eyes. He looked middle-aged. He had a feeble moustache, thinning hair and a respectable beer belly slumped over chequered shorts.

"What's ya name, mate?" said Selby.

"Humphrey Morgan."

"Humphrey, you're going to have to come with us. We're going on a helicopter ride. If you stay here you'll be toast. Okay?"

"I heard shooting. Are you guys sorting out the bloody yellow peril?"

"Sure are," said Selby. He took the driver by an arm and helped him jog up the rise.

"You'll need to keep your head down for a few minutes. The Chinks are still chasing us."

Morgan was heaving for breath when they reached the others just over the crest of the hill. They were spread out, taking up defensive firing positions. There was a black guy with them, blood clotted all over his face, lugging around a wireless set.

"Everyone, this is Humphrey," announced Selby.

"Gidday, Hump," everyone chorused.

"Hi," said Morgan lying down behind some scrub. He glanced at the guy beside him giving the orders. "Do I get a gun?"

"Can you use one?" said Blackie.

"I was in 'Nam. Course I can use one," Morgan said.

"You can have my Glock. Don't waste any ammo. Don't fire until they're really close," said Blackie unholstering his pistol.

Morgan took it and turned it over in his hands. "No safety on these buggers, is there?"

"No, so watch where you're pointing it," said Blackie.

Morgan looked down the hill. "What about my cab?"

"Gary Stone will buy you a new one," said Selby.

"Oh," said Morgan, like it was an everyday occurrence. Nothing if not adaptable, these Queenslanders, thought Blackie. If Hump had a missus he certainly wasn't worrying about leaving town in a hurry without her.

They settled in for the wait. It was a short one. They heard the screaming engines of two utes. It was as if the Chinks had never learned there were more than two gears.

The Chinese came into view at the foot of the hill, their flatbeds jammed with soldiers trying to keep their balance.

Blackie called to his squad deployed across the slope: "Listen up. It's another four minutes till the chopper gets here. When it arrives Jabril's to get on first with the radio. The rest of us will follow double quick. Jabril, tell the pilot he's to fly back toward the terminal and get as high as he can."

"No probs," said Jabril, his voice nasal from his blocked and bloody nose.

"As soon as you're sure we have enough detonation signal, light the nuke up."

Blackie checked his watch. It was 10.18 a.m.

The Chinese troops leapt to the ground and spread out across the base of the hill. On command they began to advance. Several sprayed fire across the ridge. Others concentrated on the climb.

The troopers lay still and watched. When the Chinese were a hundred and fifty metres away the troopers opened fire. Enemy soldiers fell at each volley. They were facing a line of marksmen.

Their advance halted, they attempted to conceal themselves behind clumps of scrub but the accuracy of the SAS fire was unrelenting. After several minutes the survivors stood and raced for the cover of their vehicles below.

As they retreated the loud thumping of helicopter blades vibrated the air. The evil-looking Black Hawk swooped in fast and pulled up out of Chinese sight on the other side of the crest.

Jabril pushed himself to his feet and lumbered toward the helicopter.

"Okay, Hump, your turn. Run like hell," ordered Blackie. The cabbie fired off three quick, token shots at the distant Chinese and wobbled his way frantically to the helicopter.

Blackie could hear the pilot rev the engines. Time to go. Chinese must be approaching from the other side of the hill.

"Everyone go," he called. He unleashed a hail of automatic covering fire on the surviving Chinese below and followed his troopers into the Black Hawk. It shuddered its way into the air the moment he heaved himself on board.

Jabril was kneeling behind the pilots. The helicopter pointed its nose downhill to increase its takeoff speed. It flew into a hail of small-arms fire. Shots pinged off the fuselage. The troopers at the doors began bursts of automatic return fire.

The helicopter swooped downward and then lurched up as its blades grabbed for leverage in the thin tropical air. It made for the terminal.

The senior pilot sat up and searched the horizon in a reflex motion when his headset crackled: "Bravo Romeo, you have two hostiles inbound. Shenyang interceptors. Nine minutes away."

More ground shots struck the chopper. Jabril gave a scream and clutched a leg.

Selby leapt for him and laid him flat tugging a field dressing from his jacket.

"It's okay, chookie. Dr Selby is right here," he said. Jabril nodded and clenched his blood-clotted face in pain.

"How the hell did they get you there?" Selby said cutting the uniform from Jabril's lower leg. "With those bloody skinny legs it would be a shot in a billion."

Jabril groaned and squirmed with pain.

Blackie moved over to look. Blood gushing from the wound had been stemmed by Selby's instant dressing.

"Chookie, give me the radio," Blackie said.

"Fuck no, sarge. My hands aren't hit, I'm the chook. I'm sending this signal."

"Is the radio on the right frequency?" Blackie said studying the wireless.

"Yeah. Didgeridoo FM." Jabril winced again as he pulled the set closer to him.

Selby poked Blackie in the arm. "Let the poor bugger do it, boss. It's a request programme."

The pilot turned in his seat. "We are nine hundred metres from the terminal. We're only a thousand metres up. Do you want to go higher?"

"There's no time. We'll have to take our chances," said Blackie. "Turn south and be ready for some serious turbulence."

The pilot looked up, his eyebrows raised as he swung the machine around. "What turbulence, from what?" he said.

"Okay, baby, this is it. All coal exports are cancelled," whooped Jabril.

He sent the signal. They all tensed. They could only feel the vibration of the Black Hawk fleeing at full speed. A second passed. Then another.

Then the helicopter was hurled sideways and up. A huge boom

followed. The pilot fought for control. The troopers and the ridiculously nonchalant Humphrey Morgan gripped their seats.

The ground fire had suddenly stopped. The pilot fought a stall and then the rudder answered and the helicopter righted itself and increased speed.

Blackie looked back at the terminal site. He hadn't seen the result of the first bomb he had detonated at Port Abbot. But outside he could now see a scene of utter devastation.

The Tanna terminal had disappeared. A huge black, scorched paddock had replaced it.

Tonnes of coal and coal dust floated into the air mixed with a deadly brew of radiation. It blew toward the Wiggins Island terminal.

Further north he could see the deserted Aboriginal shacks blown flat.

Beside him, Jabril was semi-conscious. Selby punched a morphine shot into his bloodied leg. The radio lay on its side beside him.

Blackie picked it up and signalled: "Comms. Gladstone detonated, 1030 hours."

The pilot beckoned Blackie: "We have company on the way. A couple of Shenyang fighters."

"Oh fuck," said Blackie.

"No probs. We'll blat it back to the gully and hide again. It's only six minutes away," said the pilot.

Blackie nodded in relief.

"Great work there," said Blackie. "I thought we were about to land in a thousand pieces."

The pilot shook his head. "Nah. Just a little shake to keep us on our toes. What the fuck did you have in that bomb?"

Blackie grinned at him. "If I tell you I'd have to kill you."

"In that case I don't want to know," the pilot said. He turned back to his controls and pressed his pockmarked machine for its last ounce of speed.

Flying too low for any radar to detect, the Black Hawk dropped back into hiding between two steep bluffs.

Jabril was carried gently from the chopper to their temporary encampment.

Everyone else began pulling camouflage netting over the machine. When they had finished it was invisible from the air. The only danger was if any Chinese patrol had spotted the last minute of their flight.

Meanwhile their original escape plan for that night had been made impossible.

The ground fire had hit the Black Hawk's fuel tank and destroyed its radio antennae. Blackie decided they would all stay put until the Chinese ground search for them had lost its steam. The gully was a safe refuge.

Meantime Selby pumped morphine into the signalman, sparing him the worst of the pain.

Blackie fell into an exhausted sleep unaware the impact of his nuke had thundered all the way to Beijing.

11.30 a.m.

Canberra Airport

It happened as he reached the bottom of the ramp. He didn't hear the shot.

Minutes before he had heard a brass band playing the Chinese national anthem as the VIP jet taxied slowly to a halt outside Canberra Airport's main terminal. From his window he saw an honour guard assembled to greet him.

The Prime Minister-elect of Australia would be among the official party at the foot of the open-air ramp that was being pushed toward the plane.

As a Vice Premier of the People's Republic, Chang Leng had been excited and confident when he set out from Townsville, knowing he carried the hopes of the Politburo — and the Chinese people, he liked to think — on his shoulders.

He would be the one to break the ridiculous impasse that had developed with the Australian Government.

When the former president had died suddenly six months ago, Chang had been part of a younger Politburo that had actively sided with Comrade Wu in his successful leadership bid.

Chang had been outspoken in support of China's long-overdue move as the Pacific's superpower to secure permanent access to the critical energy and mineral resources it depended on. The Australian north had been an empty land and an obvious choice.

He was an hour into the flight when the news came.

Three more radioactive explosions had wreaked havoc at two mines in Western Australia and a key export terminal in Queensland. The terminal had been only a hop to the south from the Townsville airport he had set out from. None of the saboteurs had been captured.

Mortified, angry and disbelieving, he ordered the pilot into a holding circle and called Jeremey Whittacker. The man who was Prime Minister-elect sounded as surprised and alarmed at the news as he was. Whittacker disclaimed all knowledge of any bomb blasts.

He frantically insisted he would be officially in control of the government in less than five hours and determined to settle a border treaty.

He was emphatic in his commitment to saving Australia from a ruinous war it could not win. Chang was desperate to believe him.

Chang then called Beijing to brief President Wu personally on the new developments. He presumed his high-priority mission would give him immediate access.

He was miffed when the Politburo Chief Secretary told him the President was not available. He could not say when he would be.

The bureaucrat added snootily that Beijing knew about the new attacks anyway. The Army High Command had already reported them.

Chang asked the Chief Secretary to inform the President he would press on with his mission to Canberra because he was certain the attacks were the result of diehards acting for the old

Stone regime. He had received a personal assurance from the Prime Minister-elect a border treaty would be signed.

The Chief Secretary had no comment. He said he would pass on Chang's message as soon as possible and broke the contact.

Chang stared at the receiver. He felt a twitch of uncertainty. The Chief Secretary was a Machiavellian bureaucratic. A survivor of many power games. Was there a new power play under way in the Politburo? Why hadn't President Wu taken his call?

Chang told his pilot to resume course for Canberra. He was the man to deliver peace and prosperity from the shambles the Australian campaign had become.

A blast of hot air struck him in the face when the jet's door swung open. He began to relax when he saw the welcoming party, the military band and the ceremonial guard of honour lined up at attention awaiting his inspection.

Chang saw a bank of television cameras swivel toward him and knew millions of viewers would be watching his every move live as the day's biggest international story unfolded.

With his entourage following him, he made his way — not too fast, not too slow — down the steep ramp that had been rolled to the jet's door.

Whittacker came forward smiling, hand outstretched. Chang gave a formal, traditional bow of his head as he stepped off the ramp. The bow saved his life.

Music from the military brass band muffled the crack of the rifle. The bullet passed Chang's lowered head missing him by millimetres. It struck the aide behind him.

Chang was still smiling when he saw a look of horror sweep Whittacker's face. Then he felt a hot wetness on his neck. Behind him his aide's skull had exploded in a red mist.

The headless man fell forward striking Chang and spraying blood down his back. Chang toppled under the weight of the falling, lifeless body. He sprang frantically to his feet. The crumpled body and the balance of his entourage blocked his escape back up the gangway.

Turning wild-eyed and panicked, he was suddenly thrown to

the ground by three Australian security guards. He lay winded and crushed beneath their protective cover.

Whittacker stood paralysed. He heard shouting and pandemonium. It came from among the honour guard who were wrestling with one of their own, cordite smoke still wafting from his rifle barrel.

The would-be assassin finally went down when struck on the head by the butt of a fellow squad member's unloaded rifle.

There was an odd silence. The music had died in jerks. The conductor, oblivious to the carnage behind him, cut a comic image as he continued to wave his baton while the band before his eyes scattered unceremoniously.

A siren wailed in the distance.

A brightly polished black GMC station wagon rolled up to the ramp. Chang felt himself being helped to his feet. A guard opened a rear door of the station wagon and waved for him to get in.

Restoring some dignity, he ignored the guard and carefully removed his coat. The back of it was soaked in blood. He felt his neck and collar. The stickiness was revolting.

An old, grumbling diesel ambulance pulled up beside the VIP station wagon. Paramedics alighted and began the grisly business of removing the decapitated corpse from a thick pool of blood.

The television crews busily recorded every moment of the drama. Chang instinctively but stupidly straightened his tie. Too late he realised the callously vain image he was portraying to the world.

Whittacker walked over to him. No handshake was offered by the white-faced Prime Minister-elect.

"Still in control are you?" Chang said. Whittacker stood open-mouthed and shook his head. Then stopped and nodded it rapidly.

"Mr Vice Premier, I am so sorry." He stopped and looked around. The guard beside the GMC was still holding the rear door open.

"Please, come with me."

"I presume this wagon is bulletproof?" said Chang. His sarcasm was lost on Whittacker.

"Of course, of course. Mr Vice Premier, you must understand there are rogue elements who will go to any lengths to wreck a meaningful peace settlement."

Rolling his eyes, Chang made for the station wagon. He got in and Whittacker followed. The vehicle made a U-turn and headed for the exit. It was joined by police vehicles front and back. Motorcycle police outriders swarmed on each side.

Overhead, three clattering television news helicopters joined the convoy. Chang demanded to be taken to his embassy.

He needed a change of clothes and to consult Beijing before there could be any further talks. Whittacker stressed repeatedly his new government wanted peace for Australia.

Chang watched Whittacker's dithering performance. The man was out of his depth and clearly not in control of events. But he was desperate to put a stop to any war. He was someone Chang knew he would have no trouble dealing with.

11.45 a.m.

The Lodge, Canberra

"Did your lot have anything to do with that?" Stone demanded.

The ASIO boss didn't have time to take his seat before the question stopped him.

"Absolutely not," Frank Church said. "We wouldn't have missed. That shot was too high. Hit the guy behind Chang right in the head."

"Any idea who did do it?"

Church held the Prime Minister's eye. "No. But it certainly wasn't any of us."

"So it was a lone wolf attack?"

"Yes," said Church. Stone believed him.

Church was overseeing a hook-up with one of the reconnaissance satellites stationed over the *Liaoning* and its four-destroyer escort.

It would give a bird's-eye view from space of the Collins' attack — an attack delayed by two hours by their skippers. They had needed more time to manoeuvre and coordinate their strike, which was now expected no sooner than 12.30 p.m.

Joe Martini had arrived in suppressed high spirits. General Thompson and Admiral Robson were on their way.

Martini buttonholed Church: "Where the hell's the Chang fellow?"

"He's at the Chinese Embassy," said Church. "Whittacker's waiting outside in the wagon. One of my men is driving him. He says Chang was going to consult with Beijing. He's then expected to go with Whittacker to Whittacker's office at Parliament. My man says Whittacker's in a state of near hysteria."

"Can you monitor the discussion between Beijing and Chang?"

"No, we can't." Church turned as three men in white overalls carrying leads entered to complete the hook-up.

Stone had watched the live television coverage of the assassination attempt. In the wake of the morning's triple bomb strikes, the latest act of violence would have had to have the Chinese strategists in a spin.

The television channels were constantly replaying the gruesome moment when the hapless aide had his head shattered. One was repeating it in slow motion.

The other favourite replay was the handcuffed shooter being led off, his ceremonial uniform carrying its own bloodstains from the head wound he suffered attempting to get off a second round.

The failed assassin would have known his honour guard comrades had unloaded rifles. They had shown courage to tackle him.

A large monitor, sitting uncertainly on a tall filing cabinet, blinked into life. General Thompson and Admiral Robson arrived as the satellite picture gave a close-up of the Chinese flotilla off Townsville.

Defence HQ was no longer where the action was, thought Stone. He had made The Lodge more like the White House.

It was easy to make out the *Liaoning*. The old, rejuvenated three-hundred-metre-long Ukrainian carrier appeared to have a number of fighters lined up on her seventy-metre-wide deck.

She dwarfed the four destroyers forming a box shape around her. The flotilla was cruising due north. It would gradually turn toward the coast to maintain its broad circular holding pattern.

The hands on the wall clock moved steadily toward 12.30 p.m. Tension in the room mounted with each flick of the second hand.

A steward brought in coffee. The room was quiet. The observers divided their time between watching the news channel replays of the assassination attempt and the newly installed satellite screen.

12.20 p.m.

HMAS Rankin, *Coral Sea*

He was wrong. He'd told midshipman Robbie Peters it would be like an exercise. It wasn't. The air had been electric since the attack orders had come the previous afternoon.

But for John Scott they came as a relief. Someone had finally made a decision. Their nerve-racking shadowing of the Chinese ships had gone on long enough. So had the stress created by the *Rankin*'s dangerously low diesel supply.

The diesel engines charged the huge battery banks to power the sub's silent electric propulsion system. The *Rankin* had spent the last hours positioning itself for the attack and was now closing silently on its prey.

It had slid only slightly deeper as it neared the enemy. The skipper had decided the undulating underwater terrain of the local oceanography would make it more difficult for surface sonar to detect them if they stayed shallow.

Scott knew what the skipper hadn't said was the terrain would also make it more difficult to guide their torpedoes to the enemy.

It was probably the reason the enemy flotilla had chosen to cruise its wide holding pattern in the area.

Scott's screen gave him a clear fix. The *Liaoning* loomed large on the passive sonar. Four destroyers surrounded the carrier. *Rankin* was positioned abreast the carrier leaving it between two of the destroyers on its starboard side.

The *Sheean* was directly behind the carrier. Three kilometres further back a large pod of migrating whales was whistling and keening.

The *Sheean* had been tasked to take out the rear destroyer to its starboard side first. This would shield the *Rankin* while it closed for a beam attack on the carrier.

The *Sheean* would then target the second destroyer behind the carrier on its port. Its third target was the most distant, on the carrier's port bow. *Rankin*'s second target was the destroyer near the carrier's starboard bow.

But the carrier was the priority. If *Rankin* was detected and attacked, *Sheean* was to turn its full attention to the *Liaoning*.

That eventuality would leave *Sheean* surrounded by defending destroyers.

Scott glanced at his twenty-year-old assistant operator, Michael Muir, beside him. Muir was staring intently at his screen, brow furrowed, his only words spoken quietly into his headset. It was Muir's second patrol.

Scott had alerted him a Chinese sub was likely to be a hidden part of the carrier's screen. The whales, oblivious to the drama, had subsequently given Muir a frightened jolt when they first showed up.

But the youngster was doing a professional job, almost certainly fighting down all sorts of fears. Scott wondered how he himself would have coped with this sort of tension on his second patrol.

The skipper was taking *Rankin* within seven kilometres of the Chinese carrier.

The stubby, bright-blue Mark 48 Mod 7 torpedoes were loaded and set in the six tubes.

It was finally happening, Scott thought for the hundredth time.

The *Rankin* pumped water from its forward ballast tank and lifted slowly to periscope depth. The pipe created a wash but they were sure it would be hidden among the white caps being whipped up by the tropical cyclone forming four hundred kilometres north.

At periscope depth the sub was only five metres below the surface. The skipper had a clear visual of the *Liaoning*.

He had raised the periscope because he wanted a last-minute, precise location check on the carrier. The best way to do this was to take a look.

The skipper pointed the scope at the carrier and pushed the bearing button, sending the precise position of the *Liaoning* to the torpedo computers calculating the intercept course.

Scott heard him over the open intercom: "Final bearings set."

The skipper stepped back. It was always the Chief Weapons Officer who gave the final order for a torpedo launch.

Their Mark 48 torpedoes, developed with the US Navy, were devastating weapons.

They streamed wire that remained connected to the sub. It allowed the *Rankin* weapons officers to see what the torpedo could see and redirect it if necessary.

The torpedoes also had their own sonar system, which would eventually lock onto the carrier when they closed on it. This would ensure an exact intercept.

Both submarines were planning to attack simultaneously at 12.30 p.m. They believed the element of surprise was critical for their success and survival.

Scott had the *Sheean* on his busy sonar screen. Its pulsing green flicker represented a sinister black monster of the deep gliding noiselessly toward its unsuspecting quarry.

Scott realised he wasn't breathing. As each second to the attack passed interminably, he knew he was experiencing the submariner's ultimate moment on a hunter-killer. The most feared warship of the sea.

He was jerked from his thoughts. In the frigid tension of the control room he heard the clear instruction of the Chief Weapons Officer: "Shoot!"

All fifty-eight souls on board braced. Scott turned to the sonar man next to him and winked. The youngster gave him a brave thumbs-up.

The *Rankin* shuddered. There was a whoosh as high-pressure water rammed the torpedoes from their tubes. Their motors started and they hurtled away.

Scott sat, his eyes fixed on the sonar screen, hardly daring to think.

He began to hear a succession of routine reports on the intercom.

"Units running normally, wire good."

The battle was under way.

"Units have merged on the bearing of the target."

No enemy surface sonar operator would miss the signature pulses of the torpedoes, particularly as they began sending out their own sonar pings to hone in on their quarry.

"Detect."

Their role as hunter or hunted would be decided in the next few minutes.

The routine voice lifted a pitch: "Acquire. We have them."

Then Scott's sonar picked up the unmistakable sound of the *Sheean's* torpedoes ripping into their first target.

Moments later, *Rankin* fired a second pair of torpedoes at its destroyer target. Scott waited. He knew the torpedoes would explode simultaneously under the carrier and the destroyer if they had got their calculations dead right.

But they didn't. Not quite. The torpedoes exploded beneath the 60,000-tonne carrier's hull four seconds before the destroyer was hit.

There was quiet jubilation at every station as the sonar readings confirmed the colossal punch of the Mark 48s detonating. They were made to break the back of any ship.

The skipper ordered periscope depth again and saw his

destroyer target had been heaved from the sea, snapped in half by the mortal double blow of the *Rankin's* torpedoes.

He swivelled to the *Liaoning*. Its flight deck was crowded by a dozen Shenyang fighters. He wanted to see the Flying Sharks drown.

But there was no sign of any impact.

He stared desperately. Nothing happened. Nothing happened. He gripped the periscope handles ferociously as he watched.

Then he detected the first telltale sign the big carrier was in trouble.

The high winds were pushing it very gradually beam on to the rising swells. She was not responding to her helm. He was certain her forward momentum had also slowed.

He allowed himself to take a deep breath and relay his visual news on the intercom.

He was about to order the *Rankin's* engines to full speed for their escape when the voice of his top sonar man, John Scott, interrupted his growing elation with news he didn't want to hear.

He swung the periscope sharply further to port and saw fires raging on *Sheean's* stricken first target. He swung further to her second target and froze as he saw what Scott had detected moments earlier.

The second, rear destroyer was turning sharply at high speed toward *Sheean's* position. They had found her.

Scott reported underwater echoes he identified as depth charges from *Sheean's* proximity.

He knew the *Sheean* had not fired her second salvo of torpedoes. She was now the subject of an attack from the surface.

Scott figured she must have made an emergency dive. He instinctively pushed his headphones closer to his ears as he studied the sonar pulse on the green screen.

Scott heard the "Periscope down" order for *Rankin* and the sub lurch on an emergency U-turn. The Chinese would expect an attacker to flee to deep water. The *Rankin* skipper ran for the coastline and the shallows.

He asked for twenty metres depth and full speed. The four-thousand-tonne steel tube was thrust forward at more than twenty knots by propellers the size of a family car. The intercom fell silent.

John Scott sensed the skipper behind him. He was leaning in for a closer view of the sonar screen.

As he did the sonar picked up more echoes that were distinctly depth charge explosions near the *Sheean*, now to their rear. And then a huge echo and the horrific shriek he knew was rupturing steel.

The *Sheean* had been struck. Scott watched helplessly as its blip fell rapidly to the ocean bed. It seemed to all happen too quickly to compute.

"She's gone, sir," he said.

"Fuck," said the skipper. He walked back the few steps to the control room.

Scott felt a shiver cross his body.

Then he heard Muir swear.

The fourth destroyer, the one that had been at the front port side of the carrier and most distant, was also turning and picking up speed. He quickly calculated it was seventeen kilometres away but steering a course directly for them.

It was impossible to say if the *Rankin* had been detected or the destroyer was reacting to the attack on the other three vessels behind it.

"Skipper, we've got a visitor inbound," he reported. He gave the destroyer's coordinates and speed. It was building up to its full speed of thirty-three knots. It was only a matter of time before it would overtake them.

12.29 p.m.

The Lodge, Canberra

The mood at The Lodge had been one of jubilation when the Collins' attack began.

Crowding around the satellite reconnaissance monitor, Stone

and his inner group watched as two of the Chinese destroyers erupted in flames and began sinking. There were high fives and applause. It was an emotional reaction after days of pent-up stress.

Then the tables seemed to turn. The atmosphere became pensive again as they realised the *Liaoning* was steaming on unscathed in the battle. And one of the destroyers behind the carrier suddenly turned a sharp one hundred and eighty degrees and accelerated.

Admiral Robson folded his arms and shook his head. The manoeuvre was ominous. Not in the playbook. He was sure the destroyer was headed for the general area from which the *Sheean* would have launched her torpedoes. The *Sheean* would have been betting on her invisibility to attack close to the Chinese flotilla.

"Oh no. I think we've been sprung," Robson said. He muttered the words but everyone seemed to hear him. A chill went through the room.

The satellite camera zoomed in to magnify the sea immediately around the destroyer. Spectacular clouds of spray exploded from each side of its bow as it smashed its way with increasing speed into the storm-tossed sea.

"It looks like the *Sheean* was detected on sonar just as she was releasing her first torpedoes ... before they even hit their target. I'm certain that's why that destroyer U-turned instantly," Robson said.

He pulled a face as he watched the distant battle unfold. "What unbelievable bad luck. After shadowing them for days completely undetected."

There was no response from the others.

They could clearly see flames thrashing in thirty-knot winds from *Sheean*'s victim as it toppled onto its side in a slow-motion death ritual.

Then someone gasped as plumes of water began exploding upward like giant water spouts behind the destroyer. The atmosphere became electric. Everyone felt helpless knowing the destroyer was unleashing depth charges in its hunt for the killer sub.

"Oh boy, the other destroyer near the bow of the carrier is now turning around as well," said Robson.

Stone said: "But what's happening with the *Liaoning*? She's the one we've got to sink. She's just cruising happily along in the middle of it all. When are they going to hit her? Or do you think they tried and missed?"

Robson shrugged. The *Liaoning* had been the priority target. Maybe the skippers had been forced to change their attack strategy at the last minute.

Stone swore under his breath. They had come this far and the biggest single naval threat to the country had escaped unscathed.

As he watched with increasing anxiety he willed it to be blown into a thousand pieces. He thought he saw it swing slightly to starboard. His imagination was working overtime with rushes of hope and desperation.

Robson moved closer to him and said: "I think our boys have already fired at her, Prime Minister. If she's been hit her momentum will push her on even if she's got a couple of holes in her. She weights sixty thousand tonnes. But I think she's slowing and being dragged side on to the swell. That's a key sign she's lost some control. Maybe she's been hit and lost some of her propellers or a rudder's been blown off."

"Fuck, I hope you're right, Admiral. And I hope the damage is enough to get her out of the war," said Stone.

He rubbed his chest.

"I can't see any change of course ... wait on, yes I think I can. I think you're right. She's coming slightly to starboard."

The seconds dragged as the tension mounted. The attacking destroyer fired off depth charge after depth charge while the *Liaoning* looked far from stricken. Robson walked up to within a metre of the screen in an instinctive effort to get nearer the remote action.

He turned suddenly. A smile cracked his face. He gave Stone the thumbs up.

"She's going nowhere. She's lost power. She's going beam on to the sea. I'll bet those Mark 48s have torn a big hole in her ass."

A cheer went up around the room.

"Sink, you bastard, and take all those jets with you," Martini yelled and danced in excitement. He had known the *Liaoning* would end up at the bottom of the sea. His sixth sense had told him. For better or worse, it was never wrong.

But any mood of joy was short-lived. A geyser of water and debris erupted on the sea's surface like an underwater volcano venting.

"Fuck, what's that?" Martini said.

"The *Sheean*," said Robson.

"Whaddya you mean?"

Robson's voice cracked and his eyes began to glisten. "They found her. She's had a direct hit."

He blew his nose. The room was shocked into silence.

Stone turned to Robson. "Would anyone survive that, Brian?"

Robson shook his head, avoiding Stone's eyes. "No, not a hit like that."

Several minutes passed. They saw the second remaining destroyer on the front port side of the carrier surge into the mounting swell. It swung across the bow of the slowing carrier and set off on a different course south eastward, obviously to search for a suspected second sub.

It began to loose off depth charges as it went.

Robson sighed. "Well, *Rankin* definitely got the big target. *Liaoning* is starting to list. She's dog tucker. She'll be on the bottom soon. Let's pray *Rankin* can get away."

The Admiral's verdict on the fate of the carrier could not reinvigorate the mood. He was clearly struggling for composure as the circle of debris marking the grave of the *Sheean* grew inexorably before their eyes. The white-capped seas quickly shoved the flotsam southward.

Stone felt empty. The Navy had pulled off a miraculous attack but it had paid a high price. He watched in trepidation as the Chinese launched their hunt for *Rankin*. The Navy might soon have to pay an even higher price.

Stone's trance was broken as Martini clasped him by the shoulder. "I know this is tough, we've lost a crew of brave men, but whatever happens now those Chink bastards can't do much invading without air support."

As he spoke the *Liaoning* began listing noticeably to starboard, her bow settling lower in the water. They couldn't see much detail but more than two thousand sailors and air force personnel were scrambling to abandon ship.

Lifeboats began to appear at her side. Several seemed to be swept away by the high winds as soon as they reached the boiling sea.

Stone called Able to his side. "Make sure the media and the Politburo know the *Liaoning* is sinking. Get them a satellite feed," he said. "But don't say anything about our subs."

He turned to Church: "Is Chang is still at the embassy?"

The ASIO chief nodded.

"Shall I tell the Deputy Prime Minister the news?"

Stone rubbed his chin.

"No, don't. He's not on our team. Let him sit in his wagon. He'll hear it on his radio or Chang can tell him."

Able gave a last glance at the satellite monitor and hurried from the room.

12.38 p.m.

HMAS Rankin, *Coral Sea*

The sonar hand swept monotonously over the green screen, dispassionately tracking the Chinese destroyer as it rushed toward them.

John Scott felt an adrenaline rush as he tracked its remorseless progress. The Chinese sonar must have picked them up as it had the *Sheean*. His heart was pounding so hard he was sure others could hear it.

Beside him Muir was gripping the arms of his seat.

Scott caught his eye and shook his head. "I'm not sure they have a reading on us. I bet they're operating on sheer guesswork. They'll be in a panic. They have to do something, so they're throwing depth charges everywhere and they're miles from us."

The young man did not respond. His knuckles whitened from his fierce grip on the armrests.

"We'll be fine, you'll see. It would take a direct hit to open up this baby. It's built like the back of a brick shit-house."

His assistant smiled but kept his eyes on the screen. He knew the Collins were built at enormous cost from high-tensile micro-alloy steel, stronger than the nickel-alloy steel used on other conventional subs.

Muir straightened his back, took a deep breath of the over-heated air and flexed his stiff fingers. He made a screen adjustment to occupy himself.

His attempts at calm suddenly shattered. A new echo was showing up about four kilometres behind them.

"Is that the Chinese sub we thought might be around the *Liaon-ing?*" he asked.

Scott squinted at his screen and raised the volume control on his headset. The echo was too indistinct to classify. It was heading north between the two surviving destroyers.

Their attention jumped back to the incoming destroyer. It was two and a half kilometres away. They both heard the crump that could only come from a depth charge.

"Oh, fuck," said Muir, "he must have made us."

Scott said nothing.

Convinced the destroyer was going to maintain its course, the skipper ordered a hard to-starboard turn. As they attempted to move away from its path, the series of underwater explosions kept up a deadly beat.

Scott looked around him. Everyone was fixed, rigid at their stations, ears straining.

Then the hulled vibrated. An alarm light began flashing in the semi-dark of the control room. The hull shook a second time. More red lights blinked.

The destroyer was now thundering somewhere close behind them. Its echo engulfed the entire sonar screen. Scott tore his headphones off.

He shook his head waiting for the final depth charge that would split them open. It didn't come. The destroyer continued to speed away.

He eased the headphones back on his damp head.

"What's happening, sonar?"

It was the skipper's voice.

"The destroyer's gone past, sir. He's still heading due west at the same speed, which means he didn't make us. He's playing Russian roulette, showering depth charges around," Scott said.

He could hear damage control teams on the open intercom. They reported three leaks. Crew in the rear quarters were being evacuated and watertight doors resealed.

"Skipper, we have another contact to our rear," said Scott.

"What is it?" There was alarm in the skipper's voice.

"We're still trying to decipher it, sir … oh no. Skipper, the destroyer has turned. He's coming back."

"Oh, fuck," the skipper said under his breath. "What's his bearing?"

"Wait one, sir," said Scott. Muir was shaking his head. He tapped his screen. Scott made a quick analysis too.

"My assistant operator has just confirmed, the destroyer's new course is slightly to the south of us."

Muir beamed with the recognition. Colour was returning to his face.

"Where's he going now?"

Scott laughed.

"Sonar, what's the joke? What's happening? Where's he heading?" the skipper repeated.

"He's going whale hunting, sir."

The new echo was becoming a series of echoes. The familiar sounds of the whales they had detected earlier behind the *Liaon-*

ing had returned. The destroyer's sonar had made them and was racing toward the new signal.

The sonar man explained the situation. The skipper turned to the navigator and said: "We'll turn back on our original course and put as much distance between him and us as we can — before he realises he's on a false scent."

Anxious smiles of relief everywhere became contagious as the tension ebbed.

Five minutes later Scott reported no further sign of danger. The destroyer that had sunk the *Sheean* was now stationary near the *Liaoning*'s original position. It was almost certainly involved in rescue operations.

He guessed the second destroyer would join in the rescue efforts when it realised its target was a pod of whales. It would hopefully assume the attack had come from a single submarine. One they had sunk.

Scott turned to see midshipman Robbie Peters staring at him.

"Some exercise," he said.

* * *

The *Rankin* would assess its damage and slow to a limp as two of its three diesel engines exhausted their last trickle of fuel. In a few hours, with no way to recharge its batteries, it would have to surface in enemy waters.

It would radio its position as soon as it surfaced. If the skipper chose to abandon and scuttle the *Rankin*, there would certainly be casualties.

Attempting to launch their emergency rubber rafts safely from the violently rolling deck of the round-hulled submarine would need impossible luck — and Scott knew they had already had their full quota from The Lady.

3.57 p.m.

The Chinese Embassy, Canberra

The air-conditioning fan blew cold air through the big VIP station wagon. It had been idling outside the Chinese Embassy for almost four hours baking in the sun.

Whittacker was growing increasingly fraught. There had been no word from his private guest since he left the wagon in his bloodstained suit.

The Prime Minister-elect had ordered the driver to kill the radio and its incessant chatter about the attempted assassination. He wanted quiet to think. What line would the Chinese Vice Premier take when he returned for their trip to the Parliamentary Offices? If he did return.

Whittacker had played a hundred scenarios through in his mind. Whatever else was going on he was certain he would be able to stop any war. But he could only guess at how many more concessions the Chinese would demand now as a price for peace.

How much longer would he have to wait? He sent an email from his iPhone requesting the Cabinet meeting be delayed for another hour. In it he claimed there were positive developments between himself and Chang to report.

He noticed a long list of messages on his screen. He ignored them. He had no time for any interruptions on this day of all days. He knew pushing the iPhone's mute button and killing the wagon's radio had been the right thing to do.

There was only one message that mattered today. And that would come from Chang. Where the devil was the man?

At 4.17 p.m. the door to the embassy's main entrance swung open. Whittacker's hopes rose — and then fell. The man walking toward the wagon was not Chang.

4.17 p.m.

Prime Minister's Office, Parliament Buildings, Canberra

A news channel pool camera assigned to monitor the Chinese Embassy recorded the man making for Whittacker's wagon.

Stone watched him on the television set in his office. He had gone there to wait for the originally scheduled 4 p.m. Cabinet meeting. His last.

The ASIO agent acting as Whittacker's driver opened the rear door. Stone's deputy remained out of sight.

Standing beside the open door the man bent down and appeared to be having a conversation. Then he nodded and got in. The agent closed the door behind him.

The wagon moved off with its police escort and followed a route directly for the Parliamentary Offices.

Frank Church was ushered into Stone's office and identified the Chinese passenger as the embassy's First Secretary, Sun Kai. He was a career diplomat. He had been passed over for ambassador in favour of Chen who had, in turn, been abruptly recalled earlier in the week. Vice Premier Chang was still in the embassy.

Stone had agreed to delay the Cabinet meeting. He had not spoken to any of his ministers. He was still unaware of any Chinese reaction to the triple radiation bombing, the failed assassination attempt or the dramatic sinking of the *Liaoning*.

But he would know shortly. From the horse's mouth. Whittacker and Sun were less than twenty minutes away. There was nothing he could do but wait.

* * *

Stone cast an eye around the office. In another hour or less it would no longer be his.

He would miss it. The expansive desk, small conference table, lounge chairs, bookshelves, the national flag adorning a wall, mementos and photographs tracing his career.

Now his time was almost up. It wasn't until the cardboard boxes arrived that the reality of his fall from power struck home.

He felt a deep sadness. He was being stretchered off for the last time. He had wanted to choose his own departure time, stepping down and handing off the leadership while still in power.

Not this humiliating ousting by a man he loathed as an unprincipled coward.

The boxes sat impatiently against the end wall. It was as though an efficient undertaker had delivered the patient's coffin early. They were the final confirmation his condition was terminal.

His office would soon be methodically stripped of his personal possessions and files. They would be stacked in the cardboard boxes and the office would be readied for its new occupant.

He was grateful Elaine had agreed, reluctantly, to stay behind at The Lodge for his last meeting. It would be an emotional and painful business for him.

He went to the outer offices and told his personal staff he was leaving for the Cabinet room. Alone. He would not need any briefing papers.

He promised to return to say his farewells properly and share a final drink when the meeting was finished. Most of the staff were fighting back tears. There was none of the usual frantic work buzz.

The wall clock said it was now 4.50 p.m., the rescheduled time for his last Cabinet meeting. Whittacker had arrived in the building with the First Secretary of the Chinese Embassy, Sun Kai ten minutes ago.

Clearly he had managed to maintain relations with the Chinese despite the last-minute attacks on them. Cabinet was about to learn what further demands China would insist on in return for a peace treaty.

Stone wanted everyone seated before he arrived. He was in no mood for pointless small talk. There was only one matter on the agenda, Whittacker's motion for a vote of no confidence in him. And that vote was a formality.

But he wasn't the last to arrive. The seat next to his, Whittacker's, was empty. Stone was furious. The PM-elect was to make a grand entrance having kept him and the rest of the Cabinet waiting.

As he made his way to the head of the big oval table he nodded to his silent colleagues. Most of them had decided his deputy would be a better Prime Minister than him. Now he would make them confirm that in his presence.

He pulled his chair out to sit down as Whittacker strode in. He looked as white as a ghost but businesslike.

He took his deputy's chair and Stone said: "Gentlemen, there is only one item of business on the agenda today."

Whittacker placed a hand on Stone's arm. "If I may, before the meeting begins ... I would like everyone to know Mr Sun, the Chinese Embassy's First Secretary, is with us this afternoon ... he's outside ... he would like to address the Cabinet."

Stone started to say something but Whittacker stood and left the room. Moments later he ushered Sun into the room and pointed to his own chair. Sun sat. The ministers and Stone watched, puzzled.

Whittacker said: "If you will excuse me, Mr Sun has already briefed me. I will leave you with him for a moment."

He turned and left the room again.

Feeling baffled and short-tempered, Stone found himself still at the head of the table.

He was unsure what to do next. What the hell was Whittacker playing at now? He saw Sun looking around the table. The Chinese diplomat seemed nervous.

Stone looked at him and raised his eyebrows. "Mr Sun, the floor is yours."

"Thank you, Prime Minister." Sun gave a slight bow of his head.

"As you know, I have been in discussions with the Deputy Prime Minister and explained our most urgent issue to him."

A dead silence hung over the room. Ministers frowned, some sat forward straining to understand Sun's accent. Sun gave an exasperated sigh and opened his hands outward.

"As I told Mr Whittacker, it isn't possible to withdraw all our forces in seven days."

No one stirred. Stone saw looks of confusion. Every person was attempting to interpret the import of what they were hearing.

When there was no reaction, Sun shook his head and turned to Stone, clearly uncertain and perturbed by his reception. He tightened his tie and shucked his sleeves and peered at the door Whittacker had disappeared through.

"You must understand, it has been three days since your withdrawal deadline was set. This doesn't give us enough time. We must have an extension."

There was a burble of surprised voices around the table. Ministers turned to each other. Were they hearing what they thought they heard? They shrugged confirmation between each other that they had had no earlier briefing from Whittacker.

Sun's voice went up an octave: "We have ourselves only been notified this afternoon of President Wu's resignation."

Stone sat forward as the hubbub grew louder and held up a hand for silence. He turned to Sun and gestured he should go on.

"The People's Republic accepts its policies under President Wu were misguided and inappropriate. As you know, I have explained to Mr Whittacker, the People's Republic will pay full compensation to decontaminate the land and repair the structures damaged by the necessity for you to implement your Emergency Nuclear Deterrent programme."

Stone did not know anything. Nor, clearly, did any of the ministers, including Whittacker's closest backers. Sun was in a dither, unable to understand his confused reception.

He pressed on: "We did not expect you to contaminate your countryside … we were unable to locate any of the bombs … they kept exploding … our whole strategy of securing guaranteed resources for our future fell apart … if you went on destroying them there would have been international shortages and higher prices … exactly the opposite outcome President Wu had promised."

Sun paused and shook his head. "We know we can't fight the whole world ... the international boycotts ... and America and its submarines ..." His words petered out.

One minister sprang to his feet and gave a whoop. Stone stood, determined to maintain order among the shocked ministers.

He demanded Sun should be allowed to finish his statement uninterrupted. Everyone needed to know what the Chinese had told Whittacker. The room went silent again amid the suppressed excitement.

Sun gave Stone a grateful look. "Your troops have been well treated you know, so we ask that you promise our soldiers safe passage as they leave."

Sun sat back, nervous eyes again sweeping the room. Perspiration had broken out on his forehead. He wiped it with a white tissue.

Stone stood again formally and stretched out his hand. "Mr Sun, please convey to your government our agreement to reset the withdrawal deadline again from today."

A look of relief crossed Sun's face.

"Also, be assured your troops will be offered safe passage. Meantime all prisoners must be freed and all hostilities cease immediately."

Sun nodded quickly. "Yes, yes, of course, of course, thank you, thank you."

"You might also let your government know the sonar signatures of the Mark 48 torpedoes your destroyers heard today were from Australian submarines."

Sun raised an eyebrow sceptically.

Stone said: "The torpedoes were developed jointly by the Australian and the US navies; this may have led to confusion among your intelligence officers."

The Chinese diplomat looked unconvinced. "But all Australian submarines are docked at their base."

"No, they're not. Two are decoys," said Stone.

Sun's confused expression suddenly cleared. "So there were

two submarines in the attack on *Liaoning* — and they were Australian."

"Yes, they were Australian. As you know only one survived," said Stone.

Sun fell silent.

The Environment Minister was unable to control himself any longer.

"Australian submarines? We don't know anything about any Australian submarines," he said. "We all thought when that carrier went down it must have been the Yanks doing something useful at last. What's been going on?"

Stone did not reply. He turned to the Chinese diplomat: "Mr Sun. Thank you. Our first task now must be to signal to all our forces that hostilities have ceased."

Stone looked at his watch. It was 5.10 p.m.

Sun nodded and produced his cellphone. "I have been instructed to call our High Command directly once I have your agreement on all the outstanding issues. There is just the one final matter."

Stone frowned. One final matter?

5.10 p.m.

Lavarack Barracks, Townsville

The men had been given only thirty minutes' notice, to ensure security. They had armed themselves with makeshift clubs, many torn from furniture, and waited tensely for the deadline: 5.30 p.m.

Each group of soldiers had been assigned a target where they would attempt to overwhelm the Chinese guards. They prayed their sheer numbers and the element of surprise would allow them to succeed before too many of them were shot.

One squad was directed to raid one of Lavarack's big armouries.

The armoury officer leading the squad had been told it would have to smash its way in. He nodded at the order concealing a knowing grin. He already held the key.

In violation of all regulations he regularly stowed a spare in his quarters. For a rainy day. He fingered the steel key in his pocket and waited patiently for zero hour. If he wasn't shot, entry would be quick.

The news of the plan to seize back their base had been greeted by the prisoners with surprise, excitement and fear. After sixteen days incarcerated humiliatingly in their own barracks by a group of Chink terrorists, they were anxious to strike back.

The previous night rumours had swept the base of an escape bid by two men that had been quickly foiled by the Chinese. The escapees had been grabbed as soon as they sneaked from their quarters.

The wilder rumours said they would face a firing squad along with twenty soldiers from their platoon as a warning to others with plans to break out.

In the short lead-up to the deadline, no one talked of casualties but medics in every platoon were ordered to stay out of the first wave of assaults.

Brigadier Silvey decided he would lead the platoon attempting to seize the headquarters building where his office was now occupied by the Chinese commandant, Major Hu.

They would go four minutes before the deadline because he wanted Hu taken before the hubbub of a mass break-out gave him any chance of escape.

5.10 p.m.

The Cabinet Room, Canberra

The room was deathly still. Every head was cocked at First Secretary Sun. A nervous tic started fluttering in his right eye. He massaged his cellphone between trembling hands. The Chinese High Command was still waiting for his call.

Stone felt a sharp jab in the chest. "What f-final matter?"

Sun had stunned them when he quietly announced there was still one, last, unresolved issue to be settled between Australia and China.

"One of our diplomats was killed today when Mr Chang's delegation arrived under an international flag of truce and your protection," said Sun.

"I raised this matter with Mr Whittacker during our discussions on the way to this meeting. He said he was the minister responsible — the man who invited Mr Chang.

"He said he would resolve the matter. But he is no longer here." Sun needlessly cast an arm around the room.

Stone sat forward. His ministers' stares switched from Sun to him, new concern in eyes that only moments ago had been filled with jubilation and relief.

Where the hell had Whittacker gone?

"Um ... Mr Secretary," Stone began, "be assured the culprit will be brought to justice. A man has already been arrested and ..."

Stone stopped. Sun was shaking his head in response to the words.

"We respect your conventions but dealing with this murder is a matter of honour for us," Sun said.

Stone felt his heart racing painfully.

Sun said: "It was a capital offence and a serious breach of international law."

The ominous words spread across the hushed room like the warning of a plague contagion. They elicited no response.

Sun breathed in deeply. "You have no capital punishment in your country to deal with such an international capital offence. China, however, does have the means for dealing with a capital offence."

Oh, Christ, thought Stone. Is he seeking the extradition of an Australian soldier to face a Chinese firing squad?

He fought to gather his wits. Was Whittacker going to sabotage their victory at the eleventh hour?

It was his personal, unofficial invitation to Chang that had led to the killing of the Chinese diplomat. His stupid insistence on hastily assembling a formal guard of honour out of a group of unvetted soldiers that included a deranged assassin.

Australia had not had the death penalty for years. And it was very unlikely to reimpose it.

So, was it back to the greater good argument?

With that rationale they could just shoot the bugger who fired the shot and peace would be restored. He would happily do it himself. It was only one renegade soldier, after all.

Sun sat stone-like waiting for a response. He was in Whittacker's seat. The Deputy Prime Minister had told him to take it as he excused himself from the room.

As Stone shifted in his chair he could think of only platitudes to explain to Sun that democracies dealt with their killers in a civilised way: they locked them up for lengthy sentences. But rarely for life. Most were eventually released.

The Chinese shot their murderers and charged the killers' families for the bullet.

He pulled himself together and tried again: "Mr Secretary, we do acknowledge this is a matter of honour for your people ..."

His sentence went unfinished. The crack of the gunshot was close and surprisingly loud. It was followed immediately by shouted commands and the sound of several people running in the corridor outside.

Several ministers jumped to their feet, looked about nervously and, moments later, sat down again.

Sun sat still, listening intently to the commotion in the corridor.

Long seconds passed. No one spoke. The row outside subsided.

Stone said: "Joe, go and find out what the hell's happening."

Martini stood and made for the door. It opened before he reached it.

The uniformed security squad commander entered, dodged Martini and strode over to Stone. He bent down and murmured in Stone's ear.

Stone looked up at him wide-eyed. The commander nodded.

He straightened up, turned and left without a look at the con-founded ministers.

Stone pushed his shoulders back and said: "Gentlemen, I have just been told Jeremey Whittacker has taken his life in the men's cloakroom. He asked to see his bodyguard's pistol and then put it to his head."

There were shocked murmurs around the table.

Sun stood. He gave Stone a small bow of the head. "We have no further business to discuss. Thank you, Mr Prime Minister. If you will please excuse me, I have some urgent calls to make."

Noble rose and escorted Sun from the room.

Stone's watch showed 5.26 p.m. He looked at Martini who was still standing by the door and said: "Joe, you're the only one here that's been in the war zone, so you can be the one to give General Thompson my compliments and tell him the war's over."

Martini looked elated. "Okay, corker, I'd love to do that."

He gleefully rushed from the room.

5.26 p.m.

Lavarack Barracks, Townsville

The platoon picked its way quietly toward the base headquarters building with Silvey at its head. As they neared its entrance, he saw a small group of guards standing casually outside.

He knew in four minutes there would be bedlam as thousands of his men charged from their barracks with makeshift clubs and simultaneously attacked guard posts all over the base.

Silvey carried a short steel rod at his side. It had been one of the arms he had torn from his mess chair. He saw another huddle of Chinese far away to his right near the main entrance guardhouse where he had originally been taken prisoner. They were milling about, talking among themselves.

With only two hundred metres of open ground to go, Silvey adopted a casual stride.

Ahead of him, a Chinese officer came down the HQ entrance

steps and called to the guards. As Silvey watched they all turned and walked back inside the building. The place was suddenly deserted, unguarded.

His instincts went on red alert. There may have been a Chinese informer in the ranks. The guards could be taking up firing positions inside the building.

His eyes swept the windows facing his squad. He could detect no movement.

With fifty metres to go he waved to his men and broke into a run. They sprinted noisily up the white concrete steps bracing themselves for a burst of gunfire.

But the foyer was deserted. His former office was at the end of a long corridor to his left. The door was closed.

Signalling the others to follow him he ran toward it. As he got close, a sergeant sprinted past him. He was about to kick it in with one violent movement when the door suddenly opened.

Major Hu stood there, shocked for a moment, taking in the scene of suddenly stalled, panting Australian infantrymen crowding the passageway.

Before anyone could react, he put his hand out.

The brigadier looked behind Hu into the big office.

It was empty apart from two Chinese officers sitting nonchalantly at its conference table smoking.

Outside Silvey could hear the roar of several truck engines starting and men shouting. He looked at his watch. It was still not quite 5.30 p.m. The din was not coming from any of his men.

"I was just coming to see you," said Hu, his hand still outstretched.

A strange silence hung over the breathless prisoners and their calm enemies. Silvey broke the silence: "You've had orders to withdraw, haven't you?"

Hu gave an almost imperceptible nod.

"Major, what's going on?" said Silvey.

Hu straightened. "Brigadier, I have just received orders from High Command to turn the base over to you."

Silvey snapped a look at his watch.

Hu withdrew his hand and checked his own watch. He looked back at Silvey and said urgently: "I must tell you, your government has this afternoon promised safe conduct for all Chinese forces as they withdraw from your country."

"Fuck," said Silvey. "Order your men to put down their weapons immediately or we are going to have a blood bath in the next few seconds."

Hu pushed out his lips. "My men have been told we're withdrawing. They will only fire if they are attacked."

"My men have been told to attack them," said Silvey.

He turned to his squad leader. "Sergeant, turn on the parade ground public address system and order a stand-down. Not everyone will hear it but it will be a start. The rest of you, fan out as far and as fast as you can and tell everyone you come across they're to stand down. No one's to attack any Chinese."

As the squad leader turned to sprint off, Silvey said: "And when you finish the stand-down announcement, play 'Advance Australia Fair' as loud as you can."

There were now four men left in the office. Three Chinese and one Australian officer. Hu offered Silvey a cigarette. Silvey took it and bent forward to a lighted match.

Through the office window he could see a convoy of his trucks idling and packed with Chinese soldiers.

He sat at the conference table with the other smokers. Hu joined them.

Silvey gazed at him. "So, what's happened?"

Hu leaned back in the chair and pushed his legs out.

"We have been ordered home. It seems the Americans have joined you. Their submarines torpedoed and sank our aircraft carrier and two of our destroyers today. We were not expecting American intervention."

Silvey could hardly believe his ears.

Hu continued: "And gangs, probably from American special forces, have been letting off dirty bombs all over the North, radiating the coal and iron regions and export ports. We've had two bombs go off just to the south of here. Killed and burned a lot of people, ours and yours."

Silvey sucked on his cigarette. None of it made any sense. A lot must have happened since the BBC announced Australia was drawing up new borders north of Brisbane sixteen days ago.

He saw the two junior Chinese officers looking vacantly at the trucks, clearly devastated at the sudden turn of events.

"And, major, you now want safe passage out of Australia?" Silvey said quietly.

"That was part of the deal that's just been concluded with your government. I was told a few minutes ago. I was on my way to get you," said Hu.

Outside they could hear loudspeakers ordering a stand-down. Then a rousing rendition of the national anthem began. The revving of truck engines added to the uproar.

"Brigadier, with your permission I will continue my plan to borrow some of your trucks to evacuate my men to the Townsville harbour. They are sending ships to take us home," said Hu.

Silvey said: "Agreed, major. But my boys will drive them and ride shotgun."

Hu scraped his chin for a moment and then said: "Agreed."

"I think we need to get out there," said Silvey standing and stubbing out his first cigarette in twenty-five years, "and make sure no hotheads decide to start a new war."

Hu said nothing. He and his officers stood and silently followed Silvey from the office, down the corridor and out to the front entrance steps.

About eight hundred Chinese were crowded into a long convoy of trucks, surrounded by thousands of Australians cheering, jeering and brandishing their makeshift clubs and spears at them.

"Advance Australia Fair" finished. Seconds later "Waltzing Matilda" began to blast from the speaker system. A thunderous, thousands-strong chorus of diggers joined in.

Hu and his officers went from truck to truck ordering their men to surrender their weapons. They were handed down from the trucks by nervous Chinese soldiers who took the precaution of unloading them.

Armed members of an Australian transport company took over the front seats of each vehicle. In a growl of engines and a cloud of diesel exhaust, the convoy moved off slowly to the main gates.

"Waltzing Matilda" finished. The noise of the trucks faded away.

Then it was oddly quiet. The sort of uneasy quiet you get in the eye of a cyclone. The freed soldiers stood in clusters, Sergeant Keith Patterson among them, his arm around his fellow best mate, Alan Morris. They had been released moments before from the cell block.

Brigadier Silvey walked back to his office. It was over. Not in a blaze of glory. But over. How and why was still not clear to him. But one thing was. He took a sheet of stationery from a desk drawer and wrote his resignation.

5.27 p.m.

The Cabinet Room, Canberra

Stone adjourned the Cabinet meeting for five minutes. There was a special text he wanted to send. His ministers were too excited and preoccupied anyway, making calls and sending texts of their own, to concentrate on an end-of-hostilities debriefing.

His text message was to Elaine. He wanted to be the first one to tell her the Chinese had capitulated. They had blinked. The biggest military bluff in history had paid off.

He called her address up on the screen and his big thumbs keyed in: "Dragon blinked. Govt furniture stays. Turkey and gravy for xmas. Home soon. Luv u. G x."

The hubbub died down and Stone signalled everyone to their seats.

"There are two items the meeting still has to cover," he said. "One is a military debriefing. There are a number of events that had to be carried out on a strictly need-to-know basis including — just a few hours ago — a sea battle and the detonation of three more radioactive bombs up north this morning. The last nails in President Wu's coffin."

His words immediately subdued the mood. They were about to learn the full cost of the victory.

"The other item is the resolution on the table."

There was an embarrassed, awkward quiet.

"The resolution calls for a vote of no confidence in the Prime Minister in the conduct of the war against the People's Republic of China."

One of Whittacker's supporters began to speak but was cut off by Stone. "Is there any mover and seconder for the resolution?"

No one spoke.

"The motion, then, lapses."

Lindsay Noble rose from his chair and began to clap. Immediately the whole Cabinet was on its feet, applauding.

Stone stayed seated, acknowledging the ovation. There was nothing like winning to unify a team.

They took their seats again and he told them the last sixteen days had been tumultuous and everyone had been under extreme pressure. The main thing was the Chinese had given up their attempted annexation of the north. Australia was a free and independent country again.

They sat politely through the military debriefing, concealing their impatience to rush to the celebrations they could hear beginning throughout the building as the news spread like wildfire.

The briefing outlined the extent of the Emergency Nuclear Defence campaign with its still unknown casualty numbers; and the day's latest Battle of the Coral Sea with the tragic loss of the *Sheean*.

As the session ended, they could hear a crowd outside cheering and singing "Waltzing Matilda" in full voice.

6.30 p.m.

HMAS Rankin, *Coral Sea*

The *Rankin* was rolling like a bastard. The submarine was under tow. The patrol boat was pulling it at a steady five knots.

An hour ago John Scott had faced the prospect of abandoning ship with the rest of the crew in emergency rubber lifeboats from the lurching deck as the night settled in.

Scott was sure lives would have been lost in the exercise in the wind-tossed seas, but it would have been necessary to clear the *Rankin* for it be scuttled and kept from enemy hands.

They had all donned bright-yellow life jackets as the submarine surfaced and radioed its status and battle report.

Under the water the *Rankin* was very stable. But on the surface, in a swell, her round hull rocked back and forth sickeningly.

As she rose from the waves, tension soared. There had been a vessel only four kilometres away. Almost certainly an enemy one. But running on fumes the *Rankin* had no choice.

Then the stunning news broke. A naval headquarters radio message warned there was to be no further hostile action launched against any Chinese ships: all enemy forces were withdrawing from Australia. The war was over.

The news was greeted spontaneously with a roar.

Aware the *Rankin* had almost exhausted its diesel, HQ requested its current status and position. A naval patrol vessel had already been dispatched to search for them. It was the nearby boat they had first feared was an enemy one.

HQ also confirmed their torpedo attacks had been a total success. The *Liaoning* was at the bottom of the sea. About half of its two thousand crew members were thought to have perished.

The destroyer they hit had gone to the bottom too, as had the second one attacked by *Sheean* in the last minutes before it was detected and shattered by depth charges. There were no survivors from the Australian submarine.

As the slow return trip dragged on, Scott found the air was even more fetid than usual but nothing would spoil his mood.

His overalls uniform was damp, soiled and stank. There was no chance in this rolling can he could sneak a shower. What he feared most was no longer a depth charge hit but the embarrassment of being seasick.

The submarine's rolling movement had not stopped a procession of crew members climbing the conning tower at the skipper's invitation to taste the fresh air. But he was staying put. The heeling at the top of the sail would be too much for his queasy stomach.

Scott knew they were lucky to be alive. Just one more depth charge from that Chinese destroyer would have broken them apart. As it was, the three leaks were under control. He thanked God nature had sent along a pod of unsuspecting whales to divert the enemy.

Shortly after the official message, a personal one arrived from the Prime Minister. The skipper had read it over the PA system.

Stone congratulated them and said their courage was an inspiration to all Australians. The sinking of the *Liaoning* had been critical to Australia's victory.

"Any time," someone had called out. They had all laughed and there were more high fives, bear hugs and a few tears.

Scott wouldn't let himself think about the fate of the *Sheean* crew or what their last moments of life would have been like. The *Sheean* had evaded detection until the last minutes of the attack. It was a cruel end.

Rankin had been lucky. It would get a heroes' welcome. That's when it would be hardest for him. The other crew of heroes would be missing — forever.

6.45 p.m.

Gladstone, Queensland

"He can't stay here."

The SAS squad's medic, Glen Selby, was holding a thermometer in one hand. He handed it to Sergeant Blackie Johnson.

"What are you showing me?"

"Jabril's temperature is getting seriously high. The leg wound's infected. He needs a doctor," said Selby.

"Christ. The chopper's fuel tank is shot up. We're in the steepest gully in Queensland with crap radio reception and it's almost dark."

Blackie looked up the terrain surrounding them and shrugged. "It's going to be a hell of a job to get him up the top of the bluff. We'll wait till first light and have a go and hope we don't run into any Chinks."

Blackie walked over to Jabril Allunga. The Aboriginal signalman was lying on his side, his forehead glistening in sweat. The eyes in his bashed face were half closed.

"Lucky he's a skinny bugger," said Blackie. "Shouldn't be too heavy."

"He'll be bloody heavy enough going up that gully," said Selby.

"Are you two discussing me?" Jabril murmured.

"Yeah. We're going to get you out of here at first light," said Blackie. "It'll be a little tough going up the gully face but we need to find you a doctor quickly."

He knelt down and felt Jabril's forehead. "You're on fire, mate."

Jabril grunted. "There're people coming down the eastern side of the gully."

"Eh? What are you talking about?"

"People are coming down the eastern side of the gully."

Blackie stood and looked at Selby.

"I'm not going to argue with the bugger again. If he says he hears someone coming, someone's coming," said Blackie pushing a hand through grimy, straggly hair.

"I'm not hearing it so much. I'm feeling it," Jabril muttered. Blackie and Selby looked down. The Aboriginal signalman was lying on his side. His right ear was on the ground.

"Okay, okay, you're feeling it," said Blackie.

Blackie looked up the steep eastern side of the scrub-covered gully. It all looked quiet and peaceful.

He sighed. "Can't tell us what nationality they are, I don't suppose?"

"There's no need for sarcasm, white fella. But I can tell you whoever it is, they're making steady progress in pretty rough country," said Jabril.

Blackie said to Selby: "You stay here. I'll take the rest of the squad and check it out."

He walked over to the others standing beside the chopper. "Jabril says we've got visitors coming down the eastern side of the gully. A Chink patrol might have seen us land."

They all turned and gazed up. They could hear nothing. And see nothing.

But they all nodded, reached for their weapons and walked around the Black Hawk toward the eastern side of the bluff. They strapped their night glasses on and went carefully into the steep bush side.

Selby and the pilots waited anxiously. The pilots had only Glock pistols. Jabril had pulled his automatic weapon to his side before he fell unconscious again.

An hour later they tensed when they heard movement in the bush.

Blackie suddenly appeared at the foot of the gully heading a column of men and gave them a thumbs-up sign. He made directly for Jabril and shook him awake.

"You've got some visitors, night owl. Some mob from outside Gladstone. They saw the chopper go down and came to see if you're okay," said Blackie.

Jabril prised his eyes open. In the torchlight he saw the Aboriginal elders he had yesterday urged to go walkabout or die. A broad smile covered his crunched face.

"You guys made enough noise to wake the dead."

The elders laughed.

One leaned over Jabril. "We didn't have to worry about noise.

The Chinks are not searching for you. They're busy packing up to leave. They've given up the war. Your bad spirits got them."

Jabril shook his head and let out a great sigh.

Selby said: "What?"

Blackie and the elders all nodded in happy unison.

"Oh my God. I've got to tell the pilots," said Selby. He sprinted off yelling their names.

They came to join the party surrounding Jabril almost in disbelief. They heard more good news. Blackie explained the Aboriginal party and local farmers had seen the chopper dive into the gully in the morning and not reappear.

When they learned on their restored radio news service the Chinese were quitting, they called the authorities. A Black Hawk helicopter was on its way. It would make a night landing and take them all to Townsville.

"Fantastic," said Selby. "When do they think it will it get here?"

Jabril said: "It's almost here, thank God. I can hear it."

"Fuck off, chookie," said Blackie. The troopers shook their heads and laughed.

They went silent listening intently. They began to hear the faint, unmistakable clatter of a helicopter.

"The bugger'll get it wrong one day," Blackie said.

He turned to Jabril: "Maybe you should become a real chook trooper."

Jabril pushed himself up on one arm. "No bloody way."

"Why?" said Blackie.

"The training's too dangerous. You told me that. I've got whacked twice in the real thing. I'd never survive the training. No, I'm going back to the fellas at Norforce. Anyway, the wages are lousy and the ..."

His voice and their laughter were drowned out by the inbound chopper's din. Selby jammed the thermometer back in his chatty mouth. Blackie kicked the bugger on his good leg.

The elders looked bewildered at his treatment.

But Jabril lay back happily as the hovering chopper's downwash fanned air over his hot, feverish body. The war was over for all of them.

25 DECEMBER

Main gates, The Lodge, Canberra

Gary Stone moaned inwardly. The bloody protesters were still there. Even on Christmas Day.

Placards were being hoisted as the Prime Ministerial convoy neared The Lodge's gates. Soon the chanting would begin as the television cameras rolled. The guards would politely but firmly clear the road.

If he went on reading the news summaries and ignored them, he would be callous. If he waved, he would be arrogant.

The first time they'd appeared noisily at the gate, three weeks ago, he had been taken by surprise and glared with annoyance at them.

Stone had not known what to expect when the deaths from the radioactive explosions were made public. He knew it would be a tragedy for many families but he expected the vast majority of Australians would understand.

The few would die so many could live. He had, after all, successfully played one of history's greatest David and Goliath standoffs.

And most people had accepted the END logic. His approval ratings had shot to seventy-eight per cent. There had been enormous celebrations in the streets of every city and town when the victory was announced.

But there were now loud misgivings about the brutal nature of the END programme. And the plight of the survivors, with their horrific burns and sickness, provided ongoing, emotional headlines.

Stone was increasingly angry at the second-guessing. The critics' favoured view held that the sinking of the *Liaoning* would have delivered a victory without the civilian deaths in the irradiated areas.

Stone was certain they were wrong.

After the success of its lightning invasion, China had become quickly convinced its resources prize was being destroyed systematically by his radioactive, scorched earth policy.

Their belief in the Australian Government's deadly intent was reinforced by the killing of its own civilians. The Chinese had no idea Australia had only six bombs.

The loss of the enemy aircraft carrier and its air cover would have halted any further invasion plans temporarily but would not have prevented China from eventually rebuilding its naval and air forces.

But the attack on the *Liaoning* had been critical in an unexpected way: the false assumption that America had entered the fray shocked Beijing, undermining any last remnant of support for President Wu.

The Chinese were now attempting to rebuild an economy strangled by international boycotts.

Stone was relieved his critics did not know the irradiation death toll of 180 was far less than the official estimate of 3000 at the start of the campaign.

There had been other losers beyond the radiation victims. Frank and Jocelyn Church's marriage was ending in divorce after Jocelyn had attempted to reveal and sabotage the END strategy.

But there had been winners too. Stone had rewarded key people from his victorious campaign. General Thompson would be the next Governor General of Australia. Admiral Brian Robson would become Chief of Defence.

John Able was revelling in his new role as ambassador to a neutered and apologetic Washington.

Suddenly Stone could hear the chanting, muted through the limousine's bulletproof glass.

"STONED TO DEATH. STONED TO DEATH. STONED TO DEATH."

He saw the familiar, bobbing placards: "WAR CRIMINAL", "INNOCENTS STONED TO DEATH", "CANNON FODDER VICTIMS DEMAND COMPENSATION".

The hard core of the demonstrators had made themselves a small camp outside the gates. The numbers had shrunk from about 120 to just a dozen but he was offended by their pointless row each time he ran their gauntlet.

He would shortly announce a compensation package. The big cheques would see the last of them off.

As his limousine passed the protesters he obeyed the instructions of his media advisers. He nodded his head politely, acknowledging them in a civil, caring manner. It played well on television. The gritted teeth were well hidden.

The convoy rolled by without incident and his mind went back to the last day of his self-exile in The Lodge when he had gone to his office for his supposed last Cabinet meeting.

By the time it ended he was still in power and fifteen of his Cabinet had offered their resignations.

He had accepted none of them, claiming he understood their dilemma. But he knew he was keeping them on in part because they would now be a very tame bunch to control. They had elected his choice, Joe Martini, to be the deputy leader without a murmur.

Whittacker had been buried with full honours at a state funeral in Melbourne. The family were grateful Stone had told the media the death had been from heart failure, probably caused by the trauma of the Chinese crisis.

Well, why not be magnanimous in victory? A bullet to the brain did cause heart failure. Eventually everyone would likely learn the truth. There were already reports surfacing about his "self-harm" episode as a teenager when he failed a school exam.

Stone had not attended the funeral. There was a limit to his magnanimity.

He cried off on his own health grounds and finally went for the heart procedure he desperately needed. The stent operation unblocked several arteries. It took less than an hour and he slept that night back at The Lodge.

He felt a fool for allowing his ego to stall the procedure for so long. But now there was no chance his health would give rise to any leadership challenge. His main protagonist was dead and his replacement had no further ambitions.

His suits were beginning to fit him again as he gained weight. And there was no question he would receive his share of the gravy today.

He began to fold up the news summaries as the limousine neared The Lodge's loggia-styled reception area. They reported the exodus south was reversing rapidly but the economy was still stalled. Nearly three million were now out of work, the tourism industry the worst hit.

Fuel rationing continued and would be an irritant till regular oil shipments were fully restored.

The value of the Australian dollar was climbing but still low, a situation resort cities were exploiting. Surfers Paradise was promoting itself as the "best, empty, holiday place in the world".

The prosecution of profiteers was proving popular. The energetic hunt for murderers and hijackers was producing results. Jeff Bolt, who had fled Sydney after killing the owner of the luxurious *Pacific Queen* superyacht, was arrested in Fiji. He had scuttled the vessel off Suva in a vain bid to escape detection.

Meanwhile Stone was enjoying another boost in his popularity after declining to meet with the US Secretary of State who wanted to visit.

New Zealand the previous week had also snubbed the US and ordered a squadron of fighter aircraft — from France. It was also adding four, lethal, short-range Japanese submarines to its navy.

Two stories in the news summary had brought a smile to his

face. One carried the headline: "Far North Moteliers Seek Govt Compensation: Chinese delegates leave unpaid bills."

The other included a photo of children running into the arms of their parents at Sydney Airport. Airline staff reported the homecoming youngsters had abandoned their luggage in their emotional stampede through the arrivals gate.

One important arrival did not make the news. Dr Peter Yu and his family flew home without fanfare and he and Lilly quietly resumed their careers; the children's Canadian holiday was the envy of their classmates.

Yu's critical role in END would remain a secret. His Lucas Heights research paper on the use of radioactive isotopes to kill off cancer cells had been published and heralded as groundbreaking.

Life was returning to normal. Stone had considered taking Martini's advice and going for an early election but, if he were honest, he was still a bit buggered from his ordeal. He needed an off-season break.

Elaine had been urging him to rest too. He looked up and saw her rushing out to meet him.

"Come on, you're late. Where have you been? Lunch is ready, all the family are waiting," she said.

Elaine took him by the arm, they walked happily toward the entrance. He stopped. "You haven't forgotten our Chinese meal deal, have you?"

"No, now come on. Everyone's waiting to start. And you should keep your voice down about the Chinese meal deal. What will the voters think if they find out your whole war-winning motivation was based on a serving of gravy?"

"I'd probably win a few more marginal seats. The voters know there are things in life that really matter."

Elaine shook her head and tugged his arm. They walked on. They reached the old "war room". It was being used for its original purpose once more. Inside, the family was impatiently seated at a table groaning under the weight of a grand feast.

* * *

Two hours later he was relaxing in his favourite lounge chair. Elaine was sitting on the carpeted floor in front of him, rocking Kati, one of her granddaughters. They were watching the televised unveiling of the memorial to the *Sheean* crew at the Garden Island submarine base near Perth.

The Deputy Prime Minister would also be pinning medals to the chests of the *Rankin* heroes, the SAS sabotage troopers, and an Army private would receive a posthumous medal for valour.

"You must be feeling very proud, darling," Elaine sighed. Stone didn't answer.

She raised her voice over the television commentator. "Gary, you must be very proud."

There still no response.

She turned and saw him slumped motionless in the chair, his chin on his chest, one arm dangling from his side.

Her hand shot to her mouth.

"Oh no," she breathed.

She scrambled to her feet almost tripping over Kati.

Elaine took a step and stopped.

She heard a faint, familiar rumbling sound.

Kati giggled. "Nana, Granddad's snoring."

POSTSCRIPT

It was 10.21 that night when Brooke Catley stumbled into the lounge breathless. The most junior of the wait staff, she had run up the stairs to the private lounge because she was delivering a very important message to the Prime Minister.

It was from a Cabinet minister. Mr Lindsay Noble. She sort of recognised his name when she answered the phone. So she must have heard it on the telly or somewhere.

Mr Noble made her get a pen and pad and write down the message. He said he was depending on her to get it to Mr Stone even though it was very late on Christmas Day and he was not taking any calls.

Stone was relaxing in a lounge chair flipping the pages of a magazine when Catley swept in.

"Excuse me, Mr Stone, the Foreign Minister wants you to call him urgently," she said.

Before looking down at her hurriedly scrawled note, she saw Stone roll his eyes. Mr Noble had warned her this might happen.

"Mr Noble says there's a bit of problem at a place called …" She paused and went a little red in the face slowly deciphering her writing. "Sounds like Bayoounder, I think."

"Bayu-Undan?" said Stone. "It's a big gas field off East Timor, Brooke."

Catley smiled and nodded. "That will be it."

"What's the problem there?" said Stone.

"Um, well, the Indonesian and Timorese navies have set fire to it."

Stone got out of his chair as she peered anxiously at the note.

"But everyone working on it is safe, Mr Noble said. They were taken off the platform … would that be right? … a platform? … before the fire was started."

Stone strode across the room and stood so close she could feel his breath. She thought he might snatch the note from her. But he said: "Go on … go on."

She was getting a little flustered, she knew. Bayoo-something must be very important. Lucky she had answered the phone. The real phone operator had gone for a smoke outside with one of the policemen.

"Indonesian West Timor and independent East Timor say the field is well within their island's territorial waters," she read carefully, "and they are … annulling … I don't know what that means … their treaty."

She looked up nervously. Stone stood back folding one arm across his chest and holding his chin with the other, looking into the distance.

He seemed worried. She wished she knew what it all meant. Turning to excuse herself, she frowned and said: "Mr Stone, sir, why would we have our platform in their sea?"

A NOTE FROM
THE AUTHOR

I hope you've enjoyed my debut political thriller. If you did, I would be grateful if you could write a review. It needn't be long, just a few words, but it would make such a difference.

I'd love to hear from you too. You can get in touch on my website. If you'd like to know when my next book is released, you can sign up to my mailing list on the link below. Your email address will never be shared and you can unsubscribe at any time.

B.C. COLMAN
www.bccolman.com

ABOUT THE AUTHOR

B.C. Colman is an award-winning journalist and publisher who divides his time between homes in the Gold Coast and Auckland. He is a former staff reporter for the *Courier Mail* and *Sunday Mail*, Brisbane.

A very successful business executive, he founded The Liberty Publishing Company which produced financial and classified papers in New Zealand. He acquired *The National Business Review* from Fairfax and Sons in 1989.

He has always had a strong interest in geopolitics and his works of fiction are set against realistic political and social possibilities.

He is a recipient of the Queens Service Medal for services to publishing.

www.bccolman.com

Made in the USA
Columbia, SC
01 September 2017